Under a Texas Star

Alison Bruce

UNDER A TEXAS STAR

http://www.alisonbruce.ca

FIRST EDITION

Imajin Books

JUNE 2011

ISBN: 978-1-926997-11-7

Cover designed by Sapphire Designs - http://www.designs.sapphiredreams.org

Praise for Alison Bruce

"A delightful Western tale that blends engaging adventure with spirited romance. Reminds me of Louis L'Amour novels...Bruce is a terrific story-teller...a complete joy to read. She immerses readers into a smoking Western that is also a spunky romance and reminiscent of the Texas Rangers television series." —Christina Francine, *Midwest Book Review*

"Filled with realistic dialog and a good attention to period detail, Bruce manages to create a believable story that captures our imagination. Well written with a compelling plot, *Under a Texas Star* brings a delightfully new and strong heroine to the literary world. Highly recommended." —Wendy Thomas, *Allbook Reviews*

"Alison Bruce's western tale of intrigue, murder, and love is a page-turning, action-packed, made-of-awesome read. *UNDER A TEXAS STAR* belongs on every reader's keeper shelf—it already has a place on mine! Love, love, loved it!" —Michele Bardsley, national bestselling author of *Never Again*

"Romance as sweeping as the Texas sky." —Gwyn Cready, Rita award-winning author of *Seducing Mr. Darcy*

"This is a rollicking adventure and Marly Landers is a girl with True Grit." —Phyllis Smallman, Arthur Ellis award-winning author of *Champagne for Buzzards*

"L'amour in the style of Louis L'Amour...Pin a silver star on this thrilling tale of love and justice in the old west." —Lou Allin, author of *On the Surface Die*

"I loved the murder mystery...as well as the sense of humor which had me either chuckling or laughing out loud." —Jacqueline Wilson, Deputy Sheriff for Publications of the Chicago Corral of the Westerners

To my sister Joanne (1961-2003),
who taught me that life is too short not to do what you love

Acknowledgments

I would like to thank Amanda and her red pen; John for insisting the story should be a novel; Janet for rescuing the lone viable copy; Frances for cleaning up the resulting digital copy and nagging me to keeping working on it; Nancy, the most constructive nitpicker on the planet; Melodie for pointing me in the right direction; Cheryl and Imajin Books for being the right direction.

To my daughter Kate, son Sam and nieces Sophie and Claire, thank you for your patience and enthusiastic support.

CHAPTER 1

Trailing from one dusty town to another in pursuit of a criminal fugitive was a job for a bounty hunter with a good horse and a small arsenal. It was tough work for a slim boy of small build, few means and fewer possessions—tougher still when the boy wasn't a boy at all, but a girl.

It wasn't the walking. Marly was used to spending most of her day on her feet in the yard of the schoolhouse her aunt taught in, tending the kitchen garden, feeding the chickens, hanging the laundry or walking the mile to town for whatever errand Aunt Adele required.

It wasn't the weight of the oversized oilskin coat or the bedroll slung across her back. They were nothing to hefting a crate of books or a basket of surplus eggs and vegetables into town to trade for flour and sugar.

It was the solitude.

Once upon a time, Marly would have reveled in the opportunity to get away from her aunt's incessant homilies, the critical stares of her aunt's cronies and even the kinder yet oppressive expectations of her friends. Now she realized that the outside clamor would be preferable to her own self-critical reflections. The long walks as she travelled from one town to another, gave her too much time to dwell on the events that put her on this solitary trail.

"As ye sow, so shall ye reap," her Aunt Adele would say.

"No good turn goes unpunished," was more like it.

It had started with a trip to the Doc's house. The two Johnnys had been fighting again. The on-and-off best friends were trying out their fledgling boxing skills. Marly blocked a stray punch while grabbing hold of the smaller John Henry. John Thomas' wrist gave way.

Despite the pain, he was quite cheerful during the trek into town.

Doc's chiding would be nothing compared to one of Miss Gumm's lectures, a fact he was quite comfortable sharing with Marly. She pointed out that her aunt wouldn't forget to punish him when he returned.

When they came in sight of the Doc's house and found Sheriff Langtree on the porch, Johnny's fear of trouble was so obvious, Marly almost laughed.

"I just sent a deputy to fetch you," the sheriff said by way of a greeting. "I brought Doc a wounded man. Victim of a hold-up. I think Doc could use your help. Rebecca's got her hands full and I've been ejected for being no help at all."

Marly gave him a quick smile and consigned John Thomas to the sheriff's care. Ever since she provided first-aid and brought John Henry's older brother Joe in—after he shot his toe off with his father's *borrowed* revolver—Marly had become the Doc's go-too person when he needed more help than his wife could provide.

"Just who we need," Doc said, looking up from his work. "Wash up, my girl. Take over for Becky so she can get back to Mrs. Applegate. She picked shopping day to go into labor. Silly first-timer mistake to make. "

"Babies come when babies come," said the childless Becky on her way out. "Except when they don't."

Marly spent the next hour assisting the removal of two slugs and the stitching of the wounds. This mostly consisted of handing implements to the doctor and the application of ether on a breathing cup when the patient started to rouse.

Doc saw to John Thomas. She cleaned up and held the basin for the man as the effects of the ether wore off and nausea settled in. She bathed his face with lavender water, known for its cleansing and calming powers.

When his hazel eyes cleared and he was fully conscious, his eyes lit with appreciation and genuine esteem.

"I must be dead," he croaked, his throat raw from the ether, "for you are certainly an angel."

Right, thought Marly, kicking a stone down the dusty road. Not an angel, but a naïve chit of a girl to be taken in by slick words and hazel eyes.

Maybe if she hadn't been taken in by Charlie Meese, neither would the townspeople of Cherryville, Kansas. She had opened the door to a trickster because he appealed to her latent vanity. That girl was left behind in Cherryville. The Marly Landers that was tracking Charlie and the money down was now a scruffy boy in oversized clothes and a droopy, weather-worn hat.

CHAPTER 2

"DO NOT ARREST—STOP—FOLLOW TO EL PASO AND
MONEY—STOP..."

Texas Ranger Jason—*Jase*—Strachan reread the telegram, then
stuffed it into one the copious pockets of his duster. Jase wasn't surprised
by the order. He was on the trail of a confidence man, who had made the
mistake of cheating some very powerful people in Austen. However,
arresting him now wouldn't recover the half million dollars he had
embezzled.

Dog Flats wasn't much. A couple of houses, a general store and a
saloon. Blink and he'd ride right by. Most people—and more
importantly, the stage—did just that. That was one of the reasons Jase
chose the town. The other walked through the door just as he settled into
the back corner of the saloon with his second beer.

The boy couldn't have been more than fourteen or fifteen, yet he
marched up to the barkeep, bold as brass, and demanded a job.

"Don't need anyone," said the grizzle-haired man behind the bar.

"I can wait tables, wash dishes, cook, clean. I'm a hard worker and
you don't have to pay me. All I want is room and board for the night."

Jase waited. The bartender stared down at the boy. The boy smiled
back at the man.

"You can start by clearing tables. Put yer stuff at the back."

For three days, Jase had watched the same scene play out, afternoon
or early evening. Arriving in town, the boy would talk himself into a job
sweeping floors, washing dishes, mucking barns—all for supper, a
packed lunch and a roof for the night. Then, at sunrise, he was on the
road, walking or hitching a ride to the next town. Town by town, he
advanced across Texas. The kid was patient and determined.

It wasn't just the boy's tenacity that caught Jase's notice. The kid
was making his own inquiries as he travelled. He was asking after the

same man Jase was tracking.

"You a Yank, boy?"

Jase's attention snapped to one of the part-of-the-furniture patrons that saloons like this attracted. The man looked like he hadn't moved from his table in years. Evidently, he still had some life in him because he had a vice grip on the boy's wrist.

"Leave the kid alone, Hayes," called another old geezer at the next table.

"I asked you a question." Hayes pulled the boy in close, breathing whiskey into his face. "Are you a Yankee?"

"Just say no," another patron advised.

"I'm from Kansas."

A hush fell over the room and Jase edged forward in his seat, ready to intervene if necessary.

"And my folks were from Massachusetts, not Missouri, so I guess that makes me a Yank."

"She-it," sighed the old geezer.

"A Yankee killed my boy," Hayes snapped.

"A Reb killed my father," the boy replied. "Another raped and killed my mother. Would have killed me too, if his sergeant hadn't found him and shot him first."

Hayes dropped the boy's wrist.

Jase sat back. Crisis averted.

"Bring me another bottle," said a subdued Hayes.

The boy stared at the man for several heartbeats, then turned toward the kitchen, not the bar. A few minutes later, he returned with a cup of coffee and a plate of cold beef and bread.

"Before you throw that plate in my face," the boy said, "let me just point out that I'm paying for this meal with my work and you would be grievously insulting my hospitality."

Hayes gave the boy a dismissive wave. For a long time, he stared at the plate as if the food might jump up and bite him. Finally, he took a sip of coffee. Then his appetite kicked in and he started picking at the plate.

Jase took his empty beer glass up to the bar for a refill and had a few words with the bartender.

Minutes later, the boy was sent over to his table. He was a scruffy lad in faded, dust-laden jeans that were a size too big and a work shirt that would have fit a man twice his size. He had hung his ground-scraping duster on a hook at the back with his bedroll—the only luggage he seemed to have. But he was still wearing his hat, which was an indeterminate brown and shapeless except for the turned up brim at the front. For all that, his face and neck were clean and his long red hair was neatly braided, Indian-style, down his back.

"You want me for something, mister?"

"I'd like to buy you a good meal. I thought steak and potatoes. If there's something else you would prefer—"

"I eat in the kitchen, sir."

"You just gave away your supper," Jase said in a dry tone. "I've arranged it with your boss. I'm taking care of your dinner and accommodations so you have the rest of the night off. You would be grievously insulting *my* hospitality to refuse."

The boy's mouth twitched. He didn't sit or leave. Head tipped slightly to one side, he gave Jase a speculative stare.

"You've been following me. Why?"

"Hardly following you. I generally make town several hours ahead of you. Why are *you* following me, Marly Landers?"

The boy's eyes narrowed. "What's your business, mister?"

Jase pulled his jacket aside to reveal a tin star. "I'm a Texas Ranger."

The kid was unimpressed.

Jase broke the stare-down and leaned back, running his fingers through his shaggy, sandy-brown hair.

"I reckon," he drawled, "that if I was to make inquiries in Kansas, I might just turn up something on you, Marly Landers. *If* I made inquiries."

Landers shrugged and sat.

Through dinner, they parried each other's questions. Landers admitted that he was headed in the general direction of El Paso.

"Personal business," the boy said. "Of no interest to a Texas Ranger."

"I'm probably gonna end up in El Paso," Jase admitted. But he didn't share the nature of his business. "What do you say to travelling together? I supply a horse and tack. You agree to work for me 'til we get to El Paso."

The boy was reluctant, so he added, "It's either that or I hog-tie you and carry you across my saddle."

The kid grinned and rocked back on his chair. "Okay. You'll have to teach me how to ride."

Jase held out a hand. "Deal."

No one had a horse to sell in Dog Flats and Landers refused to ride with Jase. No amount of cajoling or coercion worked on the boy. Fortunately, Mr. Hayes came to the rescue. He had a small farm, which he leased out for drinking money. Hayes persuaded his tenant to give

Landers a ride to Abilene.

It meant a late start because the farmer wasn't going to waste a day without taking trade goods with him. Jase took it in stride.

They set out just before noon. Landers sat beside Farmer Jorgen with a basket of cold chicken, peaches, black bread and pickles between them. Jase rode alongside where the road permitted and he accepted whatever food was offered.

His attention was focused, not on the mobile picnic, but on Landers. The boy, who would barely give Jase the time of day last night, was relating his life history to the fatherly Jorgen, including the story of his mother's death.

"It happened after the surrender," Landers explained. "There was a group of Gray-coats heading home, still armed. They were hungry and my mother fed them, then asked them to move on, which they did. Then a couple of them came back after dark."

"You remember this?" Jorgen asked, shocked. "You couldn't have been more than two or three years old."

"A little more than that." Landers pursed his lips, holding back a further comment. "Anyway, their sergeant came back too late to save my mother, but just in time to stop them from hurting me. He shot them."

"What happened to you then?"

"Sarge took me with him. Didn't want to trust me to the Yankees."

Jase bit his tongue.

"You were a brave little boy," Jorgen remarked. "Did you have no other family?"

"I have an aunt—my mother's sister. I had never met her. There were letters from her with my mother and father's wedding picture."

The boy reached into one of the pockets of his duster and pulled out a small leather-bound folder. Inside was a tintype photograph of a young couple on their wedding day. He flashed it at Jase as though to prove he did indeed have parents, then held it for Mr. Jorgen to have a look.

"Sarge took it from the house, along with the little bit of jewelry my mother had. He kept it safe until Aunt Adele sent for me."

"Sent?" Jase asked.

"Sarge was going to take me west with him. He said we could make a new family. He wrote my aunt, using the most recent letter for the address. He let her know I was alive and being taken care of, and that we'd stop in Waco for a spell before heading west if she wanted to write back. He didn't expect anything to come of it. Nothing did at first. We travelled together for almost a year before her letter caught us up."

Jase frowned. "What did it say?"

"She asked him to bring me home, which was stupid because she never liked me."

By the time they made Abilene, it was late afternoon.

Jorgen stopped at the closest livery, bid them a safe journey and continued on his business.

"You take care of Grandee," Jase told Landers, handing him the reins of his horse. "Can you do that?"

"Yes, sir."

"I'm gonna arrange our accommodations. Stay put 'til I return."

Jase sought out a cheap hotel and booked a room. Then he strolled over to the telegraph office and wired a short report to his superiors.

Back at the livery stable, he found Landers mucking stalls. A stable hand was chewing a straw and cleaning tack as he chatted with the boy. When he noticed Jase, he made himself look busy, checking a bridle for signs of wear. Landers, on the other hand, paused in his work and nodded a greeting. Sweat streamed down his face, cutting rivulets in the trail dust.

Jase shook his head. "You don't have to do that."

"Yes, I do. You might have expense money, but I have to earn my keep."

"Fine. Do what you have to and I'll do what I have to. When you're hungry, make your way to the hotel. We're staying at the DeSoto." He picked up his saddlebags and Landers' bedroll. "Wash up before you come."

It was well past suppertime when Landers made his appearance in the hotel restaurant. Though his clothes were soiled, his hands, face and neck were scrubbed clean. By way of greeting, he handed Jase the quarter dollar in change he had earned at the stables.

Jase pocketed the coins. "I hope you'll let me buy supper."

He summoned the waitress. A pretty woman in plain clothing brought a coffee pot and an extra cup to their table. She filled their cups while he placed an order for cold beef and fried potatoes. He laid on the charm and his Texas drawl, since she was holding the kitchen open for them.

Conversation was spare. The kid was obviously exhausted and Jase was busy with his own thoughts. His quarry had passed through Abilene two days ago, still headed for El Paso. Jase was taking a chance of getting too far behind by taking Landers. He told his Captain that he thought the boy might be an accomplice.

Truth be told, he suspected that Landers was heading west to find the old Rebel who saved his life. In the boy's eyes, Sarge was a hero, but Jase knew of more than one discharged gray-coat, who had found it hard to leave the war behind and had taken to the outlaw life. He didn't want to see the boy fall into the wrong hands. It offended his honor.

It wasn't a brilliant career move to let a wayward kid slow down a criminal investigation. Yet, there was some connection, however tenuous, between the boy and his quarry.

That thought paced back and forth in Jase's mind, until Landers nodded off over his apple pie.

"Come on," Jase said, prodding the boy. "Go get some rest."

He sent Landers up to the room, alone.

Jase had to see a man about a horse.

Landers was gone when Jase awoke. The boy had packed his bedroll and left it by the washstand. Jase found him in the dining room, pouring coffee for other early risers.

"Kid," he said between yawns, "you're unnaturally productive. Don't you ever give it a rest? Speaking of which, you didn't have to sleep on the floor. I would've shoved you over when I came to bed."

Landers shrugged and fetched two cups of coffee, leaving the pot on the counter for someone else to wield. After a large and greasy breakfast, Jase dissuaded the boy from any further labor.

It was time for him to learn to ride.

The gelding was a short, sturdy gray mustang with a definite mulish look to him. The owner fit a similar description. He was asking forty dollars. Jase talked him down to twenty-five, then spent another twenty-five on a saddle, bridle and saddlebags. The tack he bought used from the livery owner. With a little dickering, Jase managed to get him to throw in a saddle blanket.

Throughout this procedure, the boy stood out of the way, in awed silence. His expression was one of near panic.

"Stop gaping and saddle his horse," Jase ordered.

"S-sir, I c-can't—"

"Sure you can. You seem to have made stable work a part-time career. Next to clearing tables, that is."

He looked down at Landers and could almost see the mental calculations the boy was making. Fifty dollars was a lot of money. A month's pay for a Ranger. Mucking stables, the boy might make that in four.

"Don't fret it," Jase added. "You take care of that horse and I'll get my money back for it in El Paso. Now hoof it!"

Within an hour of trying to teach Landers how to ride, he started to wonder if he shouldn't trade the saddle tack in on a buck-board. It wasn't that the boy was slow-witted. Far from it. All things considered, Landers learned fast.

Blame, Jase had to admit, lay partly at his own door. To him, riding was as natural as walking. He took most of what he knew for granted. That didn't make him an ideal teacher. Nor did it help that they were drawing an audience. The livery owner had cleared a corral for them. Bit by bit, the fence started filling up with folks who had nothing better to do on a sultry Friday morning.

Most just watched for a time and moved on. Some cheered, while others taunted the boy. The worst ones shouted well-meaning but contradictory words of advice.

Then there was the horse. The beast didn't just look mulish. He had a temperament to match. With more intelligence and malice than Jase had ever thought a horse could possess, this one did his best to make things even more difficult for the boy.

Jase was losing his patience.

When Landers tried to pull the horse to a stop, the animal bucked hard and the boy was thrown over his head.

Jase jumped between the gray and the boy. "You!" He pointed at one of the cowboys. "Get the horse!"

Two men jumped off the fence. One took Jase's position as block. The other grabbed the reins and let the beast know who was boss.

Jase went to help the boy.

"I'm okay," Landers said in a shaky voice.

He waved off Jase's help, stood and brushed the dirt from his trousers. With a stubborn gleam in his eye, he marched up to the now calm horse. Grasping the bridle, he pulled the gray's head down to look him in the eye. "I've had enough. Your name is Trouble, 'cause that's all I've had from you. From now on, you better behave or I will personally slice you into horse steaks."

Fascinated, Jase and the cowboys watched Landers. Still glaring, the boy took the reins and walked around to the right side. As though hypnotized, the horse maintained eye contact until he had reached the limits of his neck's ability to twist.

Then Landers shortened the reins and with only a little awkwardness, mounted. The boy turned Trouble and walked around the corral's edge. Cautiously, he changed the pace to a trot.

"That's an old Injun trick," one of the cowboys said.

"What?" the other asked. "Mounting on the wrong side or threatening to make dinner out his horse?"

"Both," Jase interrupted. "Show's over."

The cowboy nudged his friend. "Come on, you can buy me a beer."

Jase's gaze returned to the boy on the horse. It wasn't the most graceful riding he'd ever seen, but at least the kid kept his seat.

When Jase announced it was time to eat, Landers almost fell out of the saddle. It seemed his knees had forgotten how to support him. They folded under him. Sitting in the dust, he looked up at Jase, puzzled and pitiful.

Jase shook his head and flipped the stable boy a half dime to take care of Trouble. He offered a hand to the boy. Landers hesitated a moment, then allowed himself to be helped up.

"You're doing fine," Jase said, giving the kid a pat on the back before letting him go. *What have I gotten myself into?*

Over beef stew and biscuits, he discovered that not learning to ride hadn't been the boy's idea.

"My aunt didn't think riding was a skill I needed to have," Landers said. "I don't think she approved of riding horses at all. Come to think about it, she didn't approve of anything I liked to do."

"Like what?"

"Like hanging out with the Sheriff Langtree. He let me sweep the floor and sort papers and keep the Wanted posters up to date. He knew Aunt Adele didn't approve, but he didn't stop me from coming around until she came down and told him face-to-face I wasn't allowed." He sighed. "For someone so law-abiding, my aunt had an odd aversion to lawmen."

Jase tucked away the name Langtree for future reference. There was something familiar about it, no doubt a reference from one of the many reports he was required to read. If he could place it, he might have another clue to the boy's identity.

After dinner, he took Landers to the general store. The boy needed to be outfitted properly. Jase accepted this as part of his self-assumed responsibilities. The kid didn't see it that way.

"What's wrong with the hat I've got?"

"Other than the fact it doesn't fit right?"

"You can't keep buying me things, sir," Landers complained, picking up a fancy black hat with silver medallions.

Jase bit his lip to stop a smile. He put the black hat back on its stand and placed a plain, light tan Texan on the boy's head.

Landers compared prices. "You can't tell me you're going to sell these things off once we get to El Paso."

"I'm keepin' account. I figure you can work it off over time as my unpaid assistant and stable boy. Speakin' of which, we'll add a shirt or two to your account. I can smell that one a mile away."

The boy turned red as his hair and picked up a denim work shirt.

"See if they got anything closer to your size," Jase advised.

"My aunt always believed in buying things with room to grow."

In the end, Landers allowed Jase to buy him two oversized work shirts, a hat and a couple of bandanas. Emptying out his pockets, the boy handed over almost three dollars in small change.

Jase gave him back a silver dollar. "Get a bath before you put that new shirt on." Landers looked ready to argue, so he added, "Tell them to save the water. I'll be along once I've had a shave."

When he arrived at the wash-house a half-hour later, a bath with fresh water was waiting for him. But no Landers.

Jase sat in a chair in front of the hotel and waited.

Hours later, the boy showed up. He was dirty, sweaty and smelled like the stables. Jase pretended to be asleep, legs stretched out, ankles crossed and hat pulled down over his eyes.

As Landers tried to sneak by, Jase said, "Seems I ain't ever gonna get a meal on time with you around." He pushed his hat back and surveyed the kid.

"You didn't have to wait."

Landers handed over the half dollar.

Jase shook his head, pocketing the coin. Switching from relaxed Texan to stern task master, he scowled at the boy. "The point was that you'd set down to supper clean and well dressed."

"Sorry, sir. You'll notice that I didn't wear my new clothes. I can go clean up now. You don't have to wait for me."

"You're a brat."

"Yes, sir."

"An obnoxious, stubborn brat," he said, trying hard not to smile. "Go wash up. Be down here in half an hour." He took a watch out of his jacket pocket and handed it to the boy. "I'm orderin' supper, so you better not be late."

The kid wasn't late.

Jase noted, with some satisfaction, that Landers cleaned up well. He was beginning to suspect that the boy was older than he seemed. His clear blue eyes and their intent gaze gave him an air of maturity. Then there were his memories of a war he should have been too young to experience.

Jase had known boys who claimed to be twenty or more who hadn't a hair on their chins. He adjusted his estimation of the boy's age up to sixteen, the age Jase was when he joined the Texas Rangers.

Landers was doing some sizing up of his own. Jase recognized the reaction his own transformation wrought. His beard was flecked with gray, which made him seem older. Clean, shaved, with his hair and moustache neatly trimmed, he now looked what he was, a man of thirty. Years had literally been washed away.

The waitress came over as soon as they were seated. She gave Jase a warm smile and a delicate blush. "Coffee?"

Jase returned her smile. "You're lookin' very pretty tonight. Even prettier than usual."

"Why, thank you, sir. I set aside some fresh biscuits for you. Usually they're gone by now."

"That was exceedingly kind of you."

Landers' mouth twisted into a disgusted expression.

"Give it time," Jase teased. "You'll learn to appreciate the fairer sex some day."

"I'll never act like that!"

The revulsion driving those words took Jase aback. He wasn't about to put up with rude behavior, but this was unexpected.

Before he could get his bearings, Landers apologized. "Sorry. That was uncalled for." The boy echoed the very words Jase was mustering. "I should learn to hold my tongue."

Landers was as good as his word, sitting quietly while they waited for their supper. It was stew and biscuits again. The meal was good, satisfying their hunger and cooling their tempers.

"Warmer than Kansas, I reckon," Jase remarked.

"A bit," Landers replied.

"What part of Kansas you from?"

"Cherryville. I was born on a farm further southwest."

"We got somethin' in common. I'm a farm boy too." His eyes met the boy's. "And like you, I lost my home to war."

"Where?"

"Not far south of here, on the Brazos."

"Union Army?"

Jase's mouth tightened into a hard line. "Banditos." He turned his attention to scooping the last bit of stew.

When he looked up again, the boy watched him, frowning.

"Were you slave holders?" Landers asked.

"My family was 'poor white trash.'"

The kid looked blank.

"My folks were neither slave-holders nor holding with slavery."

"Why did you join the Rangers?"

"To protect Texas."

Landers gave him a thoughtful nod. "My father fought for Kansas and the Union. My aunt tells me that my mother was an abolitionist. I can't say I remember one way or the other. My aunt, though, says that slavery is a sin. I think the sin is treating people like they're not really people."

They lingered over pie and coffee. Now that the boy had started talking, Jase only had to drop a comment here and a question there to maintain the conversation.

When they headed upstairs, their easy understanding experienced a setback. Landers insisted he was comfortable on the floor and that is where he would spend the night. Jase figured he'd let the kid fall asleep wherever he liked and put him to bed later, but Jase fell asleep first and Landers stayed on the floor.

Next day, Jase was irritated—with himself *and* the boy.

"I'm not gonna put up with any more foolishness. Sleepin' on the ground when you had to is one thing. Sleepin' on the floor in a hotel room is wasteful."

Landers neither argued nor agreed.

Jase sighed. "Saddle the horses."

They travelled in easy stages and made the quiet town of Coldwater by evening. Not used to riding all day, Landers was practically dead on the hoof. Jase had to force him to stay up long enough to have something to eat.

He paid for a room over Coldwater's only saloon. The accommodations weren't fancy, but the place was clean. Like most rooms, it was supplied with a double bed. This one also had a cradle.

"I can use the mattress in the cradle," the boy said. "I'll put it on the floor."

Unbuttoning his shirt, Jase sighed. "Kid, you're exhausted. You need to rest or you're gonna slow me down tomorrow."

Landers paused for a moment, then reached for the mattress.

Jase cleared his throat. "Do you like crossing wills with me? Or don't you trust me?"

"I trust you, sir. I never meant to imply that I didn't trust you and I don't mean to be contrary. I'm very grateful for all your help and—"

"Never mind. Sleep where you like."

Jase readied for bed. Gun and holster were hung on the bed post. He draped his outer clothes over the bottom post, with his boots tucked within reach. When he was stripped to his socks and long underwear, he climbed into bed. All the while, Landers held his bedroll in one hand and the cradle mattress in the other.

When the candle was extinguished, sounds in the dark told Jase that Landers was getting ready for bed. The mattress shifted as the boy crawled between the covers, keeping to the edge of the bed.

"Night, Marly."

"Good night, sir."

"Friends call me Jase."

"Good night, Jase."

The bed, like many old spring beds, sagged in the middle. Once they were no longer capable of consciously keeping to their sides, they met in the middle. Instinctively, they took advantage of each other's body heat as the night grew colder. It wasn't the first time Jase had shared his bed with a fellow traveler and ended up back to back, sharing warmth.

He woke the next morning with his arm about Marly. The boy's head was on his shoulder and one hand rested on his chest near his heart. It felt so comfortable that it might have worried him—if he had not just discovered that Marly Landers was a girl.

CHAPTER 3

Marly woke up in easy stages.

At some point, in what seemed to be a dream, she felt warm and safe in a secure embrace—a feeling she had not known since her mother had died.

Later, she stirred. Feeling a slight draft, she pulled the covers in closer and snuggled back down into sleep. Whether it was a minute or an hour later, she didn't know. Finally, sleep gave over to wakefulness.

She pulled herself up on her elbow. "Morning."

Already awake and dressed, Jase straddled a chair and watched her. "C'mon, sleepy head," he said with an exaggerated drawl. "We got miles to go. You get yourself cleaned up and dressed. And be quick. I'm going down for coffee and I'll be ordering breakfast. If you're late, you'll get yours cold."

After he left, Marly took advantage of the privacy to have a sponge bath. It had almost broken her heart not to take a bath the day before, but she couldn't very well use the men's room at a public bathhouse.

As she stripped down, she wished she had the nerve to ask Jase for a new set of long underwear. She made do, beating out the dust and using a damp towel to attack the worst of the dirt. She did the same with the singlet she wore underneath, a hand-knit garment she'd been given half a lifetime ago when she was ten. Being knit, it stretched to fit her and held in parts that would otherwise have given away her masquerade.

"And to think," she said, examining her modest curves, "at one time I wished I had a real figure."

Aside from feeling safer, she rather enjoyed being a boy, instead of the young lady her aunt always expected her to be. More importantly, a boy could travel alone, though she was glad of Jase's company and protection.

Of course, if she had been born a boy, she wouldn't be in this trouble in the first place. If she had been born a boy, she might have been able to protect her mother and wouldn't have needed to protect herself. If she had failed to save her mother, a boy could have stayed with Sarge, instead of being taken to her aunt for propriety's sake. And if she had been taken to her aunt, a boy wouldn't be expected to help out at the school. He might have been allowed to work for the Sheriff instead. More importantly, a boy wouldn't have been seduced by a honey-talking, city slicker whose good looks and charm were in direct proportion to his criminal motives.

So far, the masquerade hadn't been overtaxing. One of the benefits of overseeing the schoolyard was that she knew first-hand how boys acted. She modeled her behavior after young John Henry who, with three older brothers to train him, knew how to get away with murder around adults and hold his own with the bigger boys like John Thomas.

Soon, being boyish came naturally to her. She didn't have to act like someone else. Her deception was aided by the fact that no one expected a young woman to be travelling on her own dressed as a boy. She suspected that one or two women she'd met had seen through the disguise. Since they didn't say anything, she couldn't be sure. The important thing was that no man would see her as a woman and take advantage of her.

Marly didn't really think Jase Strachan would do that. She almost trusted him.

But then she had trusted that hazel-eyed snake, Charlie, too.

She remained cautious. Even if he didn't hurt her, Jase would probably feel it his duty to send her back to Aunt Adele.

She couldn't let that happen.

I reckon, she thought as she scrubbed her face, if I can pass for a boy sleeping back-to-back in the same bed, I probably don't have much to worry about.

After Marly took care of her ablutions, Jase purchased extra supplies. Flour, sugar, coffee, beans and bacon were distributed between their saddlebags. Marly's bags also carried chocolate, dried fruit and peanuts. Jase's carried extra ammunition.

She hoped they wouldn't have to use the latter.

"My man has at least four days on us now," he announced as they rode out of town. "I know he's headed for El Paso, so I'm gonna risk headin' there directly, instead of trailin' him from town to town."

"He's on the stage?"

"Good guess," he acknowledged with a nod of his head. "He's not the ridin' type. He's been travellin' the stage, stoppin' now and then to play poker and relieve more suckers of their cash."

"And that's why you are hunting him?"

Marly's skepticism was met with a derisive snort.

"If he cheats at the table, sooner or later it'll catch up with him. No, I'm on his trail for a more ambitious crime. He embezzled money from the wrong people. The kind who take this sort of thing personally and have the contacts in the Governor's house to back up their vendettas."

"So you're after the money he stole."

"He doesn't have the money with him. We caught him once and he gave us the slip. Lost him for a bit after that, then I got a tip that he was headed for El Paso."

"How do you know he doesn't have the money now?"

"I don't," he admitted with a shrug. "I'm guessin' because he's livin' hand to mouth. Game to game, in his case."

They stopped mid-afternoon to make camp.

"I'm not tired yet," she said.

"We don't have a waiter to bring us dinner tonight. Or a readymade bed. We can't just ride 'til you're falling out of your saddle."

Marly was about to protest. Hadn't she travelled a hundred miles on her own, often walking for long stretches of the day? It was true. She didn't have Jase's stamina in the saddle, but...

She bit back a retort that was at the tip of her tongue. She had only a commonsense notion of how to make camp.

Swallowing her pride, she listened to Jase and did as she was told. She committed every step to memory, from tending and hobbling the horses to clearing the area and digging a fire pit. Jase had found a slight hollow with scrub providing additional shelter. The horses were kept within sight, out in the open where they could graze on prairie grass.

"Know how to handle a revolver?" Jase asked once they were settled.

She eyed him with suspicion. "I know enough not to shoot my foot off."

Jase had two revolvers. A Colt Peacemaker, which he wore in his holster, and a Colt Navy, a relic of the war. He put aside the Navy and had Marly start with the lighter weight Peacemaker. He unloaded the gun and took it apart, explaining the various parts and their functions with the bored ease of a teacher repeating the most basic lessons.

She got the impression that Jase had been an instructor and a soldier in his past. Under his tutelage, she reassembled, loaded, unloaded, and disassembled the Peacemaker. The third time she loaded the gun, he stopped her, took the gun back and checked it over.

"Okay," he said, picking up the second gun and his rifle. "Let's see what you can do."

She followed him to a place where deadwood created a natural wall. Using large stones, he set up six targets. Then he counted off fifteen paces and signaled her to stand beside him.

He handed her the Peacemaker. "Point and shoot."

Marly reluctantly took the gun and checked it before straight-arming the revolver in front of her and pulling the trigger. The gun wobbled and a clump of dirt flew up several feet in front of the target area.

Jase stepped up behind her and reached around her waist. "Steady the gun with your other hand."

As he posed her arms, his hard muscles pressed into her back.

Torn between fear and excitement, Marly stiffened.

"Relax," he whispered. "Take your time. Speed will come. Squeeze, don't pull." He backed away and cleared his throat. "And try aiming. It helps."

With great concentration, she aimed the gun, instead of merely pointing it. The shot went over the targeted stone.

"Better. Watch me."

Marly handed over the gun with relief.

"Now draw a bead on your target. Stare that pebble in the eye and shoot it before it shoots you." He demonstrated, picking off the next target. Then he spun the Peacemaker and handed it back, grip first. "Try it. Think of it as somethin' that can shoot back."

With a fatalistic shrug, she accepted the gun and followed his instructions. The stone exploded into dust. She looked at Jase in surprise and received an 'I-told-you-so' expression in response.

"Again," he ordered.

She hit the next target, but not dead-on. It ricocheted off the log.

"Again."

She missed.

"Don't try so hard. Just do it."

Click.

"Don't to forget to count your shots," he said, setting up more targets. "You have to reload first."

Marly reloaded the gun. She hit four out of six targets, missing one and nicking the other.

"You got a good eye," Jase said. "Let's try another round, then we'll go on to the rifle."

Hitting five out of six, she smiled with satisfaction.

In a flash of blue steel, Jase drew the Navy and shot the remaining target. With a showy spin, he returned the gun to his holster.

Marly stared in awe. Returning to the business of reloading, she handed the Peacemaker back to Jase. He checked and holstered it, tucking the gun into the small of his back.

He handed her the Winchester .44 carbine. They hunted around for more targets and set them up. He counted off twenty-five paces this time, explaining that the rifle had a greater range and accuracy than the handgun.

"Ready?"

Marly took a deep breath. One. Two.

The stones exploded in quick succession.

She backed up five more paces. Three. Four. Five.

Not one miss. All hits were dead-on.

She gave him a smug grin. He acknowledged it with a raised eyebrow. Without warning, he threw two pieces of wood into the air. Marly swung the rifle up and both pieces of wood were hit, square on. Jase let out a whistle of admiration.

"My Aunt Adele," Marly explained, expertly topping up the Winchester's magazine, then cradling the rifle in her arms. "She thought that riding horses was a waste of resources and sidearms were only respectable when carried by an officer of the law. Even then, she wasn't too sure about them. But I can hitch and drive a pair, and she made sure I learned to hit what I was aiming at with a shotgun or a rifle."

Jase grinned. "Jack rabbits mostly, I expect."

"And wolves. I have to admit, I didn't aim for the animals, just the earth beneath them. I figured they could warn their kin off if they lived to tell about their near miss. Anyway, the way I see it, long as there are rabbits, the wolves will eat them. And long as there are wolves, the rabbits won't overrun the garden." She shrugged. "Still, Aunt Adele was convinced I was a lousy shot."

"What else did she teach you?"

"She's a school teacher, so she taught me reading, writing and arithmetic. She also taught me how to cook, mend, chop wood, build a fire, tend chickens, hoe, mow, fear God and mind my manners."

"Why'd you leave?"

"She told me to."

It was close enough to the truth, though Aunt Adele had another destination in mind.

"I suppose," she said, bitterness in her voice, "I didn't learn some lessons as well as I did others."

That killed the conversation for a few minutes. Marly was pensive and she was thankful that Jase was too cautious to ask the kind of questions that might prompt her to reveal her secret.

How long could she keep it from him anyway?

It was only a matter of time before he found out she was a girl.

Jase put her to work cleaning the guns and rifle as he cooked. It was not the most inspiring fare—beans and biscuits—but the coffee was good.

"Who taught you what you know?" she asked when Jase showed her how to clean dishes without water, using the sandy earth instead.

"I got a little schooling when I was a youngster. I learned to read and write and do my numbers. Then my pa was killed. I had to stay home and work the farm with my ma and help take care of my little sister. In the evening, I'd read to ma. She liked to hear stories and she wanted me to keep in practice."

"Sounds nice."

"It wasn't a bad life, I guess. Can't say I ever took to farming. At sixteen, I joined the Rangers."

"Your sister?"

"Dead. All the family I know of is dead or gone."

There was a long silence.

Jase finally broke the mood by launching into a lecture on how to pack the gear in the saddlebags so it took up the least amount of space and the weight was evenly distributed. By the light of the fire, he had her unpack and pack her saddlebags to prove she'd been listening. While she packed, he started a second pot of coffee.

"I generally sleep light on the trail. Since there's two of us, we might as well take turns sleepin'. You take the first watch. Just sit comfortable and keep the fire low. Don't stare into the flames. It's a sure way to get sleepy and it'll ruin your night vision. When the moon is high, wake me. I'll take over. Coffee will be ready soon. It'll help keep you awake."

"Are we likely to get attacked?"

"No, but chances are we'll run into trouble sometime on the trail. We'll come out all right. You're travelling with a Texas Ranger." He gave her a lazy smile. "Smart folk don't mess with Texas Rangers."

Vigilantly, Marly sat out her watch. She stood and stretched a couple of times, careful not to disturb Jase. Twice, she thought she heard something approaching the campfire. It was either her imagination or whatever it was thought better of bothering them.

It seemed Jase was determined not only to look out for her, but to teach her to look out for herself. It was unlikely that he suspected she was a girl. This left her with mixed feelings. Mostly, she was pleased she could perform her part so well. But beneath the guise of the charming, willful lad was the heart of a young woman with vanity enough to want to be considered attractive and feminine.

She replayed her shooting lesson in her mind. In her imagination, Jase's arms wrapped around her, guiding her shots. Then, taking the revolver back, he turned her in his arms and gazed lovingly down at her before letting loose her braid. Fingering the curls, he told her how beautiful she was, how much he wanted her.

Except, she thought, my hair would be matted with dust from the trail and the layers of clothing between us would hamper the kind of romantic scene I'd read about in the penny dreadfuls I'd hidden from Aunt Adele.

What she needed was a dress, but certainly not any dress she'd owned in her life. She needed a petticoat with an easy to loosen ribbon at the neck and maybe some ruffles. Though why she'd be wearing such a garment during a shooting lesson was hard to imagine.

When the moon reached its zenith, she gently roused Jase to take his watch. They exchanged a few words, then she took his place between the covers of his bedroll. She had not realized how tense or how chilled she had become until she relaxed under the blankets. They were still warm from Jase's body.

For a few pleasant moments, she dwelt on that thought.

Then fatigue plunged her into slumber.

Morning came too quickly.

Determined not to be a burden, Marly shoved aside her blanket and pretended that she wasn't dead tired. With the help of fresh coffee and biscuits, she managed to convince herself that she was well rested.

By the time the sun was visible on the horizon, they were on their way. Though she was sore in places she didn't like to mention, riding that early had its benefits. The landscape was beautiful in the dawn light. Later in the day, the sun would bleach the color out of the scenery. For now, everything was vibrant and the scent of sage wafted on the breeze.

Ahead of them lay the Sacramento mountain range. Around them, the plateau was so flat Marly could see the dust of riders far in the distance. No one came any closer than that.

Mid-morning, they stopped and let the horses graze for half an hour before setting off again. Around noon, Jase pointed out a good place for lunch, with grazing for the horses and a little shade. They dined on jerky and leftover biscuits from breakfast. Everything tasted wonderful.

But she was bone tired. She yearned for a nap.

"Come on, kid. We can get some target practice in while the horses rest."

Marly suppressed a groan. She ran through the possible responses that boys she knew might have. Target practice wasn't a chore, therefore dragging her heels wasn't appropriate. Maybe he'd put his arms around her again.

More cheerful, she hitched up her pants and set her hat forward to shade her eyes after smoothing back sweat-soaked tendrils of hair.

"Not much to shoot at," she remarked.

She pulled a leaf of dry grass and used it dislodge a piece of jerky from between her teeth—an action as unladylike as it was practical.

"We'll aim at the tops of the tall grass," Jase said.

Marly was required to repeat back all his lessons from the day before. Then he pointed to a stalk and let her shoot.

"You missed."

"I did not. I hit the one I was aiming at."

"Then you were aiming at the wrong one."

She pushed her hat back and gave him a hard stare.

Jase sighed and pulled a thread from his bandana. He marched into the long grass, tied the thread around one of the stalks and returned to her side.

"Okay," he said. "Can you see your target now?"

Marly aimed, fired and missed. She shook off her irritation, and after a moment of squinting at the grass, she tried again.

The top of the stalk disappeared.

Jase set up another four stalks. With careful aim, Marly hit each one. Then he threw a rock in the air. She nicked it, sending it spinning. She shot at it again, but was out of ammunition.

"We'll work on your loading skills later," Jase said, taking the gun. "We'd best rest a bit." Settling in the shade, he pulled a book out of his saddlebag and started reading.

Marly flopped down on the hard ground, irked at the lack of appreciation for her improving skills. After all, a day ago she had never even held a handgun, much less fired one. Jase hadn't seemed to notice how much better she was at riding either.

She considered sulking, but decided it was too much effort. It was much easier to stake a claim to a patch of shade and imagine saving Jase from some undefined danger. And rubbing his nose in it.

Jase gave Marly's shoulder a gentle shake. She opened her eyes and smiled up at him. For a few seconds, they just stared at each other and he was tempted to say something—if he could think of something that wouldn't cause trouble.

Instead, he stood and gave her a hand up.

"How long did I sleep?" she asked, her attention shifting from the sun to the saddled horses, then back to him.

"Couple of hours. You looked like you needed it."

She shuffled her feet. "Did you sleep?"

"I rested my eyes a bit."

Again, their gaze met and he resisted the urge to tell her he knew she was no boy. She broke contact first this time and began to brush dirt and dried grass off her clothes.

"Tomorrow, we'll just rest at noontime," he said. "Target practice can wait until the evenin'. You're pretty good. I might just make a sharpshooter out of you."

He saw pleasure, pride and just a touch of preening flit across her face before she thanked him for the compliment. Squelching a gallant impulse to help her into the saddle, he swung up onto Grandee. He waited as she mounted Trouble with only a little difficulty.

Jase, he thought, you are riding the trail to Perdition. And I don't mean the half-dozen mining towns of the same name.

He had told Marly that he picked this trail because it was shorter. Looking at a map, it seemed shorter than the stage route. If they rode hard, it could be a faster route—but he had no intention of riding hard.

He told himself that he picked the trail to give him time to prepare Marly for what was ahead. That plan would make sense if she actually was a boy who needed a mentor to keep him alive and on the right side of the law. Instead of teaching her to ride, shoot and track, he should have spent his time finding out who Aunt Adele was and sending the girl home. Now he was stuck with the masquerade until trail's end. Or until he admitted he was a fool.

Before stopping for the night, he shot a rabbit for dinner. The sound startled Marly, who was staring dreamily into the setting sun. It upset Trouble too and he unseated her. Both gave Jase an indignant glare.

"Get used to it," he advised, squelching the desire to apologize. Or laugh.

Later, Marly skinned the rabbit with practiced ease. She rubbed the flesh with fresh sage she'd picked. Next, she gathered fuel for the fire and salt from their supplies. She skewered the rabbit and set it to roast above the fire. After burying the head and offal away from the camp, she set to the task of scraping the skin.

"Another skill your aunt taught you?" Jase asked as he worked on his chore of cleaning weapons.

"The older I got, the more Aunt Adele expected me to cook. She was busy teaching and doing church work. Rabbit and chicken were the meats I most often had to put on the table."

"You prepare them, but you won't shoot them?"

"I'm not against hunting for food. I've killed chickens. And Aunt

Adele had me help butcher the hog she bought one year. I didn't like it much." She chewed her bottom lip. "Some folks enjoy killing. I don't. I guess I'll do it if I have to."

"You can leave the hunting to me."

After the meal, Jase pulled out the battered book he'd been reading and offered it to Marly.

Her eyes widened in surprise. "Thank you."

"You're welcome." Sensing an unasked question, he added, "Many cowboys carry the Bible on the trail. I once met a man who carried Plutarch's Lives. I prefer Shakespeare."

"I didn't know this about you."

"Well, now you do." He closed his eyes, recalling Marly's earlier words. *"Some folks enjoy killing."*

He hoped that wasn't how she saw him. He didn't think of himself as a killer, but he couldn't deny that death was part of his stock in trade.

As he dozed off, he remembered the feel of Marly's body against his. He imagined taking her in his arms, pulling her close and devouring her with kisses.

Would she return those kisses or shy away from him?

Just past midnight, Jase woke to the smell of coffee. As he stretched, Marly glanced up from the book and gave him a warm smile.

Coffee, company and that smile sure beats waking up alone, he thought.

Then he tasted the coffee. Good God.

He didn't mean to be rude. The expression on his face was a natural reflex.

"It's not very good," she admitted, "but if you sip it slowly, I guarantee you won't fall asleep."

He nodded toward the book. "Which one are you reading?"

"As You Like It."

"Maybe it's time I reread that one."

A suspicious frown creased Marly's brow. "Really."

"It's one of my favorites," he added. Although he'd always thought a girl dressing up as a boy to be a bit improbable.

They switched places. She tucked down into his bedroll and he draped the blanket around his shoulders to keep the chill off his back.

He wondered if she accepted this arrangement as convention, or whether she knew that he gave up his warm covers for her sake.

"Do you regret taking me along?" she asked, startling him. "I've been a lot of trouble and I know I'm slowing you down."

He had no idea what to say.

"It has crossed my mind," she said, "that for a fraction of the cost, you could have put me on a stage for El Paso."

"Is that what you want?"

"No!"

Trouble gave an indignant whinny.

In a softer tone, Marly said, "Though I have someplace to be, I'm not in a big hurry to get there. I have to the end of the month to get to El Paso. That's still twenty-three days away."

"I know it's not the business of the Texas Rangers, but do you think you could tell me why you're goin' to El Paso?"

Marly rolled over on her back and stared at the stars. When she spoke, her tone was detached. "At the end of the month, maybe a bit later, a package should be arriving with my name on it. I didn't send it, but I've got to receive it or a lot of people will lose their savings. If I can, I also want to catch the guy who used my name—and me—to cheat my friends."

"Sounds like it could be Ranger business."

"The crime was committed in Kansas. Notices went out. The common wisdom seems to be that the folks of Cherryville should learn from their mistakes and get on with it."

"But that's not good enough for Marly Landers," Jase remarked without rancor.

"Nope."

"What's this bandito's name?"

"Charlie Meese. Though I think he's used other names."

"No doubt." He had a bad taste in his mouth. "Get some sleep, Marly. We're a couple of days out of Fortuna and El Paso is a four-day ride from there. I'll get you there in plenty of time to take care of your business."

And his.

CHAPTER 4

Fortuna was a frontier town west of the Pecos River, a synonym for wild. Law had reached it—just barely. The town was on the Sunset Trail, the southernmost overland route to California. Spring and summer saw a seasonal growth of the town with the movement of wagon trains. The rest of the year, it was the center of commerce for the area's residents. Since these included cattle, sheep and horse ranchers, plus a few stubborn homesteaders, a handful of itinerant prospectors and 'civilized' Indians, Fortuna was a lively spot year round.

Jase's plan was to stock up and move on, which didn't impress Marly much, especially when he told her the second half of their trek to El Paso would be longer, with harder trails, colder nights and a chance of trouble from man and nature.

"We'll be stayin' at The Oasis," he said. "Friend of mine owns the saloon."

"The *saloon*?"

"One of them. Last time I was through Fortuna, there were three, not counting the dance hall that burned down. 'Course, that was a couple of years ago now."

Given the picture he drew, Marly was surprised that her first sight of Fortuna was a shining white church spire.

"You didn't say anything about a church," she said.

"New to me. There used to be a meetin' hall for services. Caught fire the same night the dance hall went up in flames."

The steeple of the church acted as a beacon. She watched it change color, graying as the amber sun set behind it. By the time they crossed the river that defined the town's east boundary, the church was barely visible in the twilight. Then it disappeared altogether as the intervening houses blocked the church from view.

To the right, lanterns illuminated front porches and windows glowed golden-yellow. On the left, open fires cast eerie flickering lights on tents and shacks built in and around burned ruins of a building.

She shivered. "Who lives there?"

"The old. The outcasts. Every society's got its fringes. That's Fortuna's."

"Was that the dance hall or the meeting hall?"

"Both. They were side-by-side. With the livery over there." He pointed down the road. "They were the town's first buildings."

Marly got her first glimpse of The Oasis just before turning down Main Street. It was an impressive two-story building set back from the road. A wide veranda wrapped around it and there was a balcony above. Both had hanging lanterns and flower baskets. It looked like a respectable but expensive hotel and seemed out of place in a frontier town.

Then they turned the corner.

The hotel was a bright star on the darkened street. The veranda widened, serving as a sidewalk. The lanterns burned brighter and were augmented by the light pouring out of the open casement windows and French doors. The main entrance was at the end of the block, angled to face out onto the intersection. Hanging from the balcony above the entrance was a sign decorated with flowering cactus and desert roses.

The Oasis, it proclaimed in flowery script.

"This place is a hotel?" Marly asked with disbelief.

"Not properly speakin'." Jase dismounted and indicated she should do the same. "There are rooms you can rent. They're kind of expensive, but they come with perks."

"How expensive?"

He flipped the reins over the rail and ignored her.

"How expensive?" she repeated, pursuing him up the stairs.

At the door, he took a deep breath. "They tend to be rented by the hour."

"Oh."

With a shrug, she followed him inside and once over the threshold, she stopped, transfixed.

The first time she tried to get work in a saloon was at the Palace in Wichita, Kansas. The size and opulence of the place intimidated her and the scantily clad ladies were shocking to a small town girl. She wasn't sorry to find they didn't need her.

The Oasis wasn't quite as big as the Palace, or as crowded. In every other way, it exceeded Wichita's finest.

Marly was knocked aside by a brick of a man in a smock coat. He grunted something inarticulate and made a beeline to one of the green baize-covered tables where other gentlemen were engaged in a card game. Beyond the card tables was an ignored roulette wheel.

"Excuse me," a female voice briskly.

Marly dodged an attractive, boldly dressed woman with a gaping bodice and a delicately painted face. She was one of several ladies that seemed to float like wheeled dolls, gliding between the casino area and the linen draped tables set for diners. They were nothing like the saloon women Marly had encountered in her travels, who at best could claim a shabby glamour.

"Don't stare," Jase said. "It ain't polite."

He had removed his hat upon entering and now shooed her with it toward the bar.

She nodded, then came to an abrupt halt.

Hanging above the mirrors behind the bar was the biggest painting she had ever seen. Rendered in vivid oil color, a voluptuous, auburn-haired Amazon was draped and posed in a suggestive manner. It was so lifelike that Marly's jaw dropped and a deep flush rose in her cheeks.

"If the boy's like that over my painting," a deep, throaty voice said, "what's he gonna do when he meets the real thing?"

Marly turned, musk perfume hitting her like a gut punch.

The Amazon woman from the painting stepped toward her. The glitter of colored sequins on the woman's skintight gown dazzled her as a bejeweled hand lifted her chin, closing her mouth. Through long, dark lashes, green eyes scrutinized Marly. Sculpted brows arched slightly. Then the hand dropped.

"A little young for The Oasis, isn't he, Jase?"

"The boy's old enough to have supper here."

Jase rested a heavy hand on Marly's shoulder. He pulled her in close to him, removed her hat and smoothed her hair.

Marly grabbed her hat back and held it in a tight fist.

"This is Marly Landers," he said. "He's in my charge for the time being. Marly, I would like to present my old—"

"Not *old*, sugar."

"My *good* friend," he corrected, "and proprietor of this establishment, Jezebel."

Still nauseous from the perfume, Marly managed a small, insincere smile. "Ma'am."

"Charmed," Jezebel replied with equal insincerity.

Jase took the woman's arm. "Got a room for us, Jez? We've been on the trail a spell and could use a bath and a proper bed."

"You always got a room here, sugar," she purred, leading them to the dining room. "Come and join me at my table. Happens I was just about to have Fred bring me my supper anyhow."

Jezebel's table was not hard to pick out. It was the only one on the raised stage beside the curved staircase. On the back wall, sconces dripping with faceted crystals bracketed long gilt-framed mirrors. The table itself was cherry wood, like the bar. So was the throne-like armchair that faced the room.

Standing next to the chair was a dignified-looking man with iron-gray hair, wearing a formal black, swallow-tail suit. He greeted Jase with a nod of recognition before holding Jezebel's chair.

Marly felt sick. It wasn't just the smell of perfume. Jase was ruggedly handsome, regardless of trail-worn clothes and untrimmed whiskers, whereas she looked plain and dirty. The only consolation she had in seeing her image in the mirror was the knowledge that her masquerade was safe. Besides, she wasn't one to spend her money on frivolous fancy dresses or face paint. Nor would Aunt Adele ever have allowed her these.

Still...

"What do you wanna eat?"Jase asked, interrupting her depressing thoughts.

"Not hungry," she whispered.

He frowned. "Since when?"

She sneezed from the perfume, gave a loud sniff and plopped into a chair. "Can I have a beer?"

Jase hesitated, pressing his lips together.

Her act was probably amusing him.

She arched one brow. "Well?"

"No. And don't try tellin' me you're old enough either."

Marly had a good ear and managed a fair imitation of Jase's thickest accent. "I reckon you ain't got any call to chew me out. I just stretched the truth a mite."

"Do we have sarsaparilla, Fred?" Jezebel asked the man in the suit.

"Milk," Jase said.

Marly pouted. "But I want beer."

"Milk," he repeated.

She sniffed loudly. "I'm leaving."

Jase caught her by the wrist as she stood. He looked puzzled and not at all amused.

"I'm not hungry," she said, giving him a look of quiet desperation.

He relented. At least, his eyes told her that he relented.

"Fine. Go." He spoke as though he were talking to a recalcitrant child.

This infuriated her, but she stifled a response.

Fred cleared his throat. "I've taken the liberty of having your things taken up to room five, Master Jason."

His accent was British, Marly reckoned, and well-educated.

"Your mounts, of course, are being seen to," he added. "I will have bath water sent up after I take your orders for supper. Master Landers, I'll show you to your room."

Jezebel sighed. "Ain't he a jewel?"

"I'll be up later," Jase called out as Marly followed Fred up the stairs. "And I'll be checking behind your ears."

She paused, biting back a retort. Then she took the stairs two at a time.

Jase watched Marly leave, wishing he could follow her. He also wished he had forewarned her about The Oasis. He should have known the place would overwhelm her.

"Quite a handful," Jezebel said. "Where did he come from?"

"Kansas."

"I mean, what's he doing with you?"

For a moment, he was tempted to tell Jezebel the truth.

"His parents are dead." He moved to Marly's abandoned seat. "You might say I'm his self-appointed guardian 'til he finds other relatives."

A waiter bearing a silver tray placed a goblet of wine before Jezebel and a tankard of beer in front of Jase.

"You're a Ranger," Jezebel said, taking a sip of wine. "Didn't you tell me once that Rangers can't tie themselves down with family?"

"It's temporary, Jez. He's looking for a relation in El Paso. That's where we're headed."

Jezebel's brow puckered. "You mean you're not here to replace Strothers?"

"Ellery Strothers? I thought he left the Rangers."

"Strothers accepted the post of town marshal last fall. He didn't exactly endear himself to everyone around here. About a week back, he was killed. I thought you knew. Rumor has it, one of Egan's men shot him."

"Good lord, Jezebel, how was I supposed to know that?"

"Well, I wired the boys in Austin right off, Jase. When I saw you, I figured they sent you to handle the case. I asked for you particularly." She smiled. "I had to get you back here somehow."

Jase sighed. "I'll wire Austin tomorrow. I'm here now and I suppose the other business can wait. You better fill me in."

"Later."

As if on cue, a convoy of waiters ascended the stage and set out a repast fit for a queen.

"We got plenty of time, Jase."

"All right. We can talk business first thing tomorrow, over breakfast."

Jezebel glared. "You know I don't do mornings, sugar."

When he said nothing, she heaved a sigh, then nodded.

He suspected she wasn't through trying to change his mind.

At the top of the stairs, Marly and Fred were met by a stately woman with raven hair streaked with silver. Unlike the ladies downstairs, her gown was modest and simple.

"You are with Señor Strachan?"

"Yes, ma'am," Marly said.

"We will get you settled. I am Señora Consuela Mercedes Domintado de Vegas."

"Marly Landers."

"Come, Señor Landers. This way." She eyed Fred. "I'll take things from here. Gracias, Señor Fred."

With a rustle of silk, Señora de Vegas led Marly down the hall to the last door but one. It had no number.

"What's that?" Marly pointed to the unmarked door.

"That is Señorita Jezebel's quarters." She opened the door to room five. "This is your room. It is reserved for special guests of the Señorita."

Marly gave a long whistle.

The room was impressive. A four-poster bed was the centerpiece. Draped with red velvet, it dominated the room. An ornate footed bathtub with a cherub decorated cover sat between a bronze trimmed stove and the window. Closer examination revealed a pipe leading from the tub through the exterior wall.

"It drains?"

"Si," Señora de Vegas replied. "It drains."

Marly shook her head in wonderment. She explored the rest of the room and found their saddlebags sitting in the wardrobe. Hanging above them was a red-striped nightshirt and red quilted satin dressing gown.

She gave the Señora a questioning look.

"They belong to Señor Strachan," the woman said. "He left them here."

"Oh."

"He and the Señorita are very close friends."

Marly wondered how close.

"I will leave you, Señor Landers. Señor Fred will be up soon. He will see to your needs."

"Señora de Vegas, could you tell me something?"

"Si, if I can."

"Are all the ladies here..." Marly stalled, unsure how to put it.

Señora de Vegas blushed. "Some of the ladies who are employed at The Oasis are fully employed. Many are not. If you are wondering, I am not employed here as such."

"I'm sorry. I didn't mean—"

"I know what you meant," she said with gentle dignity. "Señorita Jezebel has kindly let me stay, since my husband was killed a year ago. I try to help out. The Señorita calls me her den mother. Please let me know if you need anything."

As the door closed behind the Señora, Marly let out a long sigh and slumped onto the bed, stroking the velvet coverlet as she gathered her thoughts.

What was Jase doing downstairs? Was he still with Jezebel?

A campfire and a starry sky would suit her fine right now. A cup of Jase's coffee would be heaven.

A soft tap on the door interrupted her reverie. Before she had a chance to answer it, Fred came in, leading a parade of shirt-sleeved waiters bearing cans of hot water, while he carried a tray laden with sandwiches, cookies, milk and a pulp western.

As the waiters filled the tub, Fred arranged the repast on a side table, folded back the bedding and fluffed the pillows. With a snap of his fingers, he summoned a young man loaded down with a stack of thick white towels. On top was a blue striped nightshirt. Fred took the pile and dismissed his entourage. The towels he placed on a chair beside the tub. The nightshirt was laid out on the bed.

"If you will produce your laundry, Master Landers, I will have it taken away with the wet towels later. *All* your laundry." He gave Marly a hard stare. "I assure you, we will have clean clothes for you by tomorrow morning."

"Yes, sir. Thank you."

"Will you require anything else, Master Landers?"

"No, sir. Thank you, Mr.—"

"Fred."

"Thank you, Mr. Fred."

"Just Fred."

"Thank you, Fred.

He bestowed a sympathetic smile on her, then left the room.

Alone, Marly bolted the door against further intrusion.

By the time she had soaked, scrubbed, dried and dressed, Marly was starving. She ate half a roast beef sandwich before combing and braiding her damp hair. Then she climbed into bed with the dime novel in one hand and the remainder of the sandwich in the other. That's how Jase would have found her if she hadn't locked the door.

"Open up, you infernal brat!" He gave the door a good rattle for emphasis. "If I gotta break this lock, it's comin' out of your hide."

Marly crawled out of bed and headed across the cold floor.

Opening the door, she scowled. "Oh, it's you."

Jase strode into the room. "I take it you're comfortable."

"Uh huh."

She hopped back into bed and stuffed the last bit of sandwich into her mouth.

Fred and his young assistant entered the room. The boy drained and cleaned the tub, while Fred laid out shaving gear.

"Sir," he said, his cultured accent more obsequious than ever, "Miss Jezebel invites you to make use of her apartment tonight. I can have a bath drawn for you there if you prefer."

"My thanks to Jezebel," Jase said, "but I'll be quite comfortable here."

"As you wish."

Fred whispered instructions to the boy, who went off immediately, taking the wet towels and Marly's laundry with him.

"Sir?' Fred pointed to a chair.

"I can shave myself."

"Please, sir. I've seen what happens when you shave yourself."

Marly sputtered on a mouthful of milk.

Jase grumbled something unintelligible and sat down.

"I'm thinking I'll keep a moustache," he said.

"As we well know, Master Jason, a moustache does not become you."

"That was years ago."

Marly watched in fascination as Fred lathered Jase's whiskers. Despite Jase's protests, the moustache was the first to go.

When she had first met Jase, she assumed he was about the same age as Doc Pincus, who was old enough to be her father. Clean and trimmed, she put him at Sheriff Langtree's age, which she knew to be thirty-two because he once told her that he was twelve years her senior.

Fred was right. Jase looked better clean shaven.

Meanwhile, the boy had returned with a fresh stack of towels and a second parade of water bearers. Bringing up the rear was one of Jezebel's ladies. She carried a silver tray with a cut glass decanter and two glasses. With a few whispered words, she handed this to Fred.

Fred turned to Jase. "Miss Jezebel is wondering if you would care to share a nightcap with her. She could join you. Or if it would disturb the young gentleman," he cleared his throat, "you could meet her in her private parlor after your bath."

Jase trailed a hand through the hot water in the tub.

"Please let Jezebel know that as temptin' as her offer is, I'm hittin' the sack soon as I'm clean."

"Very well, sir.

Fred gathered the kit and shaving towel. He stayed long enough to make sure the bath was full and Jase's nightshirt, robe and slippers were laid out. Then he retreated with a dignified bow.

Marly took a long gulp of milk. "I love the way that fella talks. What is he doing in a place like this? He should be in the Governor's mansion."

"I think that's where Jez found him." Jase bolted the door and leaned against it. "I can't quite remember which governor."

"Miz Jezebel," Marly said, drawing out the zeds in an affected way, "is awfully persistent. Does she throw herself at all her guests?"

"Not all of them." Jase stripped off his shirt and the top of his long johns. "Just the special ones."

Marly snorted and buried her nose in her magazine. She listened to him undress, resisting the urge to peek, but the sound of him climbing into the tub drew her eyes off the page.

She'd seen plenty of bare torsos in her time. The thickly muscled field hands and soft, smooth boys didn't affect her the way Jase's lean, sharply defined back did. All too quickly, he sank into the tub and she had to hide behind the book so he wouldn't see her blush.

"What's it matter to you anyway?" he asked.

"Huh?"

"Why does it matter what Jezebel does?"

Marly shook her head, doubly embarrassed now. "Doesn't matter. None of my concern if a woman wants to make a fool of herself over you."

"Careful. Jezebel is our hostess and my friend."

She bit the inside of her cheek. The reprimand was deserved. That didn't make it easier to take.

"When are we leaving?" she asked.

He sank lower in the tub. "From the look of things, not for some time."

She put aside the book and fixed him with a hard stare. "I thought you had business in El Paso."

"I do. It'll have to keep."

He dunked his head underwater, his knees pushing the cover up. When he re-emerged, he soaped the washcloth and started scrubbing his head and neck.

"The marshal, an ex-Ranger, was shot here a week ago. I've gotta stay and find out who was responsible."

"Was he a friend of yours?"

"Not exactly. I served with him once, but we didn't actually get along."

"Oh."

"Doesn't matter. I still have to investigate his murder. It takes precedence over my other case. Question is, are you gonna stick around with me? Or is your business in El Paso too urgent? I'm hopin'," he flashed a charming grin, "you'll decide to stay."

Marly settled back against the pillows. "I'll stick. After all, I still have time. And who knows what trouble you might get into without me around."

Jase laughed. "How about pouring me a glass of that brandy? Care to join me?"

Marly got up and filled one of the brandy snifters.

"You said I was too young," she reminded him, holding the glass just out of his reach. "Remember?"

"Yeah, well, in public you *are* too young."

He took the delicate snifter from her hand, leaned back and inhaled its fumes. A twist of his lips suggested that he was either laughing at her or himself, maybe both.

"Don't bother telling me how old you really are. Just put a drop of that brandy in your milk. You might like it. Anyhow, you gotta admit," he lifted the glass in a toast, "Jez sure knows how to entertain."

"I suppose."

She poured a generous dollop of liquor into her cup. Sniffing it, she wrinkled her nose and took a cautious sip of the spiked milk. It sent a cold tingle down her back and a hot one down her stomach, making her shiver and flush at the same time.

"Best sit before you fall down," Jase advised.

It was times like this when she just couldn't figure him out.

After all, she thought, he either thinks I'm a boy or he's discovered I'm not. If he thinks I'm a boy, I have to keep him thinking that way. If he knows I'm a girl, then he's pretending not to know, and I have to keep up the act anyhow.

Sighing, she climbed back into bed.

Jase opened his eyes and shot her a questioning glance.

"Just tired," she said.

"Finish your milk and go to sleep. You can turn down the lamp, if you like. I don't need much light to dry and dress."

She nodded.

There wasn't much milk left, so she downed it in one gulp, sending another wave of heat through her body.

She turned down the lamp. "Night, Jase."

Marly had little expectation of sleep. The sound of Jase sloshing the water and lifting the lid told her he was getting out of the tub. The lid slammed down and she filled in the visuals.

That sound was Jase rubbing his hair, neck and face with a towel, while droplets of water ran in rivulets down the valleys of his muscular back. *That* sound was him putting on his nightshirt. And *that* sound was him picking up his brandy glass and setting it on the silver tray.

She could fill in some of the details about his body from what she'd seen. But she had trouble imagining the difference between a young boy needing her help with his pants and a grown man.

She wished she could sneak a peek.

Marly closed her eyes just as Jase extinguished the lantern on her side. A cool draft breezed over her when he pulled back the covers. The mattress shifted as he slid in beside her. His back met hers and the warmth of his body dispelled the momentary chill. A subtle shift and she could feel his taut buttocks pressed against her.

If Aunt Adele could see me now, I'd be damned to hell.

But then, her aunt had already done that, hadn't she?

CHAPTER 5

Perhaps it was the comfort of a feather bed or the warmth of Marly's body curled up next to his, but Jase didn't wake until an insistent knocking forced him to consciousness. Reluctantly, he crawled from the covers and unlocked the door.

Fred's young assistant greeted him with a nod. He held out a water jug and some fresh towels. "Your laundry isn't quite ready, sir."

Taking the items, Jase said, "Bring us up some coffee, please."

The boy disappeared.

For a long moment, Jase stared at the sleeping Marly. If he slid back beneath the covers again, he wasn't sure he'd have sleep in mind. It had been a long time since he'd found comfort in the arms of a woman. Too long.

With a sigh, he shrugged into the satin dressing gown and put on the matching slippers. He was reading the western Fred had produced for Marly the night before when Marly finally roused.

"Mornin', sleepyhead."

She cracked a stiff smile. "Good morning."

A knock on the door indicated the coffee had arrived. Jase answered it, took the tray and dismissed the boy. Then he sat down in the chair and proceeded to ready two mugs. He pulled the robe tighter across his lap, afraid he might be revealing more than he should.

For a second, Marly looked pained and his smile faded. He had no idea what he'd done to vex her, but the girl was sorely vexed.

"Coffee?"

"I'll get it," she said, starting to get up.

He held up a hand. "You stay put."

Whatever was bothering her, it wasn't modesty. She wasn't wearing long johns, and her nightshirt only came to her knees. He had felt the smooth skin of her legs against his thigh when he woke. She appeared innocent of the effect that contact had on him.

So why was she upset?

Maybe he had unintentionally crossed the line in his sleep. In his dreams, she had practically dragged him across that line, wrapping her legs around him, pressing small, firm breasts against his chest. He had protested feebly, pointing out the impropriety of him taking advantage of her. Marly had laughed and took the decision out of his hands...and into hers. Then it was his turn to takes things in hand—like her rosy nipples and soft round buttocks.

Had he acted out any part of that very pleasant dream?

"You know," he said, holding up the pulp novel and trying to forget the blasted dream, "this stuff is nonsense. I met some of the men this guy's writin' about. They ain't like that. Not half as talented. Not near as noble."

He stirred some cream into the coffee, added a spoonful of sugar and handed a mug to Marly as she sat up in bed.

"I know we have to stay in town," she said. "Do we have to stay here?"

"You don't like the accommodations?"

"You said this place was expensive."

"We're guests."

"Let's not overstay our welcome then."

It appeared Jase wasn't the direct cause of her displeasure.

With a shake of his head, he went back to his chair and took a sip of his coffee. "I suspect you're soundin' like your Aunt Adele, brat."

Marly's lower lip quivered. "I am nothing like my aunt. I just don't like this place."

There was an uncomfortable silence.

When Jase broke it, he dropped his customary drawl and spoke like the well-read man he was. "Don't be so quick to judge, Marly Landers, lest you also be judged."

Marly stared into her coffee cup. When she looked up, her eyes sparkled with unshed tears.

Tempted as he was, he didn't let up. "Jezebel makes her bread and butter from the gamblin'. The dinin' room is gravy—and her pet project. The ladies? Well, that's just a fact of life in a frontier town. There's enough people out there that'll damn this place. I'd advise you do your judging one person at a time."

A tap on the door interrupted his homily. It was the boy with their laundry. He handed the stack of washed, pressed and neatly folded clothes to Jase.

"What's your name, boy?"

"Henry."

"Henry," Jase flipped a coin at the boy, "you tell Miz Jez we'll be down for breakfast soon."

"Thank you, sir."

When the door closed, Jase glanced at Marly. "I'm famished."

"Why don't you use the wash basin first?" she suggested, sounding like her old self. "I'd like to finish my coffee. Maybe you could give me back my book."

Marly hid behind Shakespeare, while Jase dressed.

She wasn't reading, however.

Let ye without sin cast the first stone, she thought. Well, I know I'm not without sin and I don't mean to cast stones.

Jezebel and The Oasis went against everything she had been brought up to respect. She had to admit, she would have been a lot more tolerant if Jezebel was indifferent toward Jase. Or if it were not so obvious they shared a history.

But Marly could hardly explain *that* to Jase.

"You need to put that book away," he said. "I'm goin' to check on the horses. I'll meet you downstairs in about twenty minutes. Don't be late."

"I won't."

"And don't worry so much," he added, flicking her chin. "We're good now, right?"

She smiled. "Of course."

As soon as he left, Marly jumped out of bed and locked the door. There was a long, cracked mirror on the wall. The image it reflected mocked her.

"You've been thrown into a deep pond," she told her reflection. "You just have to learn how to swim, that's all."

In the light of day, The Oasis was not nearly as intimidating as it had been to Marly the night before. If she ignored the gambling tables and Jezebel's painting, she could imagine she was in a respectable, albeit fancy, hotel.

A couple of women in calico dresses were cleaning the dining room and a young man swept the floors on the casino side. Behind the bar, a scarecrow of a man polished the cherry wood counter.

When Jase entered with Jezebel on his arm, Marly was washing glasses and chatting with the man she now knew as Arnie Hollis, chief bartender and assistant manager of the bar and casino. She'd learned that the women in calico were younger sisters or daughters of the same women who served and entertained customers the night before. Arnie's own mother had been employed by Jezebel many years previous, before being carried off one winter by the ague. Yes, The Oasis was—in its special way—a family-friendly establishment.

But when Marly saw Jezebel, she felt anything but friendly.

"Hungry, brat?" Jase asked.

She shrugged. "Suppose. I'll finish here first."

"I'll order for you. Don't take too long."

Jase escorted Jezebel to her table and Marly tried to resist the urge to stick her tongue out at Jase's back. Without a word, she returned to helping Arnie.

When the last glass was put away, she approached Jezebel's table, hunger overcoming her distaste of the woman. At least the perfume wasn't too heavy and the coffee smelled good.

Jezebel was recounting the circumstances of Strothers' murder. Neither she nor Jase paid any attention to Marly, though Jase pulled the chair out next to him.

Marly sat, absently fidgeting with the silverware.

"The prime suspect for the murder is Matthew Egan," Jase said. "He's the largest landholder and head of the richest family in the district."

"As far as Matt Egan is concerned, Fortuna is his town. Those of us who disagree don't rub his nose in it. Ellery Strothers wasn't so..." Jezebel searched for a word, "diplomatic. I think he figured that being a former Texas Ranger and the district's duly appointed marshal put him above town politics."

"So a battle of wills resulted."

"I have to admit, I am partly to blame for that. I was the one who pushed the idea that we should have a marshal appointed in the first place."

Marly did her best to hide her shock, but Jezebel's wry twist of a smile indicated that some of her feelings were well-known to the woman.

"Law and order are good for business." Jezebel paused for effect. "To a point anyways. Egan and Baker wanted the town to elect a sheriff, knowing that they could put one of their men in the spot. I could see where that was going, so I persuaded Chet Winters—he owns the bank—that a State-appointed marshal would be a better idea. In turn, he convinced the town council and I contacted a few friends in Austin. But you know that, don't you sugar?" She touched Jase's hand. "I made sure you were offered the job first."

Jase didn't rise to the bait.

"To add fuel to the fire," she continued, "Strothers was courting Matt's sister Amabelle, against Matt's expressed wishes. He forbade them to see each other. Foolish man. That jest made Strothers doubly attractive to the girl."

Fred appeared with the coffeepot and a basket of rolls. Marly, who had been watching Jase sip his coffee, gave such a look of gratitude that Fred almost smiled.

She split her attention between the rambling report and her sweet roll, the quality of which more than made up for the repeated attempts Jezebel made to get a rise out of Jase.

"The next most likely suspect is Gabriel Baker," Jezebel said.

Gabe had known Matt from the cradle. Together, their fathers had been heroes in the Mexican War and profiteers during the War Between the States, selling cattle wherever they could get the best price. Between wars they rode for a spell, married within days of each other, moved further west and started homesteads in what was then the middle of nowhere. Their sons grew up as brothers. They fought and worked side-by-side, like their fathers before them, and they collaborated in business. They drove cattle and drove out competition.

If Matt Egan was the richest man in Fortuna, Gabe Baker came in a close second. He took Egan's side in the political battle against the marshal. He also had reason to dislike Strothers personally. The younger and more dashing ex-Ranger was of far greater interest to his beloved Amabelle.

"And who can blame the poor child?" Jezebel said, exaggerating her deep-south accent and gesturing broadly. "No offence to Gabe, but he's got as much shape as a plank and he's as sweet-faced as a lemon."

"Strothers has looks, if nothin' else," Jase said.

"They'd have made a pretty couple. Miz Amabelle is 'The Beauty' here 'bouts. 'Course it ain't likely Matt would let his only sister marry a mere marshal. Especially when the Baker ranch runs 'long side theirs."

Marly leaned forward. "How old is Miss Amabelle?"

"I know their folks had plans," Jezebel said, ignoring her, "for Gabe to marry Amabelle. The old men are gone now. Mrs. Egan died long ago. Baker's mother went back East but I'd bet Matt still would like to see the wedding go off."

Jase asked, "How old's the girl?"

Marly scowled at him.

"Seventeen," Jezebel said.

"And Baker?"

"Thirty, I suppose. Word is, having given Old Man Baker a son right off, Mrs. Baker didn't see any reason to give any more." Jezebel shook her head. "Now Mrs. Egan, bless her foolish soul, kept trying to have more kids. I hear that's what killed her in the end."

Breakfast was served, halting the conversation temporarily.

When the better part of the steak, eggs and potatoes had been consumed, Jase said, "Where were Egan and Baker the night of the murder?"

"Matt was entertaining the Minister and his wife."

Marly filed that bit of information away.

Just because Egan had an alibi, it didn't mean he wasn't responsible. He could have told one of his men to kill the marshal. Or, since Egan's men were fiercely loyal to him, they might have done the job voluntarily.

Jase pushed his empty plate aside. "How about Baker?"

"Home alone. Only ones who can vouch for him are on his payroll."

"That doesn't mean anything, one way or the other."

"Personally, I prefer the theory that he was bushwhacked by drifters. I just can't get myself to believe it."

Again, Marly interjected a question. "How was he killed?'

Jezebel shuddered with distaste.

"He was stabbed," Jase replied. "I met with the doctor this mornin'. He kindly made his report while gettin' ready for church. I must say, he's a very organized and thorough professional."

"What did the report say?" Marly asked, glancing at Jezebel.

With an impatient wave, the woman indicated that Jase was welcome to continue with his story.

"Strothers was riding back to town and was knocked off his horse. The doctor found bruises on him from the fall. Then his attacker stabbed him under the ribs, just missing the heart. Given the nature of the wound and the amount of blood soaking the clothes, the doctor figures Strothers bled to death slowly."

Marly pushed down the wave of nausea that threatened to engulf her. She had seen the results of accidents and bar fights, and though she wasn't usually squeamish, the thought of someone being left to die slowly was horrifying.

"How was he found?" she asked Jase.

"One of Egan's men found his horse grazing up the road. Leading the horse back to town, the man found the body. It was partly eaten by coyotes, but there was enough left for the doctor to confirm identity and cause of death."

"There was no love lost between me and Strothers," Jezebel said quietly. "But that ain't no way for any man to die."

Marly nodded, able to sympathize with her in this, at least.

The next day, Jase opened Strothers' office and assumed the role of interim marshal of Fortuna. He set Marly to work cleaning the office and the adjoining quarters, while he ran a few errands.

Just before he left, Fred and Henry arrived with their saddlebags, some clean linen, a cot and bedding. After waking up a second time with Marly cradled in his arms, Jase decided she should have her own bed or else he'd give himself away. In any case, the bed in Strothers' quarters was only big enough for one.

To avoid arguments later, he did some further shopping on Marly's behalf. Her wardrobe needed expanding. He bought her a brown shield-front shirt, not dressy, but suitable for church. He also picked up a fresh set of combinations, a couple of new bandanas and two pairs of jeans in different sizes for her to try on. After two weeks of solid wear on the trail, not to mention hours of stable work, her jeans were looking pretty worn. To preserve the new jeans, he bought a pair of plain leather chaps.

Then he returned to the office.

"Basic, sturdy and cheap," he assured Marly, handing over the brown paper-wrapped bundle. "Nothing you don't desperately need."

She opened her mouth to object.

"It's your own fault," he cut in. "You should've packed better when you left home."

She blushed and he had to suppress a grin. He had no idea where she got her boys' clothes. He doubted it was from her wardrobe. Her aunt probably sent her off with a couple of calico dresses—one for Sunday best and one for working in. She would have been wearing something between best and worn, maybe with a cloak and sturdy shoes. After leaving her aunt, Marly would have had to make the transformation, leaving behind her dresses and petticoats—everything but the daguerreotype in its leather frame.

Marly fingered the cotton shirt like it was the finest silk, a worried crease furrowing her brow.

"I don't want you arguin' either," he added. "Besides, I bought myself a couple of necessities too."

His one extravagant purchase was a saddle holster and a new Winchester .77 carbine.

Marly's eyes widened as she looked from Jase to the Winchester and back again. He couldn't have impressed her more if he had given her a bag of gold or a diamond ring. That made it money well spent.

"Go change, brat," he said gruffly, waving her in the direction of their quarters.

Excitement overcoming her usual reticence, she rushed off to change into her new clothes.

As he waited for the results, he put away the more mundane purchases of coffee, flour, sugar, bacon, beans and ammunition. The money he'd spent put a large hole in his back pay. Fortunately, he expected to recoup his expenses via marshal's pay from the town council.

More to the point, Marly's pride of possession was payment enough for what he spent on her behalf.

Marly took time to wash up before putting on her new duds.

She'd never owned anything brand new before meeting Jase, not in her memory at least. Aunt Adele had remodeled her old gowns into dresses for Marly, turning the cloth inside out so it wouldn't seem so faded.

In a moment of maternal affection, the doctor's wife had passed on a couple of nearly new dresses and undergarments that had been part of her wedding trousseau. Though Marly had accepted them gratefully, she would rather have had buckskins, fringed jackets and the freedom to wear them—like the cowboys on the covers of the penny dreadful.

I look like a model for a recruitment poster for the Pony Express, she thought.

Sitting behind the marshal's desk, Jase gave a nod of approval.

Feeling self-conscious in her new duds, she strode over to the Winchester to check it out.

"My gawd," said Jezebel, leaning against the door frame. "Will the streets be safe?"

Marly glanced up from the rifle. With one long look, she appraised the woman, weighed what she saw and dismissed her. Then she snapped the breach of the rifle back into place.

"If you don't have anything for me to do, sir. I'm going to take Trouble for a ride."

Jase threw her a box of ammunition. She caught it deftly and shoved it into the pocket of her jeans.

"If you're willing to wait, you can come out with me," Jase said. "We'll check out the scene of the crime."

"I'll go tack up. I can also return the other pair of jeans, if you like." She mimicked his earlier remark about her choice in shirts. "They're kind of big."

Jase smiled at the shared joke.

Jezebel's mouth pursed.

Giving the lady a frosty bow, Marly left through the back door. She would have kept going, but curiosity got the better of her. She circled around to the open front door.

"That boy's got a lot of sass," Jezebel told Jase.

"You shouldn't tease him."

The lady shrugged and sashayed into the office, out of sight, but not out of earshot.

"You don't have to move here, Jase. You and the boy are welcome to stay at the hotel, even if you never take me up on my invitations. You got to be more comfortable there than here."

"Probably."

Marly heard the creak of the chair.

"But I've got a job to do, Jez, and it's best done out of this office. Speaking of which, I'd better get to work."

"I guess I shouldn't complain. If you make yourself at home here, maybe you'll stay, hmm? Settle down?"

"Like you?"

"I have been a victim of circumstance. I'm now mistress of my own fate. They couldn't beg me to return to Austin and it'd be too tragic to go back to Richmond. Fortuna suits me jest fine. Not too nice, not too rowdy. Speaking of which, the town needs a marshal. A certain amount of law and order is good for business. You could still take me up on that offer—amongst others."

Footsteps approached the door.

Startled, Marly decided it was best to move on. She wasn't ashamed of eavesdropping. Still, she didn't want to get caught either.

It was time to put her talent for listening to use elsewhere.

News traveled fast in the small town. In the general store, opinions about Jase and the murder buzzed like bees.

Marly could hardly be accused of lurking when she had a legitimate reason to be there. Leaning her rifle against the counter, she managed to blend into the background so no one noticed the stranger in their midst.

The murder had stirred up feelings. Most folks liked Matt Egan. Some thought he was a little high handed. All of them knew he had killed before, but those times were clearly cases of self defense.

She listened to the gossip and speculation while browsing through the racks and surreptitiously noting the different ways the men wore their guns.

The shopkeeper, a talkative matron at the hub of the gossip, frowned. "What can I do for you, young man?"

"I'm returning these jeans. They're the wrong size."

The woman's frown was replaced with a broad, insincere smile. "Why, you must the new marshal's assistant."

Her voice carried and the buzz of conversation ceased.

"Marly Landers." She gave the woman a small bow.

"Well, Master Landers, I'm Mrs. Temple-Quinton, proprietress of this establishment. The marshal has an account here. So if there is anything you need..."

"No, thank you, ma'am."

Mrs. Temple-Quinton took the jeans and indicated with a tip of her head where the door was.

"Any progress on the investigation?" asked a younger matron with one child on her hip and another grasping her skirt.

Marly shrugged. "I'm sure the Ranger will have things sorted out soon."

A man shot a great gob of spit into the spittoon by her feet.

Startled, she jumped back a step.

"Good shot," someone murmured.

Marly picked up her rifle. With a tight smile, she said, "Good day."

Outside, she paused to load the carbine's magazine. The task gave her time to regain her composure and demonstrate to anyone watching that she wasn't intimidated.

Not much anyway.

She strolled down Main Street, mapping out the town's core. Adjoining the general store was the barbershop. According to the graphics painted in its window, it was also the home of the dentist and undertaker. No doubt, this was all one person.

An alley separated the barbershop from the Fortuna Hotel, an ordinary looking edifice like a dozen others she had seen and occasionally worked in. The hotel completed the block between Church Road and The Avenue.

Opposite the general store was the bank. Despite its imposing facade, it wasn't much of a building. Next door was the Post, Stage and Telegraph, an office much smaller than its name implied. Completing that side of the block was the Marshal's Office. Like The Oasis, it had a corner entrance and was built in a similar, albeit plainer, style.

The door to the Marshal's Office was open and people loitered around the entrance.

Jase was probably finding it hard to get away.

Across the road from the office, at the corner of Avenue and Main with a door opening onto each, stood The Haven.

A half-smile lifted Marly's mouth as she wandered by.

It didn't have The Oasis' style or the hotel's respectability, yet, rough as it was, The Haven was the kind of place she had learned to be comfortable in. There was always work to do and however rowdy the clientele might get, they rarely picked on a youngster. If someone did, someone else would step in. That kind of bully almost always backed down when challenged.

The livery and blacksmith backed onto The Haven. The yard was empty and the smithy door was closed.

Instead of getting the tack, she decided to treat Trouble and Grandee to some currying. She was brushing Grandee down when a man came by wanting his horse. With no one else in sight, he probably figured her for a stable boy. Always accommodating, especially if a tip might be had, she saddled his mount. She had just pocketed a couple of pennies when she noticed the young man whose job she had just usurped.

"Thanks," he said, stepping forward. "Seems like folks always come along when you got to step out. Name's Hank."

Towering above her, Hank held out his hand.

She took it and tried not to wince from his grip. "Marly."

"Coffee?"

"I wouldn't say no."

He led her through a door that opened onto the backyard of The Haven where chickens pecked in the dirt near a coop, guarded by a scruffy looking terrier napping under the porch. Three young men sat on the porch, drinking beer or coffee and sharing a large plate of sandwiches.

Marly estimated their ages to range between fifteen and twenty-one, the latter being her own age. Hank seemed to be the oldest. He made brief introductions and then stepped inside to fetch the coffee.

Like everyone else in town, the murder was foremost on their minds. All it took was a few well-placed, casual questions to start them talking. The random violence theory held no water with these boys. They were sure that this was murder with a motive.

"Egan's not a suspect because he'd kill a man face-to-face," Hank said, returning with two mugs of coffee.

"That don't mean it ain't one of his men," the youngest boy said. "Too many people hated Strothers, that's the problem."

Hank shrugged. "Duke sure did."

"With reason. That sonuvabitch had a grudge against Duke and The Haven. Step one toe outta line on this side of the road and you earned yourself a night in the cells. Bet no one at The Oasis ever saw a night behind bars."

"Quieter place."

"Just noise," said an attractive blond boy. "No one ever caused any trouble that Duke couldn't sort out."

"True enough," Hank said.

Most of the young men present had spent a night in jail just for showing what they described as 'a little high spirits.'

Was that enough to kill a man over?

"Some men don't need much excuse," Hank said.

But they couldn't imagine Duke being that kind of man.

"I bet Strothers was being paid to keep his nose out of The Oasis," the blond suggested.

"I don't know, Jed."

"Maybe he wanted more money," the younger boy said. "Maybe Jezebel had him killed because he was getting greedy."

"And maybe you better catch up with your uncle, Lloyd Penrod," Hank said. He handed the empty sandwich plate to Jed. "And you better see if Duke has any more work today."

This was Marly's cue to find Jase.

"Thanks for the coffee," she said with a nod to the boys.

"You know," Hank said as they headed back through the stable, "these boys ain't gonna be too pleased when they find out you're with the Ranger."

"I don't suppose so. Thanks for not saying anything."

Hank shrugged. "Your business, not mine. Just don't take their rambling too seriously."

Marly returned the shrug. "Ranger's business, not mine. I just like to hear people talk."

Jase pulled out his watch and checked the time. The latest of his many visitors were two men claiming to be Strothers' deputies—a middle-aged man and his nephew. Neither inspired him to revise his opinion of Strothers' intelligence. He suspected that Strothers had chosen them for their compliancy, not brains.

"Thank you, gentlemen," he said, cutting into the older man's diatribe against anyone who didn't welcome the law into Fortuna.

Since neither had taken the initiative to keep the office open, nor had they looked into the murder of their employer, it was hard to take either of them seriously.

"If I ever need your particular talents, I'll keep you in mind."

Reluctantly, the pair was ushered out the door.

Unfortunately, they weren't the last of Fortuna's citizens looking for an excuse to check out the interim marshal. Since no one wanted to commit to being friendly, his visitors had to find excuses to come to the office. Most were pretty flimsy. In an effort to maintain goodwill, he tried to deal with them all. After an hour of being interrogated—not too subtly most of the time—he was sick of it.

Out of this group, a well-dressed man stepped to the fore. He removed his shallow crowned hat with a sweeping gesture and offered an immaculately clean and manicured hand.

"Marshal Strachan, allow me to introduce myself. Chet Winters, banker. I have some urgent business to discuss, if you can spare the time."

Jase took the outstretched hand and was surprised by the man's firm grip. Winters dressed like a dandy, but he pressed flesh like a working man. Jase ushered the man into his office and closed the door, assuming the banker would prefer privacy.

"So, what can I do for you, Mr. Winters?"

"Keep the peace in Fortuna," the older man said with a negligent wave. "Discourage bank robbers, that sort of thing."

Winters had a pleasant face and an easy smile. Jase placed him around fifty years of age, mostly by the lines around his eyes and the steel gray hair. Otherwise, he was trim enough for a younger man.

"Coffee?" Jase offered.

"I think dinner would be more in order. That's why I'm here. My wife is expecting me home or I'd invite you out. I reckoned you needed help getting free if you were ever going to eat today—or do anything else. Perhaps tomorrow we could meet?"

"A pleasure, sir."

"Good," Winters said. "Now, I do think we better leave through the back, don't you?"

Jase locked up and grabbed his rifle and a box of ammunition before following Mr. Winters out the back door. Then they shook hands and went their separate ways.

The banker continued down The Avenue, presumably to his home, while Jase cut through The Haven's backyard to the stables.

"You just missed Landers," the stable boy said.

Leaving a message for his erstwhile assistant to join him at The Oasis, Jase hurried across the road before he could be intercepted by anyone else.

CHAPTER 6

After leaving a message for Jase, Marly headed over to The Oasis. The cowboys had offered her sandwiches at The Haven, but she didn't feel comfortable about accepting when she only had a few cents to contribute to the bill. Watching them eat, however, had given her an appetite.

The hardened gamblers were already in the casino. Otherwise, it was quiet. A couple of ranchers sat near the windows and a lone gentleman in a black frock coat sat alone, as far away as possible from the other tables. There was a slightly sinister look to the man.

Squinty eyes followed Marly across the room, inspiring her to make a beeline toward the bar. There, at least, was a familiar face.

"Waiting for the marshal?" Arnie asked.

She nodded, glancing over her shoulder at the lone man.

"Oh, don't worry about Pervis," Arnie said, smiling. "He's just curious. Trouble is, he lost his spectacles a couple of weeks back and he don't see too good. Been waiting for his new pair to come in by mail. Hasn't done his business much good."

"What does he do?"

The bartender rubbed his stubbly chin. "He's the barber."

Marly stifled a laugh.

"Appreciated your help this morning," he said. "Why don't you set up here at the bar and I'll see if I can't round up a couple of sandwiches for you. My treat."

Her stomach growled in response.

Jase walked into The Oasis and found his protégée on a bar stool, a mug of coffee in her hand and a mound of sandwiches stacked in front of her.

Marly saw him approaching and smiled.

Arnie waved. "Want a coffee, Marshal? Or a beer?"

"Coffee is fine. You know, Landers, you're a little young to be hanging out at bars."

"Oh, he's fine, Marshal." Arnie set a mug down in front of Jase. "This time of day The Oasis is as respectable as it gets, excepting the casino side. I won't let him drift over there."

Jase wasn't that concerned about Marly's safety in this familiar place, but he felt it was part of his role to play the father figure in public.

"Where's your carbine?" he asked his charge.

"Checked it with me, Marshal," Arnie replied. "House rules. Lawmen excepted, of course."

"Arnie's been telling me about Fortuna," Marly said, grinning.

"Really," Jase replied, raising a brow in Arnie's direction.

The bartender left to sell more drinks to the gamblers.

"Did you know that The Oasis is built on the ruins of a Spanish mission?" she asked. "The mission was destroyed by Apaches, along with the original Haven, which means that The Haven and the mission are the oldest buildings in the settlement because the dance hall came later."

Jase had to work at keeping his smile from betraying his amusement at her newfound enthusiasm for Fortuna.

"Anyway, that was the last time Fortuna was successfully attacked," she explained. "The Bakers and Egans came and soon afterward the settlement grew from an outpost to a town. Those two families are pretty important around here. Cornerstones of the community. However, it was the Businessman's Committee that asked the state to appoint a marshal." She popped the rest of a sandwich in her mouth. "Headed by the banker and Miz Jezebel."

The little devil on Jase's shoulder that was just a mite jealous of how easily Marly found supporters was tempted to tease her with the information that Jezebel had asked him to come to Fortuna *before* Strothers was appointed. He mentally pushed the devil aside and pretended this was all news to him.

"When you got a place like this," he said, looking around, "you want enough order to keep it from being broke up. Makes sense the banker would want a marshal. I've met Mr. Winters already. Friendliest face outside The Oasis. The others I met today are curious. Wary too. Don't think they mind law so much as they don't like this murder business. Protective of Egan, too."

Marly washed down another mouthful of food with coffee.

"They may not mind the law," she said, "but I bet they didn't like Strothers much. Seems he applied justice somewhat unevenly. At least, that's how some look at it."

Jase's eyebrow lifted.

"Some say there's a connection between Miz Jezebel bringing in the marshal and The Haven getting picked on."

"You've been busy, Marly."

The discussion was dropped when Arnie came back to refill their cups. After he left again, they finished the plate of sandwiches in silence, then went back to the stables

The stable boy had anticipated them and had Trouble and Grandee ready. He had also taken care of Marly's holster, securing it to her saddle. Marly nodded her thanks. Jase showed his appreciation with a couple of coins.

He wanted to follow Strothers' route the night of the murder. He knew from Jezebel that Strothers always paraded down Main Street on his way out of town. Coming back, especially if he was trail-worn, he tended to use the back roads.

Jase and Marly rode the length of Main Street from livery to churchyard. On the way past The Haven, the men lounging on the porch stood and glared at them. One spat a long stream of tobacco-stained spittle and hit Trouble on the flank.

The horse was startled, but Marly kept him under control. Jase caught her eye and she turned away quickly, biting her lower lip. He didn't press her until they were leaving town.

"You wanna share somethin' with me?" he asked.

She shook her head. "Don't want to, but I should. Those cowboys didn't know I was with you. I was listening to them gossip. Now they probably think I was spying on them."

"Did any of them admit to killin' Strothers?"

"No."

"Then they'll get over it."

Marly couldn't fault his logic, so she set aside the incident.

Once clear of the houses, they picked up the pace and headed west, toward the Egan and Baker ranches. Thanks to Arnie, she knew that they'd pass the smaller Circle-X Ranch. The road had a right-of-way through the property that acted as the boundary between Egan's Lazy E ranch and Baker's Bar B.

This was where the murder occurred.

The road dipped into a gully and there was just enough of a bend to it to create blind spots in any direction. By report, Strothers would have been travelling back to town.

Jase and Marly dismounted and approached the scene on foot.

After almost two weeks and regular traffic, Marly reckoned there wasn't much sign left to read. It was easy to deduce the most likely location of the ambush, however.

Jase climbed up to that spot.

"This place has been used by at least two people several times," he said. "One spent a fair bit of time waitin'. He passed the time whittlin'. Take Trouble and ride 'round to the other side. Go back about a quarter mile, then ride up the trail."

Marly was off. Riding up the road, she scanned the ground for anything that might help Jase. On the way back, she tried to put herself in Strothers' place. He probably hadn't been expecting trouble.

Even knowing where to look, she couldn't see Jase. And it was broad daylight. When she rounded the bend, she shivered involuntarily, spurring Trouble to quicken his pace.

A moment later, Jase jumped out behind her. This spooked Trouble. The horse kicked dust into his face as he rolled to his feet, coughing.

Marly reined in and turned back, passing the canteen to Jase.

"Thanks," he said, after taking a drink. "Athletic sort, our murderer." He handed back the canteen and beat the dust from his chaps. "And a cigar smoker. Found a butt up there while you were gone. Did you see anythin'?"

She shook her head. "You had good cover. Makes me wonder, why a knife? Why not shoot Strothers? Wasn't the moon full then? It's a waning crescent now. He would have been an easy target."

"To get a good shot, I would've had to stand up."

"Still, it would have to be easier."

"For you. For me too." He rubbed his hip as he walked beside Trouble. "I'd say our murderer was more comfortable with a knife than a rifle. Besides, Strothers was a lightnin' draw. If the murderer was local, he would've known that."

"But he'd be shooting up his target. And lightning draw doesn't mean amazing accuracy."

Jase chuckled. "As a matter of fact, he wasn't the most accurate marksman when I knew him. A man as quick as Strothers can be mighty intimidatin'. Folks will attribute all kinds of things to a man who can get off the first shot. Anyhow," he swung up into his saddle, "Strothers is dead. We know a bit more about how. Now we have to work on who and why."

Marly pushed her hat back and wiped the perspiration from her face. "He was killed on his way back to town. Where was he coming from?"

"Far as we know, he was just on patrol. If he was, chances are he'd do a circuit. Up ahead there's a trail that crosses the road, then curves back onto the boundary trail, which we just crossed."

"I could take one way and you could take the other."

He hesitated.

"We could meet up back here," she added. "We're not far from town."

"Okay. If you have any trouble—other than that horse of yours—fire three shots in the air."

They turned and went back up the road.

On the way through the gully, Marly had to shake off the feeling she was being watched. For a moment, when they came to the trail crossing, she almost suggested that they ride together. But she shook off the feeling and accepted Jase's admonition to be careful.

After an hour of following the meandering track, she found a pond. She stopped to let Trouble have a drink and to fill up the canteen.

"This is private property."

She turned toward the voice, carbine ready. A young girl rode toward her. She wore a dusty-rose riding habit and rode sidesaddle. Her hair hung in blonde ringlets that framed a face that was pretty, in a china doll way. She was about sixteen years of age.

The infamous Amabelle Egan?

"Sorry, miss," Marly said, lowering her rifle. "I didn't mean to stray onto your land."

"Well, you did," the girl said coldly.

"I said I was sorry. There's no need for you to get rude." Marly swung expertly into the saddle. "See, I'm going."

"Wait!"

"Why? I thought I was trespassing."

"I just want to know who you are and what you're doing here."

Marly tipped her hat. "Good day, Miss Amabelle."

By way of making his own comment, Trouble kicked up a clump of earth, causing Amabelle's horse to shy. While the girl was busy reigning in her nervous horse, Marly followed the curve of the pond. She was able to look back, without seeming as if she was doing so. Amabelle glowered at her in an unusually inhospitable manner, which seemed odd. Most folks didn't grudge a stranger *or* his horse a drink of water.

By chance, Marly found a little used track leading away from the pond. Following it, she came to a promontory. There was a small clearing with a footpath leading to the top of the rise. She had enough tracking skill to see that a horse had been tethered there repeatedly, though not very recently.

She dismounted, secured Trouble and walked up the footpath.

Like the heroes in the pulp fiction she'd been reading, she ducked down when she reached the top, so not to present an outline on the horizon. She had a clear view of the pond and surrounding country. From this spot, she could see Amabelle heading home and the Egan place in the distance.

The large ranch house stood proudly on high ground, with the barns, sheds and bunkhouses grouped a discrete distance away. A wood lot covered the hill between the house and the pond. A bridle trail wended its way through the woods and up the hill.

Amabelle appeared intermittently as she rode up the path, then was clearly visible as she crossed the open ground leading to the stables.

"A perfect lookout over a perfect meeting spot," Marly said.

Strothers could have waited here to meet Amabelle at the pond, either by *accident* or appointment. He could have scouted ahead to make sure she was alone. With a modicum of care, he wouldn't be visible from the lookout.

Marly noticed something on the ground.

A cigar butt, half buried in the dirt.

So far as she knew, Strothers wasn't a cigar smoker. That being the case, if he had used this lookout, he was not the only one.

Jase didn't look it, but he was a man on the edge. On the outside, he was the picture of a laconic cowboy slouching against a tree and watching his horse graze on the scrub across the road. Inside, he was alternately cursing his decision to let Marly ride on alone and praying that nothing had happened to her.

"You should have known she'd be late," he muttered. "She's always late."

For a moment, his mouth pursed in a hard line.

Marly wasn't the first kid he'd used in an investigation. Stable hands, runners and busboys made excellent spies. No one paid any attention to them as they plied their trade and surreptitiously picked up information. A few coins and the knowledge they were helping a Texas Ranger were generally enough to get their cooperation. A few had seen the back of someone's hand as a result. One boy had seen worse. That tough, smart boy was a Ranger now.

But Marly wasn't a boy. She was a girl—a young woman.

A *beautiful* woman, he corrected.

Marly might be every bit as tough as any boy he'd employed, but that didn't make it easier to think of her in harm's way. Yet, if he didn't treat her like a boy, he'd unmask her.

That was another kind of danger.

He closed his eyes and went back to prayer, promising to take better care of his charge in the future. A soft snicker from Grandee warned him that he was about to have company.

A moment later, he saw Marly and breathed a sigh of relief.

Marly saw Grandee before she spotted Jase. She slowed, scanning the area for possible trouble. It was only when Jase stepped out of the shadows that she realized she had been holding her breath. For a moment she had been worried about him, which was foolish.

He's a Texas Ranger, for Lord's sake.

Jase fell in step with her. "You're looking smug, brat. You found something?"

Her smile broadened to a grin.

She couldn't very well tell him that she was just happy to see him. That was something she couldn't share and shouldn't think about. Fortunately, she had something to feel legitimately smug about.

She told him about Miss Amabelle and showed him the cigar butt.

"Same brand," Jase said, comparing the butt to the one he'd found. "Same pattern of bite marks. Same smoker. We'll drop by the store tomorrow and see if we can find out who smokes this brand. Might narrow the field a bit." He flicked a look over her shoulder. "You think Strothers was a regular visitor to the pond?"

She lifted a shoulder. "Someone was. And someone else was watching him. A horse was tethered in the same spot repeatedly over a period of at least a week or so. The last time could have been around when Strothers was murdered."

"How do you figure?"

"Well," she said, taking off her hat and smoothing back the hair that had escaped her braid, "whoever it was used the same sapling to secure his horse, as though by habit, but there were different wear marks. There's a tree nearby that's obviously been used as a scratching post. The bark is worn shiny in one spot at the right height for a horse. That probably means some of the waits were long. Maybe he scratched the saddle too."

His brow arched. "Impressive."

"The dead giveaway was the horse shit."

He barked with laughter.

"There were a few different piles in varying states of decomposition," she added. "None were very fresh, so the place wasn't used recently. Besides, there's no cattle out that way, no need to use the spot as a cattle lookout. And it's not close enough to the house to be useful, except to find out if anyone's coming down to the pond."

"So what do you think?"

"I thought, at first, Strothers used the spot to watch for Miss Amabelle, but now I think it's more likely someone else was spying on them."

Jase took a long sip from his canteen.

"The Strothers I knew was too sure of himself to sneak around. Especially if he had serious intentions toward Miss Egan." He grinned. "I'd say, Marly Landers, that you've earned your supper today."

Waiting for Marly to return from the livery, Jase sorted the contents of Strothers' desk. Spent cartridges littered the desktop, dredged up from the corners of each drawer. They rolled under the neat stacks he had made of wanted posters, reports, official correspondence and personal papers. The stacks were weighted by a couple of tin cups. And Jake's revolver.

A gust of wind followed Marly into the office. Papers ruffled, but only the unweighted wanted posters escaped. Caught like sails in the wind, they sent cartridges skittering across the floor.

"Damn!" he said.

"Sorry."

"Never mind. Just close the door."

Marly helped collect the posters and found a box for them.

"I'll get the broom for the cartridges," she said. "I guess we should fill them. Doesn't look like Strothers ever got around to it."

A smile pulled at one side of Jase's mouth. "You know how to do that too?"

"Sure. Aunt Adele didn't hold with wasting brass."

Of course she didn't, Jase thought, wondering if Marly was aware of how often she referred to that dreaded relative.

By the time they were done, he didn't feel much like cooking and Marly was looking close to done in.

"Think we'll go to The Haven for supper," he announced.

"The Haven?"

"You said it yourself. Strothers had a reputation for favorin' The Oasis. With that and the fact that me and Jez go back a long way, I gotta make an effort not to seem partial."

The Haven was busy for the mid-week. It seemed to be a favorite hangout for cowboys from nearby ranches. Jase noted a few familiar faces. The would-be deputies were at the bar. A couple of cowboys who had taken exception to Marly's snooping were at a table with some others. He didn't recognize them, but they obviously knew who he was. As he and Marly entered, an unfriendly silence descended on the room.

Jase, wearing the marshal's badge prominently on his jacket, led Marly up to the bar. She carried one of the office rifles, Jase having vetoed her wearing a gun-belt. He had almost told her to leave the rifle.

The burly man behind the bar raised thick brows. "Show of force, Ranger?"

"Just here for supper before walkin' our patrol."

"I think you're on the wrong side of the street. The Oasis is more your style."

"And I heard The Haven was a friendly place." Jase leaned against the bar and surveyed the room. "I also heard that the owner, Duke, was a tough but fair-minded individual."

The bartender responded with a shrug.

"We don't like marshals," a pinch-faced cowboy hollered. "Or Texas Rangers. Or their pint-sized spies."

"I'm Duke and this is my place," the bartender said. "I have nothing against you, but I don't need trouble." With a stern scowl, he warned off the belligerent cowboy before returning his gaze to Jase. "I suggest you leave, Ranger."

"Think I'd like to stay and have a beer. Landers will have coffee."

"Sandwiches are good here," Marly remarked.

Jase smiled. "Then we'll have a plate of sandwiches."

He led her to a table near the back door. Their drinks were brought over by a good looking boy wearing an apron.

"Hey, Jed," Marly said.

Jed's reply was to slam their order down on the table and storm back to the bar.

Jase blew the foam off his beer. "Thanks, Jed."

Marly sipped her coffee and made a face. "Salted." She pushed the cup away.

Jase took a swig of beer. "Soaped."

Drinks in hand, he returned to the bar.

"I think you made a mistake, Jed. Why don't you try again?"

It was an order, not a question.

"Duke said this wasn't your kind of place," Jed said, pouting.

Duke eyed the boy, the grabbed Jase's beer and took a cautious sip. His mouth set in a hard line. "I'll bring over fresh myself."

The boy's eyes flared. "But Duke—"

"Enough, Jed. We've been having enough trouble without you wasting good drinks. You let me pick my own fights from now on."

Jed flushed with embarrassment and anger.

"Don't serve 'em, Duke!" someone yelled.

"Yeah, you don't need their kind of business."

A cowboy strode up to the bar. Obviously he either hadn't heard or didn't pay attention to Dukes warning.

"We don't need 'em here at all," the man said. "Not in The Haven. Not in Fortuna."

Murmurs of assent and warning swept through the crowd.

The area near the cowboy and the bar cleared.

"Duke," Jase said. "You're the owner of this place. If you want us to leave, we'll leave. It's up to you whose money you wanna accept. Me and Landers can always take our business elsewhere. But even if you get rid of me," he turned toward the crowd, "the law's here to stay in Fortuna. I might add, the state of Texas takes a dim view of folks murderin' its officers."

The cowboy snorted. "Who said anything about murder? I call it a fair fight."

In an instant, several things happened.

The cowboy reached for his gun. Duke lunged forward, smashing the man's gun arm with a wooden club. Marly armed and aimed her rifle at the cowboy, the distinctive sound of the Winchester's lever action coinciding with the sickening crack of the man's arm breaking. And Jase, who had drawn reflexively, holstered his weapon almost as quickly, an action noticed by the crowd.

"Jed, take Tom here to the Doc's," Duke commanded. "That suit you, Ranger, or do you want him in jail too?"

"That'll suit me," Jase replied.

"Still hungry?"

"And thirsty." Jase tipped his hat to the man. "Thanks."

Duke shrugged. "Business is business."

Marly had sat down when Jase returned to the table with their drinks. She was doing a good job of looking calm, but her hands betrayed her, shaking slightly as she took the cup of coffee.

Jase fought the urge to steady her hands with his.

"That's better," she said after a cautious sip.

"Much," Jase agreed, not touching his beer.

He forced his eyes away from her quavering hands and determined nonchalance. Instead, he watched Duke make his way across the room, with a heaping plate balanced on one hand.

"Anything wrong?" Marly whispered.

"Plenty. Nothing urgent though. I was just thinkin', I'm getting' mighty sick of sandwiches."

Marly was up and out early the next day. She returned with a rasher of bacon and half a dozen eggs, which she cooked up for breakfast. The smell attracted Jase, who emerged from the storage room. Judging by the white foam on his square jaw, he'd been in the middle of shaving.

"You started an account with the butcher?" he asked.

She jabbed the bacon with a fork. "I tried."

"Tried?"

"He wasn't amenable to my suggestion. Said I had to pay cash up front. I almost had enough in my pocket." She shrugged. "Then Fred came along. We've got an account now."

"This bothers you?"

She cracked four eggs into the pan. "Not the part about Fred helping. Just the fact that Mr. Albie Penrod thinks he can deny a Texas Ranger credit."

"It's his business. He can do whatever he pleases. Don't get riled up on my account, brat. Waste of energy."

She flicked Jase a glance.

He was stripped to the waist, damp from washing, his lean muscles gleaming. Now that her snit was passed, she could appreciate the view. Not that she had any business appreciating how good the man looked. But he looked mighty—

Her eyes met his. Damn.

Jase grinned.

Marly's gaze snapped back to the frying pan.

"Fred's right," she said, trying to cover her embarrassment. "You shouldn't shave yourself."

CHAPTER 7

After breakfast, Jase and Marly visited Quinton's General Store. It turned out the cigar stubs were from a company called J. Fuego. An expensive brand, they sold for ten cents each. There were few people who bought them regularly.

Egan was one of them. The banker, Winters, was another. Jezebel kept a supply for special customers. Baker preferred the thinner cigarillos. There were other cigar smokers, but most ranch hands preferred to chew tobacco or roll their own cigarettes.

Having cleaned more than her fair share of ashtrays and spittoons in her travels, Marly was thankful that Jase didn't indulge in any of these habits.

The next thing on the agenda was cleaning the office.

While she scrubbed, Jase sifted through Strothers' papers.

"Don't forget," he told her, "I have a luncheon appointment with Winters. After that, I'm riding out to visit Egan and Baker."

"Can I come along?"

He shook his head. "Not this time, brat."

She didn't argue. He'd tell her the results of his interviews.

When the cleaning was done, Marly left for The Haven, hoping someone would put her to work so the time would pass more quickly.

"I don't need any more young bucks hanging around," Duke said.

Bored, she headed to the livery.

"I don't mind you bein' here," Hank said, "but I don't have any work for you. You'll have to get up earlier if you want to muck the stables."

She finally found something to do at The Oasis. It had higher standards of cleanliness, so there was always something to wash or polish.

Arnie pointed to the spittoons grouped by the door.

Rolling her eyes, she wandered over to them and was relieved to find that they had already been cleaned. Her job was to buff up the brass and place the spittoons strategically throughout the establishment.

"After that, you can help me replenish the bar stock," Arnie promised.

Before that could happen, Fred discovered her and decided that she could help him in the kitchen.

"Please wash up, Master Landers." He handed her a bar of lye soap. "And do scrub well. You may assist me with the biscuits."

Marly took the soap and scrubbed until she was pink. Even so, Fred inspected her hands and fingernails before letting her approach his counter.

Another cook worked the other end of the kitchen. He was introduced to Marly as Louis the Creole.

Louis responded with a grunt of indifference.

"He's a good cook," Fred confided once they were out of earshot. "But he has no sense of management. And he's as touchy as the devil." He smiled sadly. "Of course, my temper isn't always what it should be either."

Marly gazed at him with frank incredulity.

"It is true, Master Landers. I have learned the hard way. It is not enough to acquire skills and age in order to attain maturity. Patience and self-control are the key to maturity, good biscuits and a close shave." His lips twitched.

She grinned. "After we make biscuits, do you think you could teach me how to give a close shave?"

Going through Strothers' reports, Jase noticed a pattern. Cowboys made up the bulk of the arrests, mostly on charges of disorderly conduct. That wasn't too surprising. However, over time, a disproportionate number of those cowboys were Egan's men.

There were records of new town ordinances, each one corresponding with a spate of arrests. Most regulations were standard for promoting law and order. They included prohibitions against shooting off firearms within town limits and noise restrictions. Some of them bordered on capricious and seemed to be designed to annoy certain cowboys.

One ordinance, for instance, limited the amount of time a horse could be hitched at one post. The livery must have loved that one. To obey the ordinance, a cowboy coming into town for a drink would be best to stable his horse than leave it hitched outside and risk a fine.

Either because they made a point of defying the law or because Strothers picked on them particularly, it was usually Egan's men that were charged.

Promptly at noon, Chet Winters walked into the Marshal's Office, ready to take Jase to lunch. Dining with the banker gave him invaluable insight. First and foremost, he learned never to eat at the Fortuna Hotel. An undoubtedly respectable establishment, it served the worst food he'd ever tasted. The only people who went to the hotel's restaurant were the straight-laced and the unwary.

In a town that had built a church and brought in a minister, he determined that the tolerance toward The Oasis was largely due to the Fortuna Hotel's cook.

Winters agreed. His wife, however, was the leader of the church committee.

"She would drum Jezebel out of town on her own if she thought she could get away with it," the banker said.

"Who's stoppin' her?"

"Me for one. Miss Jezebel is one of my largest depositors. Her reputation has kept her out of the parlors, but that doesn't mean she lacks influence in other circles. She's not afraid to spend money to make money. As her banker, I know all her eggs are not in the same basket. For all its vices, The Oasis has helped keep Fortuna going."

"I'm sure the vices have helped," Jase remarked dryly.

"Well, this is still predominantly a cattle town. The men that ride the ranges count on their entertainment. On pay day, The Oasis empties a lot of pockets. And they don't spend much of it on food." Winters pushed his plate away and signaled the server to bring more coffee. "Fact is, the ranch owners wouldn't be too happy if Jezebel packed up and left. Ironically, Egan was Jezebel's biggest supporter against my wife and her lot."

"Why ironic?"

"He's the one who got the new church built."

Jase's eyebrow lifted.

"I am sure that he was pushed to do so by his aunt," Winters said, leaning back and sipping his coffee. "And it wasn't as if he was opposed to the church. He and his family were regular attendees at the old meeting hall before it burned down. They also attended the tent meetings that were held to raise money. I've always felt that he and I shared the similar outlook that virtue has to be balanced by a little vice. And, if you'll pardon the pun, vice versa."

He gave Jase an apologetic shrug before continuing.

"On the other hand, there is no doubt that the extent of Egan's generosity and timing was suspect. He pushed to have the new building completed and underwrote the balance of expenses right after the town council requested the appointment of a marshal."

"It was another way to exercise power."

"Exactly. And it was a way of telling Jezebel that she had better watch herself."

After Winters left, Jase lingered, sipping his coffee—which was passable. He considered the information the banker had given him and when he couldn't put it off any longer, he headed back to the office.

He'd decided to take Marly with him. But she wasn't there.

The company would have been nice, but he wasn't prepared to track her down, so he headed out alone.

Marly held the straight razor and contemplated the foamy chin of the young man sitting before her. She ignored his wide-eyed, barely contained fear. Fred had already warned her that confidence was as important as a sure eye and steady hand in the art of giving a close shave. A scarred melon sat on the counter by the shaving bowl, testament to her first trials.

She did her best to ignore the melon, Louis and the two ladies who had wandered over to watch her performance. With a deep breath, she made the first scrape.

Henry, her less than willing victim, closed his eyes in resignation to his fate. She couldn't help but feel sorry for him. Fred had railroaded him into volunteering. He'd made it sound like the prospect of being sliced and diced was preferable to the chore of peeling potatoes, adding that if Henry paid attention, he might have a hope of being more than a busboy and scullery hand.

"Watch the angle of your blade, Master Landers," Fred said, causing Henry's eyes to widen. "Don't forget to keep the skin taut."

She tried to heed the advice without letting it make her nervous. She especially didn't want to appear as ill at ease as she felt. Henry was having a bad enough time as it was.

She wiped the blade and made another scrape. Then another. Henry hadn't screamed and the shaving soap was untinged by red, so she figured she was doing okay.

"Remember that shaving isn't merely about scraping whiskers off the face," Fred said. "At its best, a good shave is a sybaritic experience, relaxing the nerves and invigorating the senses. Stop fidgeting, Henry, lest you end up with a slit throat."

When the shave was done and his face was rinsed and slapped with rose water, Henry felt his chin. "Smooth as a baby's bottom."

This drew a snicker from the ladies because his chin was that smooth before Marly had started.

"Very good, Master Landers," Fred said, patting her on the shoulder. "If you are willing to be here early tomorrow morning, I might persuade Arnie to sit on the stool for you."

"Perhaps Señor Landers should shave you, Señor Fred."

Marly turned abruptly. She hadn't noticed that her audience had grown. Señora de Vegas and a couple of the front room ladies had joined them. The ladies looked amused, while the Señora seemed perfectly serious.

"It would indicate your confidence in him," she added.

"Of course," Fred said with a bow. "In which case, Master Landers, you should be here at first light, since that is when my day begins."

Marly hesitated. She wasn't sure if she was ready for Fred's face, but she couldn't very well turn down the offer. She was about to agree when her stomach rumbled. "Let's eat."

"I have not yet dined," the Señora said. "Perhaps you would join me, Señor Landers? Join *us*, I should say, since Señor Fred usually takes his lunch with me in the garden when the weather is fine."

Henry turned a snort into a cough and excused himself to get back to the potatoes. The ladies also dispersed, leaving Louis to hang about in hopes of watching Fred squirm.

Not that Fred really squirmed, Marly noted. He remained his usual impassive self, except for two spots of pink that appeared on his cheekbones.

"I probably should be working," she said.

Louis smiled. "I think the boy has earned his dinner, n'est pas?"

"I think you have work to do, Louis," Fred snapped.

However, there was no sharpness in his tone when he addressed Marly. "Since it would be easier for my bookkeeping if I paid you in trade, the least I can do is make sure you are well fed."

Marly helped Señora de Vegas set the table. Playing the gentleman, she held the Señora's chair. Fred brought out the food and served them before sitting down.

Well trained by her aunt, Marly fell into the formal politeness Fred and the Señora affected. For the first time in a long time, she found it hard to remember she was playing the part of a boy. It was just as well that Fred insisted on calling her 'Master Landers'. Señora de Vegas was similarly formal.

"Señor Landers, I hear from the Señorita that you and Marshal Strachan are settled in. You are comfortable, I hope?"

"Most comfortable. Though I think I'm going to miss the bathtub."

"No need to, sir," Fred assured her. "Room five has been set aside for your use any time you need it. I know the marshal has his reasons for not staying at The Oasis. None of them should interfere with either of you using the room for baths."

"Thank you."

"And please do not hesitate to make use of our launderer either. Just bring your things to Henry."

"Thank you, sir."

Fred coughed gently.

"Er…thank you, Fred," Marly amended.

"Think of it as a title," the Señora advised when Fred left them to get coffee. "You are not being disrespectful."

"It would be easier if he called me Marly."

"Señor Fred follows his own set of rules. He does not talk about his past. He has mentioned that he was a gentleman's gentleman—a personal servant. He said his temper got the better of him. I believe he was forced to leave England."

Marly frowned. She couldn't imagine what Fred could have done to warrant being kicked out of his home country. On the other hand, maybe he had been falsely accused, as she had been.

"Whatever his reason, Señor Fred is determined to be the servant and he has cast you as the young gentleman."

"He's more the gentleman than me," Marly said.

Señora de Vegas made a small choking sound, like a hastily swallowed laugh.

Fred brought coffee, biscuits and fresh fruit. After dessert, he gave them a tour of his rose garden, pointing out the different varieties and describing their origins and qualities. As they walked, he paused occasionally to pull a weed or nip a faded bloom.

Beyond the roses was Louis' kitchen garden and herbary. It was as esthetically laid out as the roses. If she could ever bring herself to write Aunt Adele, Marly would have to send her the plan.

Between the two gardens was a path that led back to a chicken coop, pig pen and a shed for the goat that was kept staked out of reach of the flowers and produce.

"Who takes care of all this?" she asked.

"The pigs belong to the Trilby twins," the Señora explained. "The chickens are owned by the ladies, collectively. The goat is mine. We trade with The Oasis against our room and board. The Señorita doesn't mind how we contribute to the business as long as the bills are paid and the customers are happy."

"Different from what I expected," Marly admitted.

"Quite," Fred said. "Now, if you ladies will excuse me, my chief contribution to the cause is keeping the mistress happy. She should be rising from her postprandial nap about now."

He bowed and left.

It took several seconds before Marly noticed his slip.

After Fred departed, the Señora took Marly around and made introductions. Whatever Fred and possibly the Señora had divined, the ladies treated her like the young man she pretended to be. They were curious about the kid who had been taken under Marshal Strachan's wing and was now an interest of the taciturn Fred.

In the late afternoon, when it was time for the ladies to dress for the evening, Marly was kicked out. She left The Oasis via the gate in Louis' garden and checked at the stables on her way to the office. Grandee was still out. Trouble was in the corral and came to her expectantly.

That was encouragement enough for Marly to decide to meet Jase on the trail. She let Hank know she'd be back for Trouble and went to get her Winchester.

The office was locked up tight.

To go, or not to go, that was the question.

Chances were she would meet Jase just outside of town. He'd been gone all afternoon and must be on his way back. Hank had saddled Trouble for her, refusing her coin for his services. It would be churlish not to go out.

Marly swung into the saddle with something almost like grace and let Trouble set the pace out of town.

Jase was having mixed luck. When he reached the Lazy-E Ranch he discovered that Matt Egan was visiting outposts on his far ranges. The ranch foreman, Tierny, reluctantly entertained him and though the man was neither communicative nor overly cooperative, he did show Jase around and answered direct questions.

It was obvious that Tierny was loyal to the Egan family. Matt Egan Sr. had given him his start almost forty years ago. Tierny had grown up working the Egan ranges. His prime was spent ramrodding Lazy-E cattle. Now he managed the ranch, answering only to Matt Jr.

As he was shown around, Jase observed the man. Though on the shady side of fifty, Tierny was still powerfully built. Iron muscles matched iron-gray hair and eyes. He looked strong and agile enough to take Strothers down. He didn't strike Jase as the murderous type, but Jase knew his kind. Tierny had given his loyalty to the Egan family. He would do anything he felt necessary to protect them.

"What kind of men does Egan hire?" he asked Tierny. "Are there any new faces around?"

"There are new faces every season. Not every cowboy is willing or able to stick to one place."

Jase knew many were drifters, hired on as needed.

"I'm choosy about those I hire," Tierny said. "If there's even a whiff of the outlaw on him, he can go elsewhere. Mr. Egan trusts my judgment, but if I ain't sure, all I got to do is introduce the buck to the boss. Mr. Egan knows his men. He's a canny one."

All it took was a well-phrased remark to encourage Tierny in extolling the virtues of his employer.

"Egan's a tough and fair. Above all, he rewards loyalty. He demands the best of his men, and generally got it. He's generous to a fault."

In the same breath, Tierny assured Jase that the boss wasn't likely to have the wool pulled over his eyes and he could be ruthless as he was generous.

"Would you like some coffee, Marshal?"

"No, thanks." Jase paused. "What do you remember about the night of the murder?"

The man's mouth shut tighter than a miser's purse.

"Well?" Jase said.

"Don't remember a thing."

"Where were *you* that night?"

Tierny shrugged. "Maybe I was in town. Maybe I wasn't."

"Did you see anyone strange that night?"

"I can't rightly recall."

Jase gritted his teeth. "Well, thanks for your hospitality. You'll have to drop by the office some time."

Tierny scowled. "I will, will I?"

"For a friendly chat. Share some of my coffee. Maybe you'll remember something."

"Doubt it."

Looking back over his shoulder as he rode off, Jase noticed Tierny leaning against a corral post, lighting up a cigar.

He wondered if it was a Fuego.

At the Bar-B Ranch, Baker's house was nearly as impressive as Egan's. While flowers, shade trees and a neatly scythed lawn had surrounded Egan's home, Baker's landscaping consisted of a couple of half-dead trees, a flagstone walk and a lot of hard-packed earth.

At the Egan place, everyone was busily employed, but Baker had several men hanging around, on call for a show of force. One of those men was Tom Tyson, the man who had drawn on Jase at The Haven. His right arm was in a sling, but judging by his left-handed rig, he could compensate.

Before Jase reached the yard, Tyson barked, "Boss!"

His master appeared.

Baker was as dry and hard as his yard, greeting Jase with a scowl. "What are you doing here, Ranger?"

"Investigating a murder, Mr. Baker. Your cooperation would be appreciated."

"Would it?"

"I'd like your permission to talk to your men about the night Ellery Strothers was killed."

Baker gave him a half smile. "We work for a living around here, Ranger. If you want to talk to my men, you'll have to find them in town on their time off."

"Won't take long and I won't interfere with their work."

Baker shook his head. "I'd prefer it if you got off my land."

"You can make that request right now, sir, but it doesn't look good when supposedly upright citizens are so uncooperative. Makes it seem like you're hiding something. Think on that."

"The law hasn't been anyone's friend around here. It's brought this town nothing but distress. Strothers gave few people reason to trust him." Baker cocked his head. "You haven't fared much better. Think on *that*, Ranger."

Jase did. He also thought the man *was* hiding something.

About the same time Jase was leaving the Baker place, Marly was riding up the road, approaching the site of Strothers' murder. A trickle of sweat tickled her back. As the gully closed in, she felt a chill. Trouble felt it too and balked.

"Don't want to go there?" She reached down and patted his neck. "That's okay by me. Shall we go back or go on?"

She found a place to scramble up the bank they took to the open country. Trouble's impatience to run decided the issue. She pushed her hat firmly down and let the horse have his head. As they galloped over the hill, the breeze blew away the ghosts.

Trees cut them off from the road for a stretch. Further along, Marly had to circle around a patch of scrub and stone. She intended to rejoin the road on the other side, but was intercepted by three cowboys riding south.

They came on her suddenly.

Looking down at her saddle holster, she winced. She'd left her rifle behind at the office.

She continued at a fast trot, but they veered off, blocking her. She slowed Trouble to a trot, reigning in about six feet away.

One of the riders was Jed, the freckle-nosed young man Duke sometimes employed. Another cowboy she remembered from the livery. He was the one who had spat at her from The Haven porch. The third man was a stranger.

"Afternoon, gentlemen," she said politely.

She couldn't fight and flight wasn't practical. That left hoping for the best and trying to act braver than she felt.

"So here's the marshal's spy," said the spitter. He pushed his hat back, revealing greasy brown hair. "Don't look like much, does he?"

"Not much at all, Roy," Jed concurred, obviously the most junior of the three.

The third cowboy was older. He had a leathery tanned face and small black eyes. He hung back slightly, watching and chewing on the end of a cigar.

Marly eyed him with some curiosity. She also spared Roy enough attention to notice him gathering up a wad of spit.

She jerked Trouble out of range.

"Excuse me, gentlemen," she said, giving them a nod. "I'm meeting Marshal Strachan up the road."

She started to wheel Trouble around, but Roy blocked her and signaled Jed to take a position blocking the other direction. She backed up. The third cowboy moved in behind her.

Surrounded, she shivered.

Roy gave a low chuckle of amusement. "Scared?"

Beyond fear, all she could think of was how angry Jase was going to be. She had been so stupid, riding out without a rifle. Forget the trouble she was in now, what if she'd met a wildcat or a coyote? What if Trouble had disturbed a rattler?

Well, a rattler won't bother you if you don't bother it, she recalled Aunt Adele telling her repeatedly.

That dark-eyed cowboy struck her that way—a coiled snake who wouldn't strike without reason.

Best not to give him reason.

Roy was another matter. He was a classic bully, intent on playing a cat and mouse game with her. She wasn't sure what she would do about him. Jed, on the other hand, reminded her of the boys attending her aunt's one-room schoolhouse. They'd strut like the cock of the yard, looking bigger and tougher than they really were.

Marly fixed Jed with a hard stare. "Is this as good as you were brought up? Did no one teach you better?" She turned to Roy and shook her head. "You think I'm an easy mark? Maybe, but you'd be borrowing a lot of trouble messing with me. You could beat me, even kill me, it wouldn't stop the marshal's investigation. Besides, attacking an unarmed man, three against one, that's just plain cowardly."

Roy sidled forward, reaching out as if to pull her off her horse, but Marly backed up toward Jed, who hastily stepped out of her way.

She had her opening. All she needed was a small diversion.

As if in answer to her prayers, she heard the faint clip-clop of hooves in the distance.

"Let's go," the third man said, tossing his cigar.

"Not yet," Roy said. "You got a badge under that bandana, boy?"

Marly stood her ground, waiting for Roy to reach out. When he did, she grabbed his arm with both hands and yanked hard. Instinctively, Trouble backed away and Roy was unseated. With a shriek of rage, the man thudded to the ground. Jumping to his feet, he grabbed at her foot. Trouble was having none of that and knocked Roy over.

Marly spurred Trouble between Jed and Roy's horse.

"Get him," Roy hollered.

Jed started to follow, but Trouble seemed to have sprouted wings. The horse flew toward the road, gliding over the rough ground, sailing over the berm and crossing the wheel-rutted trail.

Marly blew out a pent up breath.

Jase heard shouting and urged Grandee from a trot to a canter. The next thing he knew, Marly and Trouble were flying toward him, followed closely by two cautious riders, who skidded down the short embankment and ended up staring down the business end of Jase's carbine.

One man managed to stop. The other wasn't as quick. Panicking, he reined in sharply with little regard to his horse's mouth. In retaliation, his beleaguered mount bucked and threw him. The young man sat up, a stunned expression on his face as his horse rode off without him.

Jase ignored him and kept his rifle trained on the man still mounted. "Who is the instigator of this melee?"

Before the man could answer, a third man rode up, halting on the top of the grassy ledge.

Jase waited until Marly wheeled Trouble abreast of Grandee.

"So, brat, what trouble have you got into this time?"

His eyes flicked from one man to the other.

"We were just having a little fun with the boy," the man on the ground said. He attempted a smile. "No harm done."

"Well, brat?"

"I thought I might meet you on the trail. Instead, I met these fellas. I don't think they like me."

"No accountin' for taste. Where's your rifle?"

"I couldn't get into the office."

Jase grunted and handed her the Winchester.

"Sorry," she said.

"We'll discuss it later."

He hunched forward, leaned his hands on his thighs and addressed the cowboys. "All right, boys. Let's have a few introductions. I'm Marshal Strachan. This is my assistant, Landers. Who the hell are you?"

CHAPTER 8

Marly waited, but there was no answer from any of the men. Roy played deaf and looked sullen. Jed couldn't seem to find his voice. The black-eyed man acted as if the question didn't apply to him.

Roy moved, maybe to get ready to make a run for it, maybe to try his luck against Jase's draw.

Marly took no chances. She swung the rifle level with his face.

Roy froze.

"We can do this nice," Jase continued, as if nothing had occurred. "Or I can take you in and you can do your talkin' from a jail cell. What'll it be?"

Roy's eyes moved from Jase to Marly, his contempt obvious. "Won't be the first time I've seen the inside of that jail."

Jed, who had since scrambled to his feet and backed off to a safe distance, looked up sharply. He didn't seem to like the direction things were going.

"He's Roy Parker," the third man said, his voice betraying a trace of a New England accent. It sounded odd coming from a man who otherwise blended in. "That's Jed McKinley. Jed works where he can get it. Parker and I are with the Bar-B."

Jase's eyes narrowed. "And you are?"

"Locke." The cowboy made a point of keeping his hands where they could see them. "These boys got out of hand, Marshal. Landers has put up a few backs. They just wanted to scare him a little. I wouldn't have let them hurt the boy."

Marly stole a sideways glance at Jase.

"All right," he said. "I'll let it go this time. But you mark me, boys, and set the word 'round. I only have so much patience. Less when it comes to bullies. Get on your way."

Jed headed back to town, while Roy and Locke veered south.

Once they were out of earshot, Marly said, "Can we go back the way I came?"

Jase nodded, taking the lead until they reached open country.

"I suppose," he said after a few minutes silence, "I should get you a key to the office."

"I suppose." She brought Trouble abreast of Grandee. "But I shouldn't have gone out without a rifle."

"No. You shouldn't have."

"I sure was glad to see you." When Jase didn't respond, she added, "Want your rifle back?"

"Nope. Hold on to it. We're not home yet."

Marly slowed when they reached the place the cowboys had stopped her. She searched the ground, but couldn't find what she was looking for.

The cigar butt.

"Which way were they headed when you met them, brat?"

"Southeast."

"Egan's place."

"You think they're messengers from Baker?"

"If they are, it ain't Egan they're takin' word to. He's gone 'til the end of the week. Baker would know that, I expect."

They rode toward town.

"What do you think's going on?" she asked.

"I don't know what to think. Seems most folks 'round here would rather aid a killer than the lawman after him. Knowing Strothers, can't say I blame 'em much. That hombre had a real talent for setting backs up."

"What did he do to get on the wrong side of you?"

Jase didn't answer at first and she wondered if she'd overstepped some boundary.

"He abused his power," he said finally.

Marly set her mouth in a firm line and waited.

"I knew Strothers back in my Battalion days. Even then, he thought he was something else. A handsome smooth-talker and quick draw, which always impresses. He knew how to look good to those who could help him on his way. The flip side of that coin was that if you couldn't help him, he didn't care about you. He didn't care whose toes he trod on to get ahead. He got himself promoted based on *that*, not his abilities."

Jase took a swig from his canteen and offered it to her. He must have just refilled it because the water was cold and fresh.

"I don't know how much you know about the Texas Rangers," he said. "We've been the law, order and militia almost since there was a Texas. Since there's not too many of us and a lot of state to cover,

Rangers wield a fair amount of power. We've also been known to stretch the bounds of our jurisdiction."

"And Strothers stretched it a bit too far," she guessed.

"He used his position to raise a posse to recover some stolen cattle. He wanted to make a name for himself—be another McNelly crossin' into Mexico with thirty men, retrievin' the cattle and returnin' a hero. Except Strothers was no McNelly and most of his men weren't Rangers. I was given a dozen men and the job of cleanin' up his mess. We got most of his posse home, maybe half of 'em in one piece. Then he acted like we messed up his grand plan. He got some people to buy his story."

This tarnished the image Marly held of the Texas legends.

"The Rangers kept him on?"

"In a manner of speakin'. He was never put into a position where he could exercise that kind of power again. I think that's why he took the marshal's job. It put him back in the limelight."

"Back where he could stir up trouble."

"Speakin' of which," he said, "you better watch yourself or you're the one who's gonna stir up trouble. This ain't the end of the matter, you know. Roy Parker, at the very least, still feels he has a score to settle with you."

"I'm sorry I let you down, sir."

Jase reached over and clasped her shoulder. "You haven't let me down yet. You made a mistake and you recognized it. You won't make the same one again."

The next morning, Jase rousted Marly at first light. She got up with a guilty start, mumbling something about a chore for Fred.

"Just remember who you're working for, brat."

"Sorry...promised...important..."

The words came out between pulling her jeans on and trying to put the left boot on the right foot. Then she used his wash basin to wash her hands, face and neck.

"I'll be right back," she said on her way out the door, buttoning her shirt as she went.

After a good head shake, Jase washed, shaved and strolled over to the hotel for coffee. A half hour later, he returned to the office and found Marly at the desk, stuffing a fried egg sandwich in her mouth.

"When I got here," she mumbled, pushing a greasy paper package toward him, "this was hot. Not so sure now."

"How was I to know you'd be on time for once?"

The sandwich was warm and smelled pretty fine.

"You had coffee yet?" he asked, feeling guilty.

She nodded, mouth full again. She mumbled something and pointed to the chair she was sitting in.

"I'm fine," he replied, taking another chair. "I don't wanna dally much longer. I have Hank saddlin' the horses. We're gonna ride a patrol this mornin'—get the lay of the land."

"Can we do some target practice too?"

Jase grinned. "It's already on my list of things to do."

In the middle of the night, he had lain awake, worrying about Marly and her close call. It's not that he thought those cowboys would have seriously hurt her, but any roughhousing would have revealed her secret. He couldn't let that happen.

Watching her sleep, he had run through scenarios where Marly wasn't pretending to be a boy. All involved them parting company. He couldn't let that happen either. That left treating Marly as his apprentice.

Once their wide circuit of the town was complete, Jase rode to a field recommended by Winters as a suitable place for target practice. An assortment of bullet-ridden empty cans and broken bottles marked the spot.

"Go set up as many targets as you can," he told Marly.

While she was busy, he strode over to his saddlebags and pulled out an extra holster and a Remington .44-40 he'd found in Strothers' personal armory. It was shorter and weighed less than the Colt Navy—easier to draw.

When Marly returned, he handed her the gun and holster without preamble. She took it without a word, though there was some grunting as she tried to do up the buckle and support the weight of the revolver at the same time.

"Here," he said, trying not to laugh.

For a moment, they worked at cross-purposes. Then Marly raised her hands and let Jase buckle the belt. Her fingertips were so close to his shoulders that if he leaned forward, he could slip his arms around her waist and—

He pushed away the thought.

"You can practice the art of quick buckling tonight," he said, backing away. "For now, we'll work on your quick draw. To start, let's test your reflexes." He emptied his Peacemaker and re-holstered it. "Catch it when I draw."

It took several tries before she could grab the barrel.

"Now it's your turn," he told her.

The first time she drew, Marly could barely get the gun free of the holster. Jase adjusted the angle of the holster and the second draw was much better. He had her repeat the exercise until her actions were smooth.

"This is harder than it looks," she said, massaging her wrist.

"You just need to work at it. Let's see how you accurate your aim is."

They loaded, then took turns drawing and shooting the targets. It wasn't long before Marly was showing acute signs of frustration.

"Something else that's harder than it looks," he said, patting her on the back. "You're doing fine."

She looked up at him, leaning in to his touch.

Jase hissed in a breath. The temptation to end the masquerade was almost irresistible, especially with her looking so soulfully into his eyes.

"I'll never be a great gun fighter, will I?" she asked.

"Marly, you don't want...I never meant..."

He stopped, not only embarrassed that he'd allowed himself to be ruffled, but that she was laughing at him.

"Brat."

They were back in time for the bank to open.

Marly watched as Jase strode down the street, his marshal's badge winking in the sunlight. He'd told her that Chet Winters had his own guards, but Jase wanted to make his presence known. The payrolls were coming in at the end of the week and he wanted everyone to know he was keeping an eye on things. He'd already told Winters he would drop into the bank during his patrol, but that he'd vary his route day to day.

"Predictability is the bane of law officers," Jase warned.

The banker passed this information along to Troy Riley, his armed clerk. Winters had hired a father-son team to protect his bank.

Mick Riley, the father, sat in a rocker all day just outside the bank. He had lost a leg in the war and needed a crutch to get around. But he was no pensioner. A busy-body by nature, he kept tabs on everything going on around town. As he rocked in his chair, a LeMat grapeshot pistol lay across his lap.

Troy Riley was a pleasant young man. Like his father, he was tougher than he appeared. He wore a two-gun rig and was an acknowledged sharpshooter and quick draw. He was the inside guard. When things were quiet, he helped with the bookkeeping and teller duties. When they were busy, Mrs. Winters stood at the teller's window and Troy stood on guard, holding a double-barreled shotgun. The thought of being shot at close range with a shotgun was a wonderful deterrent.

Jase left Marly in the office with orders to file papers and pack cartridges. Both jobs were fiddly, boring and took forever. By the time he returned, her normally even temper was wearing thin.

"I'm done," she said with a defiant scowl.

"There's always more and there's always another day," he said. "We'll use the chipped jug to collect them and wait 'til it's full before pullin' out the powder and shot again."

Marly nodded. With any luck, they'd be on their way to El Paso before she had to repeat the chore.

After lunch and the inevitable cleaning that required, she was itching to get away.

"Think I could go to The Oasis this afternoon?" she asked Jase. "I think Fred might have some work for me."

"I suppose Fred will keep you out of trouble for me."

She bit back a sharp answer. Then she realized he was making fun. In keeping with her boyish role, she stuck her tongue out at him on the way past.

Marly had several reasons to go to The Oasis, not the least of which was the possibility of enjoying afternoon tea with Fred and the Señora in the rose garden. Now that she had gotten over her prejudice, the place held a fascination for her. The people captivated her.

In exchange for a little hard work, which came naturally to her, she gained a wealth of knowledge. The Oasis staff provided valuable insight regarding the late Marshal Strothers. For instance, even if he frequented The Oasis, Strothers had not ingratiated himself with its staff.

Ella found him a dashing and heroic figure, but she was too young to work nights. Eileen, her mother, preferred keeping her out of the business, so Ella never experienced the slights and indignities meted out by Strothers to those he considered beneath him.

"Not that it stopped him from trying to get our favors," Judith Trilby pointed out.

"Except if he had to pay for them," her twin Juliet interjected.

According to Arnie, Strothers had a running tab for food and drinks that as far as he knew was still outstanding. Gambling and other entertainment, however, was strictly cash. The former was his special vice. Strothers had a fascination for the roulette wheel and unfounded faith in his own luck.

Arnie chuckled. "I'd reckon the house won enough of that man's pay to cover a few meals."

Louis wasn't a fountain of information, but like most he had an opinion to express about Strothers.

"That cochon! Sent back one of my finest dishes. Now, mon fils, take this home for your supper." He handed her one of the goose pies she had been helping him make. "But do not tell the Englander."

Only Fred saw the direction of Marly's inquiries. Fortunately for her, he took no offense.

"Miss Jezebel did not like Marshal Strothers," he said. "I doubt that the late marshal had the wit to recognize this. Miss Jezebel is a business woman and it was good business to have Strothers around."

"Would it be good business to pay him?"

"The Oasis and the bank guaranteed his wages when he was hired. Miss Jezebel allowed him to run a tab for meals to encourage his patronage. He never paid for a meal or drinks at the hotel or The Haven either, as far as I am aware. Since The Oasis does not engage in any illegal activity, bribery was unnecessary and blackmail does not apply."

Marly raised a brow.

Fred lifted his chin. "Whatever Miss Jezebel's personal feelings toward Marshal Strothers, she was quite put out that he got himself killed."

"What *are* her personal feelings?"

"I know she was disappointed when Master Jason turned down the position. Strothers was as good as anyone else, excepting Master Jason."

Marly took a moment to digest this.

"They're very close, aren't they?"

Fred gave her a look that made her uncomfortable. "I had recently been employed by Miss Jezebel when we were forced to abandon her establishment in Richmond. Being somewhat more prescient than most, Miss Jezebel was prepared for the evacuation. She had every intention of making a clean getaway, but she has a softer heart than she lets on."

"What happened?"

"We helped several wounded soldiers. Miss Jezebel took a particular interest in one. Master Jason. We nursed him when he was injured and brought him home to Texas. Over the years, Master Jason has had opportunity to pay Miss Jezebel back for her kindness and she has taken an interest in his career." Fred let out a slow sigh. "So, yes, they were close."

Marly noted the 'were', but decided to quit while she was ahead.

A thoughtful silence descended.

Fred mixed up his famous biscuits and directed her to grease the cooking pans. He showed her how to roll out the dough into a large rectangle, then cut it into diamonds. She put the first trays into the oven before asking about Señora de Vegas

"If you wish to know about the Señora, you should ask the Señora."

"I just wondered what happened to her husband," she said. "I didn't want to bring up such a painful topic with her."

"Señor de Vegas, as I understand, was a very wealthy gentleman of a noble family. Despite this, he fought for Mexican independence and later for Texas."

"He must've been quite old by the time he married the Señora."

"Yes, and she was very young." Fred paused in his mixing and shrugged as if shifting a weight on his shoulders. "Her husband and two sons were kidnapped when they were in Mexico. The Señora went to Austen to appeal to the governor for help. I was taking care of some business in Austin for Miss Jezebel and was able to use some of her contacts to get things moving. I am afraid it was too late."

"What happened?"

"Señor Fred enlisted Señor Strachan's aid on my behalf," Señora de Vegas said from the doorway. "I will always be grateful to him for that."

A slow blush crept up Fred's face.

"I-I hope you don't mind me asking, Señora," Marly stammered.

"I am neither offended, nor surprised by your curiosity, Señor Landers."

Marly concentrated on her work, hoping someone would continue the story. She wasn't disappointed.

"Señor Strachan was able to track down one of the pistoleros hired to do the kidnapping," the Señora explained. "He discovered that it was my husband's own family who made the arrangements and he confirmed my worst fear. I knew there was bad blood between my husband and his brother's family. I never imagined they would go to such lengths. They wanted the American property, of course. They were prevented from claiming it, but there was no proof of the murders, so they are still free."

"In the meantime," Fred added, "I brought the Señora here while things were being sorted out. She had no place else to go. Her family is in Mexico. There she is vulnerable to attack."

"What about the ranch?" Marly asked.

"Sold," the Señora said. "I did not want to keep it."

"You have some money left," Fred pointed out. "You could take it and start a new life."

"I like my life well enough for now. I can be useful here. Speaking of which, I came to tell you that Señorita Jezebel wishes to see you."

"Very well," he said. "Master Landers, the batch in the oven should be done. Put a few of them in this sack. I picked some tomatoes and a cucumber from the kitchen garden for you and the marshal. Just don't tell Louis."

"I won't." Louis was the least of her worries.

Leaving The Oasis, she headed for the Marshal's Office. Jase was sitting on the office porch when she arrived. He was oiling one of the spare rifles and had two more propped against the wall.

"Expecting trouble?" she asked, pausing on the steps.

"Payroll is comin' in tomorrow. Town will be a magnet for every cowboy, drifter and gambler in the area. Might be my best chance to corner some of Baker and Egan's men." He checked the action on the rifle. "Also a good chance there'll be trouble."

Jase followed her into the office.

As she divvied up dinner, he locked up the weapons. He didn't seem particularly worried, so she tried not to be. The smell of gun oil and black powder undermined her efforts.

It felt as though they were preparing for a siege.

Thursday morning, Marly was kicked out of bed before dawn. She hadn't slept well. Her mind was too busy thinking about the next day. It was still buzzing as she washed and dressed.

There were certain things she had to do to maintain her disguise. Chiefly, she had to flatten what little she had above the waist and augment what she lacked below the waist.

Bleary-eyed, she was making adjustments to the rolled sock in her drawers as she entered the office. Mr. Winters and Troy Riley were leaning over the marshal's desk and turned at the sound of the door opening.

Marly tried to back out again, but Jase beckoned her in.

"Mrs. Winters has made us muffins for breakfast."

"That's great." Forcing her voice down an octave, she asked, "Want me to pour coffee, sir?"

"We're good. If you hurry, you might have time for a cup before we leave. Strap your gun belt on first. And fetch your coat. It's cold this morning."

Minutes later, weighed down by her sidearm and the oversized riding coat, Marly forced herself to eat, even though anticipation was making her stomach roil. She had never felt so small and out of place than among these powerful men. Riding out to escort the payroll in their company seemed ludicrous, but she didn't have the nerve to raise an objection.

Outside, Hank waited with their horses.

"Good luck, gentlemen," Winters said, giving Jase and Riley a nod. He slapped a hand down on Marly's shoulder, almost causing her knees to buckle. "The marshal says you're ready for this, boy. Do him proud."

They intercepted the stage an hour's ride out of Fortuna. It took the stage twice that long to make the same distance.

All the way back, Marly rode with her Winchester carbine across her lap, one hand holding it secure, while the other handled the reins. There was an unnerving moment when she spotted a group of men riding parallel to the road.

"Unofficial escorts," Riley said. "From Baker's and Egan's ranches."

The stage rolled into town at eleven o'clock. Mr. Winters was there to meet them and help escort the courier to the bank. There was still counting and checking to be done before the doors would open for business.

In the meantime, there was a growing cluster of cowboys all wanting to be the first in line for their pay. Jase buttonholed Tierny and with his help, herded them into a long, ragged line.

Marly was relieved from duty and sent back to the office to secure the extra arms and ammunition they had carried. That included, Jase pointed out, the Remington revolver.

"Sorry, brat," he said. "You're just not ready for the kind of trouble packin' iron in town could bring you."

She made a token protest, but was happy to lay down her arms and the accompanying responsibility.

"Coming back for dinner?" she asked.

"Don't think so. Thought I might check out The Haven once I'm done here. Will you be okay?"

"Arnie owes me a meal. I'll be okay."

She had a few other chores to do besides stowing the gear, and it was almost an hour before she locked up and headed for The Oasis.

When she stepped inside, she almost didn't recognize the place. It brought back her first impressions of the saloon. The ladies were wearing their working clothes—opulent décolletage gowns garnished with a profusion of feathers and glitter. The piano had been moved to the stage usually reserved for Jezebel's table. The piano player, a handsome black man in a striped shirt and bowler hat, accompanied one of the ladies as she sang about the man who'd left her. Behind the bar, Arnie poured drinks and collected empty glasses. He was accompanied by the big bruiser, who usually only worked nights. The dining room was filling up and the casino was already crowded.

Marly almost backed out again, but Arnie waved her over to the bar.

"I'm glad to see you," he said, sounding frazzled. "Could you go down and bring up another case of whiskey? I just can't seem to get away."

Marly nodded and he tossed her the key.

From then on, she didn't stop moving. The ladies served the tables, but they didn't always have time to clear them. Breaks and spills were frequent as spirits rose and the mess kept Marly busy.

At first, she went unnoticed except for the occasional tip thrown her way. As the place got busier, there was more talk about the marshal and his sidekick. Mostly there were a jibes and snide comments. She ignored them until one man caught her off-guard with an outstretch foot. Regaining her balance, she discovered she'd only lost one glass off her tray. It had bounced onto the floor, but didn't break.

As she retrieved it, Marly was gratified to see her prankster's lap fill with beer. A lady, who had been leaning over the man's shoulder, had *accidentally* tipped her glass. With an insincere apology—and a covert wink in Marly's direction—the lady moved off to find another customer to please.

Marly hid a grin as she straightened.

"Master Landers."

The voice startled Marly. With all the bustle, she hadn't noticed Fred's approach.

"Master Landers, I could use your services in the kitchen."

She followed him, pausing long enough to slide a tray of empty glasses onto the bar. Arnie gave her a rueful shrug before turning his attention to the men waiting for their whiskey.

One of the men was Locke.

Marly's heart raced. "I'll be there in a moment, Fred."

She picked up an empty tray and followed Locke to the blackjack table. Quietly making the rounds, she wiped up spills and picked up empty glasses, all the while keeping an eye on Locke. The man was a serious player, despite the distraction of the Trilby twins. He drank the best whiskey, judging by its rich amber color, and smoked expensive cigars. It was odd he had so much money to throw around, even if it *was* payday.

Locke ground his cigar into the table leg, then flicked it toward a spittoon, but missed. When he turned away, Marly quickly retrieved it. It was crushed to the point that no bite patterns were visible, but she could see one thing.

It was the J. Fuego brand.

As if aware of her scrutiny, Locke whirled around and caught her gaze.

Uh-oh.

"Boy!" he called.

She froze.

He flipped her a quarter dollar. "Two of Jezebel's best cigars. You can keep the change."

Across the road, The Haven was every bit as busy. Since Duke didn't provide any set entertainment, the chief occupations of the clientele were drinking and playing cards.

Jase sat in a back corner, sipping on a beer and listening. He didn't go unnoticed, but it hardly mattered. He wasn't expecting to hear a confession. He wanted to discover the kind of men that worked for Egan and Baker. Payday gave him ample opportunity.

The men who spent their wages at The Haven were a rough lot. They had no need for the niceties The Oasis offered.

Jase recognized three basic types amongst them. There were the buddies. They lived, worked and fought together. All they needed was each other's company, a steady supply of liquor and maybe a pack of cards. There were the loners. All they needed was the liquor. Then there were the young bucks. The Haven had the right image for them. It was the rough and ready place. The Oasis was too civilized—and too expensive.

The smell of smoke and stale beer eventually overwhelmed Jase, so he left to check in on Winters at the bank. Everything was under control. During his routine patrol, he found that business was booming in Fortuna. For all the noise and bustle, everything remained relatively peaceful.

He was beginning to feel redundant when he was struck by inspiration. Stopping in at The Oasis, he checked on Marly, confiscated a pot of coffee, a couple of mugs and some of Fred's biscuits.

"Coffee, Mr. Riley?"

"Call me Mick," Riley Sr. said. "Troy's the 'Mister' of the family. Going to make something of himself, that boy."

For the past few days, Jase had avoided getting into lengthy conversation with the garrulous old man. But he realized he was ignoring an important source of information, and what Mick confirmed was something Jase had suspected.

Strothers was murdered within days of the last payday.

"Egan gives most of his men three days off when the pay comes in," Mick said, "and because he does, so do the other ranchers. Over those three days, just about everyone comes into town and most leave their money here—gambling, boozing, paying off their tab at the general store, putting aside their savings. One way or another, the majority of money that left the bank on payday ends up back in the bank by Monday morning."

"And you sit here watchin' the money come and go."

Mick gave a knowing wink.

Jase surveyed the street. From here, the bank had a clear view of every business from the general store to The Oasis.

"Reckon you could probably tell me the coming and goings of most folks on those days."

"Reckon so."

Jase refilled the man's cup and sat back.

Mick didn't disappoint. He gave a credible report of who was doing what in town on the day of Strothers' murder. What he hadn't observed directly, he could attribute to a reliable source. All Jase had to do was check up on those sources later.

"Who do you think did it?" Jase asked.

"Not for me to say. Didn't think much of Strothers myself, but I can't think of anyone who hated him enough to kill him. Not even Matt Egan."

Despite all denials, Jase got the impression that most people thought Egan was somehow responsible for Strothers' death. If he *was* responsible, they thought he must be in some way justified. Mick was the first who meant what he said. If his recollections were accurate, Egan had *not* personally murdered the marshal. Nor had any of the men he'd employed. They all had solid alibis.

"Not many men that Egan would have working for him would lay an ambush for a man," Mick said.

"Not even Tierny? For Egan's sake?"

Mick shook his head. "Tierny wouldn't do it and Egan wouldn't ask him. You don't ask your family to take care of business like that. Tierny's like a second father to Matt Egan."

"Someone had to do it. If not Egan or any of his men, who?"

Mick shrugged. "Young Matt's a good fella. Respected. Liked. Still, if he did hire someone to kill Strothers, it wouldn't be anyone close to him. He'd bring someone in. Maybe hire one of Baker's men. Gabe Baker ain't nearly as choosy about who he takes on."

Around six o'clock, Jase rescued Marly from The Oasis kitchen. She had been peeling potatoes and washing dishes for three hours and still hadn't eaten. Louis, under whose supervision Fred had left her, was chagrined. He assumed Marly had lunch before coming back to the kitchen. To make amends, he packed up a selection of cold meats, cheese and pickles, along with a half-dozen of Fred's biscuits.

Back at the office, Jase lit the stove and started a pot of coffee, while Marly washed up and changed her shirt. After supper, he left her to do the dishes, while he strolled into The Oasis to do a little eavesdropping and information gathering. He learned nothing new.

When he returned, Marly was fast asleep with last year's Colt Firearms Catalogue in her hands. Ever since he had given her the carbine, she started reading the back issues of the various firearms catalogues that Strothers collected. He removed the book from her grasp and dog-eared her page before setting it aside.

She stirred, causing a tendril of hair to escape her braid and fall over her brow. He crouched and tenderly smoothed the curl back. Making sure she was securely tucked in, he indulged in watching her for a few minutes.

Marly was beautiful in sleep. Peaceful. Innocent.

How innocent?

When he left to do rounds, he couldn't get her out of his mind.

CHAPTER 9

Marly woke early to find Jase in a dead sleep, fully dressed, on top of his covers. He'd taken off his boots and gun belt. That was all. She took the blanket off her bed and draped it over him. Of all the things she wished she could do for him, she settled for stoking the fire and setting beans and biscuits to warm for his breakfast.

Guessing that there would be no morning ride, nor likely one on Sunday, Marly went to the livery to make sure Trouble and Grandee were exercised.

"Wanna work?" Hank asked by way of greeting. "Seems everyone's been waiting for payday to get stuff taken care of. Mr. Sloan's out in the smithy and needs my help. That means somebody else has to do my job."

"How much?"

"Fifty cents for the day, plus tips."

"Done."

Working for money would be a nice change. At The Oasis, she had exchanged labor for groceries and laundry services. Handy as that was, it didn't help pay off Jase for the money he had spent on her behalf.

Jase wasn't quite as pleased when he found out.

"Look, brat, I told you before, you're workin' off that debt already. That's why you're an *unpaid* assistant. 'Sides, all those goodies you keep bringing back from The Oasis are worth somethin'. I haven't spent two bits on food since I stocked up the first time."

"We have enough for now," Marly assured him. "Miz Jezebel sent you that pound of her special coffee, we've got lots of fruit and vegetables and goat cheese and that sausage thing. And I'll bet you weren't even going to come home for dinner."

Jase sighed. "Fine. Don't expect me to accept the money you make today. Keep it. You earned it."

While Marly mucked stalls, forked hay and doled out oats, Jase checked out the information Riley Sr. had given him. Armed with knowledge, he was able to narrow the field of possible suspects.

Tierny was proficient with a knife. He was also well respected. By suggesting that he might have done the deed, Jase prompted others to put forth other less popular candidates. Many men could fight with a knife, but few were known as knife fighters. Of those few, Jase eliminated any that were also good shots. As Marly had pointed out, one well-placed bullet would have done the job with less risk.

By late afternoon, he had a short list of suspects. None of them, however, had any obvious motive to murder Strothers. The questions still remained. Did Egan instigate Strothers' death? And if he did, how could Jase prove it?

He mulled the problem over and engaged in the mindless task of cleaning his guns. He worked his way through two rifles, his Colt and Marly's Remington with only a few interruptions. Reassembling the Remington, he noticed it was past suppertime and Marly still hadn't returned. He was debating whether to go look for her or fix a meal for himself when she walked into the office.

He didn't immediately look up. The distinctive and familiar damp-smelling cocktail of sweat, manure and horse preceded her through the door and was enough to signal her presence.

Marly cleared her throat and he lifted his gaze.

Sure enough, she was damp, dirty and disheveled. *And* she sported the beginnings of a black eye.

Slamming the Remington on the desk, he jumped up so violently that he knocked his chair over. "What the hell happened to you?"

Marly winced. "You should see the other guy."

"What did you do, kill him?"

"No. But he'll be singing high for a couple of days."

It was Jase's turn to wince.

"And limping."

"Uh-huh."

"And I think I broke his friend's nose."

"What?"

Jase strode toward her. He examined her hands, which were scraped and starting the bruise. Roughly, he held her chin and checked her eye. She had a small cut on her lip.

"He tried to grab me from behind," she explained. "So I elbowed him in the gut and stomped on his foot with the heel of my boot. His friend got a punch in. I sort of blocked the second. Hank evened the odds and flattened them. They woke up in the manure pile."

"Hank?" He let go of her chin and leaned against the desk.

"You know, the guy who works at the livery. We've struck up a friendship. When he heard some of Egan's boys were looking for me, he came over from the smithy."

"Good for Hank. How many of Egan's boys were there?"

"Four all together. Only two jumped me. The other two disappeared when Hank showed up."

"Do you know who they were?"

She hesitated.

"Does Hank know them?"

"Yes," she said. "Hank knows them, but he suggested it might be better if I didn't mention any names to you."

Anger welled up in Jase's throat. "He did, did he?"

He wanted to punch something—someone. Failing that, he wanted to pull Marly into his arms and remind her that she was a woman, not a boy. Instead, he crossed his arms and held back all the intemperate things he knew he'd regret saying.

Marly shut the office door. "Hank only pointed out what I already knew. In the schoolyard, nobody likes a tattle-tail. If it can be handled without calling on the teacher, then you do so. This wasn't like the thing on the trail. This was schoolyard stuff and it has been handled."

"Pretty rough schoolyard, Marly Landers. Are you sure you wanna play with the big boys?"

"I figure I don't have much choice. I did okay though. I think I earned some respect. Best keep going."

He took a deep breath and let it out slowly. "How do you feel?"

She gave a shaky laugh. "Well, my left eye hurts and I want to wash and change. Mostly, I'm just hungry. Do you mind cooking?"

Jase jabbed a thumb toward their quarters. "How 'bout you clean up and I'll take you out to dinner."

"Steak?"

"Sure." His mouth twisted in a wry grin. "One for the plate and one for your eye."

Fifteen minutes later they were seated at a table in a corner of The Oasis dining room. During the meal, Marly explained how she had been looking for scratch marks on the saddles at the livery. Problem was, *too* many saddles had scrapes. There were a couple of promising ones with scratch marks above the stirrup, where the leg would normally cover the leather.

"One of the scratched saddles belongs to Locke," she said. "And he smokes the right brand of cigar."

He stared at her, amazed. Damned if she wasn't turning into a fair investigator. That thought gave him the solution to his problem—how to protect Marly without treating her like a girl.

After supper, he took her on patrol of the town. They walked up Main Street, looking in on the hotel as they passed by. At the church, they strolled over to the butcher shop, then cut back through the alley.

"It's important to cover the back and front of the bank and stage office during rounds," he warned. "But we can't take the same route twice in a row. Or go on patrol at the same time each day."

"Too predictable," she said with a nod.

"We'll loop around the livery and stop in at The Haven. Later, we'll check out the back of the hotel and general store."

Everything was quiet at the front of the livery. Sloane and Hank were visible through the open doors. They were drinking beer with a few cronies on The Haven's back porch.

Sloane called them over, offering Marly a beer.

"I'd offer one to you, Marshal," he said, "but you're on duty."

"As it happens, so is Landers."

Marly's brow furrowed in confusion. "What?"

Jase smiled. "Do you swear to uphold the law as laid down by the State of Texas and the Town of Fortuna?"

She blinked.

"The proper answer is 'I do'. It's a bit like a weddin'."

Marly blushed to the roots of her auburn braids. "I d-do."

He pinned a deputy's badge on her shirt.

Marly gave a small gasp of delight. "I'm a deputy?"

"As duly witnessed by Mr. Bill Sloane and Mr. Hank…"

"Bjornsen," Sloane said.

"Mr. Hank Bjornsen," Jase said. "You've practically been doin' the work of a deputy. Besides, now if anyone makes trouble, it's up to you whether or not to arrest 'em."

Sloane and Hank raised their glasses in celebration.

"Now, Deputy Landers," Jase said, "if you'll follow me."

They headed into the saloon.

It wasn't hard to pick out Marly's attackers. Apart from the lingering smell, they were the ones eying the new deputy with some concern. At a glance, Jase could tell that she had pegged them correctly. They were no more than teenagers, trail-hardened youths, with no particular malice aside from wanting to put a stranger in his place.

Marly gave them a nod. Jase didn't acknowledge them.

After they left The Haven, Marly wanted to show off her badge at The Oasis. Jase vetoed the plan.

"There's plenty of time for that. We don't wanna stir up too much trouble tonight."

Instead, he put her in charge of minding the office.

"This time there's no fallin' asleep."

Marly spent the next couple of hours sipping coffee and reading the available material on legal procedure, jurisdiction and jurisprudence in the state of Texas.

When Jase came back, she skipped the usual pleasantries and asked him if Locke was still at The Oasis.

"Yep. Why?"

"Because yesterday I tried to get one of his cigar stubs. Too bad he pulverized it. I thought if we could get one of his stubs, we could check the chew marks against the ones we found." She frowned. "I doubt I could get away with following him now and you stick out like a sore thumb. But Arnie might be able to do it without raising suspicions." She took a deep breath.

Jase smirked and pulled a rag out of his pocket, setting it on the desk. "Two cigar butts."

Marly gasped. "But…who…where?"

"Locke. At The Oasis."

Trembling with excitement, she rummaged through the desk and unwrapped the other butts they'd found earlier. Comparing them, she said, "The bite marks match."

"I figured they would."

"We've got the killer, don't we?"

"All we know for sure is Locke was there. Can't hang a man on the evidence of a few cigar stubs, especially when he has no compellin' motive for murder."

"Still," she said, "it looks like we got the weapon. Now we need to gather proof and find out who aimed Locke at Strothers."

The next morning, Marly decided to do the patrol on her own.

"Can I wear my gun belt now that I'm deputy?"

"Not around town," Jase replied. "Not yet. Keep the rifle with you when you're out and about. Oh, and as deputy, no stall muckin'."

"No stall muckin'," she drawled. "How 'bout workin' at The Oasis?"

"Part-time, only after the weekend. And only so Fred will stop you from talkin' with my drawl all the time."

She laughed, then pulled the brim of her hat down low. "I reckon Fred will oblige."

At the livery, Marly broke the news to Hank.

"I understand," he said, though he sounded disappointed.

Sloan, his boss, gave her a hearty slap across the shoulders. "I like you, boy. You're a hard worker. A bit scrawny, but a scrapper. There'll always be a job for you here if you want one."

"Thank you, sir."

As soon as Sloan and Hank were out of sight, she flexed her shoulders painfully. As big as Hank was, his employer dwarfed him. She was only thankful that the two behemoths counted amongst her friends, not her many enemies.

Jase's instructions had been minimal. He expected her to walk three circuits of the town, taking a different route each time. It was up to her how to space the patrols through the morning. Between patrols, he expected her to keep an eye on Main Street.

Unsure what else to do, she took a seat on the bench outside the general store. She had an excellent view of the bank across the street.

Mick Riley tipped his hat to her.

She tugged her brim in response.

Sitting and waiting didn't come naturally to Marly. To keep busy, she pulled out a knife and whetstone. There are few things more useful than a good knife. That was probably the only reason her Aunt Adele had let her keep this one memento of her time with Sarge. He had given it to her the first night he'd rescued her. To make her feel safe, he'd said.

"That's a Bowie knife, isn't it?"

Marly raised her head. "Miss Amabelle."

"So is it?"

"What?"

Amabelle gritted her teeth. "A Bowie knife?"

"Yup."

The laconic reply didn't daunt the young lady.

"How's the investigation coming along?"

"You should ask the marshal. He's in charge of the investigation."

"And here I got the impression you knew everything."

"Nope, not everything."

Amabelle gave a huff of disgust.

Marly's lips twitched with a suppressed grin. She'd had her fair share of snubs from girls like Amabelle Egan. Dressed as a boy, she realized it was whole lot easier dealing with Amabelle's sort. And she wouldn't get in trouble for hair pulling.

She glanced up, expecting to see frustration on Amabelle's face. She saw fear instead.

A tall, plain-faced man was making a beeline for them. Marly recognized him as Gabriel Baker, though they had not been introduced.

Out of respect for her elders, she stood.

"It's not proper to talk to strangers, Amabelle," Baker said.

"Oh, Mr. Landers isn't a stranger, Gabe. He's the marshal's deputy."

"More reason not to speak to him. Come with me." He offered Amabelle his arm. "I'll help you find your brother."

"No need," a deep voice announced from the doorway. "How do, Gabe? I didn't know you'd be in town today."

Marly hadn't noticed Amabelle's brother before. Now, she wasn't sure how she could have missed him.

About as tall as Jase, yet not as tall as Baker, Matthew Egan had his sister's coloring and was as handsome and muscular as Amabelle was pretty and petite. He wasn't as slick a dresser as the banker, but Marly knew enough about quality to recognize it in his coal-black suit and pristine white shirt. She felt very small and scruffy in comparison.

"I wanted to check on the boys," Baker explained. "Perhaps you and Miss Amabelle would join me for lunch?"

"With pleasure," Egan said. "Aunt June is also with us."

"She is most welcome, of course."

"Good. Then we'll meet you at the hotel in an hour?"

Having been politely dismissed, Baker was forced to move on.

Amabelle let out a tiny sigh of relief.

Marly could hardly blame her. It was obvious that Baker had a proprietary interest in her. Equally obvious was the fact that far from returning his affections Amabelle was intimidated by him.

Egan watched his business partner cross the street and enter the Stage, Post and Telegraph Office. Then he turned and a troubled expression flickered across his features before he put on his company face.

"So you're Marly Landers," he stated.

"Yes, sir."

They took a moment to size each other up.

"Amabelle," he said, "go help your aunt with the shopping."

"But—"

"Go on. I'll be along soon."

Reluctantly, Amabelle walked past her brother and into the store, casting a wistful glance over her shoulder

Marly turned the Bowie over in her hand, unsure what to do with it. Was it impolite to hold a knife when talking to a murder suspect? She wished Jase were with her, but settled for affecting his mannerisms.

"What can I do for you, Mr. Egan?"

"Sit down, son."

"I'm fine standing." She waved the knife in the direction of the bench. "You go ahead."

He didn't sit, so she leaned against a post in order to look him in the eye without developing a crick in her neck. To alleviate her nerves, she cleaned her nails with the blade.

"You're not making this easy," Egan said, folding his arms and giving her a stern gaze.

"Making what easy?"

"I wanted to apologize for what my boys did. What they *tried* to do. Believe me, there was hell to pay when I heard about it. They won't bother you again."

Marly looked up from her task and pushed back her hat, displaying the shiner. She knew Egan's men had worse.

"No, sir. I don't suppose they will."

She flipped the Bowie, caught it by the hilt and sheathed it.

Egan sat down, taking in the black eye and what she hoped came across as indifference to getting in a fight. He smiled, making him twice as handsome and half as intimidating.

"I'm beginning to see what Amabelle sees in you, Mr. Landers. I don't suppose you'd like to come work for me, would you?"

"No, sir." She thumbed her badge. "I already got a job."

Egan nodded, his smile broadening. "Didn't think so. Are you figuring to become a Ranger?"

She stifled a snort. "Don't know that they'd have me. But it's an honorable profession."

"So I understand, Mr. Landers. In fact, I'm hoping you and Marshal Strachan decide to stay in Fortuna."

"Don't think it's likely. We've only stayed this long because of the murder. Once that's solved, we've got other business in El Paso."

"And afterwards?"

She shrugged, suspecting Fortuna was one place she'd never return to. But there was no reason to tell that to Egan.

"Think about it," he advised, rising. "I'm hosting a community dance next week. I count on seeing you there, Mr. Landers. I'll make sure that you and the marshal receive personal invitations."

This announcement surprised Marly so much that she didn't have a chance to respond before Egan disappeared into the store.

It surprised Jase even more when she told him about it later.

"I heard about the dance," he said. "I figured we'd be *personas non grata*."

After lunch, it was Marly's turn to mind the office. Jase gave her a list of chores to do, which she spaced out between periods of reading. A few people poked their heads in, but most left once they saw the marshal wasn't there.

She was sweeping when Jase returned from his patrol of the town, his face pinched with suppressed emotion.

"What is it?" she asked, worried.

He let out a gust of laughter, then shook his head. "I do believe, Marly Landers, that in a couple of years when you're both ready for it, Mr. Egan would look favorably on you marryin' his sister."

"I thought I was too young and not near rich enough."

"I suppose Mr. Egan sees the potential in you."

He threw his hat on the desk and sat down, wiping his eyes with the back of his hand.

Scowling at him, she dropped into the other chair. "I don't see what's so funny."

"You don't, *Miss* Landers?"

Marly let out a hiss of air. Damn.

She had come to the working theory that Jase must have realized she was a girl by now. If nothing else, his reaction when she came in with a black eye seemed to bear it out. He wouldn't have been so shaken if he believed she was a boy. But she'd doubted he'd bring it up.

And she certainly wouldn't. Until now.

"Have you known all along?"

"No," he said. "If I had known back in Dog Flats or in Fort Worth when I first saw you, I would have sent you back to your aunt's."

"Good thing you didn't know then. It would've only made things more difficult. See, I really can't go back. I told you, she kicked me out."

"Your aunt kicked you out." His tone was skeptical.

"She sent me away. I just didn't go where she sent me." She gave a bitter laugh. "She was sending me to a *convent* school, for heaven's sake. Can you imagine?"

His expression was a mix of amusement and something close to fury. Was he angry on her behalf?

"You know," she said, trying to make light, "except for letting you think I was a boy—or trying to—I've never lied to you."

"I know."

She knew he had a dozen questions. She only had one.

"Why didn't you tell me you knew?"

"For better or worse, I thought it was safer for both of us if I pretended you were a boy. It wasn't proper. It's too late to change the past. Both our reputations as decent folk depend on keepin' up the deception."

"I know."

He got up and checked the coffee pot. It was about half full and didn't smell burnt, so he poured them each a cup. Setting his on the desk, he crouched beside her chair and held out her cup as if it were a peace offering.

"I apologize if you think I should have told you earlier," he said. "I certainly never wanted to breach your trust."

"I trust you." She took the cup, half sorry, half relieved that he didn't feel it necessary to make an honest woman of her.

"I'm glad." He rocked back on his heels and stood. "It might have been wrong and it was definitely unwise, but I'm not sorry I did it, 'cause I'm not sorry you're here."

Marly managed a small smile. Neither am I.

CHAPTER 10

Whatever hopes Marly harbored, come sunrise it was as if the disclosure never happened. Jase checked behind her ears and under her fingernails, treating her like a scrubby schoolboy. Fred had come by to give the marshal a shave and trim before church, so she knew Jase's actions were partly for show.

"I am sure Master Landers is well scrubbed, sir," Fred said.

"He's clean enough, but that braid is messy. Maybe you should give the boy a haircut, Fred."

Marly backed up into the door. She had considered chopping off her hair as part of her disguise, but it was her one vanity. According to Aunt Adele, her hair was just like her mother's, except the color had been inherited from her father.

"No time," Fred said, packing his kit. "You need to get to church and I need to get back to Miss Jezebel."

"We'll see you in church?" Marly asked.

"No, Master Landers. Miss Jezebel went to church once, when it first opened. Her presence was," his lips twitched, "controversial. The minister was gracious, however. He is giving a brief service in the rose garden, even as we speak. Miss Jezebel and several of the ladies are in attendance."

"And you?"

"I take care of my spiritual needs on my own."

"Sounds good to me."

Jase shook his head. "We need to be at church, to see and be seen."

Fred bowed and disappeared.

"Come here, brat," Jase said. "I'll fix that braid. I was only jokin' about the haircut."

"And I was only joking about shooting you if you tried."

"You never said that."

A L I S O N   B R U C E

"I was thinking it."

Marly cautiously approached him and turned so he could work. His fingers combed her hair in gentle strokes as he unwound the braid. He smoothed her hair into three columns and gave each a twist as he braided them. Now and then, his knuckles would brush the back of her neck and it was all she could do not to lean into his touch.

"That's better," he said, giving the finished tail a tug.

Sorry that the experience was over—and sorrier still that Jase sounded so matter-of-fact about it—Marly grunted her thanks and went to get her hat. If they were going to keep up the pretense that she was a boy, it was better that he didn't see the effect his touch had on her.

After services, many of the congregation set out blankets on the grounds of the church and ate box lunches. This was a popular choice of venue for families with young children or young people courting. Those who could afford to eat out and were more concerned with comfort went to the hotel. Marly had heard about the establishment's food and was glad that Jase's sense of duty didn't extend to having breakfast there.

They headed for The Oasis where, in deference to the day, Jezebel's portrait was draped and the casino was closed for the morning.

Standing in the doorway, Marly had just taken these details in when Matt Egan approached.

"Would you do me the honor of being my guests for breakfast?" he asked.

Marly glanced over her shoulder and saw that Amabelle and an older lady were picnicking with the minister and his wife on the grass.

"Amabelle and I come here sometimes," Egan said, ushering them ahead. "But Aunt June has a stricter notion of propriety." He waved at someone. "Gabe! Come and join us."

Great, Marly thought as Gabriel Baker headed for their table.

"Hope, you don't mind, Marshal," Egan said in an undertone. "I know you two didn't make a good start, but Gabe's a good man and a good friend."

Baker agreed to sit with them only because Egan didn't give him any chance to refuse. But he didn't appear too happy.

"Marsha Strachan is a welcome addition to the town," Egan said in a carrying voice. "This town needs a little law and order."

He re-issued his invitation for Jase and Marly to attend his community social, letting everyone in the room know that he, for one, was not giving them the cold shoulder.

Marly ate as quickly as possible, wanting nothing more than to leave the men to their business association meeting. Jase didn't seem in a hurry.

A waiter appeared with shots of brandy and the cigars.

"I'm going to do my patrol," she said, gulping back the last swig of coffee.

Outside The Oasis, Marly noticed that Amabelle and many of the other young people had escaped their elders. They were now congregated on the boardwalk outside the hotel, gossiping. They didn't pay Marly much attention.

But Amabelle did.

"Come on over, Deputy Landers."

With a heavy sigh, Marly obeyed.

"This is my dear friend Kate O'Brian," Amabelle said.

Where Amabelle was blonde and delicately pretty, Kate was an auburn-haired, buxom beauty.

From her local research, Marly knew that the O'Brian family owned the Circle-X, a breed ranch. Their chief concern was horses, which the family trade brought with them from Ireland, but they also bred cattle, pigs, and dogs.

Marly's introduction interrupted an argument between Kate's older brother Shea and Bob Johnstone, heir to the Slashed Bars Ranch. The two young men paused long enough to give her a polite howdy-do, then ignored her.

"I must leave now," she said. "To do my rounds."

"I surely would like to go on patrol with you, Deputy Landers," Amabelle simpered.

Shea's head jerked up. "Now you don't want to go do that, Miss Amabelle. I'm much better company."

Marly felt a little sorry for him when the lady ignored him.

"You should offer a lady your arm," Amabelle said coyly, as she matched Marly's pace.

"Can't, Miss, I'm on duty."

It was all Marly could do not to laugh at the girl.

"Marshal Strothers always offered me his arm," Amabelle countered, "and he was always on duty."

"I carry a rifle. It's not practical. Besides, I'm not Marshal Strothers."

This point was unarguable, even for an Egan.

They walked in silence, Marly intentionally changing pace from time to time, trying to shake Amabelle off. The last thing she needed was the town belle throwing herself at her. Eventually, Amabelle tried flirting again. Then, when that didn't work, she limited herself to impatient huffs and mumbled insults.

Marly spotted Gabriel Baker and closed ranks.

"Miss Amabelle, well met. I was hoping to see you."

Baker tone was warm, his smile broad.

Marly didn't buy it for an instant. It was a forced smile, pasted on to charm and manipulate. His eyes were still cold and angry.

"You shouldn't bother Deputy Landers while he's working, my dear. Let me take you back to your aunt. I believe I saw her in the church garden. We can take a stroll by the schoolhouse, see how construction is coming along." He offered Amabelle his arm.

There was nothing overtly threatening about the gesture, yet Amabelle shrunk back.

Marly shifted her rifle so she could take Amabelle's arm.

"That's mighty kind of you, Mr. Baker," she said, adopting her Jase-like drawl and laying it on a little thick out of nerves. "Happens I already offered to accompany Miz Egan to the hotel to join her friends. Thank you all the same."

She led Amabelle along Church Road and down Reynold's Lane. She paused in front of one of the smaller homes and pointed out some flowers. It was a clandestine move to check if Baker was following.

He wasn't, but he stared after them.

Resisting the urge to hurry, she led Amabelle at a strolling pace until they turned the corner onto The Avenue.

"Thank you," Amabelle said. "Not that I can't handle Gabe..."

Marly snorted. "Right. Let's go find your friends."

Amabelle's friends had moved on, and despite her assurances that she could handle him, Amabelle showed no interest in risking another encounter with Baker.

"I'll take you to your brother," Marly said.

"No. He is far too busy for me. I'm happy to join you on your rounds."

"I'm far too busy," Marly insisted. "I'll find your friend, Miss Kate, and bring her to you."

Amabelle sighed. "Fine. Thank you."

Marly set off, relieved the young lady wouldn't be following her around all day. She couldn't understand Amabelle's interest anyway.

She found Kate O'Brian and her young gentleman friends in the church yard.

"Miss Amabelle is feeling a little unwell." Marly lowered her voice. "A feminine matter."

Kate bid the men farewell and followed Marly.

"I have a confession, Miss Kate. Miss Amabelle isn't really unwell. She just needed to get away from Mr. Baker. I know it's none of my business, but she seems to be afraid of the man."

Kate's expression was one of concern.

"I can tell your brother is sweet on Miss Amabelle," Marly continued. "I'd like you to know I have no intention of cutting him out. Miss Amabelle is above my touch. I know that."

Kate stifled a laugh. "Actually, Deputy Landers, I don't think Shea *should* marry Amabelle. I love her dearly. I just don't believe they are well suited." She frowned. "As for Mr. Baker, I used to think he was just the sort of man Amabelle needed. He dotes on her. He would indulge her every whim and would never have to count the cost. Then Marshal Strothers came along."

"I heard she used to meet him on the sly."

Kate stopped sharply. "Heard from whom?"

Marly shrugged. "Perhaps *heard* is inaccurate. The information just sort of turned up in the course of the murder investigation. I've heard nothing slanderous against your friend. My guess is that Mr. Baker started showing another side of himself after Marshal Strothers showed up. A jealous side."

Kate nodded. "Shea and the other boys never concerned him. He was in no hurry and he knew they were no threat."

"Was Marshal Strothers a threat?'

"I don't think Amabelle was in love with him, if that's what you mean. He was handsome though, and Amabelle liked to think she had him wrapped around her little finger." She paused. "Whatever Amabelle was thinking, it was obvious that Mr. Baker thought Marshal Strothers was a threat. He started acting as territorial as a skunk."

"Just as well he didn't see your brother as a threat then."

"Shea can take care of himself."

"So could Marshal Strothers" Marly said.

Kate blanched.

"And so can I," Marly added with a grin.

Kate's eyes widened. "What have you got in mind?"

With an inclination of her head, Marly suggested they walk on. "I want to give Mr. Baker a new object of jealousy. You and I know that I'm not the right man for Miss Amabelle, but I've got a feeling that Mr. Baker already sees me as a threat. Maybe it's the badge. You could help me out by pretending you thought I was a serious suitor, and perhaps by letting your brother know that I don't mean to tread on his toes. This is for Mr. Baker's benefit only."

They crossed the road and Marly helped Kate onto the boardwalk, as befitted the gentleman she pretended to be.

"This could be fun," Kate said, patting Marly's arm. "I will help you.

However, I don't think I'll say anything to Shea unless I have to. It might do him some good to see more of Amabelle's flirtatious side." She paused. "If I could make a suggestion, Deputy Landers..."

"Please do."

"If you want to be convincing as a suitor, try sprucing yourself up a bit."

"Yes, Miss Kate."

They rounded the corner and Kate slowed.

"Something else, Miss Kate?"

"Amabelle *is* frightened of Gabe Baker. She's said as much. It's a feeling she gets around him. He doesn't actually cross the line, but..."

"But he makes her feel like he might."

"Yes. She doesn't like being alone with him. The trouble is, she's known him all her life. Her brother trusts him. Her aunt trusts him. It has always been assumed they would marry."

"And I bet no one has asked her if she wants to."

"Exactly."

Once again, Marly was subjected to one of Kate's searching examinations. She could just feel the questions welling up in the young woman's mind.

"Your friend is waiting," Marly said.

When Jase finally extricated himself from the business meeting, he found Marly gazing in the window of Quinton's General Store.

Looking over her shoulder, he said, "Missin' your skirts?"

Marly's only answer was a disgusted expression.

He shrugged. "Since it's quiet, why don't we go for a ride?"

"They'll brand us sinners for sure," she replied, following him to the office. "It's the Sabbath. Good Christians don't ride on Sunday."

"We've got a duty to uphold. To serve and protect—even on a Sunday."

"And that's why we're going riding?"

Jase opened the office door and ushered her inside. "That's what we'll tell anyone who asks. Since when have you been so particular?"

There was no answer. Marly had gone to their quarters.

Minutes later, she returned wearing her chaps and buckling on her gun belt. "You going like that?"

He was wearing his best trousers and a white shirt.

Returning to their room, he changed into something more appropriate, then they set off out of town, riding southeast.

As soon as they were in open country, he challenged her to a race. Later, he had Marly practice her marksmanship from the back of a horse.

Trouble wasn't too thrilled.

"It's all right," she said after she was thrown to the ground.

Holding the reins, she tried to calm the jittery horse. "Okay, I'm not crazy about the noise either. But if you don't calm down, you idiotic animal, I'm going to nick your ear. And it will probably be an accident."

Jase bit back a chuckle. "He'll get used to the noise in time."

After an hour of practice, Trouble was better at keeping still and Marly was better at compensating. Both were tired and fed up, and Jase was tempted to suggest they rest a spell before heading back to town.

He and Marly could sit in the shade. Maybe she'd fall asleep with her head on his shoulder. Maybe she would tuck herself up against him and he'd have to put an arm around her, just to make her comfortable. If she woke up and turned her face up toward his, maybe their lips would meet. Then again, maybe he'd been alone with Marly long enough for one day.

"Time to get back to town, brat. We've got a patrol to walk and supper to make."

Over Sunday breakfast, Egan had invited Jase and Marly out to the Lazy-E ranch the next day to question his men. In doing so, he forced Baker to relent and allow the law on his property.

Monday morning, Jase made use of the offer and headed out, sure that Locke had killed Strothers and almost as sure that the man had been hired to do so. Matt Egan was the best bet, but Jase had to establish a connection between the two men.

Circumstantial evidence had piled up. Locke was a knife fighter. Since coming out west, he had learned to handle a handgun well enough to get by. He wasn't a marksman by any means and he preferred hand-to-hand combat if he had to fight. But he was athletic enough to have done the killing.

Rumor had it, Locke came west after killing a man. Other accounts gave him a more various criminal career, though he was not known for being a bruiser. In fact, he tended to avoid fights, but if he got into one, he'd win—by fair means or foul.

Jase planned to interview the man directly. To be honest, he was inclined to believe the bad over the good in Locke's case, since he'd been part of the group that attacked Marly.

Jase needed to get his own take on the man.

However, before he could talk to Locke, he had to find him.

When Jase told her he was heading out to the ranches without her, Marly wanted to argue, but he made it clear she had to stay in town.

"Don't go getting' it into your head to ride out and meet me," he warned. "And don't go off on your own."

After what had happened last time, she agreed.

When he was gone, she thought of the duties that were expected of her. For the day, she was the law in town. She was to make the rounds, looking reasonably clean, tidy and armed. She also had to take care of her usual chores.

After currying and feeding the horses, sweeping the office and cleaning out the ashes in the stove, she had a head-to-toe sponge bath and dressed for the day. Then she took her first walk about town, stopping at the bank to pass the time with Mick.

Afterward, Marly headed to the hotel.

Nellie poured her a cup of coffee. "On your own today, Deputy Landers?"

Nellie was one of the few townspeople who used Marly's new title without making it sound like a joke.

"Yes, Miss Nellie. Marshal Strachan is interviewing ranch hands about the late Ellery Strothers."

"Seems like a quiet day."

"Seems so. I'll bet you're kept pretty busy though."

This wasn't just an idle comment on Marly's part. Her own varied job experience had given her a keen appreciation for the amount of work needed to keep a hotel and restaurant running. So far as she had seen, Nellie was the only one doing it.

"If you don't mind me asking, who runs the hotel?"

Nellie wiped down the table. "We're currently between managers. There's Cookie in the back. Me out here, and then there's Mrs. Jones. She cleans the rooms and takes the desk overnight."

"Who *owns* the place?"

"That would be Mr. Egan and Mr. Baker. They bought it from the guy they ran out of town a few years back." She stopped her busywork and gave Marly a quizzical look. "Anything else, Deputy?"

"Well, you could tell me what Cookie has made today that's edible."

Nellie laughed. "The sweet rolls and chili are always good."

"I'll have the roll."

A minute later, Nellie returned with a small plate dwarfed by a huge sweet roll. "You got the last one."

Thanking her, Marly said, "It doesn't seem very business-like for Mr. Egan and Mr. Baker to let this place go unmanaged. Not like the gentlemen at all."

Nelly shrugged. "One or the other comes in regularly to do the books. They've been having trouble keeping anyone, especially since

Marshal Strothers arrested Mr. Chalmers."

"Mr. Chalmers?"

"Pete Chalmers. A really nice man. Our last manager. Seems he robbed a bank a few years back and there was a wanted poster with his face on it." Nellie leaned down to refill Marly's cup. "Folks thought it was rather churlish of Marshal Strothers to serve the warrant, seeing as Mr. Chalmers had turned over a new leaf. Mr. Egan tried to intervene, but Marshal Strothers was having none of it."

Nellie left Marly with her coffee, roll and something more to think about.

When she returned to the office, Marly looked up the file on Pete Chalmers. It was a half inch thick.

Prior to living a blameless life in Fortuna, Chalmers had a brief career as an outlaw. For a couple of years, starting immediately after General Lee's surrender, Chalmers had ridden with a gang of former Confederate soldiers. Their one big heist was a bank robbery that went bad. After escaping custody, he disappeared—until Strothers found him at the Fortuna Hotel.

What if Chalmers had escaped custody again? Would he come back and take his revenge against Strothers? Was he the one who hired Locke to kill the marshal?

She clamped her lips into a hardened line.

Maybe Arnie could help her.

Jase returned to the office, greeted by a meat pie, a bowl of sliced cucumber, a warm apple pie and no deputy.

He cursed beneath his breath. "She never listens."

Then he waited.

By the time Marly returned, he'd cleaned up and put coffee on.

"That smells wonderful," she said. "You wouldn't believe how much bad coffee I had today."

"I would. I've been doing this a lot longer than you."

Marly hung up her guns. "My coffee is awful. The hotel's coffee is a bit weak, but okay. The Haven's is strong and bitter, while The Oasis' coffee is good. And yours is even better."

"Why, thank you," he said, bowing.

She set the plates out and carved up the pie. "How was your day?"

He groaned. "Wearin'. I'll say this for Egan and Baker, they inspire loyalty in their men. None is inclined to share anythin' they think might reflect badly on their bosses or their compadres. I'm used to it. There's ways of getting folks to talk. But you know that, don't you?"

"I'm good at listening," she admitted. "I heard something that might be important today."

She told him about Pete Chalmers.

"After Nellie told me about him," she said, "I chatted with Mr. Riley. He told me Chalmers was well liked, a good boss and manager. He didn't think he was the type to jump out and knife a guy. Wasn't sure Chalmers was up to that kind of thing anymore, though he thought he might inspire someone else to do so."

"Really."

"Not intentionally, but out of misplaced loyalty. Mr. Riley said Chalmers was a fellow veteran. A sergeant, actually."

Jase's eyes widened.

She shrugged. "I did wonder if it was my sergeant. Sarge is about the right height, weight, coloring and age, according to the wanted poster."

"But?"

"But Mr. Riley's physical description was a bit more complete and it's not likely. I'm kind of relieved, I suppose."

Jase understood how she didn't want Sarge to be languishing in jail. Though at least she would have known where he was.

"Point is," she said, "Strothers made a long list of enemies. Locke could have been hired by anyone."

Early the next morning, Jase rode out to Baker's ranch, promising Marly an evening ride and telling her to keep up the good work. This time he was blessed with good luck. He found Locke and another man mending fences on the stretch adjoining the Cleary property, a dairy and feed farm.

The air was still cool, but the men had stripped off their shirts. Locke wore a singlet that showed off beefy muscles. His friend wore red combinations, sleeves pushed up, sweat stains darkening the armpits and center back.

Both men paused to see who was riding up.

Ignoring Jase, the man in the combinations directed Locke to hold the post while he hammered it down. They filled the hole and tamped the earth, Locke's friend testing the post for stability.

Jase waited until they were done.

"Birke, we still got company," Locke said.

Birke leaned on the newly sunk post. "What can we do for you, Marshal?"

He was likely not more than a year or two older than Jase. Sun, wind and the trail had carved deep wrinkles around his eyes. With his big brown eyes rimmed with dark pouches, he resembled a hound.

"I'd like to get a sense of where you were the day Strothers was killed," Jase said. "Who you saw, who saw you. I'm buildin' up a picture. I might have a couple more questions after that, but let's start there. Which one of you would like to go first?"

Locke and Birke looked at each other.

With a nod, Birke said, "Don't mind if we keep working, do you? Day's only gonna get hotter."

"I don't mind."

Birke directed Locke to dig a hole a few feet down the line.

"That's the Cleary Farm, ain't it?" Jase began.

"Yep."

"And a field of hay."

"Uh-huh."

"Strikes me it would be Cleary who would be most interested in keepin' the fence repaired, not Baker."

"The Cleary boys will be out here to mend the ties after the milking. Mr. Cleary leases this stretch from Mr. Baker in exchange for feed. Gotta make sure there's something left."

"Sure enough. So where were you that day?"

Birke stared over the marshal's left shoulder. Then he made eye contact. "Can't remember exactly."

"Try."

"It was payday. I probably got drunk. Might have played some cards."

Jase knew from Tierny and a few of the other men he had talked to that Birke didn't drink whisky and could nurse two beers for a whole night. And he only played poker for chicken stakes. On payday, according to several witnesses, Birke was working. He had made himself popular by volunteering to work most paydays and taking his time off midweek, while his acquaintances recovered from hangovers.

In other words, Birke was lying.

"Suppose that means you can't remember what anyone else was doing."

"Suppose."

"How well did you know Marshal Strothers?"

Birke shrugged. "No better than most. He never bothered me and I never bothered him."

Jase absently picked some dirt from under his thumbnail, letting silence sit between them like a glass waiting to be filled.

"Well," he said finally, "you don't know me either, or you'd know better than to indulge in foolish lies. Wanna try again?"

"Maybe I was in town. Maybe I was working. I can't say who I saw or who saw me."

"Can't? Or won't?"

"If I can't, I won't." As if handing a stray dog a bone, Birke added, "I don't know that anyone I work with—or for—is guilty of murder."

"And if you did know, would you tell me?"

Birke raised tired, sad-dog eyes and nodded slowly.

"I'll take that as a promise," Jase replied.

Birke cocked his head toward Locke. "You won't get much more out of him. Baker inspires almost as fierce a loyalty in his men as Egan."

"You been with him long?"

"Mr. Baker? Couple of years now. He's got a reputation for asking few questions when he hires a man. That can give a rancher trouble sometimes, but there are some of us that are very grateful for a second chance and it gives us that much more reason to be loyal to the brand."

"How 'bout Locke? And, yes, I will be asking him the same questions."

"Don't!"

The man's outburst wasn't temper; it was an order.

Birke rubbed the back of his neck. "Ask him about me, by all means. Locke is on his second—maybe third—chance. He grew up on the streets of Boston, ran with a gang. I know that much. He got away, but his reputation followed him."

Again, silence sat between them.

"I like Locke," Birke admitted. "Mr. Baker trusts him. The younger hands look up to him. One more thing I'll tell you so you know why I suggest you use care with your questions. He doesn't start fights, but he won't run away from one either. Trouble with the law, on the other hand, will make him rabbit. He doesn't stick around to explain himself."

"So he never had any trouble with Marshal Strothers."

Birke shook his head. "None at all."

Jase helped the men sink and tamp the next post. When Birke went ahead to the next post and Locke took the opportunity to light a cigar, Jase opened with a friendly query.

"Your accent is familiar, but I can't seem to place it."

"Boston," Locke said.

"Big city. Nice place?"

"Very nice if you got money to enjoy it."

"Is that why you came west, Mr. Locke? Lack of money?"

"Mostly."

Jase shrugged as if the question was idle. "Birke tells me you came to the Bar-B about a year ago."

"That's right."

UNDER A TEXAS STAR

"In that time, have you known Birke to be in trouble with the law?"

"No."

"Was he in town the day Strothers was killed?"

"No. We were working."

"Together?"

"No. Payday. Those who work are pretty stretched out."

"Fair enough. What kind of man is Birke?"

"The good kind."

Jase had that impression too.

"How about Jed McKinley?"

"Okay kid. Green."

Jase sighed. "You gentlemen aren't exactly bendin' over backward to be helpful, are you?"

A hint of a smile broke up Locke's usually passive expression.

"Does McKinley work for Baker often?" Jase asked, exasperated.

"Not often. Not much of a cowboy. Just a wanna-be. Mr. Baker throws him some work now and then. Mr. Egan too. Jed works at The Haven when Duke needs him, often enough to have a bed in the back. Used to get stable work before your boy came along."

"Did he ever get in trouble with Marshal Strothers?"

"Nope. Strothers didn't take Jed seriously."

"Interesting."

Jase looked over Locke's shoulder.

Riders were approaching.

"Looks like the Cleary boys are here. I'll take the opportunity to ask them a few questions and then get out of your way."

CHAPTER 11

Marly was beginning to miss stable mucking. It was hard, dirty work, but time passed quickly and there was extra money to be made in tips. In comparison, being a deputy was a relatively clean, easy job that could drag on forever. And nobody tipped.

She checked out the bank and passed a few minutes talking to Mick Riley. After patrolling the town, she stopped in at the hotel and chatted with Nellie, not wanting coffee bad enough to drink the watery stuff the woman served. Midday, though there was still leftover pie in the office, she made a point of stopping for sandwiches and coffee at The Haven.

She wasn't exactly welcomed.

The one friendly remark she got was from Duke, who told her Hank was out back if she'd care to join him. Unsure whether to thank him for the suggestion or be offended because Duke didn't want her in his saloon, she nodded and moved out to the back porch.

Hank and Mr. Sloane were slouched in their chairs, sipping beer and working their way through a large stack of sandwiches. Hank straightened as soon as he saw Marly and waved her over.

Sloane touched his forelock in a mock salute. "How do, Deputy Landers?" He chuckled. "Liking the new job?"

"Not as interesting as I'd hoped," she admitted. "I suppose that's a good thing though."

Duke came out with a mug of coffee and a very thin sandwich.

Sloane rolled his eyes. "That won't feed a growing boy, Duke. Bring us out another stack. We'll share with Landers. Bring us some of your pickled eggs too." He turned to Marly. "Hank and I are on our own for a few days. My sister Kathy usually packs us lunch, but she's taken the girls to visit their Grandpa."

"Miss Sloane is a good cook and kind enough to include me at meal time," Hank added.

"And why not?" Sloane slapped Hank on the arm and rocked him in his chair. "Hank is practically part of the family. Heck, I'd adopt him, except Dolly would be heartbroken. She wants to marry Hank when she grows up."

"How old is Dolly?" Marly asked.

"Eleven last month. I told her she can't marry until she's at least fifteen."

"By the time she's that old, she'll have so many beaus, she won't want me," Hank said.

"Dolly and Sally are the cutest girls you could hope to meet," Sloane said, beaming with pride. "Clever too. Both know how to read and write, though they haven't had a regular teacher in over a year."

"Miss Mary ran off with a cowboy," Hank interjected.

Sloane snorted. "Who can blame her? She spends all day teaching a bunch of brats, then goes home to take care of another bunch. Big family, the Livingstones."

"As in Nelly Livingstone?" Marly asked.

Sloane nodded. "Mary's sister. Mary was the oldest and expected to be second mother to the younger ones. Nelly escaped that by living and working at the hotel. I think she had hopes of marrying Pete Chalmers someday, until Marshal Strothers got in the way."

"Mr. Chalmers was a lot older than Nelly, wasn't he?"

"No harm in that. He was a good man, able to take care of her, and they had an affection for each other. That's all that's important. You keep that in mind, Hank, when Dolly's old enough to lay her hooks in you."

After lunch, Marly poked her head in at The Oasis.

"Looking for work, Master Landers?" Fred asked.

"I wish. I'm not sure I can accept it, since Jase is out of town."

"I don't think Master Jason would mind, so long as it didn't interfere with your work. There's no question of you working out front, of course."

"Of course."

That meant kitchen work, which was harder than helping Arnie out, but more rewarding in perks like produce and baked goods.

"I should complete my patrol first." She shifted her gun belt on her hip. "Better drop by the office too."

"You can put your weapons in my office, Deputy Landers. That way, if you are called to duty, they will be handy."

Searching Fred's expression for any hint of mockery and finding none, she thanked him. "I'll be back as soon as possible."

This turned out to be later than she expected. Concluding her rounds with a visit to the bank, she bumped into Egan.

"Good afternoon, Deputy Landers."

"Good afternoon, sir."

"I thought you might be out our way with Marshal Strachan."

"No, sir. I'm on duty here in town."

"Can you stop for a cup of coffee?"

Marly hesitated. She was expected at The Oasis, but the opportunity to interview one of the prime suspects was irresistible. Trusting that Fred would understand, she followed Egan to the hotel.

Nelly gave her a wink as she brought them coffee. She recommended the sweet rolls, but Marly declined.

"None for me, Nelly," Egan said, grinning. "Got to watch the waistline. Lately, I've been spending too much time at a desk and not enough out in the fresh air."

If he were fishing for a compliment, he used the right bait.

"You're looking fit as ever," Nelly said. "A fine figure of a man."

Marly stifled a smile.

She was beginning to see that Nelly's comments were not so much directed at charming a prospective mate as eliciting a generous tip. In that, she was as successful as Egan in setting her bait. He dropped a fifty-cent piece for two cups of five-cent coffee and Nelly pocketed the coin, then wandered off.

"Tell me about yourself, Deputy Landers," Egan said, his tone commanding without being rude.

"What do you want to know, sir?"

"Frankly, I want to know if you are worthy of my sister's attentions."

"Probably not," Marly said, hiding a grin.

Now she was in trouble. She didn't want to lead the Egans on, but her plan to take Strothers' place as an object of jealous or protective wrath meant she couldn't be honest about her intentions.

"I'm an orphan. I have no money or prospects other than the work I do for Marshal Strachan. On the other hand, Miss Amabelle seems to like me as much as most of her suitors and better than some."

"And do you like Amabelle?"

"Well, of course. She's beautiful, smart and rich. What's not to like?"

When he gave her a stern look, then grinned, she realized she couldn't pull off roguishness. She probably came across as precocious, maybe even cute.

She sighed and tried a different tack.

"I like your sister too well to see her imposed upon by the likes of Mr. Baker."

Egan set his coffee cup down hard, spilling some of the weak brown liquid. "Be careful, Mr. Landers. Gabe Baker is a good friend of mine."

"No doubt with good reason. But he is no friend of Miss Amabelle's—also with good reason. As far as I am able, I intend to be a friend to your sister, whether or not you approve. *And* in the face of Mr. Baker's disapproval." She pushed aside her coffee and stood. "If you'll excuse me, Mr. Egan, I better get back to work. Thank you for the coffee."

She had almost made it to the door before Egan reacted.

"Deputy Landers," he called, "I'm bringing my sister into town tomorrow for a church council meeting. I thought I'd bring Amabelle with me and take her out to lunch at The Oasis. Will you join us?"

Marly stopped in the doorway. "Yes, sir. Thank you, sir."

As soon as she was outside—and out of sight—she leaned against the hotel wall and let out a slow breath.

The next morning, after Jase left to continue his interviews, Marly spent a portion of her hard-earned cash on a fine white shirt with blue pinstripes. Before putting it on, she took Fred up on his offer and had a proper bath.

"Master Landers has a sweetheart," Fred's apprentice, Henry, ribbed while filling the tub.

Fortunately, Fred appeared and waved Henry off. With professional discretion, he left Marly a bar of sandalwood soap and a bottle of hair tonic.

A half hour later, Marly greeted Matt Egan and Amabelle outside The Oasis, she was cleaner, neater and sweeter smelling than she'd ever been and both were duly impressed.

As they stepped inside, Arnie left the bar to greet them. He showed them to a window table, forestalling both Egan and Marly by holding Amabelle's chair.

"Would you like something to drink?" Arnie asked.

Egan smiled at Marly. "Deputy, care for a beer?"

She refused with a shake of her head.

"Coffee for you, Deputy Landers?" Arnie asked. "I know you don't like anything else when you're on duty."

"Thanks."

Fred arrived to take their orders. He served their meals personally, splitting his attention between their table and Jezebel's.

At first, Marly thought this was all for Egan's benefit. He was, after all, the richest man in Fortuna. It was the wink that Henry gave her as he cleared away the dishes that clued her in. They were doing this for *her*.

They were trying to help her impress the Egans.

If they only knew, she thought, feeling guilty.

After the meal, Egan stood up abruptly. "I have business to attend to. Perhaps, Deputy Landers, you could entertain my sister until our aunt is ready to go home."

"Miss Amabelle might like to see the rose garden," Arnie suggested as he cleared the table.

Even Fred, who was hovering nearby, agreed.

Marly was outnumbered.

"Miss Amabelle." She offered the young lady her arm and escorted her out into the garden.

Oddly, Señora de Vegas also decided to go to the rose garden. She didn't join Marly and Amabelle. Instead, she admired the blooms, always staying in sight.

Marly almost laughed out loud at the thought that she and Amabelle were being chaperoned.

"Deputy Landers," Amabelle said in a hesitant voice. "Did you say anything to my brother about Gabe?"

"I might have let it drop that Baker's attentions were not welcome. Why? What did your brother say?"

"He told me that I shouldn't let Gabe bother me. Our parents thought Gabe and I would make a match, but that was when I was little more than a baby. Even Papa acknowledged that Gabe isn't the right man for me. If Gabe was under another impression, Papa would have dropped a hint to the contrary. Since Papa's not around, Matt said he'll talk to Gabe."

"That's good."

"Yes," she agreed. "Even though you were sticking your nose into my business without talking to me first, thank you."

Marly bit her tongue.

It was mid-afternoon and Marly had to make her rounds.

"I'll join you," Amabelle said.

Marly would have preferred to have the Señora present as chaperone, but as it turned out, it wasn't necessary. Kate O'Brian was in town buying ribbon for her dress. Since she had nowhere in particular to go until her mother was finished her business, she fell in with them.

After her patrol was completed without incident, Marly took the ladies to The Oasis for cold drinks. Kate wasn't allowed to go in, so Arnie served them lemonade on the veranda. This allowed Amabelle to flirt with any admirer who passed through town, while she showed Marly a measure of indifference.

That indifference disappeared when Gabe Baker showed up.

Suddenly, Amabelle only had eyes for Marly, who was steadfast, attentive and protective as a guard dog.

"Amabelle," Baker chided, "this is not a proper place for you to be."

"My brother brought me here."

"It's not like we went inside," Kate added in defense.

Marly moved between them. "The ladies are under my protection. If that isn't proper, I'm sure their families will tell me."

"Your protection?" Baker lifted a derisive brow. "Fine words, bantam."

"I think you should move along, Mr. Baker. Go in and buy yourself a drink. I think there's something in the town ordinances about loitering outside places of business."

"You are going too far, whelp."

"No, I'm almost certain there is such an ordinance. Shall we go across the road and check? I'm sure the ladies will excuse us."

Baker towered above Marly, but she held her ground, though he didn't hide his disdain or his shock. If anyone had stood up to Baker in the past, it was someone like Egan or Winters. It wasn't a scrap of a boy, which was all she was to Baker.

"It's late," he said, scowling. "Your aunt will be looking for you, Amabelle."

"In that case, ladies," Marly said, "I'll escort you to the general store. I believe your aunt is there, Miss Amabelle, probably with Mrs. O'Brian."

"That will not be necessary," Baker stated.

"I think it is." Marly shifted her gun belt to a more comfortable position before offering the young ladies an arm each. "If I've kept Miss June waiting, I ought to apologize, don't you think?"

Not waiting for a reply, she gave Baker a nod and led the ladies off. Baker followed, only to be further humiliated by Miss June, whose smile faded when she noticed the hovering man.

"Thank you, Deputy Landers," Miss June said, smiling, "for taking such good care of the girls." She turned to Baker. "Now stop being such a fuss-budget.

"You know," Marly told Jase that evening after giving him an account of her day, "I don't think it was Egan that put Locke up to killing Strothers."

"You just wanna get your future brother-in-law off the hook." He grinned, unable to resist goading her. "But I agree. For one thing, murderers don't tend to want the law to marry into their families."

She shook her head. "The reason I don't think Egan is involved is because he isn't the type."

"Uh-huh."

"I'm not saying he wouldn't kill. I just got the impression that it's a family trait to handle things personally. If he wanted Strothers dead, he'd do it himself. He'd provoke a fight or something straightforward like that. I know Strothers was a fast draw, but Egan is a dead shot."

"So I've heard. Take it he told you that."

"Of course not. I asked Mick Riley. Seems Baker is a marksman too. Or was. He's more the gentleman rancher now. Not the type to get his hands dirty."

Jase frowned. "Still, it seems you're spendin' a lot of time with the girl. If I didn't know better, I'd say you were playin' fast and loose."

"Well, you do know better," she snapped. "And I'm not. I've got my reasons for hanging around Miss Amabelle."

"I can just guess."

"I hope you can 'cause part of the reason is for her protection. I might be wrong about Baker being the one who ordered Strothers' death, but I know he used his position to put pressure on Amabelle and I don't think that's right."

"You seem to be speakin' from experience," he said. "Did Meese put pressure on you?"

"Not so crudely, but yes. He was sweet to me, but he made it clear to my aunt and others that I should marry him—that I *had* to marry him. Funny thing was, I probably would have if he hadn't tried to force the issue."

"Didn't you tell your aunt you weren't interested in him?"

"Aunt Adele impressed upon me that I would have to marry someone someday. Might as well be Charlie. But I didn't like the game he was playing."

Jase gripped his cup a little tighter, but otherwise kept his feelings on this matter to himself.

"There was no one else?" he asked.

Marly smiled enigmatically. "Well, I was awful sweet on Sheriff Langtree, but I was just a kid to him. No, there was no one else. And according to Aunt Adele, there never would be in Cherryville once Charlie had ruined me, which she was sure he had, thanks to him."

Jase made a conscious effort to unclench his hands. "He hadn't?"

"No!"

He breathed again. "Good. I don't like walkin' into a situation knowin' I'm gonna have to kill a man."

After three days of riding over the better part of the Egan and Baker ranches, Jase decided to stay in town on Thursday. Marly suspected he wanted to keep an eye on her.

But she wasn't going to let that happen.

After a morning ride and target practice, she said, "Can I take the day off to work at The Oasis? I want to work off the lemonades I had with Amabelle and Kate the other day."

Jase shrugged. "Take the day off, but don't work too hard."

With a nod of thanks, Marly stepped outside and made her way to The Oasis. Once in a while, she checked over her shoulder to see if Jase was following her. He wasn't in sight.

Inside the saloon, Arnie had glasses to clean and wood to polish in preparation for the busy weekend ahead. Marly rolled up her sleeves and set to the first task, while the bartender buffed up his bar.

"You know," he said, "Ella's starting to get jealous. She thinks you're the sweetest fella and she's as green as anyone that you're seeing Miss Amabelle. It's heartbreaking."

Marly rolled her eyes.

"It's true."

"Well, I just hope you don't tease her the way you tease me. Anyway, she's a little young to be thinking of beaus. She can't be more than ten."

"Women generally like older men."

"I've been hearing that a lot lately. Tell her to hold out for young Liam O'Brian. If his sister is half right about the lad, he'll be perfect for her."

Arnie stopped his work and stared at Marly. "Liam? I'll bet the boy's not more than a couple of years younger than you, Mr. Landers."

"That's *Deputy* Landers," she said. "And it's more than a couple. I'm older than I look. Throws people off."

Jezebel swept into the room. "Fred!"

Fred appeared and took up a position beside her. "Yes, Miss Jezebel."

"I hardly think it appropriate that the marshal's deputy be doing bar work in this or any other establishment. It ain't fitting. If you must trade our hard-earned goods for his labors, have the discretion to put him to work in the kitchen or the storeroom."

"Yes, Miss Jezebel."

Jezebel nodded curtly at Marly and strode off toward the stairs. Pausing at the bottom, she turned, saying, "And, Fred, make sure Louis packs up some of those pastries for the boy before you let him go." She smiled at Marly. "He's a good worker, even if he does have a lot of sass."

When Jezebel was out of sight, Arnie took the cloth from Marly's hand and steered her out from behind the bar.

"You heard the boss" he said. "You got any work for him, Fred?"

"I'm sure I can find something appropriate for Deputy Landers to occupy his time with so he can earn a roast chicken to take back for dinner. Louis' pastries deserve a better introduction than beans and bacon."

Marly couldn't agree more.

CHAPTER 12

Jase was busy with Winters after dinner and since Fred had no work for Marly, she wandered over to the livery. Jase had said she couldn't work there anymore, but she figured that didn't include taking care of their horses. She also decided it didn't preclude her helping Mr. Sloan and Hank shoe a difficult mustang.

"If you make a fool of me," she whispered to the horse, "I will recommend you to the hotel cook and you will either become good chili or a really bad pot roast."

The mustang snorted, eyes drawn to a spot over Marly's shoulder.

"You're being watched," Hank said, grinning.

Amabelle stood nearby, her arms resting on a fence rail.

"How do you know it's not you I'm watching, Hank?"

Hank's grin faded and Marly almost laughed at the look of panic on the man's face.

With the critical eye of someone who knows horses, Amabelle watched them work. She didn't make any more comments, but Hank was clearly discomfited by her attention. As soon as the job was done, Marly took pity on him and led the young lady away.

"What are you up to, Miss Amabelle?"

"I came into town to shop with Aunt June, but she's been invited to supper at the Minister's house. If I go, I will be preached at. On the other hand, if you escort me home, my aunt will let me leave."

Marly rolled her eyes.

"Please," Amabelle said. "The minister is *very* boring."

Marly shrugged. "Let me check in with the marshal."

Jase wasn't in the office, so she left a note for him. She couldn't see that he would have an issue with her going. They would be taking the Egan's gig with Trouble tied up behind. Miss June would be taken home by the minister. She made a show of reluctance, but seemed happy to have a night out without her niece.

She let them go with the one condition.

"Deputy Landers has to get you home in time for supper."

Marly agreed.

As it turned out, they drove into the Lazy-E home yard just as the dinner bell was ringing. The hands were lined up at the cook house. Egan was sitting on the front porch.

"Where's Aunt June?" he asked Amabelle.

When she told him, he turned to Marly. "Thank you for bringing my sister home safely, Deputy. I surely appreciate it."

"My pleasure," Marly said.

"You must stay for dinner," Egan said. "Nothing fancy. The cook made biscuits, corn chowder and pecan pie. I'll fry some steaks to go with that."

"Matt's a better cook than me," Amabelle said. "Aunt June keeps trying to improve my skills. So far we've discovered I am best at making pickles."

Marly laughed.

This was the most comfortable she had ever been with the Egans. Amabelle wasn't trying to impress and after a few remarks about how much time Marly was spending with his sister, Egan let the subject drop.

Over supper, he tried to find out more about Marly's past and her connection with Jase, but that was to be expected. Marly gave him the official line that she was an orphan and Marshal Strachan was her self-appointed guardian.

"How did you get together?" Amabelle asked. "Is he a friend of your parents?"

"We met on the trail to El Paso. He decided I needed a protector. I was a lot greener when he first met me. Just a farm boy from Kansas."

"Why El Paso?"

"I might have a relation there," Marly replied, remembering what Jase told Jezebel.

"Mighty kind of the Ranger to escort you to El Paso," Egan said, sounding skeptical. "Didn't think they had time for that kind of thing."

"He has business there. It's not like he's going out of his way. In fact, I'm waiting on his convenience. That's why I'm still here."

"Will you stay with this relative when you find him or her?" Amabelle asked.

Marly hesitated. She couldn't think of an answer that would fit fact or fiction. She preferred not thinking about the road ahead. Not that road anyway. Her only answer was a shrug.

Egan gave Marly's shoulder a squeeze. "Don't fret it, boy. You've always got a place here. If that relation doesn't come through, or Strachan can't keep you on, my job offer's still open."

"That's mighty kind of you, sir."

"If Marshal Strachan doesn't stay," Amabelle added, "maybe my brother will recommend you to the new marshal."

A wave of depression swept over Marly. She didn't want to think of Jase leaving town. Or leaving her.

It was eight-thirty by the time she left the ranch. Egan would have had her stay the night.

"You can sleep in the guest room," he offered.

She declined politely, saddled Trouble and left with the knowledge that Jase would have a few things to say when she came in past nine o'clock.

Jase had run the gamut of emotions. He was more disappointed than surprised when Marly was late for supper. When she wasn't back after he returned from his evening patrol, he became concerned. Though the Egan ranch was extensive, it wasn't that far from town. Even allowing for Marly's naturally social disposition, she should have been back by now.

He looked at his untouched supper. Irritation swelled. She should have turned down a dinner invitation, if not because it was dangerous and unwise, but because she hadn't asked him first.

The sun descended and with it his mood.

He should have gone out to fetch her.

Intelligent enough when she chose to be, the girl had more guts than brains most times. What was she thinking of, staying out this late? What was he thinking of, just sitting there? She could be hurt or dead or in the clutches of damned Egan.

As he strode out the office, fear and anger clutched his heart with an iron grip. None of that showed. His expression was impassive, his gait purposeful, but not rushed. A Texas Ranger didn't run from danger or into it. He certainly didn't do anything to make others suspect he was in a panic. Nor did he succumb to his anger or relief when he met Marly leaving the livery.

"You're late."

"Sorry." She yawned. "Got invited to supper, then lost track of time."

He put a hand to her back and propelled her along the sidewalk. He didn't say another word until they were in the office and the door was locked for the night.

Then his calm reserve burst like a balloon.

"What were you thinkin', Marly Landers? I've been worried all evenin', not knowin' where you were."

"Didn't you get my note?"

"Your note said you were escortin' Miss Amabelle home. It said nothin' about bein' out for supper, socializin' with a suspect in a murder case and ridin' home alone in the dark."

Sleepily apologetic, but hardly contrite, she said, "I would have sent you a message if I could. You knew where I was. Besides, it's not like I knew I'd get invited for supper."

"And ridin' home after dark?"

"I rode with my rifle across my lap."

Marly checked the pot for coffee.

"I drank it all," he said with no apology. "But I saved you a plate of chicken and French pastries left over from earlier. I didn't know how long you'd be gone."

"The Egans did invite me to stay the night, but I thought that would worry you more."

"You thought right." He slapped his hand on the desk. "Egan ain't stupid. Spend enough time with him and he'll discover your secret. What then?"

Marly lifted a shoulder. "Egan accepts me as a boy. Wants me to marry his daughter, remember? You know, I bet I could go to that dance tomorrow."

"Forget it!"

"All I have to do is refuse to dance."

"And what are you gonna do, Marly Landers, when some matron comes up to you and presents you her daughter, hmm? Or are you gonna go off with the boys and try some corn whiskey and chew tobacco?"

Jase took a base pleasure in the way Marly turned a little green and dropped her fork.

"Okay," she said. "I'll stay behind."

To make up for not going to the social, Jase took Marly to The Oasis for lunch on Friday. Truth be told, he selfishly wanted her company and perhaps to impress her a little. They ate ham steaks glazed with honey and sweet potato fritters flavored with fresh herbs. It was a nice break from sandwiches, stews and pie.

Afterward they went to the general store to restock. The staples like beans, flour, sugar and ammunition were running low. While he ordered the necessities, Marly wandered off to look through the clothing.

Minutes later, she returned with a red and white striped shirt.

"You're not tellin' me you need another shirt, are you?" he asked.

"It's not for me. I have a new shirt already, remember?" She held it to Jase's shoulders. "I think it should fit."

He shook his head, but added the shirt to the other purchases.

Back at the office, Marly announced that she had arranged for them to have baths at The Oasis that evening.

"Fred will be giving you a haircut," she told him. "Mr. Pervis finally has his glasses, but Fred will do the job for free."

Jase tugged at his hair. "I'll be all right. I'll get a shave tomorrow. Before the dance."

She tilted her head to one side. "Want me to braid your hair?"

"Fine. I'll get it trimmed. Who you tryin' to impress anyway?"

"I'm not trying to impress anyone. I'm not going, remember?"

Jase had a sudden thought, one he didn't want to broach with Marly, but had to.

"You know," he said, "Jez will expect us to use one room, 'less I take her up on one of her offers and use hers."

Marly rolled her eyes.

"I don't particularly want to," he said. "It's just that…things are different now. I know you're a girl. We can't pretend it's fine and proper. It ain't."

"I know."

"But we have to keep up the act. Anything else would be a disaster."

She gave him a calm nod.

Why wasn't Marly flustered?

"No problem," she said. "If you don't mind sharing the bath water, I don't."

Marly took the late afternoon patrol.

At the bank, Troy Riley was closing up. He asked her about her ride with Miss Amabelle, but Marly gave a noncommittal reply and moved on.

The general store was closed early, probably so Mrs. Quinton could make preparations for tomorrow's social event. Marly checked to make sure the doors were securely locked, then did the same at Penrod's Butcher Shop, the rear door of the bank and the stage office.

Next, she checked in on Mick Riley, who had been feeling his rheumatism earlier in the day. He had a shack backing onto the alley behind the bank. He let her know that a nip or two had taken the edge off, but he'd get an early night if it was quiet.

Marly decided to pass through The Haven, check on Hank at the livery, then loop around to make sure all was quiet at The Oasis and hotel before returning to the office. Jase's rule was for her to stay out of The Haven in the evening, unless she was with him, but the sun had not yet gone down so Marly strode through the doors, unprepared for trouble.

She should have remembered it was Friday.

Ranch hands worked a six-day week, excepting pay-week. Their days started at sunrise and ended at sunset. However, on Friday, it was common for the boys to take off a little early—if they could get away with it. Hands from the Bar-B, Lazy-E and Circle-X were close enough to town to come in for the evening and some still had money burning a hole in their pockets. The up-coming social was greatly anticipated. It was clear that spirits were high. Had she been able to get away with it, Marly would have backed out the door and given the place the go-by.

Tom Tyson, arm still in a sling, homed in on Marly like a dog finding a soup bone. Once he made eye contact, she knew there was no backing away.

She stepped forward. Giving Tyson a polite nod, she walked up to the bar and greeted Duke, who automatically set her up with a cup of coffee.

"Give the boy a whisky on me," Tyson called. "Make a man of him."

"Kind of you," Marly drawled, "but no thanks. I'm still on duty."

"Turning down a drink could be seen as an insult."

"No insult intended. I'll drink with you, so long as I'm drinking coffee."

"But I *am* insulted," Tyson insisted.

He had been sitting at a table with Roy Parker and a couple of other hands from the Bar-B. Parker had moved away. Now Tyson stood, tucking his jacket back to give him clear access to his revolver. Marly noticed that Parker was sidling around behind her.

"Leave the kid alone," a man at another table said.

"Shut up, Birke. This is my business, not yours."

Marly had not met Hugh Birke, but Jase had told her about their conversation. In his estimation, Birke was trustworthy, closed-mouthed. She spared him a glance and decided that was good enough. She had to keep her attention on Tyson and Parker.

"It would be helpful, Mr. Birke," she said in a steady voice, "if you persuaded your compadres to rejoin your table. Marshal Strachan isn't going to appreciate his deputy being goaded into a fight."

"What you complaining about? You got the advantage, boy." Tom flapped his broken arm. "My left ain't my best hand."

"You're right. I got the advantage."

Marly raised the rifle and cocked it. She backed up a couple of steps, putting Roy immediately behind her. She heard his hand slap his grip. She stepped aside and jabbed him hard in the stomach with the rifle's stock.

As Tyson drew his gun, the rifle was back up, but she didn't have to shoot. Tom found himself facing down not only Marly's Winchester but also Duke's scattergun and Birke's Smith and Wesson Frontier.

"You're dead, Birke," Tyson snapped.

Birke sighed. He really did look like a hound dog, Marly thought, a bit giddy from the mixture of fear and relief washing through her.

Behind her, Parker started to unfold.

She tapped his chest with the barrel of her rifle. "Unbuckle that gun belt and don't try anything stupid. Mr. Birke?"

"I still got Tom covered."

"Thank you, I appreciate that." She directed Parker around so she could watch both men. "I could use your help getting these gents to the office."

Birke looked sadly from Tyson to Landers. He nodded at the latter and gave the former a resigned shrug. Tyson scowled in response.

Marly tipped her hat to Duke and indicated that Tyson, Parker and Birke should go ahead. Behind her, a troop of patrons from The Haven followed them out onto the boardwalk, watching Deputy Landers' first arrest.

Jase looked up as the office filled up. "Now what?"

Marly cleared her throat, which for some reason was closing up on her. "I'm arresting Tom Tyson and Roy Parker for attempted murder."

"What?"

"They drew on the deputy," Birke explained. "That is, Tyson did. Parker tried. Never got the chance. Landers dropped him with a blow to the gut. Still, two on one." He shook his head. "Not right."

Marly avoided Jase's gaze. He might be angry, amused or frightened for her. It didn't matter. She could barely deal with her own emotions right now.

Instead, she covered Tyson and Parker while Birke relieved the men of hidden weapons. She noticed Birke didn't have to be reminded not to cross in front of her line of sight as he stripped them of potential weapons with a proficiency that spoke of prior experience.

"Thank you, Mr. Birke," she said, once Tyson and Parker were locked up. Her voice squeaked a little, but she managed to lower it. "Couldn't have done it without you."

"Sure you could. I was just insurance. And Duke doesn't like his place shot up." He gave her a smile that barely lifted his mouth, but reached right up to his eyes. "You done good today, Landers." He turned to Jase and gave him a nod. "He did you credit."

Jase nodded. He hadn't moved since they came in.

Birke left.

As soon as he was gone, Marly collapsed into the nearest chair. She dared a glance at Jase. He had a white-knuckle grip on the edge of the desk.

Jase followed her gaze and relaxed his grip. "Coffee?"

Without waiting for an answer, he poured the coffee, giving them each an extra helping of sugar. Then he set the cups down before sitting.

"Report."

She did, trying to be matter-of-fact and giving credit where credit was due. When she was done, he stared at her.

After a long pause, she filled the gap. "Do you think I could ask Troy to watch the office so we can have our baths?"

As soon as Marly left, Jase sank his head into his hands and gave a long shuddering sigh. Once he had collected himself, he went back to see the prisoners.

They were talking quietly and didn't notice him at first. He managed to pick up a few words about the boss not being happy and nothing turning out the way it was supposed to.

"You gents seem to have a particular distaste for lawmen," he said loud enough to make the two men jump. "First you draw on me, then you gang up on my deputy. It makes me wonder how you felt about Strothers."

Tyson spat at the bars.

"Thought as much," Jase said dryly. "You boys look like the best candidates for Strothers' murderer. You knew you didn't stand a chance in a fair fight, so you set on him at night and killed him with a knife. Maybe Egan paid you to do it. Or Baker. Maybe you just hate the law that much. Doesn't matter. You're the ones that'll hang."

"Now hold on," Parker warned.

"Never mind him," Tyson snapped, stepping in front of Parker. "We didn't do it and he can't prove we did."

Jase pushed away from the wall, reached into the cell and grabbed Tyson by his shirt front. With a jerk, Tyson slammed against the bars.

Jase smiled grimly, inches away from his face. "Fact one, everybody knows you tried to kill me and my deputy. I'll bet you tried a similar tactic with Strothers. A few questions to Duke should answer that."

Parker blanched. Jase had made a hit.

"Fact two," he said, "you two are part of a small group of people who can't account for themselves the night of the murder. Fact three, maybe you didn't know this, but as a Texas Ranger, I got judicial powers.

I may be the only judge and jury you ever see."

He wiped the spit off the bar with Tyson's shirt front, then let him go. The man fell back, losing his balance and hitting the floor.

"Now," Jase said, his tone deceptively pleasant, "if you boys didn't kill Strothers, I suggest you come up with the person who did."

He slammed the door to the jail cell and let the bar fall noisily. It had done him good to vent his anger, but inside he was still shaken.

He was glad when Marly returned with Troy Riley.

Time to retreat to The Oasis.

CHAPTER 13

"You can have the tub first," Jase told her. "I'll be in Jezebel's room getting a shave and haircut."

A hot surge of jealousy raced through Marly. She tried to convince him to have his shave and haircut in their room at the same time, but he said it wouldn't be proper.

Like anything else they'd done was proper.

She fumed.

Things hadn't gone exactly as she planned. Jase was supposed to come back and catch her in the tub. He would only have seen her head and shoulders, but maybe he would have stolen a peek as she dried off.

She soaked in the tub, waiting for him for a very long time. Too long. Jase's shave and haircut took forever and she wondered what else he was doing in Jezebel's room.

Was Jezebel with him?

Henry came to warm the water. It turned cold again, so she climbed out and dressed in her combinations.

When Jase finally returned, she was sitting cross-legged on the bed, furiously trying to comb out her hair. She tugged impatiently at a knot, her eyes watering from pain.

He grabbed the comb. "Before you yank every strand from your head, let me try."

Methodically, he took her hair by sections and combed them free of tangles. On one bad knot, he disentangled the strands with his fingers. He continued to comb her hair, long after the last tangle was out.

Maybe the evening could be salvaged, she thought.

Jase stopped and passed the comb back to her.

As she took it, her cool hand touched his warm one.

Then he was over at the dresser, removing his gun belt and emptying his pockets, as though they'd never touched.

Jase caught sight of Marly in the mirror. It was the first time he had seen her when it was clear she was a girl. As baggy as they were, the combinations couldn't hide her feminine curves.

With a sigh, he pointed a finger at her and motioned her to turn her back. Then he stripped and stepped into the tub.

"Bath hot enough?" she asked, back still turned.

"Just great." He watched her braid her hair, then he leaned back. "You're missin' a strand."

"Shit," Marly swore, pulling apart her work.

Jase chuckled.

She swiveled around and glared at him. "What's so funny?"

"You are. You really aren't much of a lady. Or did you used to be prim back in Cherryville?"

She grinned. "My aunt kept threatening to wash my mouth out with soap because my language slipped every time I got excited."

"Did she?"

"Once. I threw up all over her nice white pinafore."

Jase laughed.

"How's this?" She showed off her braid.

Jase tilted his head and squinted. "A little messy at the end."

"Damn."

He sat up. "Come over here. Maybe I can fix it."

Marly pulled up a stool and sat with her back to him.

"No good," he said. "I can't get at it right. Give me a second. Just gotta give myself a scrub. I'll do your braid when I get out."

He started from the top and worked down, paying special attention to the back of his neck and behind the ears. Then he put down the wash cloth and reached for the brush.

"Damn." No brush. "How did you manage?"

"If you're willing to contort yourself, the cloth will work. But I've got a better idea."

She stood and pushed the stool aside. "Give me that."

Before he could protest, she pushed her sleeves up, soaped the cloth and started rubbing his back.

"This ain't proper," he said halfheartedly.

"Aunt Adele used to say I had no sense of propriety. She raised me well enough, but I was always getting into trouble. Least, that's what she called it. She blamed it on Sarge. I was with him for the better part of a year before she found out about me and summoned me back."

She worked the cloth over his shoulders and down his back as she talked, pushing her sleeves up higher as she descended below the water line.

"Aunt Adele blamed Sarge for my parents' death and my shortage of lady-like manners. She thanked him for bringing me home, but she wouldn't let him come back."

Jase glanced over his shoulder. Marly's scrubbing had slowed to a halt. Her eyes were far away. With a blink, she rinsed his back and started on his shoulders, this time cleaning his upper arms and chest.

"You know," she said softly, "he was going to take me west and we were going to have our own little ranch. I told you that, right?"

"Yep."

Jase was distracted. Marly had reached his buttocks.

Where was she going to stop?

"Yet, the only name I ever knew him by was Sarge," she said. "Isn't that odd?"

She rinsed off his upper torso and soaped the cloth again.

Marly's ministrations were creating a surge of heat in his lower extremities and it was getting a bit uncomfortable.

He took the cloth from her hand. "Get dressed, brat. I'll take it from here."

Saturday was remarkably quiet due to the Egan party. The festivities started mid-afternoon when families began arriving with foodstuffs to contribute toward dinner. There were games for the children and horse races for the men. The dance was to start after supper and continue past sundown, though some families would leave in time to drive home in the light.

That left little time to raise trouble in town.

Or so Marly thought.

She had agreed to keep an eye on things.

Just about everyone in the community was invited to the Egans and all were intent on looking their best. Mr. Pervis was busy, more than making up for lost business after he had lost his spectacles. The general store was open in the morning to allow for last minute purchases of ribbons, string ties, pomade and perfume. The hotel, however, closed after breakfast and The Oasis and Haven were not expecting much business. Bill Sloane had given Hank the evening off and was closing the livery early to join his sister and her daughters at the dance. And by three o'clock, Fortuna was as quiet as Boot Hill and just about as lively.

Marly held the door open as Jase put the finishing touch on the knot in his silk bandana.

"I should ask Riley to stay with you, or at least do the patrol tonight," he said.

"Can't," she stated. "Troy is going to the social. Probably already gone. Mick is watching the bank. Just in case, he says."

Jase frowned.

She waved him out the door. "It's okay. Fred said he'd drop by later. I can handle it."

Jase mounted Grandee while she waited, arms folded, wearing her deputy badge and looking every bit the part she played.

He tipped his hat and rode off.

When he was out of sight, Marly hugged herself tightly, not nearly as sanguine as she acted. She hated being left behind and wanted nothing more than to dance all night long with Jase.

She went inside the office.

It was close to an hour's ride to the Egan house and when Jase rode up, the party was in full swing. He handed Grandee over to one of Matt Egan's men, securing his riding coat to the saddle.

He strolled over to the house, exchanging greetings with everyone he met. Some, he had never seen before. They were probably from ranches further out of town.

But they knew him.

Since Jase was wearing his Texas Ranger star and the badge of office as Fortuna's marshal, most greeted him by name.

The yard was decorated for the event with Chinese lanterns. A dance floor had been built on the front lawn, with a space for the musicians on the porch. The back porch was set up with tables for food and drink. Trestle tables and benches for eating supper lined the lawn. Beyond that, children were running a sack race.

The community had put on their festive best for the occasion. This ranged from worn calicos to new satin gowns and bright bandanas over work shirts to suits and string ties. The men stood in groups, talking. The women bustled back and forth, laying out food for the coming meal.

Matt Egan met Jase with a hearty handshake, but his cheerfulness diminished when he was told Marly Landers would not be at the social.

"Someone had to mind the office," Jase said.

"Why didn't you say so before? I could've let you have one of my men."

"Well, sir, no offense, but I'm investigatin' your men—amongst others—for the murder of Ellery Strothers. Kind as the offer is, it wouldn't exactly look right. Would it?"

Egan acknowledged the point with a half-shrug. "Amabelle will be disappointed. To be honest, I'm disappointed. I've grown rather fond of young Landers. There's just something about that lad."

"Kinda gets under your skin," Jase said.

An awkward silence fell between them and he immediately regretted his candor.

"Well," Egan said with a forced smile, "enjoy the evening, Marshal. Don't work too hard."

When the guests started to seat themselves, Mr. and Mrs. Winters invited Jase to join them. Mrs. Temple-Quinton was close at hand and the three each took turns trying to persuade him that he should take over the town marshal job—permanently.

Jase gave them a polite nod and thanked them, then excused himself as soon he could.

More than ever, he wanted to get out of Fortuna.

He was accosted by Amabelle Egan next.

"I need your help, Marshal," she said, slipping her hand into the crook of his arm.

"What's wrong?"

"Wrong? Not wrong exactly. I need your help persuading my brother to get the band to start playing. I know for a fact that they ate earlier."

Jase stared down at the girl. She put on her most charming smile and batted her eyelashes. Her mannerisms left him cold.

"Please, Marshal. I've got a brand-new muslin dress with silk ribbons just waiting to be twirled."

With a silent curse, he allowed her to lead him to her brother.

"People are still eating," Egan complained.

"Some of them will be eating all evening," Amabelle said.

In response to a prompting pinch on the arm, Jase added his entreaty. "I did promise Landers that I'd ask Miss Amabelle to dance. On his behalf."

"Good," she said. "After that, you can dance with me on your own behalf."

"Yes, ma'am."

Amabelle blushed.

Jase and Egan exchanged a look over the girl's head. In a word, it said, "Youth."

"I'll go ask the band to set up," Egan said. "You will wait until I lead Mrs. Winters or one of the other ladies to the floor before you start dancing. Understand?"

Amabelle nodded meekly. The moment her brother's back was turned, she dragged Jase over to her friends to show off her latest conquest.

Though the sun was setting, there was no lack of light. Lanterns glowed throughout the yard, along with handmade candles set on each table.

While musicians tuned their instruments, a crowd gathered around the boards that had been assembled into a large square-dance floor. Young girls in short skirts and ribbon sashes stood at the edge, dreaming of long skirts and courtiers. Their would-be beaus roamed in packs, trying to appear older and tougher than they were, totally oblivious to the girls' occasional glances. Many of their older brothers tried to be similarly nonchalant.

Jase observed this with some amusement and a touch of wistfulness. At their age he had been fighting.

Finally, the music started.

Moments later, Egan asked Mrs. Temple-Quinton to dance, and Jase and Amabelle joined them—to the obvious chagrin of her many young beaus. Jase led her around the floor in an energetic polka. Other dancers joined them in short order until the floor filled and the steady thump of feet on wood accompanied the music.

Shea O'Brian claimed Amabelle's hand next and Jase beseeched Rose Quinton's hand for the two-step, seeing her hovering at the side with the girls in short skirts. Though flustered at first, Miss Rose danced well and seemed to enjoy herself. He felt no compunction, therefore, presenting her to Shea O'Brian as a partner for the first waltz, though dinner conversation had made it obvious that Mrs. Temple-Quinton hoped that Rose would catch Matt Egan's eye.

Miss Amabelle was now dancing with the oldest Johnstone boy. Standing this dance out, Jase was able to observe Gabe Baker as he watched Amabelle. He was appreciative, but not obviously jealous. Young Johnstone was a handsome lad. After some moments, Baker lost interest in the dance, with its changing partners, and stepped back to converse with the men.

When Jase took Amabelle's hand for the next dance, he could feel Baker's eyes on them. When he glanced over during the dance, the man's attention was on Amabelle, not him.

It was true what Marly had surmised, Jase thought. Baker didn't feel threatened by any of the ranchers' sons, though they were a natural match for Miss Amabelle. The man didn't seem threatened by Jase either, which might have damaged the ego of a lesser man.

Baker *had* been jealous of Strothers. And by report, he was now jealous of Marly.

How jealous?

There were certain aspects of her new career that Marly found dead boring. Having to stay in the office and guard prisoners was at the top of that list. Jase had warned her to check on them periodically and to give them the silent treatment.

That was easy. Every time they saw her, they either swore a blue streak or stared at her in sullen silence. They did try to cajole Duke when he brought them each a bowl of soup.

Duke shook his head. "Not this time, boys."

Later, Fred came over with a basket. "Why don't you do your rounds, Deputy Landers, while I lay out your supper?"

"Thank you, Fred."

"I can only stay a half hour this time. Miss Jezebel will be needing me. I shall return later, however."

"That sounds fine, Fred."

"If you would permit, Master Landers, I will stay and converse at that time."

Marly was grateful for the company. She had already finished three short stories about the daring career of Wild Bill Hickok that afternoon and the sameness of the adventures were beginning to tell. There were no new gun catalogues to peruse and she'd already read two of Shakespeare's plays.

Fred might not be lively, but he was intelligent. And he might be persuaded to talk about Jase's past.

It was a relief to get out of the office. Once outside, Marly breathed in the warm night air, grateful for the light breeze that cooled her skin. The Egans had been blessed with perfect weather for their party.

She wondered how it was going.

Was Jase dancing with one of the young ladies?

She scowled, not wanting to think about it.

Marly patrolled the streets, but all was pleasant and quiet. Mick Riley chatted with her, but was more intent on having a postprandial nap. The livery was quiet. At The Oasis, the only greeting she got was the admonition to get back to the office quick because Miz Jez wanted her dinner. She returned to the Marshal's Office and passed the message on to Fred.

"Miss Jezebel can wait a few minutes," he said.

Marly's eyes widened, but she said nothing as Fred served up a plate of cold roast beef, pickles and thickly cut bread. A jar of milk sat on the desk. He poured half the contents into one of the mugs.

Satisfied, he stepped back. "Enjoy your meal."

"You best be going," she warned. "I'll be all right."

"Of course you will, Master Landers. I will return in a couple of hours. Don't try to make coffee without me. I have it on the good authority of Marshal Strachan that your coffee is worse than his shaving."

Jase leaned against a pecan tree and watched Miss Amabelle juggle her admirers. What attracted the cowboys and ranchers' sons was obvious. Amabelle Egan was the prettiest and wealthiest girl in the district. It was to her credit that most girls liked her. A couple of them were clearly devoted to her.

If Amabelle lapped up this hero worship, she also made sure her devotees were not left out of the conversation or dancing. With those young ladies who were more on a par with her in popularity and position, Amabelle engaged in friendly rivalry. At the moment, this included a light-hearted competition for the interest of one Texas Ranger-turned-Marshal.

Kate O'Brian was the liveliest of the lot and the most intent.

Jase innocently flirted with her, admiring her earthy beauty and pragmatic nature. He could tell she was clever enough not to take him too seriously.

"You know, Miss Kate, you'd make a good match for Landers. You're both redheads." He gave Amabelle an apologetic look.

Amabelle frowned. "I don't think he's your type, Kate."

"Oh, I don't know," Kate said with a smile. "I think he's very sweet."

"Who is this fellow?" asked one Kate's admirers.

"Haven't you been listening, Will?" she chided. "Marly Landers is the marshal's assistant."

"Just a kid," Bob Johnstone added.

"My *deputy*," Jase said sharply. In a lighter tone, he added, "And Miss Amabelle's latest beau."

Amabelle waved a hand in the air. "A slight exaggeration, I think."

"No offence intended, Marshal Strachan," Johnstone said, "but your deputy *is* rather young."

"Old enough to face Tom Tyson," someone piped up.

Johnstone glared at the speaker, whom Jase didn't recognize.

Probably one of the Slashed-Bars' crew, one of Johnstone Sr.'s employees.

"He may look young," Amabelle snapped, "but Marly Landers is old enough to be a gentleman to a lady. And he doesn't back down to anyone. Not even my brother or Gabe Baker."

This remark caused a few feet to shuffle. A blush suffused Bob Johnstone's face. There probably wasn't a man there that didn't keep a respectful distance when either Egan or Baker showed up.

The band started playing a slow waltz and Jase asked for Amabelle's hand. The pace allowed them to converse as they danced.

"My deputy tells me that Mr. Baker is bothering you some."

Amabelle's eyes narrowed. "He did, did he?"

Jase gave her an encouraging smile. "Marly is just concerned—doesn't like to see a lady put under any undue pressure. In that respect," he said, carefully watching her face for her reaction, "I think he sees you as a sister."

She nodded, lost in thought.

"When you say Landers stood up to your brother and Mr. Baker," he continued, "how do you mean exactly?"

She gave a tiny shrug. "I don't know what he said to Matt. I just know that afterward my brother showed Mr. Landers more respect. I was there when Gabe tried to intimidate him. He stood right up to him. For a moment, I was afraid there was going to be a gun fight. It was very exciting."

Jase didn't trust a reply to that.

The dance ended and he returned Amabelle to her friends, leaving to circulate in more mature company. He appeared at her side later to exclude Baker from taking her to the late supper. He collected up the O'Brians, commanding Shea to find and hold seats for the group.

Soon, Amabelle was safely surrounded and Baker, defeated, left the party. After a brief and unsuccessful attempt to find his host to say good night, Jase left also.

As promised, Fred came over to the office so Marly could do the evening patrol. All was quiet and the chore was quickly accomplished. When she returned, Fred set out a sweet plate, then taught her how to make drip coffee.

"You might have better luck with this than the modern percolator from the office," he said.

After checking on her prisoners and making sure the back door was firmly locked, she put her rifle on the rack. Fred insisted that she take the more comfortable chair behind the marshal's desk. When he had poured the coffee and trimmed the wick of the lantern, he sat opposite her and nibbled on a biscuit.

"Nothing is going on in town tonight," she said. "The only ones left are the hardened gamblers and the quiet drinkers. I might end up bringing in one or two of the drunks if the night gets cold."

"And the gamblers?"

"Any trouble they cause will be amongst themselves and over before I can do anything."

"You learn quickly. You and Marshal Strachan make a good team. But for two things, I would have your appointment as the town's lawmen become permanent."

"Two things?"

"One, neither of you would accept the appointment," Fred said.

She shook her head, bemused. It was difficult to shake the feeling that in his terribly stiff English way he was laughing at her.

"I suspect I know what you are thinking," he said. "If I have learned nothing else, I've learned that age does not always bring wisdom. Nor has my experience supported the idea that there is a weaker sex. I hear you've learned to play chess. Would you like a game?"

She suspected the game had already started.

"The second reason," Fred continued, setting up the board, "is that it would be a waste of talent. I assure you, murders are not normal in Fortuna. I doubt Master Jason would quit the Texas Rangers in any case, especially now he has such an able partner."

"Well..."

"There may come a time when it will no longer be, shall we say, convenient for you to be traipsing all over Texas. Perhaps then you will consider making Fortuna your home. By that time, Miss Amabelle should be married and you might safely return."

She stared at him, wondering what he was getting at.

The next half hour was taken up with opening moves and counter-moves. Marly was painstaking with her moves, not yet comfortable with the game and its strategies. Fred gave her pointers, usually after she had made a mistake. She lost the first game quickly.

During the second game, she asked him about his adventures.

"You seemed to have been many places."

"You might say I am well traveled. Is there something in particular about me that you are curious about, Master Landers?"

That might have quelled someone else. Not Marly.

"I am a little curious why you left England. I'm not asking. It's your business if you want to tell me."

"Rest assured, I will give *your* privacy equal respect."

Marly studied the board, pondering her next move.

"Let us just say that, like you, I can't go back," he said.

She took her queen out of danger, threatening one of Fred's knights in the process. "If you can't go back, maybe it's time to go forward."

He squinted at her.

"It seems to me" she said, "that you haven't entirely left your past behind. Yet, there's a future waiting for you."

A small smile lifted the corners of his mouth. "Perhaps the same could be said of you, Master Landers."

"Maybe. I've got some things to work out with my past. Old debts, I guess you'd say. How I'm going to settle them, I don't know. And we still have a murderer to catch."

"It has been my experience," Fred said, taking her bishop with his endangered knight, "that the solutions to life's problems are generally achieved by winning one battle at a time."

Marly took his knight with one of her pawns.

One battle at a time.

Despite a gallant effort on Marly's part, Fred was the better player and eventually took the game.

Age may not bring wisdom, she thought, but experience certainly had its advantages.

She checked on the prisoners again, leaving them fresh water.

When she returned, Fred decided he could no longer shirk his duties at The Oasis and took his leave. Alone again, she tossed aside the penny dreadful and retrieved Jase's copy of Shakespeare's comedies. She finished Fred's coffee and *Much Ado About Nothing* about the same time.

She was debating whether to put on a fresh pot when the office door opened.

"Very good, Marly," Egan said, eying the barrel of the Remington, "but I come as a friend, not a foe."

It surprised and frightened Marly how fast her hand had found the gun. It took her a moment to recover before she smoothly holstered her weapon.

She hid her nerves by affecting Jake's lazy drawl. "Evening, Mr. Egan. Didn't expect to see you here. Dance over so soon?"

Egan removed his hat and placed it on the desk, leaning toward her as he did. "I wanted to see you in private."

A shiver of fear swept through Marly. She fought the feeling, along with the urge to pull her gun again.

"We missed you, Marly. *I* missed you."

He was nervous, she realized. There was something she couldn't quite define. His control was only surface deep. She wasn't out of danger.

Still, the knowledge calmed her.

"That's very kind, sir. I hope you're not going to tell me Miss Amabelle pined away with no one to flirt with."

Egan's smile was automatic, devoid of real humor. "No. My sister had plenty of fellows to keep her amused, including our new marshal." He waited for a reaction.

Marly shrugged. "Good for her."

"In any case, I think it best if Amabelle and you don't get any closer."

"Oh?" She folded her arms and sat on the desk. "You going to bar Miss Amabelle from seeing me like you did with Marshal Strothers? I wouldn't count on it working, Mr. Egan."

"What I count on is your discretion, not my sister's. *Miss* Marly."

CHAPTER 14

Marly only betrayed her shock for a moment. As Egan's polite smile broadened into one of triumph, she knew she'd lost the high ground.

"I think you've made a mistake, Mr. Egan."

He moved around the desk, closing the gap between them and stopping no more than a foot away. He breathed in deeply as if sniffing out her femininity.

"Have I?" His voice purred like a cat. "I don't think so, though you play the part of a young man very well." He reached out and smoothed a stray curl that had escaped her braid.

Marly sidestepped away from him and went to the stove. She stirred up the flames and added a piece of wood, keeping the poker in hand.

"I don't know why you're masquerading," he said. "I'm not sure I want to know. The point is, a man doesn't come to feel toward a boy what I feel for you."

She turned. "And what do you feel, Mr. Egan?"

"I wasn't sure before tonight. The idea you might not be a boy seemed far-fetched. Then Strachan announced that you weren't coming to the social and I smelled a rat. It was more than that." There was an odd tension in his voice. "I recognized my feelings for you. I had to be right. I had to know if there were breasts beneath those boy's clothes."

She dropped the poker, the sound startling them both.

Marly recovered first and gave Egan a long, hard stare. He had stepped over the line. What she saw in his eyes flustered her and made her blush. No one had ever looked at her like that. It was both flattering and frightening.

She turned away, covering her confusion with the mundane task of cleaning the pot of old grounds and refilling it.

"Would you like some coffee, Mr. Egan?" She kept her voice devoid of emotion.

"Thank you. What I'd really like is for you to stop calling me Mr. Egan. My name is Matthew. My friends call me Matt."

She shook her head.

After that, Egan kept a respectable distance.

Once the coffee was brewing, Marly took down her carbine and made a show of checking and topping up the magazine. Ignoring Egan, she sat at the desk, her leg propped on a drawer in a characteristically unladylike pose.

Egan pulled a chair around. "Does Strachan know?"

"He doesn't act as though he does. I think he accepts that if I dress like a boy and people think I'm a boy, then that's how I want to be treated." She eyed him. "If he knows, then he's too honorable to take advantage."

He snickered. "That's telling me off." He leaned back, adopting a more casual tone. "Will you tell me why the disguise then?"

"It's safer. I've travelled as far on my own as with Ranger Strachan. When I first set out, I figured I'd attract less attention travelling alone as a boy. It's easier too. I may be a girl, Mr. Egan, but I'm not much of a lady."

"You may not be a lady, but you're one hell of a woman."

Marly locked the breach in place less gently than usual.

"Despite the disguise," he added, leaning toward her. "I don't know why you are taking part in this charade, but you must have a very good reason. I only wish you would trust me with it."

"Thank you, Mr. Egan," she said as steadily as she could manage. "I do appreciate your faith. I would appreciate it more if you keep this to yourself. While I am in Fortuna, I must continue to be Mr. Marly Landers."

"And after? How long do you intend to keep playing this role? As interesting as this is, I look forward to seeing you in your petticoats. You make a very attractive boy. I do believe you'll be a beauty as a girl. I'm anxious to be proved right and you must be anxious to drop the pretense. You say it's easier, but it's hardly natural."

She scowled. "I am Deputy Landers until Ellery Strothers' murderer is brought to justice. Then the Ranger and I have business in El Paso."

"And then?"

The door opened and Jase walked in, saddle over his shoulder.

Marly breathed a sigh of relief. She stood, still holding the rifle, and checked on the coffee. At no time did she entirely turn her back on Egan. She trusted Jase observed this and would treat the situation with caution.

"What brings you here, Mr. Egan?" he asked.

Egan stood. "My horse."

Marly detected the unspoken challenge in his voice and body language. It was one thing to let the Texas Ranger play marshal. It was another for him to question Fortuna's leading citizen on a personal matter. The tension was so great she almost cocked the rifle when Egan pulled aside his jacket.

Jase didn't react, however.

Egan removed a small parcel from an inside pocket. "I wanted to make some compensation to Deputy Landers for having to miss the party."

He stepped toward her, holding out the package. Since her hands were full, he had to settle for placing it on the desk. Then he paused for a response.

"Thanks," she said.

That was clearly less than he wanted from her.

Egan turned his attention to Jase. "Marshal, could you grant me a small favor? Could you stretch your rules so you and Marly could join me and mine for dinner Sunday night?"

"I think I can find someone to mind the office for the evenin'."

"Good." Egan gave Marly a brief smile. "Then I'll be off. See you in church."

She watched as Jase locked the door and shuttered the windows for the night. He took her carbine from her slackened hold and put it on the rack under his.

Finally, she moved. She poured the coffee, her hand shaking as she passed Jase his cup. He steadied her hand in his, then took the cup and put it aside.

"Figures you wouldn't wait for me to get back before makin' coffee."

Coffee was the least of their worries.

"Sit down before you fall down," he ordered.

He pushed the package toward her. Then he sat down in the seat Egan had vacated.

"What happened?"

Marly took a deep breath. "Egan knows I'm not a boy."

"Are you all right?"

"Yeah."

It was hard to tell how Jase was taking the news. He wouldn't meet her eyes. Instead, he risked a sip of the coffee she'd brewed. His expression said he was prepared for the worst.

"This ain't terrible."

"Fred gave me some pointers."

Jase took another sip.

"Well," he said after a moment, "Egan's not stupid and he's a hell of a lot more observant than most. Does he know I know?"

"He asked. I was evasive. I told him you treated me like the boy I pretended to be."

He let out a sharp laugh and she winced. He reached out for her hand and gave it a quick squeeze, as if to say he was laughing at himself, not her.

That isn't much better, she thought. She hated it when he started chastising his own behavior. It was as if he didn't acknowledge it had been her choice.

"What about the party?" she asked. "Anything happen?"

"Baker left early. I thought he might try and pay you a visit, so I followed him." He shook his head. "He went straight home."

"You think he arranged Strothers' murder too, don't you?"

"Yep."

"There's a quiet evil about the man. He frightens Amabelle."

"Didn't frighten you though, did he?"

She searched his face. "I didn't back down when he was trying to intimidate us. Kate O'Brian tried to stand up to him too, though poor Amabelle trembles every time he comes near her."

"I noticed."

"I didn't do anything reckless or inappropriate. Honest."

"I trust you." He gestured toward the cells. "Did Egan say anything about those two?"

"No. Should he have? They aren't his men."

"He's probably the only one in a fifty-mile radius who hasn't heard by now," he replied. "You're starting to get yourself a reputation. If he knew you had locked those two up, he would've had a few words with Baker, but they hardly spoke tonight. And I'm sure Egan would have said something to you about putting yourself in danger like that."

"It's my job."

Jase shook his head. "It's *my* job."

She didn't point out that he had made it her job too. She didn't want to give him any ideas about taking away her badge.

She leaned back in the chair. "You think Tyson and Parker were under orders?"

"Could be. Hard to say. Tyson's mean enough to do it for spite, but that doesn't mean he wasn't encouraged. Parker's just his shadow. I'm hoping he's scared enough to tie Locke to whoever hired him."

"Baker," she asserted.

"Egan ain't clear yet," he said, his tone suggesting he wasn't too pleased at how easily she dismissed Matt Egan as a suspect.

"Egan doesn't hire the kind of men you'd think of as cold-blooded killers," he added. "That don't mean he wouldn't use Baker's hands."

Marly hid a grin.

There were times when Jase laid on his Texas drawl with a trowel, just for effect. Other times, like now, it came out because he was dead tired.

"I'll buy that Egan might have wanted Strothers out of the way," she said. "He is just as ruthless as Baker in his way. Still, Egan doesn't strike me as the type who'd get someone else to do his dirty work. He'd want to best Strothers personally. Baker, on the other hand, wouldn't rely on besting the man. He backed down to me, after all."

Jase was suddenly alert. "He was gonna draw on you? I thought Amabelle was exaggerating."

"If she said he was about to draw his gun, yes she was exaggerating. If she just said Baker looked like he wanted to kill me, she was correct. He was trying to intimidate me, that's all."

Jase rubbed his eyes. "Now he's jealous of you."

That had been her intention.

"I don't like it," he said. "But I did my best to encourage the rumor at the party while letting Amabelle know your interest was brotherly." His mouth turned down in a scowl. "Unless something else comes along, I guess it's the only way to tie Baker to the murder. I could arrest Locke tomorrow on what we got. There's no guarantee he'd let himself be taken. Less that he'd implicate Baker. 'Sides, without a motive, the charge might not stick anyway."

"I figured as much."

Jase stared at the package. "What did Egan bring you?"

Marly opened the paper and revealed a squished piece of chocolate cake. She stuck her finger in the icing and tasted it. Her nose wrinkled slightly. She pushed it away. "Too sweet."

"Ironic, ain't it?" Jase said, looking into his coffee cup. "Baker is jealous of you because of Amabelle, but it's her brother showing real interest in you."

She squeezed her eyes shut.

Why did he have to bring that up again?

When she opened her eyes, he was gazing at her, his expression every bit as intense and almost as frightening as Egan's had been. For the first time since they met, she realized how tightly Jase kept himself reined in. She wished he wouldn't. She wished he didn't have to. She wished she had the nerve to hang it all and throw herself into his arms.

For Jase, she would be happy to be a woman.

What she had told Egan was true. Since Strothers' murder was unsolved and they were in Fortuna, she had to remain Mr. Marly Landers. After that, she had to settle with Charlie Meese. Then, if Jase was still interested...

She tucked away the thought.

"You look beat," she said. "Why don't you get ready for bed? I'll wash up the cups and take a last look in on our prisoners. I imagine they're passed out from boredom by now."

"I'll check on the prisoners," he countered. "Leave the cups for the morning and you get ready for bed. I'm gonna sit a spell and have another drop of your not so bad coffee. I'll be in soon."

She didn't argue.

In their private quarters, Marly washed and undressed. She looked at Jase's bed and wonder what would happen if he found her in it. Folding down the covers, she sat on the edge. It was a narrow bed. Still, there might be room enough. He would have to hold her close, but that didn't bother her.

No. More likely he would sleep on the cot.

She stood, smoothed his sheets and fluffed his pillow before retiring to her own bed.

What had been quietly circulating at the Egan social was common knowledge by Sunday morning. Everybody knew how Tom Tyson, backed up by Roy Parker, had made a play for Deputy Landers. Not only had Landers taken care of Parker without firing a shot, to hear Birke tell it, the young man didn't need any help with Tyson either, though both Duke and Birke had been ready to stand by the young deputy.

Jase and Marly heard the rumors via Hank, who stopped at the office at first light.

Gabe Baker, who was hardly a fan of Landers to start with, came very close to losing his temper. No one thought he put Tyson and Parker up to the job, but there were a few well-meaning folks who suggested he should be more careful about the kind of men he hired. Baker's temper wasn't improved when Egan pulled him aside Sunday morning, telling Baker he held him partly responsible for Tyson and Parker's actions.

Hank had overheard Egan tell Baker that his friend's attitude toward the Ranger and his Deputy laid the groundwork for the attack. Then Egan made it clear that whatever their parents' scheme, it was up to Amabelle whom she married.

"Don't get your hopes up, Marly," Hank said. "When Baker asked if Egan intended his sister to marry a penniless deputy, Egan said he didn't think you were the right person for Amabelle, though he did add that he thought she was safe with you. So that's something."

Whatever his feelings, Baker recovered sufficiently to be politic when—followed by Egan and family—he stopped by the office to bail his men out. He made a show of telling the troublemakers that the money would come out of their wages, which they could pick up Monday morning. They were no longer in his employ.

Egan rewarded his friend with a nod and a pat on the back, making it clear to everyone where the idea had originated.

Jase would rather have left Tyson and Parker in their cell. He had questioned them again that morning and though nothing concrete came of it, he was convinced that Tyson knew Locke had killed Strothers. Unfortunately, Tyson wasn't intimidated.

Parker was afraid of the noose, but more afraid of his friend. Jase made sure the man believed that his fear of hanging was founded, *unless* a better suspect was produced. He hoped Parker would come around when Tyson was no longer standing next to him.

The only advantage to them being released was that Jase and Marly were free to go to church. And they could have breakfast at The Oasis afterwards. That meant warning her that she was likely to be the center of attention.

If there was any doubt that everyone knew what had happened, it was laid to rest during the sermon.

"'Let your light shine before men, that they might see your good works,'" the pastor quoted. "'Think not I come to destroy the law or the prophets, I am come not to destroy, but to fulfill.' So sayeth the Lord, amen."

He went on to abjure his fellows to make peace with their neighbors and live righteously. He warned the wicked to mend their ways before judgment fell upon them. It was a rousing service and thinly veiled plea for the violence to stop.

Previously indifferent and suspicious folk made an effort to greet Jase and Marly after church, with hopes they would stay in town. In part, they were following Egan's lead, but many were sincere in their desire to make their temporary lawmen permanent additions to the town.

With Jase's help, Marly escaped the crowd outside the church, only to be waylaid by Matt Egan. She scowled as he caught up with her outside the office.

"Why didn't you mention the episode with Baker's men when I was at the office the night before?" he demanded.

"I wasn't in much danger, Mr. Egan."

"Any danger, as far as I'm concerned, is too much. What did they do?"

Marly's attention was split between Egan and the scattered groups approaching from down the street. She hoped that Jase would be amongst them so that Egan's interrogation would end.

"They didn't do anything I couldn't handle."

"You could have been killed," he growled.

She shrugged and would have moved off, but he clamped her arm in a vice grip.

"Give up this charade, Marly." When she shook her head, he swore under his breath. "Tyson and Parker had better leave town and keep going. If I see them again, I'll..."

"You'll do nothing," she said more calmly than she felt, "unless they do something to you. That's the law."

Egan let out an angry huff.

"You know," she drawled, "if you're tryin' to break my arm, you ain't bein' very efficient."

With a guilty start, Egan released her.

Without seeming to rush, Marly beat a hasty retreat. She went straight to Miss Amabelle, who was having her own troubles with Gabe Baker. Mindful of the comments Amabelle had made about Deputy Landers standing up to Baker, Shea O'Brian remained doggedly, though ineffectually, by her side. In all fairness to young O'Brian, Baker was behaving in a respectable, if not cloying, way. Not deserting the lady was about all a gentleman like Shea could do.

Marly, however, was no gentleman.

"Excuse me, Miss Amabelle, you promised to let me buy you breakfast. Shall we go?"

"Oh, Deputy Landers."

"You didn't forget, did you?"

"No...of course not."

Beaming a smile at Baker, Marly said, "I'd hoped not. I hope you missed me a little last night. I was looking forward to dancing with you and never got the chance."

"We'll have other dances." Amabelle said this with such warmth that Baker's face flushed with anger. "You'll have to tell me about your adventure. I'd love to hear it."

Baker was not a gunman by nature, but his hand reflexively found the grip of his revolver. Marly noted this and gave him the blandest look she could muster.

Amabelle responded with a gasp of fright.

This caught Shea's attention. He moved beside Landers. With slow deliberation, he pulled the skirt of his frock coat out of the way of his holster, making it clear whose side he would be on if there was to be any shooting.

Baker backed off and left.

"Thanks, O'Brian," Marly said, wiping her brow with the back of a hand. "You think you and your sister could join us at breakfast? I might have enough to treat us all."

Shea O'Brian gave her an inquisitive look. She could practically see the gears move. Now that Baker was gone, she wasn't acting like a serious suitor.

Amabelle's hand had dropped from her arm.

"My treat," Shea replied finally. "We'll meet you at the hotel."

Jase had observed the scene with Baker, giving half an ear to the minister as they strolled from the church. It didn't surprise him to see Marly escorting Miss Amabelle into the hotel after a brief conference with Aunt June. He only hoped his deputy enjoyed the company because he was sure she would be disappointed with the food.

Jase joined Egan and Baker at The Oasis, without their invitation. Neither greeted him with more than the barest of welcomes and both found reason to leave early. Baker was the first to make his excuses. Egan's came so quickly afterward, Jase suspected the man was worried about what his friend might be planning.

Jezebel joined Jase afterward.

Sharing a fresh pot of coffee with him, she said, "'Gabe's moody at the best of times, though Matt's pretty even tempered. You're not gonna pin this murder business on him, are you, sugar? Or maybe he's having second thoughts 'bout hitching his only sister to your young deputy?"

Jase sighed with exaggerated fatigue.

"Don't sigh at me. The boy's far too young for the girl. Though I will admit, he's got a lot more going for him than I first thought. Jest wish he wouldn't keep sticking his nose in everybody's business. Bad enough the gals think he's a pet and he's got Louis eating out of his hand. The boy's even won over Fred."

"Makes friends easily."

"Well, that's fine, but now Fred spends as much time on your brat as he does on me."

Jase snickered.

"You can laugh," she said, scowling. "I am not accustomed to having to fend for myself."

"Poor Jez."

"It gets worse. Fred's bin kind of dreamy 'bout Consuela ever since she came here. Fact is, I invited her to stay 'cause I was afraid he might leave with her when she went. So far, he thinks he's beneath her, which is fine with me. However, since that boy's bin 'round, Fred and Consuela's bin spending more and more time together. Your deputy has tea with 'em, then leaves 'em alone together." Her eyes widened. "Today, Consuela called Fred 'Señor' and he didn't correct her."

"Shocking."

"It ain't funny, Jase! That boy is subverting him. Good help is hard enough to get these days without losing Fred."

"Offer him a partnership."

Jezebel shook her head. "Wouldn't work. He don't really approve of my business and I know Consuela wouldn't go for it. Fact is, she don't belong here, though she stays and helps out where her conscience will allow her. I think she's got a touch of martyr in her. Both of 'em do, I suspect."

This wasn't Jase's area of expertise. Still, this puzzle was a welcome change from the grimmer challenges of the murder. Besides, he owed Jez something for not confiding in her about Marly. When she eventually found out, she was going to be mighty annoyed. Best he get on her good side now.

"Buy them the hotel," he said.

"What?"

Jezebel's shriek rose above the din and a small party of ranchers, the only ones left in the dining room, turned around in unison. Henry, who was serving them, was also startled by Jezebel's sudden outburst. He recovered quickly and turned the ranchers' attentions to their bill.

"I can't imagine the present owners get much income from it," Jase said. "The Señora has some money, doesn't she? She can contribute. You can be their silent—*invisible*—partner. It'll be an added source of income for you and you'll keep Fred handy. He's been training Henry, hasn't he? He can be your personal servant. And you can let Arnie take up some of the slack."

"Buy 'em a hotel?"

Jase leaned back and sipped his coffee. "It's either that or throw yourself on the mercy of my deputy."

"I'll think about it. I'll consider both your suggestions. I'm not so proud as I won't go to the kid, if it'll help. Maybe the little runt'll talk Fred into being happy here."

Back at the office, Jase shared Jezebel's tale of woe and his suggestions with his deputy.

"I feel sorry for her plight," Marly said.

That surprised him a little.

"But I'm glad that Fred might finally leave his *'station'* behind him," she said.

"I think he'd be quite satisfied running the hotel."

She nodded. "Your solution sounds perfect. I can't see Fred totally deserting Miz Jezebel. He's very loyal. This would make them all happy."

Jase watched her clean the carbine. She was entirely unguarded around him now. She didn't bother with the mannerism of a young man or worry about how she carried herself. To the casual observer, there wasn't a lot of difference. She certainly wasn't ladylike, but there was something more feminine about her at times like this. Maybe it was the way she smiled at the thought of Fred finding love.

"What'll make you happy?" he asked.

"Well," she looked up at him, "this is a good start. I think Fred and the Señora deserve to be happy and Arnie deserves more recognition for his work and Henry will be delighted and Louis will be glad to get 'the Englander' out of his kitchen..."

He held up a hand to stop her.

"I mean, brat, what'll make *you* happy?"

"Oh." She blushed slightly. "Being your brat's enough."

His face grew warm in response. *My* brat.

"I'd also like to see this business with Baker finished up," she said. "I really want us to be able to prove he was involved, before he forces me into a gunfight."

"What?"

She gave him the rundown on her morning's activities, including the confrontation with Baker.

"Amabelle told me Baker took advantage of being alone with her to make his intentions very clear. It was no great surprise to me. Even Miss Kate had a pretty good idea what was going on 'cause Amabelle had confided in her before. Shea O'Brian, on the other hand, was very shocked. He was also sorry Baker hadn't drawn on me."

"Shea O'Brian wants you dead?"

Marly bit her lip. "Well, he said he would've avenged me."

It was either laugh or hit something.

Jase opted for laughter.

Dressed in their best clothes, Jase and Marly left Troy Riley minding the office and headed out for the Egan place at three in the afternoon. Jase wanted to ride out via the Egan's pond and check the promontory Marly found. Satisfied no one had been using the look-out lately, they rode along the bridal trail.

Approaching the rear of the house, Jase noticed the yard had been cleaned up, but the lanterns still hung in strings, blowing in the wind.

One of the ranch hands arrived to take their horses.

Marly started toward the back door.

"You're expected around the front," the man said.

Jase and Marly exchanged glances. In unison, they began beating the dust off their coats. Catching themselves, they grinned at each other.

"All right then," Jase said, giving the ranch hand a hat tip.

Walking around the side of the house, they climbed the steps to the porch. Jase paused to straighten his bolo before knocking on the front door.

Matt Egan was suited up in black, with his blond curls slicked back. He greeted them at the door, took their riding coats and directed them toward the parlor.

"Hello, ladies," Jase said when he entered the room.

Amabelle was a confection of pink ruffles and ribbons. Her hair was dressed with flowers and she smelled like Fred's rose garden. Aunt June was almost as ruffled in deep purple and redolent of lavender.

He couldn't imagine Marly fitting in with them.

Nor did he want to.

"Please, take a seat," Egan said behind them.

"I've saved you a place, Marshal," Aunt June said, patting the seat beside her on the settle.

While he struggled to keep from falling into the plush cushions, Marly picked an ornate, delicate-looking chair. She fidgeted, trying one position and then another, unable to get comfortable. Jase was more practiced at sitting still, no matter what the circumstance. But that didn't make him any more comfortable.

"Sherry?" Egan offered.

"That's a fine treat," Aunt June said. "Amabelle, you may have one small glass."

"I'd prefer whiskey," Jase said, especially if it's that fine Scotch in the cut glass decanter."

"I'll have a beer," Marly said.

Jase flicked her a tight smile. "No you won't."

"Surely, Marshal Strachan," Aunt June said, "if the young man is old enough to be a sworn deputy, he's old enough to have a little beer."

"That's all right, ma'am," Marly assured. "I don't need anything right now."

"I'm not sure Marly is old enough to be deputy," Egan said.

"Now that's funny, Matt," Aunt June said. "Just a few days ago, you were telling Gabe Baker that you thought Mr. Landers was a fine deputy."

"Well, yes, but..."

Jase's mouth twitched and Marly's face reddened. He suspected that it wasn't embarrassment but the effort not to laugh that raised her color.

Egan turned to Jase. "Surely even you, Marshal, must admit that Marly shouldn't be facing the likes of Tyson and his ilk."

"But Deputy Landers *did* face him," Amabelle stated proudly, "and he faced down Gabe Baker when the man would have drawn on him."

Dead silence followed her announcement.

Egan's eyes flared in shock. "What? Is this true, Marshal?"

Aunt June stood up, ruffling her skirt like a hen might ruffle her feathers. "You must be mistaken, Amabelle. Gabriel would never do such a thing. Now, if you gentlemen will excuse us, Amabelle and I shall finish the preparation of supper."

Jase rose to his feet. Marly and Egan quickly followed suit.

When the ladies had gone, Egan went to the sideboard and fetched the whiskey. Without a word, he topped up his glass and Jase's.

"Gabe is an excellent shot," Egan said in a dull tone. "Not fast, but accurate. We used to compete against each other. For marksmanship, we were close to evenly matched. And I consider myself a sharpshooter."

"Rifles or revolvers?" Jase asked, sipping the whiskey.

"I used both."

"I meant Baker. What did he use when you competed?'

"Rifles. Why?" He gave a slow nod. "Oh, I see what you mean. At that range, he wouldn't have to be too accurate, would he?"

Conversation lapsed into awkward silence.

Jase ignored Marly's stare, while Egan appeared anxious.

Aunt June's call to the table was greeted with relief by all.

CHAPTER 15

When Marly had supped with the Egans before, they had eaten in the kitchen and sat around the table after the meal, sipping coffee, munching on cookies and talking comfortably. She hadn't even seen the parlor and dining room. Tonight, she was treated not only to the company rooms, but also to the company china, silver and napery. Without a doubt, the Egans were out to impress.

As Jase held Aunt June's chair for the woman, Marly just beat Egan to Amabelle's chair and forestalled him from pulling out the young lady's chair.

"Aren't you the gentleman," Aunt June cooed, making Marly blush. "You've picked a good one this time, Amabelle."

Marly sneaked a glance at Amabelle.

Except for a tight smile, she didn't react.

"So sad to be all alone in the world," Aunt June said, heaping Marly's plate with potatoes, summer squash and three thick slices of roast beef.

"Not all alone," Jase corrected.

"Not anymore," Egan added. "I've told Marly that if her relative in El Paso doesn't pan out—and even if he does—she always has a place here."

"Oh, yes," Aunt June said. "Of course, we all hope you'll stay too, Marshal. If you can't, perhaps Mr. Landers will stay on as deputy. I suppose he's a little young to take the job of marshal."

Marly choked on a bite of beef. Egan and Jase stood quickly, but she waved them off. "I'm all right."

The meal seemed to take forever. Miss June was a chatterbox. Amabelle alternated between being embarrassed and egging her aunt on whenever the woman tried to get information from their guests. Egan competed with everyone for Marly's attention, while Jase tried to distract the elder Miss Egan's determined attempts to delve into Marly's background.

Marly couldn't have been more grateful for his efforts.

As awkward as supper was, there was worse to come.

Jase could hardly blame Marly for trying to help the ladies with the dishes, even though it was out of character for a young man. Her offer was firmly turned down. They had a girl for that and the deputy was a guest. Miss June did let Marly help clear the table, but it wasn't long before she was dismissed to join the gentlemen in the parlor.

After a brief glance at the chair she had sat in before, Marly chose to sit next to Jase on the settle. He gave her a welcoming look, though it caused a responsive frown to flit across Egan's face.

This didn't go unnoticed by either of them.

Minutes later, Amabelle appeared with a tray laden with fine china cups and a coffee pot. She poured, while her brother dispensed the brandy. When Egan went to open the window, Jase tipped a bit of his brandy into Marly's cup. Amabelle caught him in the act and let out an involuntary giggle.

"Best go back and help your aunt," her brother said.

Amabelle gave a sarcastic curtsy before complying.

Egan shook his head. "That girl."

He offered Jase a cigar from a humidor he kept beside his chair. Jase glanced at Marly. "Fuegos are an expensive brand. No thanks."

Egan fetched a second humidor. "Want one of Gabe's cigarillos?"

"Not one of my vices. That Baker's brand?"

"I keep them on hand for him. We're good friends, as you know. There have been times when we spent more time together than not."

"Then he probably keeps the cigars you like at his place," Marly suggested.

"Of course, though I imagine by now they're getting pretty stale. These days, Gabe usually comes here. "

"Maybe he's giving them to someone else."

Jase wondered the same thing.

Egan's brows pulled together, puzzled.

"I don't imagine many smoke your brand of cigar," Jase said.

"Not many. What's your point, Marshal?"

"Someone smoking your brand of cigar was watching your sister. I suspect the same man laid in wait for Marshal Strothers."

Amabelle returned to the parlor.

Egan opened his mouth to snap at her, but saw Aunt June.

Standing for the ladies, Jase checked to see that Marly did the same.

She was already on her feet, giving Miss June a polite bow.

Marly had once told him she'd learned the mannerisms of a boy from schoolboys. Had she learned the manners of a gentleman from young men courting her?

After a half hour of idle chatter, Jase said, "We best be headin' back to town. Thank you for your hospitality."

"I'll see to the horses," Marly offered.

Amabelle offered her arm. "I'll take you to the stables, Deputy Landers."

Jase had every intention of following right behind the pair to save Marly from embarrassment. Miss June had other ideas.

"Let's give the young folks a few minutes, Marshal. Come, I have some leftovers in the kitchen. You can take them home with you."

With a glance in Marly's direction, he allowed the woman to lead him back to the kitchen.

Marly would have to fend for herself.

Outside, Marly buckled on her gun belt and took several deep breaths of the cool night air. Then she swung her arms, stretched her cramped calves and worked the cricks out of her neck and shoulders.

"We aren't usually that stuffy," Amabelle said.

"Your Aunt June seems to like the formality."

"Well, yes, but this was my brother's idea, not hers. I don't know why he wants to impress the marshal so much. He never cared about Marshal Strothers' good opinion."

"Is that why you let Marshal Strothers court you, because your brother didn't care for him? Or did he not care for Strothers *because* he was courting you?"

Amabelle's pace slowed. "Marshal Strothers was different from the men around here. More polished. And he was more flattering in his attentions."

"From my experience, flattery is like gravy over bad meat. Makes the worst seem good until you dig into it."

"You think Marshal Strothers was 'bad meat'?"

The girl's question was sincere. Marly hadn't been thinking of Strothers particularly when she made her observation. Now she did.

"I don't know that he was really good meat or really bad."

"Maybe just a bit overdone?" Amabelle suggested, mouth twitching.

Their laughter was cut off by Amabelle's gasp of surprise when Egan appeared out of the shadows.

"Matthew!" Amabelle thumped her brother on the arm. "Don't do that." She turned to Marly. "He knows I hate it when he does that. You wouldn't think such a big man could walk so softly."

Cursing herself for being caught off guard, Marly didn't comment lest her voice betray how shaken she was. She was more sanguine facing Baker than having to deal with Matt Egan.

"You go back to the house now, Amabelle," Egan said. "I'll see Mr. Landers off."

"Sometimes you are so stuffy," Amabelle complained. She gave Marly a curtsey. "Deputy Landers."

"You don't have to stick around, Mr. Egan, I can manage on my own," Marly said, closing the distance to the barn at a brisk walk.

"I'll bet you can. Do you really want to? Wouldn't it be much better to have someone to take care of you?"

Marly found Trouble and led the horse out of the stall. She smoothed his back before placing a blanket over him and securing the saddle.

"You're a stubborn one," Egan growled before fetching Jase's horse and saddling it.

Marly checked Grandee, tightened the cinches a notch and examined the stirrup lengths. When she straightened, Egan was staring at her, pinch-faced.

Good, she thought.

"Is the marshal any closer to solving Strothers' murder?" he asked.

"Closer."

"And then you have business in El Paso."

"Yep."

She led the two horses out into the yard.

"*You* have business or Strachan does?" Egan asked.

"Both."

With a few long strides, he passed her and blocked the way. Trouble didn't take kindly to this and stepped forward, aiming for Egan's foot. Egan glared at the horse and Trouble backed off.

He turned his attention back to Marly. It was all she could do to hold her ground against the intensity of his gaze. It irked her that he could intimidate her as easily as her horse.

"If I must, I'll take matters into my own hands," he warned. "For now, I'll wait. But I won't wait forever."

"Won't wait for what, Mr. Egan?" Jase asked, as soft-footed as Egan.

Marly almost swooned with relief. She took a deep breath and responded as calmly as possible. "Mr. Egan has made me an offer I cannot accept."

"Then Mr. Egan better learn to take no for an answer." Jase turned to Egan. "Landers has a job to do. He's not free to take up any other offers at this time. Thanks for your hospitality all the same."

Jase let Marly lead the way until they were well beyond the ranch house. She was anxious to get away and he could hardly blame her. He had questions, of course. He hoped she would provide the answers without prompting. So, even when they were riding abreast, he let the silence hang between them.

It became clear she wasn't volunteering anything.

"What you have, Marly Landers," he said, "is an embarrassment of riches."

She gave an impatient shake of her head and urged Trouble forward. The horse was happy to oblige.

"Marly!" Jase called.

If she heard, she gave no notice. She was covering ground, reckless of the poor light. He didn't have much choice. He had to catch up to her.

Damned girl.

When he reached her, he grabbed Trouble's bridle, forcing Marly to rein the horse in or suffer the humiliation of him doing so.

"What the hell do you think you're doing?" she demanded.

He felt the heat of her anger and realized he had pushed her too far. Bad enough that he teased her, interfering with her handling of the reins was like a slap across the face. Had she been a man, no one would've blamed Marly for taking that as a challenge to a fight.

He let go the bridle and sat back. "I'm sorry."

She lifted her chin, but said nothing.

In silence, they continued along the road at an easy trot.

When they were halfway to Fortuna, Jase said, "I know this is awkward for you. It ain't easy for me either."

"It's more than awkward," she said, sounding tired. "Egan has threatened to reveal my secret, though I think he'll wait for now. In the meantime, what if Amabelle is getting too attached to me? I don't want to hurt or embarrass her."

These were the same arguments she had dismissed a few days ago when he had made them.

"We've been here too long," she said. "We—*I* should go."

"Where would you go?"

He dreaded the answer.

"I need to be in El Paso soon. I should take the stage when it comes through. I'm only complicating things here."

She bent down to pat Trouble's neck.

Was that for the horse's benefit or her own? Was she regretting her suggestion? Was she waiting for him to object?

He tried to think of an argument against her plan, but she had a point. Even though it felt like she had stabbed him in the heart.

An explosive crack startled Grandee. Trouble bucked in fear, while Marly barely kept her seat.

"Go!" he shouted.

Without hesitation, Marly dug her heels into Trouble's flanks, spurring Jase into a ground-eating gallop. She kept her head down and hugged the horse's neck to reduce her profile. He half willed and half herded them onward, shooting over his shoulder to discourage the riders behind them.

Once he felt they had gained enough ground, he wheeled Grandee around and headed back toward their pursuers. Confused, the men panicked, spreading out in a chaotic pattern.

This gave Jase the advantage.

He counted three men wearing bandanas across their faces.

One man collided with another, their horses jittery. The third man turned in the other direction, then decided to brazen it out. He rode at Jase, firing wildly in his direction. As the man passed, Jase shot him right out of his saddle. The man hit the ground with a sickening thud.

Turning Grandee, Jase pulled out his Winchester. Grandee took this as his cue to stand still.

The first two men had separated. One was still having trouble with his horse, trying to rein the animal in with one hand, while holding a gun on the other. He glowered at Jase and shot wide. Jase raised the Winchester, winging the man and upsetting the last of his precarious balance—and his horse's nerve.

The horse bucked and the man dropped to the ground.

Jase turned to the last rider. The man tossed his gun and raised his hands. When he lifted his face, the bandana slid down.

It was Locke.

Knowing the man's fighting style, Jase was prepared when Locke launched from the saddle and lunged at him, bellowing with rage. Grandee backed up and Locke hit the dirt, face first. When he started to get up, Jase knocked him across the head with the stock of his rifle.

"Stay down!" he ordered.

He tied a rope around Locke's hands and arms and jerked it tight. Locke ended up eating dust.

"Dumb move, Locke."

"Had to try."

Jase strode toward the man he had winged.

Jed McKinley.

The boy was clutching his shoulder, almost curled up in a ball from fright. When he realized that Jase wasn't going to finish him off, he almost fainted with relief.

McKinley's mount had run off, so Jase took the saddle from Locke's horse and propped Jed against it. Using two bandanas, he bound up the boy's wounded shoulder. Then he used Locke's bandana as a makeshift sling.

"Don't move, boy," he warned. "Not if you value your life."

"Yes, sir," came the faint reply.

Jase went to check on the other man he'd shot.

The man was lying on his stomach. Dead.

He rolled the body over.

Roy Parker.

"Marshal," Locke called. "Jed didn't know we were supposed to kill you. He isn't a killer. Fair is fair. He just came along to frighten you."

Jed nodded in assent.

"Another thing," Locke said, "this ain't over yet. The boss wanted to take care of your deputy personally."

Jase's stomach churned. "What do you mean by that?"

"I suggest you ride."

Marly rode hard. She'd only be in the way if she followed Jase. That did not mean she had to like it. She had every intention of circling back if he didn't catch up soon, but before she knew it, she was in the hollow where Strothers had been killed.

A chill crept over her.

Trouble slowed. Marly spurred him on, intending to get through as fast as she could, then double back over the high ground.

But it was too late. Trouble's hesitation killed him.

Marly heard the shot after she felt the bullet hit.

"No!" she cried.

Trouble leaped forward and skidded as he fell.

Shocked, Marly didn't kick her feet out of the stirrups in time and her leg was trapped as the horse collapsed onto his side. Trouble lifted his head and heaved a ragged breath. Marly tried to free her leg, but failed. The horse's weight fell back before she was clear. She shifted, straining to reach the saddle holster.

"Don't bother."

Gabriel Baker strode from the bushes, his rifle pointed in her direction. Marly closed her eyes and flattened her body against Trouble, using the horse's body as a shield.

The report sounded like a cannon.

But Marly was not the target.

She opened her eyes. A dark hole pierced Trouble's head, and the shudders that wrenched Marly's heart and pounded her pinned leg stopped.

"At least you have some sense of decency," she called out. "Even if you are a coward."

"Well," Baker said, moving closer, "it looks like I have you at a serious disadvantage. You can't talk your way out of this one, Deputy Landers, and you have no friends here to—"

The sound of hoof beats interrupted him.

In his moment of distraction, Marly reached for her carbine, but Baker was quicker. He took the rifle from her saddle holster and ran back into the shadows.

Jase rode up, his rifle ready.

"Watch out!" Marly cried.

Baker emerged from the brush. "Welcome, Marshal. Please throw down your guns and dismount. I will kill your deputy if you don't obey." He waved the rifle from Jase to Marly, then back again.

"I'm not playin' your game, Baker," Jase said, sounding unnaturally calm to Marly's ears. "You're gonna kill Landers no matter what I do. And now you gotta kill me too. What makes you think I'm gonna make it easy for you?"

"Wishful thinking," she retorted. "Just like Baker wishes Amabelle loved him instead of me."

Marly's taunt hit home. Baker shifted his stance and she could see him well enough now, even if Jase couldn't. Determined to get Baker's attention, she twisted into an awkward semi-sitting position, propped up by one hand and holding onto the saddle horn with the other.

"It must really burn you that not only does Amabelle prefer me, but her brother wants me in the family as well. Even if you kill me, she won't marry you and you'll never get to add Egan's land to your own."

She got what she wanted—Baker's rifle pointing at her head.

Jase caught the dull glint of gun metal. He fired a quick shot.

Damn. He missed.

Baker stepped out of the shadows and took aim.

In the second it took for Jase to drop his rifle and draw his Colt, another shot rang out in the night.

Baker dropped to the ground.

Jase moved so fast, he wasn't aware of his feet hitting the ground. He didn't holster his Colt until he had checked Baker.

The man was dead. One bullet through the head.

Jase ran to Marly's side.

"You okay?" she asked, a tendril of gun smoke hanging over her like a halo.

Shaky laughter upset his balance and he fell back onto the dusty road. "You are the coolest hand I ever met, Marly Landers. A natural born Ranger who doesn't need any help."

Marly gave a snort. "I could use some help getting free."

Muttering an apology, Jase hefted the Trouble's body enough to allow Marly to get her leg free. The dead weight of the horse hit the ground again with a tremor and a puff of dust.

"Let me check your leg," he said.

With practiced hands, he palpitated her leg from knee to boot top, then cautiously flexed her ankle.

Marly winced.

"You seem to have full range of motion in your joints," he said.

With a little help, she was able to stand. She took a few tentative steps on her own, then returned to Jase's side.

"Well?" he asked.

"I've been better," she admitted. "But I'll do. How about you?"

"I'm fine."

She grabbed his right hand. "You're bleeding."

"Just a scratch."

With a tug, she guided him out of the gully and examined the wound in the pale starlight. Before he could stop her, she returned to the dead horse and retrieved the canteen from her saddle.

"I'm sorry about Trouble," he said in a quiet voice.

She shrugged.

Jase knew this wasn't Marly's usual stoicism. She was on the edge of being overwhelmed. Her hands were shaking as she cleaned and bandaged his wound, using a clean handkerchief and her bandana to hold it in place.

"That's great," he told her.

No matter that he wanted to hold and comfort her, this wasn't the time for sympathy. They had miles to go and she needed to hold it together for a little while longer.

"You take Grandee and ride back to town—"

"No," she argued. "Not without you. There might be more of Baker's men. We shouldn't split up."

He blinked, taken aback. "I have to go back. I left a wounded man back there. Young Jed caught one of my bullets in his shoulder. Roy Parker's dead. Locke's back there too, tied up. There's one horse left between them. The others ran off. Baker's should be around here..."

Marly limped up the road and ducked into the brush.

"Marly!"

She reappeared with Baker's black gelding.

"Dammit, Marly."

Leading Baker's horse, Marly went to Trouble and gave the horse a last gentle pat. "You done well."

She picked up her carbine where Baker had dropped it and took his longer rifle as well. After topping the magazines of both and replacing the spent shell in her revolver, she shortened the stirrups and mounted the black. Placing Baker's rifle in the saddle holster, she kept hers across her lap.

Jase stared at her for a moment, then gave in to the inevitable.

If he'd wondered why Locke had warned him about Baker, he got his answer soon enough. Locke had taken advantage of Jase's absence to make his escape.

Jed McKinley had passed out. They slung him across Baker's horse and tied him to the saddle.

Marly mounted Grandee, behind Jase.

"What about Baker and Parker?" she asked.

"The dead will have to fend for themselves," he said. "For now, at least."

When they came to the hollow and had to pick their way carefully around Trouble's body, Jase could feel Marly's face press against his back. Her tears couldn't penetrate his jacket, but he felt the tremors that shook her.

He clamped her arm to his side, covering her hand with his injured one. If the bandages had allowed it, he would have clasped her hand. Instead, her fist clenched a handful of his shirt.

Marly managed to pull it together and was riding upright by the time they reached town. The first order of business was seeing to the injured man so they went straight to the doctor's house.

Leaving Marly with the doctor, Jase made a beeline for The Haven. He hoped to find Tierny. The Lazy-E foreman wasn't around, but he saw Birke and deputized him on the spot.

"Your first task," Jase said, "is to retrieve Baker and Parker's bodies and their effects."

Birke wasn't particularly honored.

"Round up a few men," Jase added, "And get some lanterns and a buckboard from the livery."

"I know the drill," Birke assured him.

"Good, 'cause I'm making you responsible for retrievin' Landers' saddle, holster and bridle too. And I want Trouble buried off the trail."

"I could round up the hands I need from the shanties and pay them in horse meat."

Jase hesitated.

Birke cleared his throat. "I don't think Landers would grudge a few poor families fresh meat."

"I don't suppose he would. But we're not gonna tell him, okay?"

Doc Whitney summoned his son to help Jed McKinley into surgery. Then he turned his attention to Marly.

"Marshall says a horse landed on you."

Marly shrugged. "I'm okay, sir."

"Doubt it. But you're walking, so follow me. If Jed starts babbling out a confession, you'll need to take notes. I'll have my hands full."

She figured the Doc's son was about her age. Taller, broader and sporting the beginnings of a moustache, he looked older. A handsome young man, she thought with amusement, if his complexion wasn't so green.

"Dad, can I..."

"Go!"

Jed was awake and trying to sit up on the examining table.

Doc pushed him down gently. "Stay put, son. I don't want you passing out on my floor." He started gathering up equipment.

"I can help," Marly offered. "I often helped our doctor when I was living with my aunt."

"Bullet wounds?"

"A couple of times. Mostly broken bones and cuts. I'm not squeamish."

Doc's face broke out in a broad grin. "Let's put that to the test."

Marly passed, but Jed fainted again.

By the time the bullet was extracted and Jed was sleeping with the aid of laudanum, Doc Whitney seemed to have forgotten he was going to examine Marly.

That was fine with her.

Bone weary and wanting nothing more than her bed, she thanked the doctor and assured him she'd be back to see the patient in the morning.

"Afternoon will do," he replied, yawning. "Practically morning already and I gave him enough opiates to put a horse down."

Jase was waiting for her on the front porch.

"Doc says Jed will be out until the afternoon," she told him.

"Okay."

She looked down at her bloody clothes. "I helped Doc."

"I can tell."

He took her by the elbow and guided her back to the office. While she washed and changed, he made coffee. He hardly spoke until she was settled in an armchair.

"Baker was driven to murder by insane jealousy," he said. "Although he never admitted to orderin' Locke to kill Strothers, Locke made it clear he was actin' under orders. He said Baker planned to kill you himself."

"Locke said all that," she asked.

"He said *most* of that," he conceded. "I didn't stick around for a full statement once Locke made it clear you were a target. You and I know Baker killed Strothers as surely as if he held the knife. Locke was just the instrument. But for you makin' him jealous enough to come after you personally, I might never have been able to prove Baker's connection."

"You would have done the same."

"Maybe. But you're the one who saved our lives tonight. I'm proud of you, Marly Landers. Very proud."

She was warmed by the compliment. Jase warmed her further by placing a blanket around her sore shoulders and handing her a hot cup of coffee, generously laced with Jezebel's best brandy.

She took a cautious sip. "What about Locke?"

"I've wired El Paso and Presidio. The border companies can look for him and I'll send a posse out in the mornin'. We've got other fish to fry."

Marly nodded.

"First we'll have to find you a new horse," he said, pulling a chair around to sit beside her.

"I still haven't paid you for the last one," she replied wryly.

"No, you earned Trouble a couple of times over."

Marly smiled. Then the smile dissolved into tears.

Jase gathered her in his arms and pulled her close. She felt his warmth comfort her, easing her sobs of grief. They remained like that until her tears were spent.

She must have dozed because she wasn't aware of being picked up, only that Jase had carried her to the bedroom. He put her in his bed and tucked her in, kissing her forehead.

Maybe he will climb in beside me, she thought.

Exhausted, she drifted off.

Jase watched Marly until he was sure she was fast asleep.

"If you had any sense," he whispered, "you'd have taken her to The Oasis tonight."

Of course, if he had the honor he always laid claim to, he wouldn't think those thoughts.

He got ready for bed and glanced ruefully at the cot. With a sigh, he crawled between the covers, hoping the damn thing wouldn't turn over in the night.

Sleep came easier than he expected.

He dreamed of Marly's head on his shoulder, her hand over his heart.

CHAPTER 16

First thing in the morning, with Mr. Winters' blessing, Jase sent Troy Riley and Hugh Birke out with a posse. He didn't hold out much hope they would find Locke, but he had to try. The telegraphs he sent out the night before were more likely to be productive.

Next, he went to The Oasis where the first order of business was smoothing Jezebel's ruffled feathers. She had roused herself from her room early because of the shocking rumors and required a full explanation of the events before she would let Jase leave. If Egan hadn't shown up, she would have kept him longer. Instead, she had to bow to his greater claim on the marshal's time.

When Jase got back to the office, Marly was awake, sitting at the edge of the bed.

"How do you feel?"

"Like I was sat on by a dead horse," she said, forcing a smile. "Everything seems to hurt."

"Understandable. Think you're up for breakfast? Egan's gonna meet us at the hotel."

"Egan?"

"Yep."

She sighed.

"You don't have to," he said quickly.

She smiled weakly. "If he doesn't treat me like a deputy, can I shoot him?"

Jase laughed. "With my blessin'."

"Then I'll come."

Matt Egan looked worse than Marly felt. His eyes were pouched and he kept running his hands through his hair, causing it to stand on end. Regrettably, she wasn't required to shoot him since he barely paid attention to her.

Nelly, her usual friendly manner subdued, kept their coffee cups filled as Jase explained what happened the night before. With what Marly considered extraordinary forbearance, the young woman didn't linger or eavesdrop either. She just seemed to know when cups were empty and when there was a lull, she came to take their breakfast orders.

"I'm not in the mood to eat," Egan said.

Marly, on the other hand, ordered steak, biscuits and chili, all the things she knew Cookie prepared well. She was famished.

"Make that two," Jase said. "And bring some biscuits right away, Miss Nelly. A little food might do you some good, Egan."

Egan shook his head and pushed his coffee away. "It had crossed my mind that one of Gabe's men might be responsible for Strothers' death. I hoped I was wrong. It never occurred to me that my friend would order someone's death."

"Mr. Baker was obsessed with your sister," Marly explained. "He had every intention of pressuring Miss Amabelle into marrying him and he had no compunction removing the obstacles to his end."

Egan shot her a murderous glare. "He should never have gone after you. You should never have given him cause."

"If not me, then it would have been someone else. At least I was expecting trouble and I knew Marshal Strachan had my back."

Egan gave her a look that hinted at his own obsession.

She suppressed a shiver.

"Baker was your friend," Jase said. "It's understandable that you should find it hard to accept his death, even if it was his own doing. I assume you will wanna take care of his burial arrangements?"

"I've talked to Purvis already," Egan said. "I told him I'd take care of Parker's burial as well. Now, if you'll excuse me, I have to compose a telegram to Mrs. Baker telling her that her son is dead."

After breakfast, Marly and Jase went to check on Jed McKinley. With the doctor's permission, Jase took the young man's statement. McKinley was cooperative, but not as helpful as Marly would have liked. Having shot a man, she wanted to know beyond all doubt that he was the one responsible for Strothers' death.

"I never talked to Mr. Baker," McKinley insisted. "Ray let it slip that they were doing this for the boss, then Locke shut him up. To be honest, Tom Tyson suggested me as his replacement and I was truly honored. I really didn't think about what I was getting myself into. Not that I'm making excuses. I suppose I got what I deserved." He wagged his shoulder.

"What did they tell you?" Jase asked.

"That we were giving a bit of payback for Tom. I should've known they would have roughed Landers up." McKinley tapped his forehead. "I was damned stupid. And I'm lucky to be alive. But I got to say, I don't want to die at the end of a rope."

Jase rested a hand on the young man's shoulder. "If Tyson didn't tell you the attack was with intent to kill, and he'll swear to that, you might still die of old age."

Once they left the patient, Marly said, "Is there really a chance that Jed will hang?"

"No. Locke told me Jed had no knowledge of their plan to kill us. I believe his story and I think he's learned something."

"I'm glad. Still, I think you should let him worry a bit longer."

McKinley had been willing to rough her up and for that he deserved some punishment.

"What about Tyson?" she asked.

"I'm gonna bring him back in as a material witness. He's got charges against him already. With this, he might rabbit and we don't want that. I'll head out now, if you're okay."

Marly didn't really feel she was okay, but she waved him off anyway.

Little more than an hour later, she returned from a very slow patrol of the town and found Grandee and a second horse hitched to the rail. The office was empty, but the door to the jail was ajar. She found Jase guarding, while Doc bandaged up Tyson's left forearm.

"That was quick," she said to Jase.

"As it happened, I met Tyson on the road. Curiosity got the better of him. He was on his way into town to find out what happened to Parker, Locke and McKinley. When he saw me, he panicked. Drew his gun and yelled out that he wasn't gonna be taken alive." He gave her a self-satisfied smirk. "He was."

"Now he's up for attempted murder of two lawmen," Doc said, staring the wounded man in the eye. "Sounds like he better be very cooperative when he gives his statement."

"That's 'bout the only hope this fellow has," Jase said.

When Doc left, Marly retrieved a notebook and dragged a chair to the cell door. Jase said nothing and Tyson watched, while tapping his foot with noticeable unease.

Sitting, she readied the pencil. "All right, Tyson, what's your story?"

Tyson was not nearly as cooperative as McKinley. Aside from saying that he didn't know anything about the attack the night before, he wouldn't talk.

She turned to Jase. "If he doesn't cooperate, there's no reason for showing leniency in the two attempted murders, right?"

"Right."

"Well, that's all right by me. How about the murder of Marshal Strothers? Is the circumstantial evidence sufficient to hang him?"

"If McNelly wires me to go ahead with the trial, then it's up to me. I might just go for a life sentence. If he sends a judge, chances are he'll hang."

"In that case, can we skip this and go have lunch? It's been a long morning."

"Fine with me."

With rising concern, Tyson watched the play and almost rose to the bait. Then he scowled and clamped his lips.

Marly was disappointed he hadn't felt more pressure to talk.

Damn. They were so close.

Marly preceded Jase out of the cell hallway. When she staggered slightly and leaned against the wall, he could have kicked himself. How could he be so stupid to not notice the pain she was in?

"Here, let me help you."

Jase put an arm around her waist and half carried her to their living quarters.

"Hang up your gun belt, strip off your pants and tuck up in my bed." Even to him, his voice sounded gruff. He attempted a calmer tone. "I'll be back in a couple of minutes to check that leg."

It took more than a few minutes to do what was needed, but he returned with the news that Fred would be bringing over lunch and a liquid painkiller—namely Jezebel's best brandy.

While he was gone, Marly had changed into her original, vastly oversized shirt. So far as he could tell, that was all she was wearing.

Her face reddened. "I thought if you needed to look at my leg, you'd better be able to get at it."

She shifted the covers so her legs were exposed. One was muscular, curved and pale. The other was mottled purple and swollen.

He swore. "Look, I gotta check..."

"I understand. It's not like we can call Doc."

Jase gently manipulated the swollen leg, feeling for any shift in the bones or lumps in the tissue.

"We need to do somethin' about that leg," he said, covering her again. "I'm sure nothin' is broken, but that swellin' ain't good."

"Hurts like the devil," she admitted between clenched teeth.

He smoothed a stray hair from her forehead. "I bet it does."

Pulling a chair to the bedside, he sat with her until Fred arrived, then was shooed out with the suggestion that he take care of the horses.

Fred met him in the office when he returned.

"I've seen this kind of injury before, Master Jason. Recovery requires a delicate balance between rest and exercise. Too much of either could leave her with a permanent limp."

Jase was unable to find the words he wanted.

"I've wrapped her leg with liniment," Fred said. "She had a little broth and I gave her some laudanum. She's asleep now."

"Just tell me what I have to do."

"For now, eat lunch and think on how you will charm Miss Jezebel when she inevitably complains of my repeated visits here."

Marly woke up and found Fred sitting beside the bed. He was reading Shakespeare by the light of a lantern.

"Sorry," she said, "I must have dozed off."

"For several hours. The marshal has been sitting with you for most of the time. I returned so he could do his evening patrol." He set the book down on the table and stood. "I have some supper for you, but before Master Jase returns, I think you should try a little exercise. Though you need to rest, your leg should not be allowed to languish. A short walk will do it good."

Marly didn't argue about getting up, but she did object when Fred held out the silk robe Jase kept at The Oasis. She hadn't seen it since their first night in Fortuna and she would have been happy never to see it again.

"It's only a robe," Fred pointed out. "A very nice one."

She let him help her into the hated garment and the silk caressed her skin.

Maybe it wasn't so bad after all.

After a brief, pain-filled stroll about the room, she was happy to get back into bed and have liniment and fresh flannel applied.

As a reward for her effort, Fred brought her a new book.

"This is from my own library, one of the few books I brought with me when I came to this country. It should make your stay in bed more enjoyable."

Marly read the cover. "*Pride and Prejudice* by Jane Austen."

"Master Jason read it when he was convalescing with us. My personal favorite is *Persuasion*." Fred held up a second book. "But I am currently in the midst of that novel myself. Now, if you will excuse me, I will go warm your soup. If you need anything, please call."

With a bow, he left the room.

Marly opened the book and started to read. Before she had finished a chapter, she had fallen asleep again.

The next day, Jase conferred with Fred.

"The swelling has gone down, Master Jason, but except for brief turns about the room, Master Landers still needs another day of bed rest."

When Jase told Marly, she didn't argue, which concerned him until he noted her reading material. Besides, he had bigger problems to deal with—like keeping Doc from visiting after rumors spread that Deputy Landers was injured.

That night, after almost two days of being mostly ignored, Tom Tyson decided he wanted to make a statement.

"I can't speak to whether Baker hired Locke to kill Strothers," he said, "but I was present when Baker arranged the ambush of you and your deputy. Parker, McKinley and Locke were supposed to distract you. The boss wanted to deal with Landers his self—without you around to interfere."

"Like Birke interfered when you drew on my deputy at The Haven? Was that Baker's idea too?"

Tyson sniffed. "The boss might have mentioned that he'd bail us out of any trouble we might get into if we made trouble for Landers. The boy was treading on the boss's turf. Anyway, you have no proof I was going to draw on Landers because I didn't. I was just trying to scare him."

"You managed to convince Duke and Birke you were gonna draw," Jase said. "Let's leave it at that. Tell me about McKinley's involvement."

"Tell you what?"

"Baker went to you, Parker and Locke to arrange the ambush. How did McKinley get involved?"

Tyson flapped his broken arm. "I couldn't ride and shoot with this, so I got McKinley to take my place."

"That was taking a risk. What if he turned you in?"

"Hah! He was so excited to be one of the gang he practically peed himself. 'Sides, if I didn't know Baker was in a killing mood, I couldn't very well pass it onto McKinley, could I? If he's saying I roped him into something more than a night-time chase, he's lying."

Jase reported the results of his questioning to Marly over beans and bacon the next morning. She was up and dressed, slowly lifting and flexing her bruised leg to keep it from stiffening. Fred had come by earlier to apply more liniment and replace the flannel bandages with fresh ones. As a result, her knee had limited mobility and the smell from her bandages was eye-watering.

"There has to be a hearin'," he said. "Until Locke is caught, there's not much more we can do."

"How long do you think it'll take for the hearing?"

"I'm settin' it for Sunday, after church. It'll be held at the hotel. Troy Riley and the men should be back by then, with or without Locke. Everyone who is able will be in town. Justice will be seen. If you can wait that long, we'll head out for El Paso Monday mornin'."

"I can wait." She moved her wounded leg and let out a small groan. "To be honest, as long as Egan stays out of my way, I don't mind staying in Fortuna a little longer. It'll give my leg a chance to heal. I just hope Charlie doesn't pick up that package and move on before I get there."

Jase grinned. "Now that's where knowin' a Texas Ranger can come in handy. I wired El Paso and made sure that Meese can't pick up that parcel without you. He'll just have to kick his heels 'til we get there."

Marly rewarded him with a quick smile that made him want to please her more.

"I think I can keep Egan busy too," he said, "if you don't mind takin' care of things 'til I get back. I've told him he can't go through Baker's papers 'til I have a chance to look at them. I'll send word to meet me at the Baker house this afternoon. If you think you're up to resumin' your duties, Deputy Landers."

"I can do that, Marshal Strachan."

He eyed her leg and wrinkled his nose.

Time for some fresh air.

Nelly brought three bowls of chili and a basket of biscuits at noon. Marly thanked her and dug into the food before it hit the desk. Being injured certainly didn't affect her appetite.

"You going to give Tyson a bowl?" she asked Jase.

He rewarded Tyson's lack of cooperation by eating the man's share and offering him a biscuit and stale coffee afterwards.

Before leaving for Baker's place, Jase gave Tyson a fierce glare. "I'll show you seven kinds of hell if you cause trouble for my deputy while I'm gone. Understand?"

Tyson gave a nod.

After Jase left, Marly settled down with *Pride and Prejudice*.

Mid afternoon, Fred came by with Señora de Vegas.

"We'll look after the office so you can do your patrol," the Señora offered.

"But please take things slowly," Fred warned after checking her bandages.

As it turned out, Marly didn't have much choice. Her leg was stiff and the tight bandages slowed her down.

Then there were all the people who stopped her to talk.

Giving credit where credit was due, Jase had been scant on details when relaying their run-in with Baker and the others to the townspeople. It was Birke's report that had raised her to heroic status. Before leaving town with the posse, he had confided in Duke and a couple of cronies about what he saw when he went to fetch the bodies.

He had investigated Baker's body first. From the wound, he deduced that Marly had not only shot the man, but killed him with a single bullet to the head while lying on the ground. The shot would have been tricky even in broad daylight, let alone in the dark. And Marly did it trapped under a dead horse.

It was the bar incident magnified by ten.

After Birke's departure, his story was repeated and embellished, until Marly was being called 'the man of the hour.'

She couldn't wait until her hour was up.

Under the watchful eye of Matt Egan, Jase sifted through Baker's personal papers and accounts, building his own picture of Gabe Baker. He was looking for hard evidence of Baker paying Locke to kill Strothers. Unsurprisingly, there was no ledger notation saying, *"Paid to Locke for services rendered."*

The letters he received indicated he was a generous friend and an implacable rival. According to the accounts, the man paid fair wages and was a canny businessman. Instead of appointing a secundo, Baker spread management of his ranch between a handful of men who were paid extra for the responsibility. Birke, for instance, was Ranch Maintenance Boss. There was the Home Farm Boss. There were a couple of field bosses in charge of the stock. And there were men out on the range.

Finally, there was Locke.

Not long after Strothers took up his post in Fortuna, Locke had been listed with the managers.

There was no mention of what he managed.

Not exactly conclusive evidence, Jase realized, but interesting. It was about the only interesting thing he found before giving up and riding back to town.

Mick Riley stopped Marly on the street.

"Deputy, you must tell me what really happened."

"I wonder how your son and the posse are getting along," she said, changing the topic. "Let's hope they find Locke."

The man agreed and she moved on.

At the Stage Office, Mr. Dunstan, who had never exchanged more than a handful of words with her, was suddenly interested in her health.

He gave plenty of advice for ensuring that no permanent damage was done to her leg.

"Before settling in Fortuna," he told her, "I rode shotgun on the stage and had my fair share of work-related injuries."

At the general store, she bumped into Mrs. Temple-Quinton, who was very curious about Marly's adventure and would have kept her there all afternoon if her daughter hadn't distracted her.

Marly tipped her hat to Rose as she beat a hasty exit.

Mr. Penrod, the butcher, had some sausages he was prepared to part with for a very reasonable sum. He held the package ransom as he confirmed the details of Marly's Sunday night rendezvous with Gabriel Baker. Knowing they had plenty of provisions, she would have left the butcher and his sausages if she hadn't been schooled by Aunt Adele on the importance of good manners.

Before carrying on, Marly stopped in at the Marshal's Office. Fred and the Señora were playing chess and conversing quietly until they noticed Marly.

"Just checking on the prisoner," she said.

Tyson was asleep, so she left them to their game.

In The Haven, Duke set her up with coffee. Grateful, she sat down for a quiet half hour. The place was almost empty. Most of the regulars were working or had been rounded up by Birke for the posse.

After a lengthy silence, Duke asked, "How's Jed doing?"

"I'm told he's resting well. I'm going by there later. I'll let him know you were asking after him."

"He's a good kid."

"I think Marshal Strachan might have come to the same conclusion."

Duke nodded, satisfied.

"Has he got family around here?" she asked.

"Nope. He's a farm boy from Kansas. Left home to become a cowboy."

"I started off on a farm in Kansas. What about Tyson?"

"Came to Texas, like most of 'em looking for adventure. He's a better ranch hand than McKinley, but he's a bully. The Double-Diamond and Slashed-Bars wouldn't take him. Mr. Baker isn't that fussy. He likes—*liked*—his men rough and tough."

"Birke is with the Baker outfit," she pointed out.

Duke chuckled. "Don't let that hangdog face fool you. Hugh Birke is plenty tough. Just smarter about it."

"You won't find me showing Mr. Birke any disrespect," she said. "He strikes me as an honorable man. And I believe you when you say he's smart and tough."

"He's all that. So was Gabe Baker most times."

When Jase headed out again after breakfast on Thursday, Marly was left to watch Tyson, read and do her rounds of the town, although instead of Fred, Arnie showed up to mind Tyson. He pulled out the checker board and drafts with the intention of entertaining the prisoner.

In the afternoon, Troy Riley and Birke reported to Marly that Locke had beaten them to Mexico, slipping past the Texas Rangers that patrolled the border. She thanked the gentlemen for their services and accepted Troy's badge, allowing him to go home or report to Mr. Winters, as he willed.

"Do I get to go home too?" Birke asked.

"Marshal Strachan told me specifically to let Mr. Riley go. He knew Mr. Winters would need him. He left you to my discretion."

"Uh-huh?"

"Thing is," she drawled, "I have a bone to pick with you."

He gave her a look that encompassed trail weariness, mild surprise and amusement.

"Oh, sit down, Mr. Birke," she said, relenting. "Coffee?"

He accepted a mug. "What have I done to piss you off, Deputy Landers?"

"You made my life a bit complicated telling everyone how I killed Baker with one shot in the dark and so on. Everyone thinks I'm damn hero."

"You are. Now, me, I'm just a ranch hand—a job I should return to." He started to take off his badge.

Marly raised her hand. "No, Mr. Birke, you are still a deputy. Marshal Strachan thinks I need help and I choose you."

Birke narrowed his eyes. "Why me?"

"I trust you. The marshal trusts you."

He sighed and she knew she had him.

"If you can come back for an hour to let me do the afternoon rounds, I won't impose on you further," she assured him. "Marshal Strachan arranged for you to have a room at the hotel while you were in town."

Birke's grim look relaxed. "You eaten?"

"Not yet. I was about to fix some lunch."

"You feed me and let me wash up, I'll stick with you 'til the marshal returns. I could use a clean shirt, but if you can live with the smell, I guess I can."

She wrinkled her nose. "Go to the hotel. The marshal took the liberty of fetching some of your stuff from the Baker place. I'll have lunch ready when you return."

Jase rode into town as the sun was casting an orange glow on the church steeple. He let Hank take care of Grandee and went straight to the office, hoping there was hot coffee waiting for him. He was greeted by the smell of coffee, stew and fresh biscuits.

Even more welcoming was the quick smile that came to Marly's face when he walked in.

Then he noticed Birke. The man spared him a quick glance before staring at the chess board on the desk.

"I resign," Birke announced, tipping over his King. To Jase, he said, "Landers tells me you want me to hold onto this badge for a couple of days." He fingered the piece of tin on his shirt. "Seeing as the boss isn't in any state to fire me over it, I figure I can help out for a bit."

"Birke has stuck around most of the afternoon," Marly said. "He even cooked chicken stew. We saved you some."

"Smells good. How's the prisoner?"

Birke and Marly exchanged glances and pulled almost identical expressions of distaste.

"He's...grumpy," Marly said diplomatically.

"He's a foulmouthed sonuvabitch," Birke muttered. "He quieted down fast enough when we told him he wasn't gonna get supper until he shut up. I think the smell of fresh biscuits did the trick."

Marly grinned at Birke. "My biscuits, your stew."

Jase clenched his hands, struggling to remain calm.

"You look tired and you must be hungry," she said.

As she stood, Birke patted her arm. "Stay put, Landers. Rest that leg of yours. I'll get the marshal a plate."

"I can serve myself," Jase said dryly. "You can call it a night, Birke. If you can be back here tomorrow afternoon, I'd be obliged."

"Suits me." The man grabbed his hat and waved it at Marly. "I expect a rematch, Landers."

"You're on."

"You and Birke seem mighty cozy," Jase said when Birke was gone.

Marly shrugged. "We get along fine. I'm sure Miz Jezebel is happy I won't be stealing Fred from her twice a day."

"She was a bit put out."

"Well, I'll miss conversing with Fred. He has been telling me about you."

Jase sank into the other chair. "Oh, yeah?"

"Yeah. It's nice to know you weren't always this squared away, trail-wise. You were young, foolish and made mistakes."

"Still do."

"I hope you don't still think I'm a mistake?"

"Never a mistake. A whim, maybe."

Marly grabbed a stray shell casing that had lodged between a weighted stack of papers and an ink well.

"Or an error in judgment," he teased. "A morally questionable decision."

She whipped the shell at him. He caught it deftly.

"But never a mistake. At least, not one I regret."

CHAPTER 17

Jase stayed in town Friday morning. Though not a pay week, Friday was a big banking day for merchants. Also, Jed McKinley was discharged by the doctor and moved to the jail. He was given his own cell, since Tyson was inclined to want to kill him.

Jase was tempted to leave the prisoners unattended.

He and Marly took turns patrolling Main Street and keeping Tyson in line until Birke joined them after lunch. Then he rode out to wrap up his investigation of Baker and his men.

Jase had to give Baker his due. Until Marly had pushed him, the man had played it cool and close to the chest. No one but Locke knew about the killing of Strothers. Only a couple of men knew that their boss had asked about Locke's background before giving him a promotion.

Without the urging of their new boss, Matthew Egan, the ranch hands wouldn't have revealed what Baker knew about Locke. Now Jase knew that Locke was a former enforcer for a Boston gang leader. The man had headed west to escape the life, but he could never quite get away from his past profession.

Locke had been a killer for hire. And Baker used him.

At the end of the day, Jase thanked Egan for his help.

"If you really want to show your gratitude," Egan snapped, "take that deputy badge away from Marly Landers. It isn't safe."

"Can't do that, Mr. Egan. I need Landers. Don't worry. I always take care of my deputies."

Saturday morning, Marly slept late. Her leg had given her a bad night. It was looking a lot better and she could get around fine during the day, but it seemed the better her days were, the worse the pain was at night. Or maybe it was because Fred stopped coming by with laudanum in the evening.

There was coffee in the pot. The first mouthful was so bitter that shivers ran down her back. She forced down a couple more gulps, then dumped the remainder out the door and started a fresh pot.

"Hey!" Tyson called from the cells. "Who's out there? When the hell do we get breakfast?"

Marly poked her head around the heavy door that separated the office from the cells. "You might want to try that greeting again."

"Shee-it, it's the snot-nosed deputy," Tyson jeered.

"Shut up," Jed McKinley said, his voice tired.

She guessed his night wasn't any more comfortable than hers.

"My belly's eating a hole in me," Tyson whined. "Strachan said we'd get breakfast hours ago."

"One hour ago," McKinley corrected. "If that. Though I could go for some of that coffee I've been smelling."

"I'm making a fresh pot," she said. "Breakfast won't take much longer."

She had biscuits, bacon and beans ready by the time Jase returned to the office. McKinley was drinking his coffee. She'd told Tyson he'd get his with breakfast. If he was lucky.

"That smells good," Jase said, eying the plates.

"Good timing. I'd rather I had backup when I give Tyson his food. He's not exactly a model prisoner."

Jase gave a dissatisfied grunt but didn't say anything as he followed her to the cells. McKinley was polite and appreciative. Tyson was unnaturally silent. When she turned back to the door she saw why. Jase had his hand on his sidearm. His narrowed eyes and grim sneer said, "Just give me a reason."

It gave her a warm feeling knowing he had her back.

Back in the office, they ate breakfast in companionable silence. When the sauce and bacon grease had been mopped up with their last bites of biscuit, Jase made a startling announcement.

"I'm givin' you the rest of the day off. I've got Birke comin' in."

"But I've got reports to file. And there's our laundry. Fred picked it up yesterday afternoon."

"Yeah, and he told me last night that you were pushin' yourself too much. You need to rest up for the ride to El Paso."

"I don't want to spend any more time in bed."

"Not bed rest, just a day off."

She waved a hand over the pile of dishes. "You sure you don't want me—"

"Want you, yes. Need you, no. Not today."

A hot flush settled over her cheeks as she gaped at him.

He flicked her chin with his thumb. "Go. The day's your own, but Fred's expectin' you for lunch. Best wash up and put on a clean shirt."

Marly disappeared into their quarters, pressing her back against the door and contemplating his odd choice of words.

"Want you, yes."

Did he really want her? In what way?

As she cleaned up, Marly discovered she was out of clean shirts. She considered buying one, but it was a frivolous expense. Instead, she decided to see if their laundry was done, before reporting to Fred.

With a quick goodbye to Jase, she left for The Oasis.

"I am very sorry, Deputy Landers," Henry said with great formality, "but your laundry isn't quite dry yet. However, it should be ready after your bath."

"My bath?"

"Marshal Strachan made arrangements with Mr. Fred for you to have the use of room five for the day, including a bath. I believe hot water is available now. Mr. Fred is expecting you for lunch in the garden." He gave her a low bow.

When they reached the second floor, he dropped the stiff formality. "I've been promoted. I served Miss Jezebel's breakfast this morning."

Marly congratulated him.

Henry left her with a hot tub of water, fresh towels, fresh clothes and the promise that no one would be allowed to disturb the deputy on his watch. She took advantage of the time to take a long and glorious bath.

She was considering taking a short nap when there was a pounding at the door.

"Marly!"

It was Matt Egan.

Now she had a serious problem—besides the fact that she was buck naked. It wasn't enough to scramble into her clothes. She had to dress properly to hide her true gender.

But he knows, she reminded herself.

Though Egan *had* already worked out her secret, she wasn't about to let her guard down or show him he was right.

"Mr. Egan, please," she heard Fred say. "We do not appreciate you disturbing guests of The Oasis."

Egan growled something Marly couldn't make out.

"Allow me to escort you downstairs," Fred said. "Then I will ascertain if *Master* Landers is available to join you for coffee."

During the lengthy pause, Marly dressed. When a discrete tap sounded on the door, she was ready to open it.

Fred entered and bolted the door behind him.

"You know that he knows, right?" she said.

"And he knows that I know," Fred replied. "He also knows what I will do if he jeopardizes your charade. I considered telling him what Master Jason would do, but Mr. Egan is not the sort of man to fear death."

"What *you* would do?" she repeated.

"Nothing I can describe to a lady." He winked.

Dropping all pretense of being anything but a woman, Marly reached for Fred's hand and kissed him on the cheek.

"Thank you," she said. "I am so glad I have you."

He blushed. "I know how we can get rid of Mr. Egan. You stay here." A mysterious expression crossed his face.

"You have another idea, don't you?" she asked. "Something more suitable for *Deputy Landers*?"

Fred grinned.

After years of lacking a father-figure in her life, Marly suddenly felt she'd found one—and a smart one, at that.

The rule about leaving all guns at the bar did not apply to lawmen, so Marly was fully equipped when she descended the stairs. Her gun belt was slung low on her hips, her hat was at a rakish angle and there was a lady of the house on her arm.

Angela, with whom Marly had worked in Louis' kitchen, was dressed for the evening in a low cut, high-hemmed gown that showed off a pair of elegant ankles. She parted with Marly at the bottom of the stairs, giving her a seductive smile.

Marly couldn't help blushing, but she managed to say, "Thank you, ma'am," without giggling.

One glance at Egan told her he was livid and embarrassed by his assumption that Marly was female.

With a swagger, she crossed the room, secure in the knowledge that her burning face wasn't out of place on a young man caught in this situation. The smattering of patrons threw her appreciative and amused glances.

"Sorry to keep you waiting, Mr. Egan," she said, tipping her hat, "but this is my day off."

As she sat, Fred brought coffee.

"I need to talk to you," Egan said, impatience clipping his words.

"Go ahead, Mr. Egan."

"Not here."

Marly sipped her coffee. "Anything you can't say here, you probably shouldn't say."

"I don't like the way you set my friend up, Deputy Landers."

She wasn't expecting that.

"I know that you used my sister to make Gabe jealous," Egan said. "Your intentions toward her were not serious, though you did protect her from Gabe's inappropriate advances. For that I thank you."

Marly hitched up her gun belt. "You're putting the cart before the horse, Mr. Egan. I protected Miss Amabelle from Baker's advances and then realized that he might have been responsible for her last suitor's death. It's true I made myself a target, but only when Baker was present. My behavior toward your sister when he wasn't around was merely friendly."

"So she says. Always the gentleman."

Marly didn't rise to the bait.

"I always tried." Taking pity on the man, she added, "Your friend was obsessed with your sister. I know the Gabriel Baker you knew was a good friend but given the chance I think he would have taken Miss Amabelle by force. If that had happened, it would have been you—not me—that ended Baker's life."

When Egan didn't reply, she took refuge in her coffee. Without warning, he reached for her hand and she leaned back in the chair, holding the cup close to her chest like a shield.

"Hey, Landers, can I buy you a beer?"

Birke's shout across the saloon startled Marly and she slopped coffee on her clean shirt.

Swearing softly, she yelled, "Good question. Can you?"

"I think I can scrape together the coins," Birke replied.

Several chuckles flitted across the room.

Relieved to have the tension broken, Marly gave Egan a polite nod and took her coffee to the bar.

"The marshal says you're off duty 'til tomorrow," Birke said, sliding a glass of beer in her direction. "He warned me to keep you from getting drunk and disorderly." He punctuated his last remark with a slap on Marly's back.

She was glad she'd already put down her coffee cup.

Arnie refused Birke's money. "Deputy Landers' entertainment today is on the house."

To cover her embarrassment, Marly took a mouthful of beer and almost spat it out. It was all she could do to swallow it. The beer reminded her of the time Aunt Adele washed her mouth out with soap.

"It's an acquired taste," Birke said, grinning at her. "Strachan told me you had a teetotaler for an aunt."

She took a more cautious sip and shuddered. It was bitter and slightly soapy tasting, but it did feel good going down. On the whole, she preferred brandy-laced coffee.

When Egan left, Marly gave a sigh of relief.

To her surprise, so did Birke.

"We got word Egan was harassing you," he admitted, lowering his voice. "The marshal thought there might be a confrontation if he came over. He sent me to help you shake him off. You looked like you were handling things okay."

"I think so. I was still glad to see you. So, what now?"

"I got rounds to do and Fred looks like he wants your attention. How 'bout dinner later? Strachan suggested as much."

The way he invoked Jase's name made Marly wonder if Birke had figured things out.

"I think Deputy Landers has got enough credit at The Oasis to cover a couple of steak dinners," Arnie said. "I'll let Fred know."

Marly figured Jase and Fred had planned the dinner as another way to protect her from Egan. She would have preferred Jase's company, but understood his choice to stay out of it.

There had been enough killing in Fortuna.

Fred beckoned her to the kitchen and led her through to the gazebo where Señora de Vegas was waiting for them. The Señora wore a new cotton dress that made her look years younger. Fred was in shirtsleeves, a radical departure for him. It didn't make him look any younger, but it did make him seem more approachable.

"Come, Señor Landers," the Señora called. "Louis has made a special lunch for us. He was fretting you would sleep through it."

Marly was mystified. "What's this all about?"

"Señorita Jezebel has planned a special party for after the hearing tomorrow."

"Oh, no."

"Oh, yes. We have all been busy preparing for it. That is why we want our own little party with you before. To thank you, Marly Landers."

She stood there, speechless.

"Marly might not know yet," Fred said, shocking her by using her given name. "Consuela and I are buying the Fortuna Hotel with some financial help from Miss Jezebel. She's making the down payment. We will use our joint savings to make renovations and the income will pay the mortgage."

"We are going to make the hotel a worthwhile place to visit," the Señora stated proudly.

"And you can be assured the food will be better," Fred added.

"This is wonderful," Marly said. "Why are you thanking me?"

Fred and Consuela exchanged glances.

"We have it on the best authority," Fred said, "that it is all your fault."

She snorted. "Well, you're welcome then."

Jase must have known what these two had planned.

"This is why Jase gave me the day off," she murmured.

That realization did a lot to restore Marly's spirits. She was ready to set aside the weight of killing Baker and the pressure Egan was applying to celebrate with her friends.

Jase, taking pity on McKinley and Tyson, ordered a plate of sandwiches from The Haven, rather than subject the prisoners to another bowl of thin stew. He took one of the sandwiches, but didn't have much appetite.

The day was tedious without Marly's company.

He had a fair idea that Egan would be coming into town and he wanted to spare her his advances. Not only did she seem to be uninterested, Egan might let the truth out and that would be disastrous.

When he got the message from Fred that Egan had forced an interview on her despite their efforts, his first instinct was to take care of Egan himself, but that might result in an even bigger confrontation. In fact, he was pretty damn sure he'd force a confrontation if Egan stepped over the line by even a toe.

There was only one reason for Jase's protectiveness.

He was in love with Marly.

The warmth he'd felt that first time he woke up with her head on his shoulder had grown until he knew his life wouldn't be whole without her. Trouble was, she was under his protection. He'd stretched his responsibility a bit, bent his rules of engagement, but not broken them.

When this was all over, he'd ask her to marry him. If she still wanted that little ranch in west Texas, the one her sergeant had enticed her with, he'd retire from the Rangers and give it to her. If she'd rather travel as a Ranger's wife, as he suspected, they'd do that.

First, they had to get out of Fortuna and settle Marly's business with Meese.

For the second time, a determined Matt Egan walked into the Marshal's Office unannounced and was greeted by a rifle barrel.

"Is this standard behavior in this office, or is it just me?"

"You should learn to knock first," Jase said. "You come to visit Tyson and McKinley?"

"I've come to discuss Marly Landers' future."

"Landers has the day off. Come back tomorrow."

Jase approached the door of the jail and shook it, making sure it was securely closed and barred. He had a feeling Egan wasn't going to be brushed off and he didn't want eavesdroppers.

Then he went to the front door and opened it.

Egan didn't take the hint.

Jase sighed. "Might as well get it off your chest then."

"You know Marly isn't a boy," Egan stated. "You must. You've been living with her for weeks. I don't like that arrangement.

"Think about what you are sayin', Mr. Egan. Think very carefully."

Though Jase was not pointing the rifle at Egan, he had not put it down either.

"If things are as you seem to be suggestin', Marly would have as little reputation as one of Miss Jezebel's ladies."

"I would still marry her," Egan said.

Jase let out a dry chuckle. "And here I thought you were a better man than your friend Baker."

Egan's hand went to his holster.

"Don't try me, Egan. You're threatenin' someone in my guardianship. So, in the interest of peace, I ask you again to think of what you are sayin'."

Jase placed his rifle across the desk and turned to face Egan, who had taken up his position at the door.

"Durin' the war," he said, "I heard stories of wounded soldiers who turned out to be women. None of their comrades suspected anythin' until they were laid out for burial or the doctors treatin' 'em for wounds discovered the deception. They fought bravely too. How many went home after the war with no one ever learnin' their secret, we'll never know."

"What's your point, Marshal?"

"Those women lived, fought and died alongside men and they didn't have anythin' to worry 'bout besides gettin' sick or bein' injured in battle—so long as they were just one of the men."

Egan's lips were pursed. He wasn't buying everything Jase was offering, but at least his hand was away from his holster.

"Landers and I have business in El Paso," Jase said. "Until that's complete, I will take it as a personal attack on my honor if anyone suggests that my deputy is anythin' other than presented."

"And afterward?"

Jase sighed. "That's Marly's business."

Several hours after sundown, Jase heard a knock on the door.

It was Marly. She was flushed, wobbly on her feet and grinning like a lunatic. Birke followed, holding her steady by the back of her gun belt. Both smelled of beer and tobacco smoke.

"When I told you to take care of Landers," Jase snapped, "this wasn't what I had in mind."

Birke slumped against the door, closing it with a bang. Marly's grin twisted into a painful grimace and she reached out for the support of Jase's arm.

He slipped and arm around her waist and led her to a chair.

"It's my leg," she reported, quite sober. "And Birke did take good care of me. He made sure I only drank two of the many beers bought for me this evening, figuring that was all I could handle. When I turned my knee, he helped me graciously exit The Haven." She grinned. "Well, maybe not graciously. At least no one knew how much pain I was in."

Birke coughed. "Gotta keep up your heroic status. Right, Landers?"

She winced. "Right."

"Okay, hero," Jase said with a snort, "I'll help you limp to your cot. Birke, pour yourself a coffee and sit for a minute."

Holding back a curse or two, he helped Marly up and assisted her into their living quarters, kicking the door shut behind him.

"What happened?" he demanded once she was on the bed.

"Someone thought I should make a speech from a chair top. When I jumped back down, I landed badly. I think I'll be fine by tomorrow."

"And Birke?"

"You sent him to look out for me. He did. After dinner at The Oasis, he took me out drinking with the boys. Except that he kept switching glasses on me so that out of every beer bought for me, I drank maybe a quarter and he had the rest. He was pretty slick about it too."

"Do you think he...?"

Marly shrugged. "You sent him to look out for me and he did. I also think he takes a perverse pleasure in sending me up." She caught his eye and held it. "Reminds me a little of you."

"Get undressed. I wanna look at that leg before bed."

Out in the office, Birke had poured two cups of coffee and was flipping through the stack of wanted posters when Jase entered.

"The rancheros will respect him more now," Birke said.

"I trust Landers. And I trust you or I wouldn't have given you the job."

Birke sniggered. "If that was a job, I was well paid. Got a good dinner and Landers is good company."

"Well, I have another job to offer you. How would you like to be marshal of Fortuna? After the hearin', Landers and I have to move on. I'd be happy to recommend you for the position."

"Not me. No way. It's been an interesting experience, but too much responsibility for me."

"Sleep on it."

Later, Jase locked up and went to check on Marly. She was already asleep—in his bed. He kissed her lightly on the forehead, then crawled between the covers of the cot.

Word had spread that Fortuna's interim marshal was presiding over a hearing for McKinley and Tyson after Sunday services. As a result, the church was filled to capacity. A half hour later, it was standing room only in the hotel restaurant, which served as the courtroom.

Waiting for the hearing to begin, spectators were able to order coffee, fresh biscuits and jam. Though the ownership of the place had not yet been officially transferred, changes in the restaurant fare were already evident.

At eleven o'clock, Marly and Birke escorted the prisoners to a reserved table. With his Texas Rangers' star prominent, Jase entered from the kitchen and took his place at the bar.

"Attention everyone!" he called out. "Listen up!"

Silence fell over the room.

"I am now actin' in judiciary capacity of the Texas Rangers. Since both prisoners have pled guilty to the charges against them, this is just a hearin', not a trial. The purpose is to make an official record of their statements before sentencin'. Troy Riley will be takin' notes. If you have a question, get my attention. I don't wanna make this more formal than it needs to be, but remember this is a court of law."

At least, he sure hoped it was.

McKinley testified that Parker and Tyson had involved him in chasing down the marshal and his deputy.

"But I never dealt directly with Mr. Baker and I don't know what orders were given."

Tyson confirmed that McKinley hadn't been told anything more. He made it sound like an insult.

"Neither me or Parker was told that Locke intended to kill the marshal or that Baker intended to kill the deputy," he said. "The idea was to put a scare into 'em. That's all."

His actions, and the others, were sanctioned by Gabriel Baker.

"I only knew of Locke's contract to ambush Strothers *after* the fact," he insisted. "Though I have no love for either the marshal or his deputy, I swear I'm not the kind to dry-gulch a man."

In the course of the hearing, evidence against Baker and Locke was presented and Jase knew they had Locke dead to rights if they ever got their hands on him. The evidence against Baker was more circumstantial. It hardly mattered anymore. Whether or not he ordered Strothers' death, he had been killed while trying to murder Marly and Jase.

There was nothing to connect McKinley or Tyson with either Strothers' murder or the willful attempt to murder Jase and Marly. On the other hand, neither was exactly innocent either.

"Is everyone satisfied with the proceedings so far?" Jase asked.

There was a murmur of assent.

"All right then. Troy, take a break."

Troy laid down his pen as Jase walked around to the front of the bar and leaned against it. There was a small rise in ambient noise that immediately ceased when he started speaking.

"I've been givin' this a lot of thought. Investigatin' his death, I've discovered that Strothers wasn't exactly a model lawman. He abused his power and behaved in a manner unbefittin' an officer and a gentleman. I am not sayin' that was an excuse for killin' him, but he didn't endear himself to this town and his actions might have invited a little resentment." He glanced at Marly. "That resentment seemed to spill over to Deputy Landers and me."

There were murmurs of agreement. A few people protested that Jase and Landers were welcome in Fortuna.

Jase held up his hand. "What these two gentlemen here did was wrong, not just illegal. That doesn't mean they are bad men. You folks know better than me whether these are good men who made a mistake or bad men that need to learn from their mistake the hard way. So..." He returned to his place behind the bar and nodded to Troy, who picked up his pen and dipped it in ink.

"It is the judgment of this court," Jase said, "that Thomas Tyson and Jed McKinley be sentenced to one year imprisonment for assaultin' officers of the law. This sentence will be suspended if, and only if, a five hundred dollar bond is posted by a member, or members, of the community. That's five hundred dollars each, to be paid to the school fund and worked off by the prisoners."

Egan stood. "I'll post the bond for both men."

Jase turned to Tyson and McKinley. "Remember, you're not off the hook. You're on parole until your bond is repaid. If you leave town, renege on the bond or engage in any illegal activity, you'll be hunted down as criminals."

And hanged, he finished in his mind.

The decision was well received. Tyson was known to be a dangerous man and few cared what happened to him, but Jed McKinley was generally liked, even if he was wet behind the ears.

Troy Riley finished off his notes, gathered them into a neat pile and handed them to Jase. While Marly directed some of the spectators to help put the tables back where they belonged, Jase skimmed over Troy's notes.

"You've done a good job," he remarked. "Seems like you got everything. And in clear print too. I reckon you've got a fair notion about how things are handled. Ever thought of pinning on this badge when we go?"

Troy took a deep breath and let it out slow. "I can't say the thought hasn't crossed my mind. You and Landers have given the law a good name around Fortuna. But no thanks, all the same."

He looked over at Winters, who was engaged in an animated discussion with Mr. Pervis and his sister-in-law, the proprietor of Quinton's General Store.

"Mr. Winters has put a lot of time and trouble into training me," he said. "What I know of legal procedure, I know because of him. It may not be as exciting, but I plan to be a banker."

"I know you'll do well, whatever you put your hand to, Troy." Jase held out his hand. "Good luck."

"And to you, Ranger."

Jase looked over at Marly. She was navigating the crowded room with three mugs of steaming coffee in her hands.

"Here," she said, setting a mug on the bar.

"Thanks. I need it."

He could have used a stiff shot of whiskey too.

Chapter 18

Marly put the other two mugs down on a table. Hank claimed one of them. She pushed the other in front of Jed McKinley. He was still recovering from his wound and looked pale and thin. He had his bad arm propped on the table for support.

He reached for the coffee with his good hand and raised it to his lips. "No salt?"

Marly grinned. "No salt."

He gave her a puzzled look. "You been awful pleasant, considering."

She found a chair and pulled it up to the table. "It's nothing."

"You got Quaker blood?" he prodded.

Hank looked as if the question had also crossed his mind.

"I don't think so," Marly said. "The way I look at it, you acted foolish and you paid for it. And you'll continue paying for it 'til you take care of that bond. That's good enough for me."

Jed smiled crookedly. "Well, at least I got a regular job now."

Tyson wasn't quite as stoic. He glared across the room at Marly and McKinley, as though he were trying to decide which one he hated more.

"Give it a rest," Birke advised him. "You got better than you deserved. You try anything and you're likely to find yourself buying a six-by-three plot of land."

"Don't count on it."

Birke scowled. "But I do. You know the marshal can outdraw you. And I suspect Landers can too. If not, I promised Marshal Strachan I'd keep the boy out of trouble. I reckon that includes keeping him alive."

Marly observed the two men.

What had she ever done to deserve such animosity? Or such devotion?

"Don't come between me and Landers, Birke," Tyson growled, "or

I'll shoot you too."

Birke squared his shoulders. "Then you better kill me with the first shot, Tom, 'cause you won't get a second."

Tyson spat.

Birke sidestepped and the gob ran down the wall behind him.

"You'll clean that, Tom Tyson, or do another night in jail."

"You can't—"

"Yes, I can. Marshal ain't taken that deputy's star back yet and you're on a short lead."

Jase made a beeline for Birke once Tyson had gone for a rag.

"You handled that well, Birke. Like you got experience in this area."

Birke shrugged. "Got experience in most areas, one time or another."

"You know, I think I'm gonna let you hold on to that badge. Least until a new marshal is appointed. Unless you change your mind about takin' the job yourself."

"Aw, shit."

Jase leaned against a clean stretch of wall. "Thought you'd say that."

The Oasis had been specially prepared for the evening and it was a sight that Marly thought she'd never forget. Everything that could be polished was mirror bright. Every bit of glass was crystal clear. The ladies wore their best gowns, without any gaudy embellishment, and many with lace collars that made their necklines more demure.

Señora Consuela de Vegas graced the lower rooms in her fine silk and jet beads. Fred wore a formal black suit, tailor-made, with a pristine white starched shirt and silk cravat. He continued to serve Miss Jezebel, but he could have as easily been a lord as a butler.

Jezebel graced the event by wearing one of her most spectacular gowns. Satin threads and glass beads formed peacock feathers encircling the enormous hooped skirt of blue satin. With her bare shoulders draped in a lace shawl, her costume was as appropriate for an antebellum ballroom as a bordello.

All the prominent citizens of Fortuna were present in their finery. Winters had even persuaded his wife to attend. Her puritanical upbringing showed in the tightness of her polite smiles.

"Stop being a prig and enjoy yourself," Marly overheard the woman's sister, Mrs. Lily Quinton, say. "New England is miles and years behind us."

Then the indomitable lady dragged her hapless daughter off to corner Matt Egan.

Amabelle and Kate bore down on Marly, who was listening to Nels

Penrod tell her about a colt he had helped his brother foal last spring.

"Nels," Amabelle interrupted, "I think you better watch Lloyd and Ruthie. They've been trying to convince the bartender that they're allowed to drink beer."

"Oh, lord!"

Nels was responsible for his adolescent twin cousins, though he was only a few years older. He said something unintelligible to Marly, then hurried off to rescue the bartender.

"They won't be sitting for supper yet," Kate said.

Amabelle smiled. "Let's go for a walk, Deputy Landers."

The young ladies each took one of Marly's arms, giving her no choice but to accompany them outside. They escorted her to a private stretch of veranda, overlooking the flower garden. Only then did they let go of Marly's arms and face her.

"You should have told us," they said in unison.

"Told you what?"

"That you aren't a boy," Amabelle snapped. "Matt told me after the shooting. He was afraid I was getting too attached to you."

Marly tried to think of something to say.

"I told him I knew all along," Amabelle said. "I wasn't going to let him know I was fooled. Besides, if you were a boy, you'd be too young for me. I haven't met the man I'm going to give my heart to. To be fair, I did think you made a sweet boy and I am grateful for all you did about Gabe—even killing him."

Kate gasped. "Amabelle!"

"That does not excuse you from not telling us," Amabelle said. "It's possible you might not have trusted me, but you *were* conspiring with Kate. Yes, she told me! Surely you could trust her?"

Marly chewed her bottom lip. "It's not a question of trust. I never wanted to lie to either of you. It's not just me I'm protecting. What would it do to Marshal Strachan, a Texas Ranger, if it got around? Besides—and I don't expect you to understand this—I prefer being a boy. I'm more comfortable."

Kate and Amabelle exchanged glances.

"I'll believe you're more comfortable," Kate said. "And you are good at it. I think we should forgive Marly, Amabelle."

"I think so." Amabelle smiled. "Whoever you are, Marly Landers, you've been a good friend to me. Thank you."

The girls took Marly's arms again as they went back into The Oasis. Just before letting her go, they gave her a kiss on the cheek.

Marly heard Bob Johnstone swear.

"Don't let the girls wind you up," Shea O'Brian said.

Marly raised a brow.

Maybe Shea was getting over Miss Amabelle like his sister hoped.

Soon, Marly and the other ladies were helping people find their seats. Jezebel offered a full course meal at a price most guests could afford. Egan and a few ranchers pitched in to cover the guests of honor and supply beer and champagne.

Knowing they wouldn't have to pay, Jase had offered to buy Birke's supper so he could attend. However, it turned out the man had a saving disposition and a streak of pride. He took care of his own expenses.

Before sitting down with the ranch owners and business proprietors, Birke leaned over to Marly. "I wish I'd stayed at the hotel."

She felt much the same.

The tables were arranged in a horseshoe with Jase and Marly at the head. Jezebel sat on Jase's other side. Amabelle had been placed next to Marly, but Egan changed places with his sister.

Since Mrs. Temple-Quinton had already finagled to put her daughter beside Egan, the lady took it as a personal slight. Miss Rose Quinton, on the other hand, was relieved. When Amabelle hurriedly invited Kate and Shea O'Brian to sit with them before the seats were taken, Rose was made happier still.

Seeing a hint of a blush touch Rose's cheek when Shea sat down, Amabelle seemed inspired to put someone else's romantic interests before her own. After making introductions, just as the soup was being served, she asked Shea to change places with her so she could talk to Kate more easily.

Marly watched Amabelle's machinations with approval.

"Mr. Landers," Egan announced in a loud voice, "I think I have just the thing to cheer you up."

"I didn't think I needed cheering up," she replied.

"I don't know 'bout that," Jezebel interjected. "You seem unnaturally quiet for such a mouthy kid."

"I know that the loss of your horse was a blow to you," Egan said, reclaiming the conversation. "I would like to make it up to you. I'm offering you your pick from my stable."

"No, sir," Marly said. "I couldn't do that."

"Please. It would mean a lot to me."

"Go on, boy," Jezebel urged. "Horses ain't cheap, honey, and Matt here has some of the best breed stock in the district."

There was a murmur of agreement.

Marly looked to Jase for support as everyone started expressing their opinions on Egan's horseflesh and the propriety of Marly accepting such a generous offer.

"I reckon you're too late, Egan," Jase said. "I've already taken care of Landers' mount. You'll get to see her tomorrow."

Perking up, Marly asked, "Her?"

"Yep. O'Brian gave me a good price on a sorrel mare, perfect for your weight. You both got the same color mane."

Marly smiled with delight, while Egan frowned in disappointment.

Whether out of devilry or to divert, Jezebel turned the subject.

"What a darling couple Mr. Landers and Amabelle make," she remarked in a carrying voice that would do an actress proud. "He's a little skinny." She leaned across Jase to pinch Marly's arm. "I'm sure he'll fill out. You just wait, Miss Amabelle, the boy's gonna make a handsome man some day."

Amabelle blushed.

Her brother looked just plain uncomfortable.

Jase came to Marly's defense. "Stop teasin' 'em, Jez."

"Oh, it's okay," Marly said. "She only does it because she knows I'm supposed to be polite to older folk."

"Brat!"

There was a ripple of laughter from those close enough to hear the comment. Jezebel opened her mouth, no doubt to make a snappy retort, but was interrupted by the arrival of the first course.

Fred probably did it on purpose. His timing was never off.

Once dessert and coffee were served, Jezebel stood and called for quiet. She had a few words to say.

"Fortuna owes Marshal Strachan and Marly Landers for their efforts over the past few weeks. They solved the murder of the last marshal of Fortuna, kept the peace and repaired the damage Strothers had done during his tenure as marshal. So it is with great pleasure—that is, as great a pleasure as I could ever get from giving money away instead of making it—that I present Marshal Jason Strachan with fifty dollars in gold."

She waved down the applause. "Now wait, there's something else. I just got confirmation from Austin that Mr. Landers here has been appointed to the Texas Rangers."

Marly didn't know what to say.

One look at Jase was enough to confirm that he knew nothing about this. He gave a baffled shrug as he performed the duty of pinning the star on her shirt.

"Though this is surely unexpected," he told her. "I couldn't ask for a finer partner."

After a standing ovation, Marly was dragged off by Misses Egan and O'Brian. While she was shepherded from group to group by the ladies, Jase pulled Jezebel aside.

"How and why did you pull this off?" he asked.

"I have my ways," she purred, "and my connections. I poured on the charm and cut through some red tape. Anyhow, it's not like Strothers needs that piece of tin anymore."

Jase rolled his eyes toward the ceiling. "Why go to all that trouble? I didn't think you liked the kid that much."

Jezebel gave him a look of injury. He wasn't buying it.

"I figured it's jest what the boy deserves. It's what he wants, ain't it?"

Jase's eyes narrowed, but Jezebel turned away.

"Mr. Warner," she called, grabbing an older gentleman's arm. "Do you think cattle prices might go up next year?"

Jase never heard the man's answer. He went looking for Marly instead. Since the men were lighting up cigars and cigarillos, he guessed she'd escaped for some fresh air.

Marly wasn't the only one who felt the need for fresh air. When she stepped outside, she saw Shea O'Brian and Rose Quinton inspecting the flower baskets at the far end of the veranda. Rather than disturb them, she headed toward the Fortuna Hotel.

"I've been wanting to speak to you, Marly."

Egan emerged from an alley and took her arm.

Marly pulled away. "I've been right beside you all evening. You've had lots of opportunity to talk."

"Alone."

"I prefer not to be alone with you, sir, but if I don't let you say your piece, I'll never get any peace." She indicated the gate that led to Fred's rose garden. "Shall we?"

In the garden, it was too dark to see the blooms, but their fragrance filled the air.

"I love roses," she said, taking a deep breath. "I think they're one of the few truly feminine things I do love. I sure don't like skirts much. And I hate frills. Now, you wanted to tell me something, Mr. Egan?"

Egan fidgeted and cleared his throat.

Good, she thought, I've derailed him. At least a little bit.

"Marly," he began, "I know you think it's more comfortable being a boy, but you must also know it ain't natural. Maybe your papa wanted a boy or you thought you'd be safer as one."

"I hardly remember my father."

"Maybe someone is looking for you. I don't know. It doesn't matter. Trust me with your problems and I'll sort them out for you. Under my protection, you'll be safe. I'll be in El Paso next month on business. Wait for me. We can get married there and you can come home to Fortuna as Mrs. Marly Egan."

"You're jumping the gun, Mr. Egan."

"Matt."

"I haven't said I would marry you."

"You haven't said you wouldn't. I know you don't love me yet, but I'll give you everything. I'll make you happy. You can't run around in boy's clothes forever."

Marly glowered at him. The nerve of the man.

"I—"

He placed a finger against her lips. "Don't say anything now. Just wait for me in El Paso."

Behind them, the kitchen door opened. Fred appeared.

"Ah, Master Landers, I was hoping it was you enjoying my garden." He scowled at Egan. "You like roses, Mr. Egan? It is true—you *do* learn something new every day. You must come and see them in daylight."

Marly had to bite her lip to stifle a laugh.

"Perhaps you could secure the gate when you are finished, sir," Fred said. "Deputy, I believe Master Jason wants you to do the rounds. You can come through the back way."

With a nod to Egan, she followed Fred up the steps.

"Thank you," she whispered.

"You should be more careful."

"I thought I would be safer here than any place Egan might have taken me. What I should've done is led him into Louis' vegetable patch."

"Louis would have chased him out with a butcher knife."

"Exactly." She paused. "The marshal didn't really want me to do the patrol, did he?"

"No," Fred admitted. "He's busy with ranchers and business owners, discussing what they should look for in the future marshal of Fortuna."

She bid him good night.

Stopping at the office, Marly picked up her rifle and stuffed ammunition into her pockets. If nothing else, she would be armed if Egan bothered her again. He was a persistent man who wouldn't take no for an answer.

It was a quiet night, with only a few young couples strolling down the dusty street. Mick Riley was still sitting out in front of the bank, smoking his pipe. He looked asleep, but he gave her a lazy greeting as she walked by.

As she passed the alley behind the bank and the express office, she recognized a cattleman's daughter embracing a man in a gray suit jacket. She hoped he was her fiancé.

Taking a winding route around the north edge of town, she found another couple in the alley between the barbershop and hotel. It seemed love was in the air and everyone was in high spirits this evening.

She pushed Egan's marriage proposal from her mind.

A few yards further, she exchanged greetings with an old man who was picking through the refuse behind the general store.

"The pickings will be better at The Oasis tonight," she suggested.

Walking back down Main Street, Marly realized she'd miss Fortuna. And the townspeople.

The Haven was her last stop. No one paid her any attention. Many were too engrossed in their own pastimes—drinking, playing poker or both. The rest were grouped around one table.

"Hey, Landers!"

Birke sat in the back corner.

"I'll buy you a beer," he offered.

"Coffee'll do."

"A coffee for my fellow deputy. Pull up a seat."

She sat facing the door. "Sounds like you've got used to the notion of being a lawman."

"Got my first pay. 'Sides, it's only temporary. As soon as the town gets a new marshal appointed, I'll go back to what I know best. Meantime," he raised his glass, "here's to law and order."

"Cheers!"

Birke finished his beer. "'Nother coffee here, Duke."

Duke brought the pot and a second mug.

Marly held hers up for a refill just as loud guffaws erupted from the crowded table across the room.

"What's going on at that table over there?" she asked.

"Well," Birke said, drawing out the word for maximum effect, "it seems your moment of fame is over. McKinley has the spotlight. Turns out the boy's a fair storyteller. He's been telling his side of the adventure and he has the guts to make his part in it sound foolish. Should hear him tell how he fell off his horse." He grunted.

"If he's so good, why are you over here?"

"Got tired of standing."

Marly drifted over and listened to Jed for a few minutes. He spotted her and tried to draw her into telling her part of the story. She shook her head and returned to sit Birke's side. His company was less demanding.

Later, she left to finish her rounds. Birke joined her.

It was busier on Main Street. As usual, almost everyone left the party at once. Some of the people who lived further out of town were staying overnight at the hotel. The intersection of Main and Avenue was clogged with folks taking forever to say good night, as though they weren't going to see each other at church next week.

When they saw Marly, they pulled her into their farewells.

"Make your way to the office," Birke said under his breath. "I'll finish patrolling the town."

Once inside the Marshal's Office, she leaned against the door and yawned. "Finally...peace."

When Jase came in, she was at the desk, rubbing her temples.

"Tired?" he asked.

"Drained dry."

"It's been a long day."

She got up, shuttered the windows and bolted the door.

"You staying up?" she asked.

"Nope."

She picked up the lantern and lit the way to their quarters.

"Egan sought me out again," she said.

"And?"

"He told me that he's coming to El Paso for me."

"You didn't tell him there was no point?"

Setting the lantern down, she let out a frustrated huff. "He doesn't listen and I don't know what I can say to make him listen."

She waited for a reaction, a suggestion—something.

Nothing.

Irritated by his silence, Marly began stripping off her outer clothes, getting ready for bed. She hung her gun belt on the chair by the cot. She lined up her boots so she could find them easily in the dark, if needed. Her jeans were draped over the back of the chair and her shirt hung over the jeans and belt in such a way that she could still get at the revolver.

Sitting at the edge of the cot, she fingered the tin star of the Texas Rangers. She glanced over her shoulder. Jase was watching her.

She lifted the badge. "Is it okay if I wear it?"

"Course," he said gruffly. "You earned it, didn't you?"

She wasn't sure. She wasn't sure of anything.

With a sigh, she wandered to the washstand. As she wiped the day's grime from her hands and face, Jase undressed behind her.

By the time she turned around, his gun belt was draped over the bedpost and he'd pulled off his boots. Standing in his combinations and wool socks, he smoothed and folded his dress trousers and laid his jeans out to wear in the morning. Likewise, his best shirt was replaced.

Marly didn't think a man could look so good in worn, whitish combination underwear and slouching gray socks.

She suppressed a sigh.

As Jase took care of his ablutions, she swapped out her good shirt for one more suitable for the trail. She pulled a fresh pair of socks out of her packed bag and placed them on the night stand. The odd sock she used to give herself the right shape beneath the belt was tucked beneath her pillow.

Jase turned around just as she was adjusting her drawers.

There was an awkward moment.

Finally, Marly grinned. "Egan should see me like this. That would cool his ardor."

With an intensity in his gaze, Jase closed the distance between them. He ran his hands over her shoulders, down her back.

Off balance, she held onto his hips.

"It doesn't cool my ardor," he whispered in her ear.

Her arms wrapped instinctively around his neck, their bodies pressed so close she could feel the outline of his muscles through two layers of knit. One muscle, in particular, pressed hard against her belly.

It excited and frightened her.

Charlie had often found a way of pressing against her to show how she affected him. That had been exciting at first too. Then it was intrusive and threatening. He certainly never made her feel the way she did now.

Marly raised her face expectantly. A familiar hunger haunted Jase's expression, but she also saw tenderness and...anguish?

She reached up and cupped his cheek. He had no reason for anguish. She wouldn't refuse him.

He took her hand from his cheek and pressed a kiss to her palm before letting go and backing away.

"Better get to sleep," he said.

Marly woke at dawn.

Jase and most of their gear were gone.

After a moment of panic, she washed and dressed with urgent efficiency. She was taking a last look around the office to make sure nothing was missed when Jase came in with Hank in tow.

"I've eaten already," Jase announced. "Why don't you two go have ham and eggs on me? Fred's got the kitchen open just for you."

Marly wasn't sure what to say.

Hank was duly thankful for the treat.

The Oasis was empty. Even Arnie hadn't started work yet, but there was one table set.

"I've never been here," Hank confided. "It's really something."

"Why don't you look around?" she suggested. "I'll give the kitchen our order."

Hank nodded, already absorbed in Jezebel's portrait.

"Ah, Master Landers," Fred greeted her. "Ready for breakfast? Master Jason ordered ham and eggs, biscuits, home fried potatoes and coffee, of course. Will that suit you?"

"Sounds wonderful. Is everything okay?"

"Why do you ask?"

"I don't know. Jase is acting a bit strange."

Fred paused in his task of trimming two ham steaks of their excess fat. His eyes mirrored her concern, but a smile lifted the corner of his mouth.

"Jason Strachan is—by nature, if not by birth—a gentleman. Consider what it is like for a gentleman to be put in the role of guardian to a young lady masquerading as a boy. Especially now that you'll be alone on the trail together."

Marly picked at a hangnail. "Maybe that's all it is…"

She started back to the saloon, but before the kitchen door swung shut, she turned back to Fred. "You know, I never asked him to be my guardian."

"No, I never supposed you did."

She left him, feeling more conflicted than ever.

An hour later, Hank and Marly strolled into the livery yard.

Jase, Birke and Grandee were waiting.

Bob Sloane led out a sorrel mare, whose reddish coat and strawberry-blonde mane complimented Marly's own coloring. Marly's saddle was already on the horse's back, the carbine in the holster.

As brown eyes met Marly's blue ones, the horse quieted.

Jase mounted Grandee, waiting as she stowed her gear.

"All set?" Hank asked, giving the horse an admiring once-over.

"Yep."

Marly offered her hand. Hank shook it gravely, then gave her a friendly slap on the shoulder. Resisting the urge to rub the stinging muscle, she turned to Birke. "I left my badge in the desk in case you need a spare."

He gave a nod.

"That reminds me," Jase said, leaning down with one hand outstretched. "Take care of this for now, okay?"

The marshal's badge slipped into Birke's hand before he could blink.

Marly pulled on her gloves and mounted up. "Let's ride."

Hank held the gate and waved them off.

As Marly and Jase walked their horses through town, the

townspeople lined the rode to say goodbye. Fred stood in the forefront of a small group of Oasis employees. Jezebel and her girls alternated between waving and sniffling into their dress sleeves. Other townsfolk called their farewells as they passed.

At the end of Main Street, Jase turned Grandee. Marly followed his lead. Then they galloped down the road to El Paso.

CHAPTER 19

They took their first break on the bank of a creek.

As the horses drank, Marly said, "I've thought of a name for my horse. Portia." She smiled. "I was considering Darcy."

"Darcy is a man's name. She's a mare."

"You're assuming I meant Fitzwilliam Darcy. I meant Mrs. Elizabeth Darcy."

"Why'd you change it to Portia then?"

"I remembered the Merchant of Venice and Portia, who dressed up as a man for the sake of the man she loved. Dressed up as a man of the law." She gave him a mischievous wink.

Jase winced. "The way you say that...well, you dressed up as a boy for the sake of Charlie Meese, not me."

God, he hoped that was the case.

She pursed her lips. "Maybe I'll go back to Darcy."

"Portia's good," he said, laughing at her response. "I was just teasin'."

He glanced away, realizing that they were completely alone for the first time in a long while. For a minute, the only sounds were the wind in the grass, the babbling of the brook and the quiet snuffling of two horses chewing their cud.

"Please don't tease me about Charlie," she said, breaking the silence.

"Okay."

Another silence fell.

Then it was his turn to break it.

"Do you still have feelings for the man?"

It was out before he could stop the words.

"Yep. Anger. Shame. Embarrassment." Her voice dripped with sarcasm. "Did I mention anger?"

"You did. Is that why you keep trackin' him? Out of anger?"

"Mostly. He stole money and implicated me in the theft. No one really thought I was to blame. That just made it worse. It was worse than him making Aunt Adele think he'd ruined me. "

"He made a fool of you."

"Exactly! I was so angry and hurt when I set out. Now, finding Charlie just seems like a job to do. Like catching Baker."

"Then let's go."

Jase stood, brushing the dirt and grass off his chaps. Once his back was to Marly, he allowed himself a pleased grin.

Meese was just a *job*.

Their routine reestablished, they took three breaks in the day before stopping for the night. After dinner, Marly took the first watch. Jase took the second, waking her up earlier than usual so they could be on the road as close to sunrise as possible. The break at mid-day seemed shorter and they rode longer in the afternoon.

Marly noticed that Jase was more watchful. Picking up his tension, she wasn't inclined to take naps in the saddle. The easy relationship that they shared made it easy to forget about leaving Fortuna behind them. El Paso was ahead and all that mattered were the horses and the trail. The latter gave them enough to worry about. As they climbed the Sacramento Mountains, the going was as rough as the landscape was beautiful.

On the fourth day out, Jase spotted an Apache scout. That evening, they rode well past sunset. Off the beaten track, on a site picked for security not comfort, they stopped for rest.

"Don't bother gatherin' fuel," he said. "There'll be no campfire tonight."

They ate a cold meal, then Jase settled in to sleep, while Marly sat with her back against a tree and her carbine in her lap.

"Don't worry," he assured her. "Apaches don't like fightin' at night. Just keep an eye on the horses." He yawned. "And wake me if you hear anythin'."

An hour later, Jase woke up and glanced over at Marly, who was wide awake. And shivering.

"S-sorry," she said, her teeth chattering. "I didn't mean to disturb y-you. I was getting c-cold."

The temperature had dropped considerably.

Jase shook his head at his own stupidity. Of course the weather was going to be more extreme up here in the mountains. They might even get frost, though it was almost summer.

He rearranged the bedroll so they could bundle under the blankets and lean against the saddles.

"Come here. Don't want you catching a chill."

Without objection, Marly settled in beside him and he tugged her closer, ensuring that the blankets covered them both. She kept one arm on top of the cover, holding the rifle. Jase's freedom of movement was a little restricted, but his right arm was free and his Colt was handy.

Just in case.

He let Marly doze off. His shoulder cushioned her head.

When Portia fretted at the distant sound of a coyote, Marly woke, instantly alert. She relaxed again, but didn't go back to sleep.

"If you're sleepy..." she said.

"I'm okay."

He shifted so she would be more comfortable. Then he stroked her hair, smoothing down a strand that was tickling his chin.

"I doubt this is gonna be a restful night for either of us."

They dozed on and off until the first shards of light crept over the mountains. Stiff and tired, they saddled up and rode out.

The path Jase chose was a torturous one for several miles. Once out onto open ground, the horses were itching for a good gallop. He pointed out their direction and let Marly take the lead.

At noon they stopped at a creek, filled their canteens and watered the horses. They didn't stay. It was too open, too exposed.

"We'll stop soon, Marly." He had an idea. "I bet you can't carry a full pot of water while ridin'."

She grinned. "I'll take that bet."

The first trick was mounting Portia without losing the water in the pot. The rest would have been easy, except that Jase kept changing paces on her.

"Not bad," he said when they stopped. "We'll try the egg and spoon test next."

She pushed her hat back. "You trying to make a rodeo star out of me?"

"Could do worse. At least we now have water for the coffee—without usin' our canteens. I don't know about you, but I'm overdue for a cup of coffee."

He was impressed when Marly remembered her trail lore. She built a smokeless fire and then fixed a hot dinner. Jase started the coffee.

"We'll keep going 'til we reach El Paso," he said. "That means a long ride this afternoon. You best catch a nap."

"How about you?"

"Me too."

Neither got much sleep.

Soon, they were up and on their way. Since the sun was still high, they took an easy pace, alternating between a slow trot and a walk. Once, they dismounted and led the horses, letting them graze as they walked. By late afternoon, they watered the horses again.

After that, it was time to pick up the pace.

They rode for hours, sometimes giving the horses their head.

In the evening, Marly slowed Portia to a walk and Jase moved Grandee beside her.

"Tired?" he asked.

Marly shook her head and pointed ahead to where the blazing sun seemed to set the land on fire. "It's beautiful."

He saw tears in her eyes and sidled Grandee closer.

Marly slipped her hand into his and squeezed tight. For a moment they just stopped there, legs touching, hands clasped. Then the light softened to pastels and Portia whinnied, indicating they'd stood still long enough.

"We're just a couple of hours short of El Paso," he said, urging Grandee forward in a slow walk. "Almost at trail's end."

"Maybe," Marly replied. "For me, it depends if Charlie is still there. Or if he even got there."

"The money should be there."

"That's important. But so is justice. Who knows what other foolish females he has seduced. Or *will* seduce, if given the chance."

"How *did* he fool you?"

"Vanity," she said with a shrug. "He told me I was pretty and that he liked my spirit. I never thought of myself as pretty. And nobody much cared for me being spirited. Aunt Adele called me a hoyden."

Jase was dumbfounded. How could Marly not know she was pretty? More than that, to him she was beautiful. And he delighted in her feisty independence.

Though he knew the kind of woman Aunt Adele was, she had his sympathy. Marly would be just the sort of girl to put several gray hairs on such a woman's head. He also had a fair notion what kind of girl Aunt Adele would have approved of.

He was glad Marly hadn't turned out that way.

"Just as well Charlie didn't stay in Fortuna," Marly said.

"Why is that?"

"Amabelle is very pretty. We would have had a second murder by the time we hit town."

"I'll stick with you till you find him."

"What if he's left Texas?"

Jase fingered his Ranger's star. "Won't be the first time I've gone beyond my jurisdiction."

"And when we do find him?"

"Then justice will be served." He held her gaze. "I wish he didn't have a hold on you."

"So do I. Suppose I have to sever that hold before I can really move on." Her voice was sad, almost disappointed.

"Suppose so."

She gave him a timid smile. "Have I gone back to being your young ward or can I have a beer in El Paso? I didn't like it much at first, but I have a feeling one is going to go down very nicely at the end of this day."

"You can have a beer at the El Hombre. After all, you're a Ranger now."

Her eyes narrowed in suspicion. "What's the El Hombre?"

"An old friend of mine runs the place. I'm hopin' he'll let us have the back room while we're there. El Paso is a whole lot more expensive than Fortuna."

"But they have good beer?" Marly asked.

"Yep."

"In that case, let's go."

She spurred Portia into a gallop and Jase grinned at her enthusiasm. Maybe he'd buy her two beers.

They rode into El Paso around ten o'clock. By this point, neither of them cared about finding Charlie. Priorities were on finding a room, having that beer and getting a decent meal.

Their first stop was the El Hombre.

"Stay with the horses, "Jase told Marly.

She was happy to obey.

The El Hombre was at the most disreputable end of the disreputable part of town. In fact, from the look of the dilapidated buildings that lined the streets, she wasn't sure El Paso had a respectable neighborhood.

Discretely, she loosened her rifle in its holster.

Jase returned. "All set. We just gotta take care of the horses."

"Is this place okay?"

"Sure. Just looks tough 'cause it is." He swung into the saddle. "So tough that nobody dares start any trouble. Pequeño won't allow it. Bad for business. Hard on the furniture."

They returned from the livery the back way so they could drop their saddlebags off and wash up a little before supper. Their room was a furnished shed, one of many add-ons to the ramshackle building. There were two small beds with bare mattresses. Between them, a stack of empty whiskey crates served as a dresser. On top sat an enamel tin bowl and a mismatched jug of warm water. A couple of hooks on the back of the door completed the furnishings.

"Well, it ain't The Oasis," Jase commented.

Exhausted, Marly unrolled her bedding and carefully spread her oiled groundsheet over the mattress before arranging the blankets.

"Good idea," he said with a nod.

He fixed his bed, then allowed her to use the water first to wash up. She rinsed her face, neck and hands until the water in the bowl turned a muddy brown.

"Here," he said, handing her a clean bandana. "Tomorrow you can have a proper hot bath."

After he washed up, they headed out to the saloon.

The El Hombre was most certainly not The Oasis. Instead of clapboard, the construction was adobe and might have been one of the original buildings in El Paso. In the center of the room was a fire pit. An iron flue hung above it, channeling most of the smoke up the chimney. Around the pit were rough-hewn trestle tables surrounded by an odd collection of chairs, stools and benches. The floor was sawdust-covered dirt.

The bar had been built on a section of flagstone floor and there were flagstones around the fire pit. The only wall decorations were two flags, Texas and Mexico, hanging above the bar. These were partly obscured by the chandelier. It was a huge multi-branch monstrosity, a nightmare tangle of antlers and longhorn skulls. The rest of the saloon was lit by hanging lanterns.

"I got two steaks on the grill with all the fixings," a voice boomed. "You and the chico will be set soon."

Jase pushed Marly through the crowd toward the bar.

"Marly, I'd like you to meet an old friend of mine. Goes by the name of Pequeño. It means tiny."

A lumbering, massive man strode out from behind the bar. He was a good head taller and much broader in the shoulders than Jase. Pequeño further belied his name by his coloring, which was typical Scandinavian. White blonde hair and beard contrasted with a dark, leathered complexion.

Pequeño grinned, showing off a mouthful of unusually white teeth. "Not what you expect, huh?"

His hearty laugh echoed in the room as Marly shook his hand.

"So, amigo," he said, turning to Jase, "you said something about a beer, no?"

"Make that two. Three, if you'd care to join us."

Pequeño passed the order along to one of his bartenders. With an arm around each of their shoulders, he ushered them to a table in the back corner. Marly noted that both Pequeño and Jase sat with their backs to the wall and she was encouraged to do the same.

Taking a seat beside Jase, she surveyed the saloon while the men caught up on each other's lives. Although the saloon wasn't crowded, the tables were at least partly occupied and there were half a dozen cowboys at the bar. A few more stood around the piano where a toothless man mangled a tune. Smoke from tobacco and back draft from the fireplace drifted up in clouds, hanging around the chandelier before being vented through the roof.

"Drink," Jase said, sliding a glass of beer in front of her.

Pequeño was drinking whiskey. He raised his shot in salute. "To old friends and new."

Jase raised his glass."Saludo!"

"Cheers!" she added.

Soon after the drinks came, supper was served. Marly found that beer was slightly more palatable when it washed down barbequed steaks, chili and refried beans. As she'd suspected, it went down well at the end of the day, seeming to wash away the dust of the trail.

When Pequeño offered her another glass, she shook her head. "One is enough for me. I'm beat."

"You should go to bed," Jase said.

She didn't argue and was too tired to be offended by his easy dismissal. Leaving the old friends to their conversation, she headed for the shed.

As sleepy as she was, she had a hard time settling. Noises from the alley kept her awake. Each time she heard something she'd reach for her revolver, listen for a bit and peer into the darkness.

"Haven't seen you ride with a partner for a long time, have I?"

Jase shook his head. "Nope."

"Noticed the Ranger badge too. Little young, no?"

"Maybe, but Marly came by it honestly."

"Are you going to tell me the story?"

"Part of it. Part of it is still to be played out."

He gave Pequeño the short version of Strothers' murder investigation and Marly's heroics. He might have dwelt a little longer on Marly's heroics than he needed to, but he was proud of her.

"So, you got to keep this partner, yah?"

"Gonna try."

"And then you can tell Pequeño the full story, yah?"

The two men locked gazes for a minute, no more.

When the big man smiled, Jase relented. "Someday. I promise."

A half hour later, he left Pequeño to his customers and returned to the shed. Marly was asleep, rousing just enough to be sure it was him. She grunted something that might have been "good night."

Jase tucked the blanket up over her shoulders and noticed her Remington revolver tucked under the shirt she was using as a pillow. Ever vigilant, Marly presented a tough exterior. Except when she was sleeping.

He stroked her cheek. "Good night, my sweet brat."

After breakfast, Jase arranged for baths at one of the more reasonably priced hotels. He took the privilege of having the first bath, giving Marly the chore of taking their trail clothes to the Chinese laundry. Since he trusted her to go out on her own, she deduced that El Paso wasn't as dangerous as she thought—at least not by daylight.

El Paso was nothing like anywhere Marly had been before. It might as well have been a foreign country. There were at least as many people speaking Spanish as English and a fair number speaking other languages like German, French and Chinese. The railway was coming and the city was already showing signs of things to come.

The El Hombre was just off the Camino Real. It had linked Santa Fe and Mexico City since the first Spanish colonists settled in the area. Just down the street and across the river lay Mexico. Marly put a visit to the border on her to-do list, along with finding the post office, dealing with Charlie and settling her account with Jase.

First, she had to find the laundry.

Jase had every intention of being in and out the bath before Marly returned. The hot water was too seductive. He fell asleep, briefly registered when she returned, but didn't really wake until he felt her washing his shoulders.

"Sit up and I'll do your back."

Too weary to argue, he complied.

Marly used the soapy cloth to scrub him clean. As she rinsed, her hands smoothed his muscles, her fingers easing the tension.

Jase enjoyed the luxury of the massage until his conscience nagged him. The masquerade would be coming to an end soon. Things were going to be complicated enough without him crossing the line.

He took the cloth from her. "The bath is yours now."

While Marly bathed, he checked in on the town marshal.

Frank Crowley was a good old southern boy, gracious but not polished. He greeted Jase with a beaming smile and a pat on the back. It seemed the news of Strothers' murder and Baker's death had already reached town.

"Charlie Meese?" Crowley said, scratching his chin. "Never heard of him. But I'll make some discreet inquiries."

"I'd appreciate that."

"Check back later."

"Will do."

Jase moved on to the telegraph and post office. There, he discovered that a slick-looking fellow had been asking about packet addressed to one Marly Landers. The packet was still there, unclaimed.

By the time he returned to the hotel, it was close on noon and Marly was waiting for him in the dining room.

After two slices of pie, she put her fork down. "I'm going to start looking for Charlie."

"No point puttin' it off, I guess, but you might do better if you pocket your Ranger's star."

"You coming?"

"I have some business of my own."

After she left, he followed at a discreet distance.

Marly started at one of the livery stables, asking if there was any work. There wasn't. She hung around for a bit, chatting with the stable hands. Since Jase could hardly eavesdrop without drawing her attention, he decided to check in on the marshal.

"Happens you're in luck," Crowley announced, pouring Jase a cup of coffee and offering him a chair. "He's staying at the Alhambra. Not calling himself Meese, mind you. He's going by the name of Chuck Masters. One of my deputies remembered him. Seems he lost a week's pay to our friend, Meese."

"How'd your deputy lose money?"

"Poker."

"Fair game?"

Crowley shrugged. "Or damned slick. If I knew for sure he was cheating, you'd have found him in one of my cells."

Jase stayed and they swapped stories.

Marshal Crowley, a married man, had recently added another member to the family and was proud to share the news. She was the first girl after three boys and the prettiest baby west of the Mississippi, according to her father.

"I'd be honored if you and your deputy would come to dinner tomorrow evening," the man said.

"That's might kind of you. Thank you."

He had a feeling, if he stayed around long enough, Crowley would be fixing him up with a date for the Saturday night dance.

He met Marly at the El Hombre, where she was sipping sarsaparilla and reading.

"Charlie is in El Paso," she told him as soon as he sat down. "He's at the Alhambra. Looks like he's up to his old tricks." She told him about the poker games. "There's some question as to the honesty of his games. And he pays a stable boy two bits a night to keep a horse ready for him. Just in case."

"That's a lot of money for a little insurance. He's more likely to get shot at the table if he gets caught cheatin'. Makes you wonder if he knows someone's after him."

Marly gritted her teeth. "I doubt he'd care."

"He might not know it's you. Anyway, I checked at the post office. The package addressed to you is waitin'. They've been tellin' Meese it hasn't arrived yet."

"I imagine if I pick it up, he'll find me."

"You gonna confront him like that?"

"Like what?" She looked down at her clothes. "Oh."

Pequeño interrupted with two heaping bowls of chili con carne and a plate of tortillas. "Pedro's secret recipe."

Pedro, an older man with a permanent grin, followed with a bowl of salsa and a dish of chili peppers, and Pequeño returned with a pitcher of beer to top up their glasses. "Buena appetito!"

"Hospitable, isn't he?" Marly said when the two men left.

"I told you, he's an old friend."

"Another fellow Ranger?"

"Not exactly. When I first met him, Pequeño was on the other side of the law. By the way, I wouldn't touch those peppers if I was you."

Jase let Marly take the edge off her appetite.

"So...what are you gonna do about Meese," he asked finally.

"I don't know. I suppose I had better buy a skirt or something. I can just imagine what kind of greeting I'd get from Charlie Meese if I showed up like this." She leaned back in the chair. "I guess the next step after that is to get the package and set things in motion."

"I'll buy you some clothes. I can say it's for a present. No one will question me. Then there's the problem of makin' the transition. I think for that we better find you another place to stay."

Marly heaved a sigh. "It all seems so awkward. I think it would have been better if Charlie had left town. Better for him anyway."

Jase's eyebrow lifted.

She shook her head. "I'm not stupid."

CHAPTER 20

Marly had her suspicions from the start. She knew Jase was after someone, that he was hunting that person down. He'd never told her who that someone was and it had never come up in conversation. And he'd been happy to traipse after Charlie, on her word that the man was a criminal.

That could only mean one thing.

"You're after Charlie too," she said. "Aren't you?"

"I'm after the man who calls himself Charlie Meese, Chuck Masters, Charleston Mathers and probably a bunch of other C. M. names. I could arrest him and will eventually."

"Why didn't you tell me?"

"I don't know. Guess I was worried you'd think I'd bring him in before you could work out your business with Meese. I figured you might want the first go at him."

"You're right about that."

Jase had a late night drifting from saloon to saloon and casually inquiring after Charleston Mathers. His description was a little vague. He acted as though he was happy to take his time, that he was looking for a friend. His drawl got thicker as the evening wore on. He gave the impression that he was drinking a great deal more than he had and that he wasn't too smart.

Marly was gone when he woke up the next morning. He wasn't surprised. Maybe she'd decided to go to church. More likely, she was trying to pick up some work and more information.

At midday, he headed for the El Hombre.

"Seen my deputy?" he asked.

"The chico ordered a packed lunch," Pequeño told him.

"Strachan," a voice called out behind him.

Marshal Crowley joined him at the bar.

"Thought I'd find you here," the man said. To Pequeño, he said, "I'll have what he's having. With a shot of brandy."

Pequeño set a mug of laced coffee in front of the marshal and discreetly left them to their conversation.

Over the next hour, Jase answered Crowley's questions and asked a few of his own. He decided it was time to trust his old acquaintance, so he told him about his protégée's true gender, giving a condensed version of their adventures and leaving out her name and the reason she was looking for Meese. He painted a picture of an orphan in distress and threw himself on the mercy of the family man.

Crowley's face reddened with rage as he listened.

At suppertime, Marly strolled into the El Hombre. Smudged with dirt and soaked with sweat, it was easy to deduce how she had spent her day.

Jase waved over Crowley's shoulder.

When she arrived at the bar, he stood. "This is Marshal Frank Crowley. He has kindly offered to help us out with Meese. Crowley, this is Deputy Landers."

"Howdy," Marly said, wiping a grimy hand on her jeans and offering it to Crowley.

"Landers."

Jase noticed a faraway look in the older man's eyes, as if he were trying to recall something.

Pequeño brought Marly a beer.

She reached for the beer and took a deep gulp. "You know, I think I'm developing a taste for this stuff. It really does wash away the dust."

Jase groaned, then glanced back at Crowley.

The man was staring at Marly.

Jase cleared his throat. "Marly, I told the marshal about your predicament—*our* predicament. He's—"

"Marly Landers?" Crowley's eyes flared.

Marly gave him a puzzled look. ""Do I know you?"

The marshal's mouth floundered for words.

Jase watched with suspicion. What the hell was going on?

Suddenly, Marly gasped. "I *do* know you!"

She reached a hand out and Crowley grabbed it.

"Marly," he whispered. "I never thought I'd see you again."

At this, Jase felt a surge of jealousy wash over him.

"You two mind tellin' me what's goin' on?"

"This is Sarge," Marly said, laughing. "The one I told you about. The one who saved me."

He remembered. He also recalled that Sarge had been very protective of Marly. The man had killed his companions to preserve her safety.

Jase swallowed hard.

Maybe he'd better make his will out tonight. If Crowley decided that Jase deserved to die, he wasn't sure he'd put up a fight.

"I wanted to write you, Sarge," Marly said. "But I never knew you as anything but Sarge. If Aunt Adele knew your name, she wouldn't tell me."

"I thought as much," Crowley said. "I wrote you, but I never took it personally that I didn't hear back. I reckoned that your aunt wouldn't pass my letters on." He shook his head. "I was nuts to take you back to her."

Marly opened her mouth to comment.

"Why don't we get all caught up tonight," Jase interrupted. "Marly, we've been invited to supper at Marshal Crowley's home."

Marly kissed the man's cheek before leaving. "See you later, Sarge—I mean, Marshal."

With tears in his eyes, Crowley watched her leave.

Then he turned to Jase. "You know, son, you got a lot of explaining to do."

Jase sighed. "I reckon so."

Marly was not at her best when she met the Crowley family. Women wearing trousers were an acceptable necessity at times, but not at a family dinner. That she had been masquerading as a boy was not quite acceptable either. Fortunately, Mrs. Crowley was of a sympathetic and romantic disposition. It helped that she knew about the little girl that her husband had wanted to adopt and remembered so fondly.

The marshal and missus took great pleasure in introducing baby Marly, their first daughter. There was some awkwardness when Frank Jr. wondered why their baby Marly was a girl and their guest Marly was a boy.

Mrs. Crowley explained that both were girls, but that their guest had ridden a long way dressed as a boy to be safe. She insisted that Marly stay with them, starting immediately.

After supper, Jase was sent back to the El Hombre for her things. Marly was waiting for him on the front porch when he returned to the Crowleys home with her gun belt and saddlebags.

"You probably won't need this for a while," he said, handing her the gun belt.

Ignoring him, she strapped on the gun belt and attempted a quick draw. Jase caught her Winchester between his hands as it came up. She let go. He dropped it, catching it again by the trigger guard. The revolver spun on his finger. Then he flipped it up and caught it by the barrel and handed it back to her.

"Show off," she said, giving him a reluctant smile.

She sat down on the top step and Jase joined her.

She gathered her thoughts before speaking.

"When I first went to live with Aunt Adele," she said, "I fantasized about Sarge returning to take me to Texas. I felt like I had lost a second father. This reunion, coming here..." She shrugged. "It's strange. Mrs. Crowley wants me to call her Aunt Jeannie. She says she's looking forward to making me into a lady again. As if I was ever a lady to start with."

Jase placed his hand over hers. "I'd say she wasn't puttin' too many demands on your bein' a proper lady so far."

"Proper lady," Marly sneered.

"These are good folks. Understandin' folks. I don't blame Mrs. Crowley for not wantin' you to stay at the El Hombre. It ain't a suitable place for you. Safe, though she might not believe it, but not appropriate. I know you're not a big one for propriety, but aside from the fact they care about you, the Crowleys are helpin' us out."

She knew what he was saying was true, but she couldn't help the overwhelming sadness that gripped her heart. She and Jase had never been apart for long. And now she wouldn't be sleeping in the bed next to his.

"I know," she said. "It seems like a miracle finding Sarge. I am grateful that he remembers me and that his family has accepted me into their home. But..." she glanced at him, "I'd rather have stayed with you."

He said nothing.

"That isn't proper now, is it?" she asked.

She held his eyes, willing him to argue.

"No," he agreed. "It ain't proper. Never really was."

Jase slept late, making up little for the restless night he'd spent. He got up and dressed. The silent, empty room mocked him and left him feeling aimless and sad.

Leaving the shed, he went inside the saloon.

"You look like something the cat dragged home," Pequeño remarked.

"Got any coffee?"

"Well, if I looked that bad, I'd have a temper too."

Pequeño brought out a pot and two cups, then led Jase to the back table. Setting the mugs down, the bartender looked over his shoulder.

"Where's the chico? Pedro has made burritos for his breakfast."

"Gone."

"Gone where?"

"Just gone. Stayin' with his folks now."

"With no good bye?" Pequeño shook his head. "I don't buy that, amigo. You bring him back. Pedro won't be happy if you don't. An unhappy cook is bad for business."

"I don't think I can. This ain't exactly the most respectable joint in town, you know. The family might not approve."

"Don't tell them you're bringing him here."

Jase snorted. "They'd find out. Trust me."

"Make Pedro happy," Pequeño implored. "Make me happy. Maybe even make yourself happier."

"Good idea."

"That why they call me El Hombre."

Jase grinned. "Yeah, you're the man, my friend."

He had a few errands to run, but shortly before noon he was at the Crowleys home. A young girl answered the front door.

"I'm Mary-Beth," she said when Jase introduced himself. "I'm looking after the children."

"I'm lookin' for Marly."

"Mrs. Crowley took her out shopping. You can meet them at the Traveler's Inn."

The Traveler's Inn was a modest and respectable looking edifice. The adobe was whitewashed and there were chintz curtains across the bottom of the windows. It was the kind of proper establishment a young woman should be seen in.

Marshal Crowley intercepted him in the doorway.

"A girl named Mary-Beth—"

Crowley held up a hand. "Silliest girl in the state, but the children love her. You're here, that's what counts. I promised Marly I'd find you." He put a hand on Jase's shoulder, stopping him from entering the inn. "I should warn you, she isn't too comfortable in her skirts. She might need a bit of encouragement."

Jase spotted Mrs. Crowley over the marshal's shoulder.

Beside her stood a young lady. She was stunning in beauty and grace, and the smile she aimed at Crowley's wife was breathtaking.

For a second, he thought the beauty was the shopkeeper.

Then he realized who it was.

He pushed past Crowley. "Marly?"

Marly turned and her smile froze.

She wore a blue calico dress that brought out the vibrant sapphire of her eyes. Though it was probably one of Mrs. Crowley's dresses, the woman had cinched it in where needed and it fit Marly like a glove, flowing out from her narrow waist.

Instead of one long braid, Marly's hair was plaited in two braids that were pinned up in a circlet around her head. Jase suspected that the severe style was one Aunt Adele favored. Marly probably used it without thinking.

Still, it brought out her high cheekbones and soft lips.

Lips he longed to kiss.

As they approached the table, Marly started to rise. Mrs. Crowley stopped her with a hand on her arm. Ladies did not stand for gentlemen.

Knowing he was supposed to be encouraging, Jase said, "That's a nice dress."

It sounded weak even to his ears, but he was off-balance. He couldn't think of a thing to say that would be appropriate at this time and place.

Marly seemed to be having the same problem.

"The post comes in this afternoon," Crowley said, filling in the awkward silence. "Your boy might get a bit suspicious if his package doesn't turn up."

"So this is a good time for me to claim it," Marly said. "Then Charlie Meese—or whatever he is calling himself—will have to confront me."

"I'm not sure that's a good idea," Mrs. Crowley objected.

"I have to do it, ma'am. I have a score to settle."

"She won't be alone," Jase said. "Marshal Crowley and I plan to keep Marly in sight at all times. Besides, Marly can take pretty good care of herself."

At least, he sure hoped so.

The stage brought the mail in late afternoon. Passengers debarked and most checked into the nearby Traveler's Inn. One well-dressed gentleman went straight to the Alhambra. Another man in less flashy attire spoke to the driver, then wandered down the road.

Marly observed this from the porch of the inn where she sat, ankles crossed, with Jane Austen's *Northanger Abbey* open on her lap. She had changed from calico to a brown riding skirt with a matching jacket worn open over a pleated blouse. The suit had been bought and fitted earlier in the day, the tailor putting this job above all others for the sake of the marshal's ward. Though it was fancier than the old calico dress, she was more comfortable in her new outfit.

After waiting a half hour, she strolled into the post office. She moved with the deportment of a lady and the composure of a Texas Ranger.

Ignoring a couple of waiting customers, she made her way to the counter. "You have a package for Marly Landers?"

The postmaster looked up from sorting mail. "Yes, ma'am." He glanced over her shoulder. "That gentleman over there has been asking for the same package."

She peeked at a man seated on a bench, staring at his dusty boots.

It was Charlie.

Why had she thought he was so special? He was of average height and build, with average features. Nothing special about him.

Except he could charm a rattlesnake right out of its skin.

She eyed the postmaster. "He might be looking for it, but he's not Marly Landers. I am." She pushed a sheet of paper across the counter.

The postmaster nodded. "The package is yours."

Aware that Charlie was now standing behind her, she signed for the package, tucked it under her arm and left the office, with only a bare acknowledgement of Charlie's presence.

As expected, he followed her outside.

On the sidewalk, Charlie took her elbow and guided her away from the small crowd waiting for their mail.

"I'm glad you decided to meet me," he said, his tone dulcet.

"You didn't give me much choice."

"When did you get to town? How did you get here?" There was an edge to the questions. "You weren't on the stage. I've been watching for you."

She jerked her arm away. "Don't pretend you care about anything but the money. I give you this," she held up the parcel, "and you'll be gone."

He gave her a smoldering gaze and matching smile.

Now she remembered what had attracted her. It was that focused attention, that feeling of being desired above all else.

"We're attracting attention," she said.

Passersby stared, but gave them a wide berth. No one interfered in what seemed to be a lovers' quarrel.

"Let them look," Charlie said with arrogance.

"There's a Texas Ranger after you."

"I know, angel." He put his hands up in mock surrender. "I'll tell you what, you hold onto that money until we're married in Mexico. We'll leave town right away. Can you get a horse?"

"Yeah."

"Good girl. Meet me at Kirby's Livery in an hour. It's near the

Alhambra. And don't forget to bring the money." As he spoke, he closed the gap between them.

"Yes, we can't forget that," she said.

"The money is so we can make a life together." Touching her shoulders, he gazed into her eyes. "It's always been about you and me, angel. Believe it."

When he smoothed his hands down her arms, she shivered.

An hour later, Marly approached the livery with caution, half expecting an ambush. Portia waited nearby as one of Kirby's stable boys saddled her. Charlie's horse stood ready.

She handed the stunned stable boy a dime. "Go."

"Yes, Miss."

"All set, angel?"

Charlie strode up to her. He was carrying a carpetbag.

"I have a horse," she said. "That's all. I don't even have a change of clothes."

"We'll buy what we need across the border." He patted his carpet bag. "Between us, we have plenty of money to live in the lap of luxury for years."

Marly went to her saddle and checked the cinches. "So who else did you steal from, Charlie?"

Charlie turned, his face set in a practiced expression of gentle indignation. It wavered a bit when he saw the Winchester carbine pointing at him.

"Angel, don't be silly. What I have will be yours once we're married. Besides, you can't go back and you can't make it on your own without me."

"I made it this far. Unbuckle your gun belt, please." She cocked the rifle for emphasis.

"Sweetheart, what is this? Did you think I ran off on you?" His tone was wheedling, but he unbuckled his gun belt and held it out. "I would have taken you with me if I thought it was safe."

She gritted her teeth to keep from blowing his kneecap off.

"Put it down and stand back."

He dropped the gun belt and took two steps back, then another two when she urged him with her carbine.

She reached for his belt, but her skirt got in the way. When she straightened, Charlie had Derringer two-shot in his hand. As he cocked it, she raised her rifle.

A shot rang out.

Charlie dropped the gun and clutched his wrist. "Damn!"

"Never split your attention when you're coverin' someone, Marly."

Jase stepped out into the open. "Wanna cuff him?"

He made an underhand toss and she caught the handcuffs.

Without crossing Jase's line of sight, she went to Charlie, yanked his hands behind his back and secured them.

"Jesus, angel. Do you have to be so rough?"

"It's just a nick, Charlie. You'll live."

"Charlie Meese," Jase said, "you are under arrest for extortion and fraud. I have a warrant from Austen, but I also have an extradition request from Kansas for a variety of charges, includin' kidnappin'."

"Kidnapping!" Marly blurted. "Who...?"

"I think you might beat that charge," Jase continued, "seein' as Miss Marly was trackin' you, not unwillingly travellin' with you. I doubt you'll talk your way out of the rest." He glanced over his shoulder. "Marshal?"

Crowley appeared, followed by one of his deputies.

"Mind putting this fellow up for me, Marshal?"

"It'll be my pleasure, Ranger Strachan."

Marly flicked a look at Jase and her eyes narrowed with suspicion. "You wired Cherryville when we got here?"

"Not exactly. I wired Cherryville from Fortuna."

"And I brought the extradition order out personally," a voice said from the shadows.

A tall, imposing man stepped forward.

"Sheriff Langtree?" Marly's eyes widened in dread. "You didn't bring Aunt Adele, did you?"

He shook his head. "No, ma'am."

When Jase took the carbine out of her hands, she rushed toward Langtree. For a moment, he stared at her, holding her hands. Then he pulled her into a close embrace.

"Dammit, Marly," he said in a shaky voice, "why didn't you come to me? Did you think I would believe what Adele said? Or that Meese character? Did you think Doc or his Missus would?"

Marly stared up at him, her eyes bright with tears. She felt every bit as shaky as he sounded, but her voice was steady.

"Aunt Adele told me that I was ruined. She said that no one would ever marry me now and the only other respectable profession for me was being a missionary." She gazed down at the ground and shuffled her feet. "So she sent me away."

Langtree tipped her face so their eyes met. "Adele is a wicked fool."

Watching the scene between Marly and Sheriff Langtree play out, Jase had to agree with the man's sentiment. Marly's aunt was a damned fool. And it could have cost Marly's life.

Jase cleared his throat. "Your aunt certainly is a fool if she thinks Marly Landers is cut out for mission work."

Marly laughed and Langtree let her go.

Jase tried not to heave a sigh of relief. This jealousy thing was getting out of hand. It wasn't the ideal time or place for declaring himself, but if that's what it would take to keep Marly, he'd do it.

"The doc thinks you'd make a good nurse," Langtree said. "I always thought it a shame I couldn't make you my deputy."

Jase secretly gloated as a grin spread across Marly's face.

"Sorry, sir, but I've found another callin'," she drawled.

She pulled back the front of her dress jacket. Pinned to the high-neck blouse was the tin star of the Texas Rangers.

Over the next hour, the money from Cherryville was examined, recorded, counted and put into the marshal's strongbox pending Langtree's departure. A large chunk of the money extorted from the Austen businessmen had been spent, but the remainder was taken to the local branch of an Austen bank, less the ten percent reward.

That was presented to Marly.

"You earned it," Jase told her when she started to refuse. "And don't try givin' it to me as payback. You don't owe me anythin'."

"I owe you a lot. But I won't try paying you back with this."

The party moved from the Marshal's Office to the Crowley home. Langtree and Sarge—as Marly continued to call Crowley—shared stories about her growing up, with the subject of these tales either embellishing or denying the tales.

Eventually, Mrs. Crowley told her guests to go home.

"Some people," she said with a smile, "need to rest."

"I'll walk out with you, Langtree," Crowley said. "Wait until I get my coat. I'll see you tomorrow, Strachan. Unless you want to join us?"

Jase shook his head. He wanted the opportunity to have Marly alone for a few minutes.

He motioned her to join him on the porch.

"Marly…can I take you to lunch tomorrow?"

"Just us?"

"Just us."

She nodded.

He took her hand and gave it a squeeze. He would have done more, but Langtree stepped outside.

"Excuse me, Strachan. I'd like a word with Marly before I go, if you don't mind."

Jase did mind, but he said good night and strolled toward the gate, thinking of his date with Marly. At the gate, he gave in to his curiosity and glanced back.

Langtree and Marly were standing very close. Then they parted and Marly returned to the house.

He walked back to the El Hombre, thinking about the day's events. He thought about Marly's relationship with Meese, as ill-fated as it was. She'd obviously seen something attractive in the man. Then there was good old Sarge. Crowley, he corrected. And Sheriff Langtree.

Marly seemed to have a collection of admirers. It made Jase wonder where he fit in.

He slumped into a chair at a table in the back.

"Where's the chico?" Pequeño asked.

Jase gave him a look that would have made a lesser man quake. Pequeño was not a lesser man, but he did shut up.

Later, he returned with a whisky bottle and two glasses.

Morning brought Jase sobriety, a splitting headache and a dose of common sense. With a renewed sense of purpose, he took off to the public washhouse and paid for a bath, a shave and a haircut. The attendant said he looked clean enough already, but took his money.

At twelve o'clock precisely, Jase arrived at the Crowley place wearing his best trousers and the red pinstriped shirt Marly had picked out for him in Fortuna.

Mrs. Crowley answered the door and ushered him into the front room. "Marly will be a few minutes."

Restless, he wandered the room, stopping to admire the daguerreotype of Frank and Jeannie Crowley on their wedding day.

"Marly's been playing with the children all morning," Mrs. Crowley said. "That's why she's running a bit late."

"It's kind of you to entertain me in the meantime, ma'am," he replied feeling a bit awkward.

"I would like to have a word with you about her, if you don't mind."

He didn't imagine he had much choice.

"Ranger Strachan," she started as he sat down on the settle.

From her tone, Jase knew he was going to get a lecture. He was surprised when she skipped the past and went straight to the future.

"Frank and I would be happy to keep Marly with us. I think we could both grow to love her as a daughter. Well, as you probably know, Frank thinks of her that way already."

"I know."

"I don't like to speak ill of anyone," the woman said in a hesitant tone, "but I don't think it would be wise to send her back to her aunt. I understand that the doctor in Cherryville would be willing to send her to school to become a nurse. I'm not sure that is what Marly wants. The point is, I want you to know that she has choices. She's not alone in the world."

"I understand, ma'am. But I think Marly's the one you should talk to about this. It's up to her to decide what she wants to do. It ain't—it *isn't* my place to say."

Mrs. Crowley sighed and gave him a look he suspected she often gave one of her wayward children. "Ranger Strachan—"

"Jase!"

Marly entered the room, a wide smile across her face. She wore the brown riding skirt, this time with a blue and white striped blouse. Instead of braids, her auburn hair was pulled back and tied with a broad blue ribbon that matched her blouse. The bow was lopsided.

Jase grinned. "Come here, brat."

He tied the bow and arrayed the ribbon neatly against her hair. He had never noticed how curly her hair was. A tiny ringlet twisted around his finger as he smoothed the ribbon.

Reluctantly, he stepped back. "There, all set."

They took their leave of Mrs. Crowley.

Once they were out of earshot, Marly said, "It feels so strange going out without my gun belt or at least my rifle."

Jase suppressed a chuckle. "I guess you'll have to trust me to protect you."

She gave his arm a squeeze. "But who will protect you?"

CHAPTER 21

Unlike its adobe neighbors, The Grande Hotel was all terra cotta brick and white-painted wood. Not since The Palace in Wichita had Marly been inside such an opulent building. Even The Oasis couldn't hold a candle to it.

Crystal chandeliers lit the lobby and dining rooms. All the male employees wore black and white and were spotless and clean shaven. There were no serving girls, only waiters. Damask cloths draped the tables and silver glinted everywhere.

Marly was speechless. One part of her was stunned she was in such a place. The other wondered if Jase could afford it.

"What do you think?" he asked.

"I hope the food is good."

"It is. This place was built on the promise of west Texas prosperity. I hear that everyone who's anyone—or wants to be—comes here."

"Let me guess," she said dryly, "you know the owner."

"Never met him. Last time I was in El Paso, this place was a corral for mail horses."

Marly laughed.

The waiter arrived and conversation was suspended until he took their order. Discussion resumed on trivial lines until the plates were taken away and they were left alone with their coffee.

For Marly's part, she wasn't sure what to say. Everything seemed so much more complicated since coming to El Paso. She longed to talk to Fred about what she should do next. As dear as he was, she didn't feel she could confide in Sarge the same way.

"I was talkin' to Mrs. Crowley," Jase said.

His expression filled her with dread.

"She told me that she and the marshal were hopin' you'd stay with them. She's really taken with you."

"They're nice folks, like long lost family. But I don't think I'd be comfortable staying there for more than a visit."

"I understand Langtree wants to take you back to Cherryville. Apparently, the town doctor and his wife wanna send you to nursin' school."

She frowned. "I suppose that's better than the mission school—but not by much. They are very kind. I guess I'm good at mending broken bones and cleaning wounds, but it isn't what I want to do. I've been over this ground already with Sheriff Langtree." She held up a hand. "Before you ask, I don't want to go back to my Aunt Adele either. Besides, the sheriff has pointed out that I do have other options besides nursing and Aunt Adele."

"He offered to marry you."

"He *asked* me," she corrected. "I declined. I'm not ready to go back to Cherryville. And as much as I miss Fred, I don't want to go back to Fortuna or stay in El Paso. For that matter, I couldn't stay here even if I wanted to."

He gave her a puzzled look. "Why not?"

She gave an exasperated huff. "I told you. Egan's coming here. If I'm still here..."

"He can't force you to marry him if you don't wanna."

"Well, I don't. But if I can help it, I'd rather not see him again. I was ready to shoot him last time we met."

Jase gave her an odd smile. "If he steps out of line, I'll shoot him." He signaled the waiter for their bill.

"Where are *you* going?" she asked, sipping her coffee and pretending the question was casual.

"I don't know yet."

A tense silence fell over them.

Their cups were refilled and the bill arrived.

Marly took a deep breath. "I don't suppose I could travel with you as a boy again, could I?" When Jase shook his head, she mumbled, "I didn't think so."

"Wouldn't be proper."

"Of course not."

When the bill was paid, they walked back to the Crowley home. With her hand on Jase's arm, neither spoke.

At the bottom stair of the porch, she stopped and looked up at Jase. "Thank you."

"My pleasure, ma'am." He gave her an exaggerated tip of his hat.

"I mean for everything," she said, a slight catch in her throat.

"You made all of it a pleasure." He paused. "Marly, I—"

"Marly!" Frank Jr. ran around the corner. "You gotta see this!"

The seven-year-old grabbed her hand and tugged her toward the back yard. She looked helplessly at Jase.

"I'll be 'round this evening," he said. "We'll talk then."

She wished he'd do more than just talk.

Jase watched her go. Frustrated, he kicked a stone, sending it skipping down the path.

For some reason, he thought it would be easy once Meese was out of the way and Marly was in her skirts. It wasn't. Their comfortable relationship was slipping away and it looked like he might have to start from scratch to develop another one.

So be it, he decided, heading downtown. If he had to court Marly to win her, he would do it.

First stop was the telegraph office. He had already applied for leave. If a reply wasn't waiting for him, he'd wire Austin and tell them he was going anyhow. He had enough money saved to take some time off. He had enough that he could buy a small ranch. Or he could seek an appointment as town marshal or sheriff.

Whatever Marly wanted. Whatever it would take.

Back at the El Hombre, Pequeño sent a scowl in his direction. "No chico again? Where is he? No one's seen him in a while."

"He's been busy."

"Well, Pedro is very unhappy. I am very unhappy. What game are you playing, amigo? Is the chico in trouble?"

"No trouble. I just can't explain."

Pequeño pushed Jase down into a chair. "Try."

Jase was not about to break the news to Pequeño that Marly was a girl. At the same time, he didn't want to lie to his friend. It went against the grain. He was the one who had persuaded Pequeño—formerly known as 'Big Pete', 'The Swede' and 'that crazy Viking'—to go straight.

So he settled on partial truth. He told as much as he could about Marly without revealing her gender.

"So the chico has to decide what to do with his life. Tough. Well, you tell him if he gets tired of civilized company, he can come work for me. Everybody likes him. You tell him."

"Sure."

Pequeño patted him on the shoulder. "Don't worry. The chico will work things out and everything will be better."

Jase hoped his friend was right.

He didn't want to intrude on the Crowleys for supper again, so he waited a reasonable time for them to eat before returning to the house.

With courting in mind, he arrived at the door, a hat in one hand and flowers in the other.

"Thank God," Crowley said. "Jeannie, it's Strachan!" He ushered Jase into the house. "Did my deputy find you?"

Jase shook his head, puzzled.

"He must have just missed you. I've got another one checking the livery and one looking for Langtree. Marly's gone."

"When?"

"We're not sure. Not too long before supper, I imagine. She was playing with the kids 'til Jeannie called them in to wash up and set the table. The girl has taken all her things. Left us a note thanking us for our hospitality, apologizing for leaving so suddenly and promising to stay in touch. Mentioned something about a fellow named Egan being after her." Crowley narrowed his eyes. "You didn't tell us anything about that."

"The man wants to marry her," Jase said, his mouth curling in exasperation. "He's a cattle baron, not an outlaw. It's not like he's gonna kidnap her or anything."

"I don't know, Strachan. Some of those cattlemen...I'd sooner trust outlaws."

Mrs. Crowley emerged from the kitchen, bearing a package wrapped in brown paper. "Ranger Strachan?"

"Ma'am?"

"You'll be going after her immediately, I expect."

"Yes, ma'am."

"If you can, bring her back here. If you can't, please give her this and my best wishes." With a gracious inclination of her head, she retreated to the kitchen.

"If I find out anything, I'll send word," Crowley promised. "She left a note for Langtree, but nothing for you. I expect she knows you'll find her."

"Don't worry. I'll find her, and I'll let you know when I do."

"Just remember, son, that girl is like a daughter to me." A hint of the old Confederate Sergeant stared out from the marshal's eyes. "Do right by her. Understand?"

"Yes, sir."

Jase left, flowers forgotten on the dining room table.

His first stop was the livery where he ordered Grandee saddled. The stable boy admitted to seeing Marly earlier when she came for Portia. His description confirmed his suspicion that she was one again travelling in boy's clothes. The stable boy couldn't be sure what time she left and didn't pay attention to what direction she went.

The El Hombre was much more useful. While Jase was being

grilled by Pequeño earlier, Marly had been in the kitchen with Pedro.

"What?"

"The chico came back to say good bye," Pequeño said, shrugging. "I knew he would. Pedro packed him some food for the trail."

"Where'd she go?"

"She?" Pequeño gave him a knowing look. "So, now you come clean? Perhaps if you had told me sooner..."

The look on Jase's face made Pequeño rethink his strategy.

"Pedro's brother-in-law runs a roadhouse," he said with a shrug. "It's on the way to Santa Fe. The chica said she needed to get out of town, some place safe, but not too far away."

Jase turned on his heel and left the saloon. He packed up his belongings and cleared out of the shed in minutes, almost missing the deputy who had been sent to find him.

Crowley's man was able to confirm Marly's directions.

"Thank you," Jase said. "It's nice to hear that not everyone is workin' against me."

Pedro's brother-in-law's roadhouse was just outside El Paso, in an area that had been settled by Tigua Indians up until a few years ago. Now the surrounding land was farmed by white settlers.

By the time Jase arrived, it was getting dark. The peach glow of the setting sun contrasted dramatically with the inky purple shadows spreading across vineyards and orchards. Even in the dim light, he recognized the roadhouse from Pedro's description.

It was an old mission that had been converted for commercial purposes. What had been the dining hall now served as a saloon. The chapel was being used as the family's quarters and the building that had housed the brothers was being used as an inn. From the look of the fortifications, the place was accustomed to being raided. No doubt it had protected its occupants from Apaches, Mexicans and gringos on both sides of the law.

Jase told a scruffy boy outside to watch his horse. He told a slightly older boy to saddle and bring Portia out into the court.

That taken care of, he went inside.

He was not too surprised to find that he was expected. Pedro's nephew, a tough looking hombre, greeted him with a broken-toothed grin and directed him to Marly's room.

Without knocking, he flung open the door and strode inside.

"Oh," Marly said, lowering her carbine. "It's you."

If she thought her calm greeting was going to get her off the hook, she was crazy as a loon.

"What the hell do you think you're doin' runnin' off like that?" he demanded.

"I was going to have a hot bath ready for you, but they don't have a tub. Too bad," she smiled, "you could use one."

That derailed him.

"I just had a bath."

"But it would have relaxed you."

"Maybe, but that ain't the point." He revved up again. "I wouldn't need to relax if you hadn't run away. You've got the Crowleys worried and Sarge threatenin' me with bodily harm. Thank heaven I didn't run into Langtree. And Pequeño thinks—hell, I don't know what he thinks, but I could've killed him today, not tellin' me you were there."

"Would you like a glass of beer?" she asked with maddening calm. "I asked Juan to bring up a pitcher and two glasses when I got here. I smelled the coffee. Vile stuff."

Jase slumped down beside her on the bed, took his hat off and wiped his eyes free of dust, while waiting for his racing pulse to slow.

Marly stood and he grabbed her wrist. "Why?"

"Why what?"

He gave her the best hard stare he could muster.

She blinked. "Why did I run away? Because I couldn't think of anything else to do."

She sat down again and he took her hand in his.

"Marly," he said, "I know you'd like things to go back to the way they were. But I can't treat you like a boy. That's not the way I feel about you."

"You never actually said how you feel."

"I didn't think it was right. You were under my protection. I didn't wanna take advantage."

"But I did think you might care for me," she said. "Maybe even love me."

"I do."

Marly sighed with relief. Had she really doubted his feelings?

"I hoped so," she said. "When we got to El Paso, things were too confusing. First, there was Sarge acting like Papa Bear. Then Sheriff Langtree showed up and even though I did say I was a bit sweet on him, I..." She shrugged.

Careful not to pull her hand free of his, she stood and straddled his lap. With her other hand, she reached up and touched his cheek. Then, with only a moment of hesitation, she kissed him.

Surprised, Jase pulled back. But something in her eyes must have melted the last bit of his resolve. He drew her into his arms and kissed her hard and deep.

Marly was in heaven.

Just because she dressed as a boy didn't mean she didn't have a woman's heart. It had fluttered for John Langtree. It had been fooled by Charlie Meese. For a time, she wasn't sure whether she could trust that heart again.

But she had and it was worth it.

She wrapped her legs around Jase's waist. Once more, she could feel the outline of every hard muscle, from his chest down. She touched the more familiar territory of his back, while his tongue caressed her mouth. When he let her come up for air, she gave a happy sigh.

She kissed him again, her tongue exploring his mouth. She didn't have the words to describe what this was doing to her. All the stories she had read ended with the kiss, never hinting about the excited thrum she felt throughout her body—a body that seemed to have a mind of its own.

Heaven.

Hell, Jase thought, fighting his growing lust.

He stood, still holding Marly. With a groan, he set her down.

"We should go, Marly."

"What do you mean?"

"I promised to take you home to Crowley. It'll be late by the time we get there, but he'll be glad to see you."

She stomped her foot—the most female thing he had ever seen her do. "I thought we had settled where I was staying. With you."

"It ain't proper. Not yet, anyways."

Marly stood before him, hands on her hips, giving him an exasperated glare. He had a feeling this was an Aunt Adele glare.

"Jason Strachan," she said, "we have lived together for two months. We've slept in the same bed more than once. And now we've finally settled things you tell me *this* isn't proper?"

"Well, I have kind of missed havin' you around. I could ask Juan for a cot."

Scowling, she shook her head.

"All right," he said with a sigh. "But consider yourself engaged to me 'cause my sense of propriety is a sight more particular than yours." He gave her a quick kiss. "I gotta go check on the horses."

Jase headed down to the livery and discovered that Grandee had already been stabled. His saddlebags were waiting for him by the bar. Once again, Marly's influence had proven more irresistible than his own.

When he returned to their room, Marly was in her oversized nightshirt. She sat on the edge of the bed, sipping a glass of beer and swinging bare legs.

After a moment of distracted gazing, he remembered Mrs. Crowley's package. He handed it to Marly, who opened it cautiously.

Inside was a short lace veil.

"She *did* understand," she said, smiling.

"Sarge understands, too. He told me that if I don't do right by you, I'd be in more trouble than I could handle. So if you have no objection, we'll return to El Paso tomorrow so we can be married."

"No objection at all."

Marly slid under the covers and turned down the lamp. She was where she wanted to be. Though a little nervous about what might come next, she trusted Jase. Completely.

It seemed to her that he was slow to divest himself of his outer garments. She was reminded of the first time they shared a bed and how shy she had been.

Was it possible he was shy, now that there was no pretense between them?

"I could sleep on the floor," she offered. "Or we could get that cot. I don't want to make you uncomfortable."

In answer, he hung his gun belt on the bed post.

"You don't make me uncomfortable," he said. "Anythin' but."

His boots, jeans and shirt were laid out for the morning next to her. Then he sat on the edge of the bed, took his socks off and started unbuttoning the top of his combinations.

"It's not that I don't have any idea about what's proper," she mumbled, "whatever my aunt might say."

"Marly, why are you tellin' me all this?"

"Because I want you to know that I wouldn't have got into bed with you the first time if I hadn't already started to love you. I just realized I hadn't told you yet. I hadn't actually said I love you, but I do. With all my heart."

He squeezed his eyes shut and reached for her hand.

Was Jase upset with her admission?

When he released her hand, worry turned to fear.

But it turned out he needed his hands to finish undressing.

"Jase..."

He stood before her, naked, beautiful and a bit ominous.

"Don't you ever run off on me again," he commanded. "Got that, Marly Landers—soon to be Marly Strachan?"

Marly Strachan had a nice ring to it.

"Got it."

She slowly unbuttoned her nightshirt and heard his breath catch as he watched her. Even more exciting was his physical response. He was harder, longer.

"Just because I'm not a man," she said, "don't think I won't be with you on the trail. I aim to take my duties as a Texas Ranger very seriously."

He grinned. "Yes, ma'am."

She pulled the covers back, inviting Jase into her bed, her body and her heart. He was tender, touching her face, her lips, her skin...

He made her heart race and her pulse quicken with every kiss.

When she was ready and begging for more, he took her to the stars. They moved together as one, slowly at first and then with frenzied passion. He took her where she had never been, to heights so exhilarating and glorious that she thought she would weep with joy.

As they settled down to sleep, Marly rested her head on his shoulder, her hand over his heart. In the dark, she heard him whisper, "I love you, my Texas Ranger."

Message from the Author:

Dear Reader,

The book you hold has had many adventures on the road to publication. Orphaned by obsolete technology, the original manuscript clung to life as a printout from a dying dot-matrix printer.

When it finally made it into a workable file, it had to wait while I had a couple of kids and took care of my sister and father. Meanwhile, I collected far more information on Texas, guns, riding and the price of beans and ammunition than you would ever want to see in a novel.

I hope you agree that, like Jake and Marly's journey, it was all worth it in the end.

Thank you for reading,

Alison

About the Author

Alison Bruce has an honors degree in history and philosophy, which has nothing to do with any regular job she's held since. A liberal arts education did prepare her to be a writer, however. She penned her first novel during lectures while pretending to take notes.

Alison writes mysteries, romance, westerns and fantasy. Her protagonists are marked by their strength of character, the ability to adapt (sooner or later) to new situations and to learn from adversity.

Copywriter and editor since 1992, Alison has also been a comic book store manager, small press publisher and web designer in the past. She currently manages publications for Crime Writers Canada and is a volunteer with Action Read Family Literacy Center. A single mother, she lives in Guelph, Ontario with her two children, Kate and Sam.

www.alisonbruce.ca
www.alisonebruce.blogspot.com
http://twitter.com/alisonebruce

IMAJIN BOOKS

Quality fiction beyond your wildest dreams

For your next ebook or paperback purchase, please visit:

www.imajinbooks.com

Made in the USA
Charleston, SC
26 June 2011